PROTOTYPE

ALFREDA BAILEY

Olympus Story House

Contents

THE GUARD'S WHISTLES PIERCED through the air around her. The high-pitch sound irritated the drums of her ears, forcing her to stop. Gayle Robinson pressed her small form against the rough, damp wall of the building. She looked up into the impenetrable blackness of the sky. Daylight came and went too soon. Her face twisted in disgust at the controllers, who could not even allow the citizens of the Downs a few minutes of light. If they did, maybe there would be less insanity, and the streets would be a little safer. Maybe David would be able to play awhile outdoors.

Once the warning whistles ceased, fading away into the night, she pushed away from the wall. She took in her surroundings, noting the crumbling, abandoned buildings along the avenue, most built of thick red bricks that were blackened due to the repeated coal burning in the fireplaces from the lack of heat. She took a cautious step forward, careful to avoid the jagged holes in the decaying cobble streets, then transitioned to running, hugging her carpet bag against her chest. The cleanse team would start again with their genocide. Her eyes continued to stay alert, watching for the guards and a hiding place. Then the perfect place stood before her—a tall, imposing three-story building. Unlike the other surrounding buildings, the glass windows still remained intact, and all the doors shut tight with double chains hanging on the outside.

Gayle took a deep breath and made her way across the open expanse of the avenue until a roar of an engine caught her attention, and she twisted her head around, seeing the familiar, malicious iron grill of the cleanse-guard truck turn the corner. Then a blinding white spotlight pointed at her feet, and the whistle sounded again. She rushed toward the double doors of the building trying to yank them open, hoping the chains were just prompts to discourage some of the more criminal residents of the Downs. Screaming, she sprinted around the corner of the building's edge, running down the narrow alley separating the building from its smaller neighbor. An open window appeared before her eyesight; below there were stacks of crates. They appeared unsteady, but she decided to take risk climbing up an unstable mountain of crates, slipping through the window. She scrambled through the narrow square opening, squeezing herself. She lost her grip and landed on her back on the floor, hearing the sickening thud on the ground. She let out a throaty cry as the pain rip through her body.

Then she heard the shouts of the guards and the jiggle of the chain on the door. Her eyes wide when she heard the heavy door slam open, then followed by the thunderous choir of combat boots against the stone flooring. The whirling charge of weapons reached her ears. She struggled into an upright position listening to the intruders. Her eyes adjusted to the darkness around her, because of the constant darkness in her lifetime. Her night sight was keener compared to other humans. She saw their lingering shadows around the front door. She looked around seeing the first floor was almost gutted except for a crumbling pair of stairs.

"I am certain they ran in here." A male voice spoke. His voice was filled with overblown confidence and arrogance.

Gayle gathered the last of her strength and ran to a nearby stairwell, scrambling up the crumbling steps on hands and feet. Her breath grew more labored as her progress to the second floor continued. Her hopes dwindled when she reached the second floor and found almost no walls, and what appeared to be walls were in crumbles and in ruins. The small number of furniture were broken desk and small metal cots.

Her brow furrowed as she regarded the scene. *What the hell is this place?* Below, the doors slammed open. The heavy boots echoed and caused the building to almost shake.

*****

"Somebody is here," the boy whispered.

Dr. Gregory glanced up from the rows of numbers on the screen. He frowned over at the small blond boy seated on a plush chair in the corner impeccably dressed in a gray jumpsuit. The boy's attention was focused on one of the security monitors. He looked at the monitor and saw Dome security guards enter his building. He groaned debating whether warning them away would be worth interrupting his current calculations.

"Leave those alone, boy, and get back to your studies. We have another six months before I can present you to those predators," he mumbled, deciding best to let it be. "They will be gone in a bit anyway, probably looking for another poor soul to clean away."

"But, Father, look." The boy indicated the edge of the screen where a young dark-haired woman crouched down behind a half wall. Her form was visibly shaking.

He banged on the table with his fist. "I told you never to say that to me!"

The boy glanced his way with glimmering blue eyes and, with an all too calm voice, spoke. "You need to ask them to leave."

The soldiers above made an even louder racket causing him to pay attention this time. There were always people that came inside the building—refugees from the storms that appear to only rip through the Downs, criminals fleeing from the few guards that police the small destitute metropolis. He tended to ignore it all finding some peace in the chaos.

"They will kill her," the boy said.

His eyes watched as the five dome guardsman spread out through the second floor and now approached the stairs. "I have no doubt they will, boy. Her life has meaning as all life does. It will be a waste to just end it so soon."

"What are you saying?"

"Spare her." The boy's eyes glowed. "Spare her."

Dr. Gregory felt his head implode. He saw himself reaching for his phone. He pressed a button on the screen. The phone rang until a gruff voice answered, "Chief Cleander here."

"Chief Cleander, this is Dr. Gregory. I own a building in the Downs and currently is in occupation of this building. However, I see that your men think that it is some sort of playground, and I wish to have them removed immediately."

"Oh…of course, Doctor. I will call around to see what is going on and have them leave."

*****

"They went up here." A guard spoke.

Gayle listened as the sound of the phone echoed.

"Hello, sir… We were not aware of this. My sincere apologies. I will handle it right away," she said.

She heard the man growl, and then he ordered his men to retreat to the first floor. The footsteps below receded into the night. She waited for a moment before allowing herself to breathe. Her head leaned back against the wall, and she closed her eyes to calm down.

"They are gone now." Gayle's eyes opened, and she let out a silent yelp. A small boy, about ten, stood before her.

"Where did you come from?"

"In Midtown, you will go to Saint Francis. You will find salvation and help," the boy said, then his eyes glowed.

"Wait…what?" she started.

"Do it."

Then darkness overtook her. Gayle awoke the next morning feeling strange. She peered around her and recognized her old wooden dresser that her grandfather carved himself, the heavy black drapes her grandmother made years ago, and the many small blackand-white portraits of her family for four generations living in the Downs.

"Gayle!" the deep baritone of Alfred called out to her from the living room.

She sprinted from the bed barefoot into the living room. David squeezed past Alfred barreling into her. His small arms encircled her waist in a tight embrace.

"Why didn't you come back to the hideaway, Mommy?" David shouted up at her.

"I…don't know," she whispered.

Alfred cleared his throat. "They stopped the cleanse for now, but, girl, you have to stop taking this risk. Richard would never approve."

She wanted to laugh. Richard would not only have approved, but he'd stand right on the front line goading the Dome security with his bare rear end and making stupid one-line jokes.

"Alfred, have you ever heard of Saint Francis in Midtown?"

"Of course, it's in Midtown, a church of some sort, as I recall." He shrugged his shoulders. "These days, they act as some kind of employment agency, but, Gayle, why do you ask?"

"I've been thinking." She ran a shaking hand through her curls. "I can't continue living like this for David's sake. Last night was a close call. Maybe if I try to find a legit occupation, things will get better."

Alfred's bushy brows went up into his hairline. "Gayle, they only hire for Divine Cybernetics. That company is even more evil than the Dome Council."

"I don't know why I have this feeling, but I have to go there."

*****

"What is that for?" Gabriel watched Dr. Gregory rush around the lab. His stiff white coat was open and fluttered around his small slender frame. When he did not receive an answer right away, he remained silent just watching his father.

"I cannot believe she wanted to move the date up," his father shouted out loud, then stood stiff in the middle of the lab."

"We are not ready." Gabriel spoke up, somewhat remembering what had his father upset. He wished to settle the elder man's issues, but he was afraid to push too much.

His father never responded but continued in a frustrated monologue. "Miles would never have demanded this of me. He would have honored our agreement."

"What is an agreement?" Gabriel asked.

"But no…not that ice queen. What am I supposed to show her? I have nothing. I have"—Dr. Gregory turned to finally look at Gabriel—"I have you."

"What is agreement? I need the definition."

"Later…later, child. I am trying to think. That ice queen moved the presentation to tonight and with all the Dome Council members. How the hell she got involved with them I would never know." Dr. Gregory began to pace. "Yes, we can market you as—well, what would those vampires want?"

Chapter 1

ADELINE BAKER TOOK IN the eight expressionless faces of her eight students, the open and airy classroom designed with comfort in mind, the tall floor-to-ceiling windows lined one wall that provided a pastoral scenery of the small rolling neatly manicured hills. On the opposite side, six large rectangular digital frames lined the wall, programmed to alternate among the numerous wild animals, including the large ancient cats, which were not around.

The eight children were educated apart from the rest of the upper-crust students at the academy. Another quirk of the exclusive guardian program. Although she never fully understood the nature of the program, the excitement of participating in a Divine Cybernetics experiment caused her to ignore the warnings whispered by her colleagues at Uptown Prep. *What really do they know?* she thought. They only taught the children of the more affluent employees that worked for Divine Cybernetics.

"Okay, everyone, we will do fractions today. So who can tell me how much of this pie we have now?" She glanced over her shoulder at the students. Their stone faces remained watching her.

Her lips pressed into a thin line. She hated being the only warm body in the room and secretly despise the absence of activity. It bothered her that children who generally should be hyper and lively behaved like motionless statues, and her fear of repercussions from her bosses caused her to silently accept this. Inhaling, she half turned to the broad, raising her laser to the digital board.

"Fractions are necessary when we need to take a portion of an item and divide it up." Her voice struggled to sound bubbly and bright. She pointed toward the image displayed on the board. Her fingers fluttered across the screen, causing an image of an apple pie to appear. Mathematics was never been an easy subject to teach, but with fun images, she thought it would be fun to motivate the students to be more lively. This was her thoughts last night, but trying to bring her theory into fruition made her feel silly.

Adeline glanced down at her small digital pad searching her mind for another image that would bring the class alive, but she never had a chance as the door of her classroom slid open. She twirled around and sucked in her breath seeing the brightly colored, round figure of the Uptown Preps' bubbly principal, Paula O'Neill, tumble through the door. A striking couple followed immediately behind the rotund, bright-faced woman. At first glance, she wondered if they were related to one another as they shared the same fair hair and elegant, beautiful features. Their eyes fixed on her as well, instantly causing her to have a full body shiver.

Paula briefly leaned in to whisper something to the couple who then remained near the entrance as the principal proceeded toward her. Adeline swallowed hard hoping this will not be the day for another observation

Adeline swallowed hard. "Good afternoon, Principal Paula," she called out, allowing her gaze to rake over the still faces of the children. "Children, let us welcome Principal Paula to our classroom."

"Good morning, Principal Paula," the children chimed in unison with stiff postures facing forward.

The principal gave the children a bright smile. "Good morning, class. I apologize for the interruption, but we have something very special plan for your today." She gestured the tall couple at the rear of the class. "There will be a field trip to the Grand Preservation Park in

Midtown. Guardians Delilah and Gabriel will accompany you with Ms. Baker."

Adeline immediately felt a moment of dread. She never met any of the guardians associated with the program. How was she to act? What should she say to them? She realized that Paula regarded her. She forced a smile on her face despite all the anxiety that welled up inside her.

Paula faced the class again. "Now I believe Guardian Delilah belongs to Zane and Lily. Why don't you two come forward to properly introduce your guardian to the class?"

Adeline watched the dark-haired brother and sister slid out of their chairs. They made their way slowly toward the front of the class where the guardians stood stiffly by. The principal neared her and whispered, "I need to speak with you outside for a moment."

She nodded. The principal shuffled away and hurried down to one of the aisles. She briefly looked back at the guardians and the children, then followed the principal out of the classroom. Once they stood outside the classroom together, Paula started to pace, then stopped, and faced Adeline, giving her a worried look. "I don't want you to be alarmed by this sudden development. Divine Cybernetics practically owns this school. They never plan anything in advance."

"What about permission from the parents?"

"Their parents practically signed their children over to the company," Paula said in a low voice. "They really don't have much of a say."

Adeline whispered, "The parents still need to know."

"That is not for you to worry about. Everything has been handled. Listen, the representative I spoke with want to know how some of the guardians behave out in public and interacting with other people. Apparently, being holed up with their respective tester families is not giving them much of a challenge."

"How long will they be with us?"

"The entire day and all expenses will be covered by the company. Just handle this as a normal field trip with chaperones."

Adeline hugged herself. "This is not really a normal field trip."

Paula fluttered her hands in flamboyant gestures. "What are you so nervous about? I said everything has been handled. Just do your job and what you're paid for, and the less questions you ask, the better you will come out of this."

Adeline widened her eyes. "Have I not been doing just that and to the best of my ability at that?"

"I don't have any complaints about your work, but—" Paula stopped in midsentence.

The pause did not escape her notice. "What have I done, Paula?" Her mind raced back to her first interview. A small pepper-haired doctor plastered her with questions and then listed a number of rules she had to follow. She remembered how much her head hurt trying to remember them all.

"Don't get yourself all work up, Addie. Just make sure you don't gossip more to the other teachers." Paula narrowed her eyes. "Remember the incident with Mrs. Jarvis?"

Adeline groaned. Her argument with Marguerite Jarvis, the queen bee of the teacher pool, went very far south. Last week, the odious woman cornered her in the break room while three of the other teachers looked on, trying to pump her for information about the guardians. She could not even answer them all and got so irate that she made up facts insisting the guardian program was only for special-needs children.

"I only told her the purpose of the experiment, Adeline. I did not mention the names of the testers."

Paula held her hand up then leaned in. "I know what you told her. Never mind that. Just do not make a habit of talking about the program. The less people know about the program, the fewer questions are asked. Remember what I told you at the beginning."

Adeline looked down at the sterile white floor of the corridor. "Out of sight, out of mind." Paula stepped back drawing her great body up. She brushed off imaginary dust from the long sleeves of her dark-blue blazer. "These should be simple enough. Allow the guardians to participate in the activities and such. Just sit back and observe."

"I understand." Adeline lifted her head and started to return to her class. Her hand grabbed the cool rounded door handle and stepped back into the classroom.

"Oh, Addie," Paula whispered to her, "remember, there are still eyes everywhere. Be careful."

*****

The journey to the Midtown Preservation Park lasted only an hour. Many citizens did not travel much during midday, so their small group got a chance to have their own terminal car.

Once the group arrived at the Midtown terminal, they started on foot toward the park walking along the wide, pristine sidewalks where small intimate shops lined both sides of the streets. Adeline often took this route on her way home and knew this would be a short walk to Preservation Park from the terminal.

All her hesitation melted away once she saw the children come alive. She could hear faint shy ramblings among the eight children. Guardian Gabriel even took it upon himself to interact with them. He astonished her with his gentle approach and genuine concern. When two of the children wandered off, he reacted with quick and natural instinct guiding them back to the group.

However, Guardian Delilah seemed a bit more determined to have her own way. The service bot often would linger in front of shop windows at long intervals while their group drifted away. Adeline glanced back to see the Guardian Delilah again staring inside a shop window. This time, she decided it was best to approach her and let her know that remaining with the group was important. She drew herself up and walked up to Delilah, clearing her throat to get her attention, and caught her wrathful glare.

"May I help you?" Delilah said.

"Not really, but I would like that you keep up with the group. It is enough trouble for me to ensure that the children do not wander away."

"The dress is pretty." Delilah spoke returning her interest to the window display. A slinky strapless black minidress donned the trim figure of a female mannequin.

"Please rejoin the group," she said, her voice carrying more authority than usual. However, this did earn her a chilling look from Delilah. She felt they had a standoff in the middle of a sidewalk.

"Delilah"—Gabriel's baritone voice cut through the tension—"we must continue to the park. You can look at the dress tomorrow."

The chilling dead stare in Delilah's eyes returned to normal. "You are right, brother. I shall come and purchase this tomorrow." Then as if nothing happened, the female guardian returned to the group of children waiting at the corner.

Gabriel fell into step beside her, then whispered in her ear, "She is curious about these new surroundings."

Adeline glanced over at Delilah. She shook her head and resumed her attention on the children. "I can understand that, but she must learn to follow my direction. It's dangerous here even in Midtown. If something happens to her, I will have to answer to the executives at Divine."

"Nothing will happen. I will do my duty to protect everyone," Gabriel said.

She tilted her head and met his eyes. "That is very noble of you. So…which of these children is your charge or, rather, charges?"

Gabriel looked over the children, then looked back at her. "David Robinson belongs to me, but he is unwell today."

Adeline smiled recalling the little curly-haired boy with the large curious brown eyes. "David is joy to have in the classroom."

"He is a special little one," Gabriel remarked.

"I am sorry that he is unwell today. If time permits, I can try to stop by and see how he is doing. Do you think his mother will mind?"

Gabriel regarded her. "I will speak with her tonight, but I am sure it will do no harm."

"Thank you." She smiled.

A low growl startled Adeline, causing her to jump away. She found Delilah's cool expression glaring at them. "Careful, human. We are not sexbots," Delilah said.

Gabriel and Adeline gasped. The tall blond female glared at them with frozen, glowing eyes. She felt an uncomfortable heat flash emit from Gabriel. His casual demeanor switched off in an instant. She watched his large hands tighten into fists at his sides.

Delilah's face took on a maniac delight, and then she chuckled, almost patting herself on the back. Adeline decided she had enough.

"Hey, what's going on here?" Adeline asked, looking between the two guardians.

Gabriel visibly shook his head, appearing to snap out of a trance. He straightened himself and walked away without another word focusing his attention back onto the children. They reached the entrance of the park. The eight children huddled together waiting for the adults to give them the next command.

Delilah still stood there, continuing to laugh. Adeline turned toward her. *What the hell is wrong with this bot? Was this some malfunction?* Gabriel behaved normally right until Delilah made the offcolor remark. It was almost like the female delighted in tormenting him.

"What's with you?" Adeline almost shouted. "That was not a nice thing to say, especially where there are children around."

The laughter died abruptly. The growl came again. Delilah's expression turned malicious. "I was just having a bit of fun…trying to explore what you humans call teasing."

"Teasing is an art that you may want to practice in private before you try it on the populace," Adeline said. "More so, I will for sure report this to Divine. Your behavior is atrocious."

"You cannot do this."

"I can and will. You need to either rework or reprogram. I am not sure which one will correct your attitude problem."

Delilah attempted a move toward her but then stopped. She raised her elegant chin. "I understand that you will do what you need. I will strive to remember my programming for the rest of the trip."

"Please see that you do," Adeline said, then turned around returning to the children. She inhaled three times before reaching the group of waiting children in order to calm herself. Never had she lost her temper. She refused to allow this service bot to break her calmness.

The rest of the field trip went on without another incident from Delilah. Adeline even managed to sneak in a biology lesson when a family of furry brown squirrels came close to the children. However, the time to leave came much quicker than she expected. The school was expecting them in the next hour. Adeline clapped her hands together, getting everyone's attention. "All right, everyone, get ahold of your partners,"

The children all attached themselves to their partners, all except Lily. She spotted the little girl alone and glancing around. She hurried over to Lily. "Where is Zane?"

Lily shrugged her shoulders. "He told me to wait here, then went to the lake."

Gabriel strolled up to them. "Zane is missing," he said.

Adeline stood up on shaky legs. "Lily said he went to the lake. We have to get to him. I don't know if he can swim if he falls in."

Gabriel stared down the path that would lead toward the only large body of water in the dome. "Delilah is missing as well," he said. "Wait here. I will retrieve them."

"Please hurry," Adeline said. She grasped Lily's small hand, then patted it to reassure the girl everything would be okay. She looked down at the small sable-colored hair entwined with white ribbons. "Do you—" She turned back to speak with Gabriel, but he disappeared. She never even saw him walk down the path.

*****

Zane did not like Delilah. He never did and nor did Lily. Zane's mother told him they had to deal with Delilah until the year was up. He had high hopes the year would end soon, and his family would return to normal. Then his mother and father went away a month ago. They had yet to return. He missed them at some moments, but at other times, he would forget them, almost like they were never there.

"Answer me," Delilah said. "Why are you following me?" She towered over him, appearing like a hovering skeleton.

Zane shook his head. When he followed Delilah down the path, he was determined to confront her about his parents. He knew she lied about where they were, but now his voice abandoned him and his pleading eyes went to the other guardian with the brown skin. He recalled that she belonged to Mel and Alice Peterson when he and Lily would meet up with them in the park.

"Dear, sister, calm down." Olivia spoke. "He was frightened."

"Of course, he was. He had been a naughty little boy and need to be punished." Delilah approached him. Her face started contort into the familiar mask of evil he had seen many times before.

"Gabriel comes," Olivia blurted out, causing Delilah to refocus her attention onto Olivia. "I must leave quickly, or he will sense me."

"Don't worry. I have blocked him from sensing your presence."

"He will still sense me. I must leave. Please do not continue to anger Gabriel. He is our leader, and though merciful, I believe he will hesitate to discipline you."

Delilah rolled her eyes. "Promise me that you will take care of this for me."

"I will do as you wish, but this must be the last time." Olivia glanced toward the path. "Killing is wrong. Gabriel will not like this."

"Gabriel will never know, little sister." Delilah's mouth formed a small smile. She gave Olivia a big hug. "Soon we will be free of them. Think…think of all the time we can play."

"Yes, I long to play again," Olivia whispered. "Just like the old days, right?"

"Just like the old days."

Delilah smirked. "Good. We will meet again in Father's maze. You will tell me everything."

Zane blinked his eyes, not understanding. Then Olivia disappeared on the spot. He gasped, drawing Delilah's attention once more. She gave him a slow smile revealing her sharp pearl canines. She started to approach him when Gabriel suddenly appeared behind her.

"What is going on here, Delilah?" Gabriel demanded, stomping forward.

Delilah shrugged, giving him an innocent expression. "Nothing, brother. The little one wanted to see the lake."

Gabriel glanced toward the wide sparkling blue lake, then returned his stare to them. "You should not have left the group."

"That is just what I told him," she agreed.

"I meant both of you." He stabbed her with serious eyes. "Come to me, Zane." Gabriel held out his hand to the little boy.

Zane maneuvered around Delilah toward Gabriel, taking the large hand in both his smaller ones, never wanting to release them. Gabriel spared Delilah another serious look, then continued back down the path with Zane in hand.

Once the group came into view, Zane loosened his grip on Gabriel and ran ahead to where his sister, Lily, clung to their teacher. He never looked back. Ms. Adeline kneeled down, placing a hand on his cheek. "Zane, why did you leave the group?"

Zane started to tell her about it but stopped. All of a sudden, he could not remember why he left the group. The image of the lake appeared in his mind. He loved the way the water sparkled and seeing the fish fly out of the water. "I wanted to see the lake."

"Please don't do that again, Zane. I promise you next time we'll see the lake," his teacher said, ruffling his hair.

Zane took his sister's hand. Their teacher guided them into place with the other children. He shook his head trying to shake the feeling that he needed to tell Ms. Adeline something. Again, all that came to mind was the lake, the multicolored rainbow forming over the water, and the chatter of the critters among the trees and bushes. The water was really pretty. He hoped they would see it next time.

*****

Adeline stepped away from the terminal, cuddling her coat closer to her body. Again, she found herself in the epicenter of Midtown. The false sun faded away, revealing a black void, and then the tiny white lights started to appear in the sky. The streetlights of the station flickered on around her. Everything appeared so different now, dark and abandoned than earlier. She never intended to come so late, but Mrs. Robinson never returned her call. She waited and tried to leave a message for Gabriel since he promised to speak with Mrs. Robinson, but he as well never returned her call. She was never one to show up uninvited. She finished wrapping her reports for the day and left the school. She tightened her grip on her satchel before walking out of the station onto the main stretch that led to the Midtown Preservation Park. Her apartment sat just opposite the three-milewide green area. Thankfully, some of the shopkeepers along the street kept some light on. So she found it more comforting to continue her journey, unafraid and took the chance to recollect her day at the elementary school in the wealthy Uphill district.

She hoped there would not be any more surprise field trips, especially with Guardian Delilah. There was an appointment for her to report about the field trip to the principal the next day. She realized that the disturbing behavior she witnessed cannot be allowed around the children. Someone had to look into the matter. Her mind drifted to Zane when he returned from the trip. His dark eyes and features were withdrawn and fatigued. She almost sent him to the nurse, but school was over, and he went home.

Adeline paused at a familiar corner. She looked up at the pitchblack sky. The environmental dome provided a false night as well. The fluorescent bulbs resembled stars spoken about in the history books—constellations and planets that were visible in long years past now forever hidden.

She glanced around again. The streets were empty. Midtown curfew would be in the next hour. Everyone finished their errands for the day in time to be in their habitats. She glanced up to see Midtown Preservation Park, remembering the image of the day. Now the park stood silent and empty. Often, Dome patrol shooed citizens out of the park as the sun died to not encourage the more rebellious citizens for using the park as a meeting place for undesirables.

Tonight the park would be empty, and she could hope to sit for a while and actually enjoy the night. She patted the side pocket of her jacket ensuring herself that her papers were still tucked securely away. She stepped off the curb heading for the large square. Cameras lined the park's perimeter so it would be safe to wait for a moment before she headed to her apartment. She sat down at a nearby bench, allowing her tired body to settle into the smooth curve of the back. She leaned over to brush a spot of dirt off her gray knit shoe.

"What a beautiful sky." A smooth voice spoke beside her.

Adeline stiffened, swinging her head toward the disembodied voice. A woman sat at the other edge of the bench. "Oh, hello," she said.

"Hi." The woman's striking heart-shaped face twisted toward her. The moonlight reflected the flawless olive hue of her skin. There was something familiar about the woman, but she could not place where she might have seen her. However, it was still curious that someone else was out this late when curfew time neared.

"It is a very beautiful sky," Adeline said just to make some conversation. No need to be rude. "I like to stare up at it, often wondering how close it is to our real sky."

The woman blinked her sparkling amber eyes. "There is no comparison."

"Reality is never what they try to imitate," she said, relaxing her body more. It is nice to speak with another individual without stressing about time.

"Olivia," the woman said, extending a bare hand toward her.

She grabbed the woman's hand. "Adeline."

"Your skin is very soft and pretty." The woman's grip tightened, and her thumb stroked her wrist.

"Uh, thank you." She tugged her hand away, narrowing her eyes. That was odd. "What brings you here at this time?"

"I just like to sit and stare at the blank sky. Stare at nothing," Olivia said, giggling.

Adeline froze. The giggle sounded familiar. She heard it before but from a different form. She steeled herself, ready to end the encounter and be on her way. The conversation made her uncomfortable again. She only had a couple steps to get to her apartment. That would be a good excuse to end this odd encounter. "Well, it seems to be getting late. Never safe for decent young women to be roaming about." She stood.

"Of course, predators are everywhere." Olivia stood, slowly watching Adeline closely. Adeline swallowed hard and let out a light cough. "Very well then. Nice meeting you, Olivia."

"It is always nice to meet a stranger on a night walk." Olivia moved closer; her amber eyes seemed to take on a fiery appeal.

"I cannot say the same. These nights there are all sorts of people about." She took a step back sensing some distant danger.

Olivia cocked her head to the side and blinked her eyes rapidly in the span of a second causing Adeline to jump. "You have displeased, sister. So she wants you to go away."

"Your sister?" she whispered, then before she could react, Olivia moved liked a blur toward her.

A silent scream erupted from her, only to be silenced. The world tilted. Her eyes watched the night sky fade to black.

Chapter 2

GAYLE CRUSHED THE SMALL white paper in her hand. She refused to look at it again. Instead, she remained standing inside Uptown terminal looking at the luxurious, rich landscape of the major main hub of Uptown, which was so unlike the Downs, where she lived most of her life until six months ago.

She remembered just strolling along the pristine marble walkways wearing just one layer of clothing and not worrying about some disgusting spice addict harassing her. She never wanted to leave.

The facade of perfect elegance and prestige covered the malicious intrigue and secrets. Uptown had been her home for the last six months, and the culture here often left her feeling more sour. Sue Johnson mockingly called the town Plastic City. Gayle remembered the sophisticated, tall woman crackling over coffee. Then, of course, Sue was a notorious gossip, and at that time, she never paid much attention. Then one day, they took Sue away.

Inhaling, she closed her eyes fighting the tears that once again threatened to fall, wanting to erase the cryptic message from her brain, but she could not erase the white coats bringing the elder Johnson's body out of her home and the solemn faces of her children. That's when the message took on a whole new meaning. The note read:

Divine is evil. Run away.

She knew then that David had to be saved.

"Mommy?" a small voice whispered beside her.

She jolted back to reality, glancing down into the large dark eyes of her eight-year-old son, David. His expression was full of questions, but she cowardly ignored them. Instead, she glanced back through the tall windows wanting to remember the way the glass reflected the brilliant rays of the false sun, the pure green of the vegetation that brought a mystic atmosphere to Uptown, and the scene of actual animals mixing in with the flesh-and-blood humans.

A slight pulling on her hand broke her focus again. She tightened her hand around David's smaller one. She pulled him tight to her side, turning around to face the sea of Uptown transit passengers dressed impeccably. The elite adult society crowded the expansive honeycomb terminal, marking the start of the work day. They were the cookie-cutter replica of what Dome 16 government wanted in all their citizens.

"Mommy, I'm really hungry," David whispered. His desperate plea tore at her heart. She wanted even more to turn back around and return to the utopian home given to her by Divine, but she fought the urge. They needed to get away.

"We'll eat soon, baby," she said, pulling him along, melting into the crowd. They maneuvered behind a short line of passengers pouring into a single terminal car. The car was the only route that would take individuals south of Midtown into the Downs, a desolate city at the bottom of the mountain.

She stared forward, hoping her anxiety never showed to the human security that roamed the terminal. They were a ruthless breed that she encountered before and never wanted to do so ever again.

"Your ticket, miss." A metallic voice spoke.

Gayle's head swiveled around in the direction of the robotic ticket taker. She handed her ticket over, trying to steady her shaky hands. It scanned her destination, punched the card, and handed it back to her. She pulled David through the thick metal doors. Her heart still pounded a deadly rhythm in her chest while guiding them to a seat at the very last row of the car. The five other occupants appeared older. They never looked at her or David. Maybe they were more focused on their own pursuits.

Gayle turned her head toward the long narrow windows of the car. They allowed her only the view of the sky. She was able to know the location of the train by the slow change from serene, clear-blue skies to harsh, dark, and even red at some points.

"Midtown," the metallic voice of the train called out.

The train stopped, and three of the five passengers exited. Now two elder well-dressed men, along with her and David, remained on the train.

"Last stop, the Downs." The metallic voice spoke again. "Warning to passengers: there is a protest and rebellion in progress in the area of First and D Streets. Passengers should take care to protect themselves."

"What do they mean, Mommy?" David whispered.

"No worries, honey. It's just a recording." She patted his small hand, realizing they felt almost frozen. "Your hands are getting cold. Let's put on your mittens now," she whispered.

David nodded, pulling out thick black wool mittens. She assisted him in putting them on. He also started to shiver, despite his thick gray coat and four layers of thermos wear, and Gayle noticed the ends of his thick dark curls started to frost. She retrieved his small wool cap hidden in her own pockets and secured it on his head. "This should also help."

"Thank you," he whispered.

"You're welcome, baby." She cuddled him in her hands, looking around. They were getting closer to the Downs terminal. She knew they could not leave under the normal terms. "Terminal zero, downhill." The robot voice spoke for the last time over the intercom.

She saw two other passengers gather themselves and stand up. She remarked that both had two long, heavy rectangular cases in their hands. One must have felt her regard because he turned his head to finally look at her. They held a brief stare, and she looked away, trying to busy herself with making David warmer. When she looked up again, the man focused his attention back to the doors of the terminal car. The train stopped, and the doors opened. The men stepped out in unison; their strides unusually purposeful and quickened.

"Come on." She grabbed David's hand, pulling him out of the car. She stood, watching the men leave.

Other than the men, no one else roamed the terminal. Nothing unusual, as at this time of day, no one would dare roam this area of the Downs for fear of being caught up in the cleanse.

She dragged her son toward the dark tunnel entrance of the terminal, where the tracks ended. As a rebellious teenager, she and her gang snuck on and off trains through a secret makeshift entrance hidden below the tracks. They avoided the terminal security many times, and none were the wiser. Using the same escape route, she pulled her son along, keeping their pace quick and steady. She continued to glance behind her as they slipped into the shadows, reaching the end of the platform. She stopped and knelt down, hopping into the track area, careful not to step on the third rail. She turned around, reaching out her arms to David. "Come on! Jump!"

"I can't!" David cried. His small broken voice filled the void between them.

"Yes, you can, honey. Come on. We have to go."

David sniffled, "I'm scared."

"You're hungry, honey, right? I'll catch you."

"No, Mommy!"

"David, listen to me. Please jump," she said.

He whined.

She grew impatient and grabbed his small ankle.

He let out a yelp. "Okay…okay."

"Mommy's sorry, honey, but remember, the monsters are afraid of mommies," she said.

"Okay." He launched his small body into the air, crashing into her.

She caught him, stumbling back a bit, but steadied herself. Suddenly, a loud alarm blared. The deafening sound even managed to reach them inside the tracks. Her head turned toward the epicenter, where a suspicious metallic reflection indicated the terminal's robotic security had started to gather on the platform near the car.

She staggered further into the shadows, holding her son tight. He let out a small cry, and she had to shush him during the laborious trek. "It will be over soon." She spoke into his ear. Her lungs started to burn, and her legs felt like jelly, but stopping would not be an option. The makeshift entrance came into view. Although there had been some damage, the exit still appeared functional and untouched. She set David down near the small hole. "David, listen to me. You need to crawl through this hole. It will be dark, and there may be some small animals crawling around in there, but you have to ignore them."

David nodded his head in the shadows then crouched down and started to crawl through a small hole. Gayle watched as he crawled a few feet into the tunnel then followed him, squeezing through the hole. It had been many years since she had used this illegal exit, and the extra pounds she had gained made it more difficult. The wooden sides of the tunnel left painful scratches on her thighs and back, but she bit her tongue to keep from groaning. She didn't want to scare her son, who was with them.

However, always intuitive, David called back to her, "Are you okay, Mommy?"

"I'm fine. Keep going," she said, continuing to crawl forward on her belly until she felt the familiar sting of cold from the peculiar Downs weather.

They reached the end of the tunnel, which landed them into a narrow alleyway sandwiched between the transit building and the dome guard building next door. She glanced around the alleyway, paying special attention to the sky for the air patrols. Against the forever dark atmosphere, one could see the bright-blue lights dancing across the blackness.

She dusted off her clothes and then started to do the same for David. The wind around them started to settle, but she knew that this would be the calm before the storm. They needed to find shelter fast. She grabbed David's hand once more, racing down the length of the alley toward the main throughway, which was D Street. She heard the angry cries of protesters mixed with shouting commands of Dome security officials assigned to the Downs. When they walked out of the mouth of the alley, most of the streetlights were dimmed, except for the terminal's lights. Further down, a thick crowd of Downhillers gathered at the intersection. Gayle took in the situation. They would have to go the opposite way, which was a much longer and more dangerous route, but at least, they would not be in the gallows of the cleanse party when they arrived. She steered her son away from the chaos and started walking the opposite way.

"Wrong way for you," a dark growl said.

Gayle froze. Her breathing increased tenfold. She increased their progress, only to find it blocked by a tall, broad man who stepped out in front of them. Her eyes looked frantic at the crowd. No amount of shouting would alert the security guards. She did not know if they would help or be another threat.

"Let us through." She found her voice, hoping it sounded more confident than she felt.

The man simply chuckled and advanced toward them. His baggy clothes whipped around him with the increasing winds. She got a full glance of his brown face that had pale slashes across his cheeks and over his forehead.

David let out a loud whine. She pulled him behind her as she continued to back away. Suddenly, a different set of steps caused her to stop again. They came from behind her, but her fear would not allow her to turn around.

Then a familiar baritone voice spoke in perfect syllables. "Remove yourself, Defective Citizen, or you shall be removed."

Shocked, she twirled around. "Gabriel?"

Gabriel emerged from the shadows into the dim light. His tall, intimidating form reached them in two long strides, passing her and David, and injected himself between them and their assailant. The man leered and made another approach.

"I see that my speech was not clear to you." Gabriel spoke again.

Gayle heard a change in his voice, a change that caused her skin to crawl, and she pulled her son even closer.

The would-be assailant's face form a surprise mask, then turned away and merged back into the shadows. Gabriel stood there, looking after the man. Against the darkness, his light-gray and silver-lined jumpsuit stood out. The wind caused his usually perfectly placed platinum locks to ruffle. Then he turned around. His pale face showed a calm demeanor, but she still felt unsure about him.

"Gabriel?" She stared at him. "How did you find us?" Her voice wavered. She hoped he did not notice.

"You have been deceptive. You said David was unwell. I see that he is fine." He approached them.

"He was unwell, a bit under the weather," she said, backing away.

"When I returned to the habitat, you were not there. If he was sick, why did you not take him to the medical facilities available in Uptown."

"I wanted to take David to friend, who is a doctor. David is used to him."

Gabriel shook his head. "You are being deceptive again. I also sense fear in you. What has you so afraid?"

"Now see here. This is none of your concern," she said, his eerie blue eyes staring at her.

"Gayle, I am concern for you and David. This is not a safe place, and I doubt any physician here will equal the talent of the ones in Uptown. Now what do you fear?"

"Why are you questioning me?" she screamed, then stopped.

He was a guardian created in the labs of her employer, Divine Cybernetics. Dr. Gregory, the inventor, told her that if she saw any sort of emotion from him, it was only a reflection of her own directed at him.

"You are my family. It is my job to protect you," he said. "If there is something you fear, I need to understand what I am up against."

"I have relieved you of your duty," she said.

Gabriel stopped, then glanced down at David. He held out his large bare palm. "Hello, David. Are you well?"

"Gabe! You came!" David slipped from her grip, hurling his body toward Gabriel.

"David! No!" She stumbled after her son.

David clung to Gabriel's leg, burying his face into the soft fabric of his clothes and watching Gabriel with unbiased hero worship.

Gabriel looked down at David, who was clinging to his leg. Gayle was sure her mind did not play tricks this time. Gabriel's expression changed. What was going on with him? Dr. Gregory assured her that the guardian's programs held the basic programs created only to protect and serve in the capacity of a caretaker. Was this a lie to deceive the testers and trick them into completely trusting the guardians with their offspring?

Gayle approached the pair, remembering their first meeting. She expected a female and objected in front of Gabriel to the scientists who deposited him in the foyer. Of course, they ignored her objections, holding her to the binding contract she had with Divine Cybernetics.

Until the year end was up, she was to adhere to each and every request made to her by Divine Cybernetics scientists. Then they left, leaving her staring at the guardian. He stood before her as he had six months ago—elegant, flawless, and rather beautiful, reminding her that she was none of those things, so how did they expect her to command such a thing with such superiority? She struggled to find her voice, refusing to feel intimidated. This time, she would speak her thoughts to him, and he better listen.

"Gabriel, I no longer want to be a part of this program. I release you of your duties. Please leave us alone."

"I cannot do that. I am sorry." He raised, his head to look at her.

"Why not?" she almost screamed.

"I must ensure your safety throughout this experiment." His eyes left her face to review the area. "This is not a safe place, Gayle. You are unwise in coming here."

"This is my home. I am safer here than in that castle on the hill," she threw back. She groaned. Why the hell was she arguing with a robot? Better yet, why was the robot arguing with her? She narrowed her eyes at him.

"Gabriel—" She tried to reason with him in a calmer voice.

"I cannot fail. I cannot fail," he repeated, then his voice broke. "I have already made your excuses. They believe me for the moment, but if you do not return soon, I fear their wrath upon you and David will be even beyond my help."

Suddenly, a sickening horn blared in the direction of the riot. She looked back and sensed the cleanse was starting. "Hurry! We must leave this place for now. We will go to my old home here in the Downs."

Gabriel started to protest, but he also heard the horns and nodded. "As you wish."

"Come with me. I know where to find transit." She grabbed David's hand. "We have to hurry before the cleanse team gets here. They are not prejudiced when they do their sweeps."

Turning around the corner to C Street, a lone cab was parked at the corner. The exterior appeared worn and rusted, and she flinched at the thought of even touching the handle, but they had to either ride in this cab or spend the entire night cold and hiding under some stinking rotten boards or garbage bin. She hurried to punch in her bank account information for payment and felt the cab door unlock. The driver, a robotic head, turned to look backward at them. Its large amber eyes blinked, then she heard a voice over speak.

"Welcome, Passengers. Please enter your address. Warning: I will not go on D Street, Five to Six Avenues, or the terminal at this time, as there is danger in those areas, and if forced to do so, I will remove everything from your bank account."

"Gayle"—Gabriel started—"I am not sure this is a good idea, after all."

"Quiet, Gabe," she spat, entering her old address into the computer screen. "We are not going into those areas."

"The location is acceptable." The metallic voice spoke once more. "Please buckle up." The cab revved its engines and thrust down the avenue.

"This is really fast, Mom," David said as his body bounced between her and Gabriel.

"It is," Gabriel said.

She swore he had laced his obtuse comment with a hint of sarcasm.

An hour later, the cab let them out in front of her old home located in the outer edges of the Downs. The lowest part of the Dome where light or heat never entered. Here, massive winds ripped through the areas, carrying sand and debris. When the weather got more aggressive, she remembered hunkering down in the downstairs pantry with David praying the house did not fall around them.

Despite the condition, this was her home. It saw five generations of her own family, the Carmichaels, her brief marriage, and David's birth. Approaching the rundown habitat, she noticed the lack of glass and the crooked front door. She noticed there were fewer boards on the roof, and the wooden shakes on the sides were almost all stripped away.

"This style of architecture died in the twenty-fourth century. This is a poor historical representation," Gabriel said.

"Thank you for stating the obvious, Professor," she said, rolling her eyes walking the rest of the way down the path.

"Gayle, there might be undesirables about," Gabriel said as he grabbed her hand.

Instinctively, she yanked her hand from his grip. "Gabe, no one can live here long, especially during the windy months. Trust me. There are no undesirables about. We are safer here than anywhere else in the Downs." She continued her progress toward the house.

"Let me show you my old room, Gabe," David said as he grabbed Gabriel's hand, yanking him along the crumbling stone path. They passed her bounding up the rickety steps to the wraparound porch and disappeared in the home.

Gayle exhaled, following them entering the home, hugging herself. Her eyes spotted the sand deposits under the windows. The wind whistled through every opening. She was glad her grandfather did not build the home with too many windows, or they would be shoveling sand for days just to see the floor.

"I do not sense life," Gabriel said, standing at the bottom of a single flight of stairs. He stared at her with his eerie direct blue eyes.

"I told you there should not be anyone here," she said. "It gets really cold, and most squatters don't have the skills to make a fire." She moved further to stand in the center of the room, which served as the dining room, living room, and kitchen. A large cobble fireplace sat on the longest wall. She had given away all the furniture to discourage squatters from stopping there while they were away.

She also never planned to return. The lump sum Divine Cybernetics promised would have bought them a nice dwelling and citizenship in Midtown. Now she would have to begin again from the bottom. Hopefully, her departure from the program would not end in the termination of her permanent job.

"I found my old toys!" David shouted from above.

She heard his boots stomping around his room, raining dust and sand upon her head.

"I'll build a fire," she said, turning to walk out.

"Gayle, you should not be out there alone. I will."

"Gabriel!" David called out. "Come up here!"

Gabriel appeared, somewhat confused, then followed the command, allowing her son to be the leader. He was almost like a loyal hound or rather a rabid one.

"There goes that argument," she whispered, walking out of the rear door into the backyard.

They kept a small shed outside, which had a pile of wood to use for heat and cooking. She slid past the broken door and peered into the darkness. Footsteps pounded into the shed behind her. She jumped and turned, seeing Gabriel's form in the doorway. "Why did you follow me?" she asked.

"You should have waited for me," Gabriel replied.

"I told you that I would build a fire. I am only a few feet away."

"It is very dangerous in this sector for a female. My point was proven when we were at the terminal."

"I could have handled him," Gayle said, even though she doubted her own abilities.

"Statistically, you would have not been able to handle him. He weighs 350 pounds, and you are 110. He has been assaulting females much longer than you have been alive. Forgive me if I doubted your abilities."

"Gabriel, I really do not want to argue tonight. I have to get wood for cooking and heat." She stomped over to the pile and bent down to grab a moldy piece. Her face skewered after examining the log.

"It will not work," Gabriel said as he came to stand beside her. "None are flammable." Then he turned around and walked out of the barn.

Gayle narrowed her eyes at his back, then stuck out her tongue. What did he know? She had worked with this type of wood enough to know if it would ignite. She chose another larger piece of log and headed out of the shed. When she entered her home again, David sat on the floor, playing with some small figurines.

"Is Gabe back, love?" she asked as she dropped the wood in the fireplace.

"No." He looked up at her. "I thought he went to protect you."

Or rather annoy me, she thought. "No, oh, well." She knelt in front of the fireplace.

"Ew!" David said, approaching her. "Are we going to make a fire with that?"

"It was the least gross piece," she said as she patted her thick pants. "Now where did I put that lighter?"

"In your jacket pocket." David pointed to her chest.

She smiled. "That's it." She slipped her hand into the inner pocket, producing a small rectangular metal lighter. "Move back."

"Shouldn't we wait for Gabe, Mommy?"

"Mommy has done this many times, baby," she said as she pointed the laser end toward the log.

A small cloud of smoke appeared on the rugged surface, then nothing. Her brow creased. She pressed harder.

"I have already analyzed the specimen." Gabriel spoke from behind her, causing her to fall backward on her butt. She glanced up at him with a sour face. "This piece is defective." He came from the shadows, carrying a basket, blankets, and two large logs.

"Fine." She stood up and dusted off her pants. "Have at it," she said and stomped away, feeling a bit juvenile, but he really started to irk her. She felt like exploding.

Gabriel dumped the logs in the fireplace after removing the one he deemed defective. "I found some food three houses down." He set the basket in the center of the floor and glanced up at her.

"Thank you," she muttered, approaching the basket with David. She knelt beside it and was immediately assaulted with delicious smells of bread. She reached to uncover the thick burlap cloth covering the basket. "You found this, three houses down?" she asked.

Gabriel remained quiet. She glanced up, seeing that he had the fire started.

David let out an excited whoop. He rose with his back still facing her. "Gabriel?"

He turned around. His eyes regarded them. "David is hungry," he said.

Gayle felt that she did want to let the issue drop, but somehow, the hypnotic glow in his eyes had her unconsciously taking the bread out of the basket and handing them to David. She took out a bottle of milk, followed by a block of cheese.

"The fire will go out soon. I will search for more. You will stay inside. Nothing will harm you here." Gabriel spoke again. He held her glance once more before turning to leave.

"I'll stay here, Gabriel." Gayle heard herself saying.

Chapter 3

GABRIEL CREPT OUTSIDE THE small dilapidated home. He scanned the outside yard ensuring himself there were no more danger to Gayle and David. He also allowed himself to release the pent-up guilt that lurk in the inner depths within himself. Guilt clutched at this heart. He did not want to force Gayle. He never wanted to force anyone. Despite his programming, he felt this was all wrong. He spoke with his brothers and sisters in the program, but they did not feel the same. Delilah even told him things that made life easier for her because humans were stubborn, and they did not have the same mental capacity to know what was good for them. He disagreed with her. He refused to take the easy way out, but then Gayle disappeared. He thought the worst, but as he was able to locate them, by tuning into their life force, his thoughts turned to frustration and anger. *Why did she leave? How could she just leave? Didn't she know that leaving would make their death sentence quicker?*

He glanced back at the home, then turned away once more. His mind had confusing thoughts. He often felt overwhelmed with sensations that had recently been hard for him to ignore. He never let any of the lab techs know his frustration, so it remained. It made it hard for him to work with Gayle and David.

Brother, brother. The echo of the collective voices of his siblings spoke inside his head. He did not wish to answer them with the conflicts rolling through his mind, but they sounded worried. He should have told them that he found his family and would be back soon.

Brother, please answer. Olivia's voice pierced through the chorus of pleas.

Gabriel moved away further from the home, walking until he was three houses down, then stopped and glanced around. He closed his eyes, opening his mind to the melding. *Everything is okay now, my loves. Do not worry about me.*

It is not you we are most concerned about. Delilah has been reported missing from her family hub. Divine security has been alerted. We will keep them from the Robinsons' home, but you must come back soon.

No worries, dear sister. Continue to run interference. Has Delilah responded?

She has not.

Then do not continue to contact her. Leave her to me.

Yes, brother. The chorus of voices came again.

Take care. Gabriel opened his eyes. He curved his hands in a fist. Delilah continued to defy the rules. He suspected she had already started stage 2. He reached out to his wayward sister, but continued to come up against a wall. It felt more like a void. This did not give him a good feeling. He exhaled. He would check back later. For now, his main concern was getting Gayle to return with him to Uptown. Gabriel turned to walk back to the home. He hoped his persuasion had worn off. He never wanted to see the effects of his influence on his family. It left a sour taste in his mouth, just to think of them suffering. Upon entering the small common area, he saw Gayle seated on the floor with David sleeping on her lap. She leaned against the stone wall of the fireplace. Her dark eyes instantly focused on him.

Gabriel sat in front of her, his perfectly sculpted torso stiff and upright as his piercing eyes regarded them both. "Gayle, you must come back to Uptown. I do not understand why you ran away."

"I just had this feeling…well, you know, I am worried. I"—she held up her hand—"I just want to know if they would harm the kids."

Gabriel blinked his eyelids. "We would never harm the children. We are programmed to advise, solve problems, and protect the children from danger."

Gayle inhaled deeply. "I received a note from Sue two days after the funeral. It said to run away, and Divine Cybernetics was deceiving them, and then she signed it."

Gabriel twisted his head to look at the fire. "It is all I am programmed with, to know what the truth is. I am not aware of any danger that would come to you and David." He turned to look back at her. "I do know that Mrs. Johnson may have been under the influence. She had been assigned to the care of the company psychologist a month ago."

Gayle swallowed hard. "How do you know that? I didn't, and we talked maybe once a week."

"I am mentally connected to the Johnson's guardian, Delilah. We have been since our lab days." He stopped and then continued. "Mrs. Robinson, this does not seem to be a good place to raise your child either. Divine Cybernetics has done everything to make you and David comfortable. Are you throwing it away because of a woman with possible mental issues or concrete evidence?"

She cocked her head at him, smirking. "You have to understand maternal instincts. Her note made my heart skip a beat."

"Dr. Gregory will make his rounds in lieu of the Johnson deaths. You are free to ask him anything. He is a genius doctor and brilliant scientist."

She cuddled her son closer, then glanced around the darkness of her old home. Her husband, Richard, died trying to get them away from downhill. He had broken every rule, no matter what, to ensure their safety, only to sacrifice his own. "Okay, then I will go back."

She turned her head to stare into the fire. Tomorrow they would have to return, but what would their lives be like?

*****

Downhill, or the Downs, as it had been nicknamed by the thousands of residents unlucky enough to be born there, criminals, or those who fell on hard times in Midhill and Uphill were exiled to the Downs. Periodically, the elders from Uphill visited the Downs. They rode the nonstop terminal train and went hunting for forbidden treasures that would be a death sentence in their own city, and despite desolate atmosphere, the Downs bulged hidden riches that enticed the perfect citizens of Uphill. Tyler leaned heavy on the cold, rough surface of the building. He took rapid, shallow breaths and closed his eyes. Suddenly, the door slammed, and beside him, a small chubby man shuffled out. His head was down, and his oversized gray hat slanted over his round, ruddy face. He pulled his heavy gray coat tighter around his body, though the coat provided enough warmth. The fine wool and intricate stitching would ensure the wearer years of stylish comfort.

"The money's on the stand," the man said. He nodded and hurried down the narrow alley. The "in" terminal train whirled in the distance, causing the man's steps to quicken.

Tyler shrugged his thin shoulders. He never immediately went back into the room. Instead, he shoved away from the wall and started his usual routine. His feet started in a slow shuffle, in the opposite direction from which his customer took. His eyes were pointed downward, looking at nothing, since nothing ever changed about the warped cobblestones that lined the alley, but when they changed color from black to a sheen dark gray, his pacing increased. Soon, his booted feet pounded the pavement of the boulevard. The downtrodden expressions of the defective citizens around him blurred. He saw nothing but a tapestry of smeared gray and brown that once again faded to black. He stopped, glancing at his surroundings. He recognized the old part of town, where they ran out of money. The old homes stood empty and abandoned because of the tempestuous weather and sandstorms.

It would be good to roam around for a moment, as the desperate only hung around the terminal these days. Nothing else was left for anyone there. The wind started to pick up. A shiver ran through his body, but it did not bother him much. He'd become used to the cold in his childhood. The best thing about growing up without the false sun was that one didn't miss what they never had. He stopped to lean against a rusted light post, peeking up at the starless sky, as the dome that protected the citizens also blocked the natural night. Yet for them who lived at the bottom of the mountain, it proved to be a cage, never to be opened again. He took another drag, closing his eyes, blocking away the disaster of life. A shadow blocked the light of the lamp. Tyler's eyes popped open only a second before he felt his breath leave his body. He opened and closed his mouth, trying to grasp the precious air, but it never filled his lungs, and he felt his heart slowly beat to a halt. His body became a shell in seconds. The shadow flowed away, allowing the dull brilliance of the streetlight to shine on the cold, pale body below.

*****

Morning came too soon for Gayle. She thought that it just may be nature's personal vendetta against her. She felt stiff from sleeping on the unforgiving dusty floor, but at least, the living room felt warm and dry. She regretfully thanked Gabriel's foresight to find better specimens of wood.

"We need to leave," Gabriel said, balancing on the balls of his feet before her, appearing like the perfect pendulum.

Gayle blinked twice at the large hand holding a plate. Her eyes followed up the arm to the serene, handsome face of Gabriel. He cocked his head to both sides, regarding her with those intense blue eyes that made her feel more vulnerable than necessary. She pulled her limp body to a seated position and glanced around for David.

"He is saying goodbye to his old room," Gabriel said.

She peeked up at him. "You are remarkably intuitive."

"I am programmed to anticipate my family's needs."

"Is that how you found us?" Gayle asked Gabriel.

He rose, straightening to his full height. "Yes, Gayle. I sense your imminent danger."

"We weren't in danger." She struggled to gain her own footing, and she immediately felt her body being lifted. Gabriel stood by her with the plate of food balanced in one hand, and steadying her in the other.

"I was created to perfectly monitor you and David wherever you are. I know you were in danger." He came back into view and extended the plate of food toward her. "You must eat now."

"I really—"

"You must eat now. We need to leave," he said. "Please."

"Please?" she said, surprised. "I didn't know that was included in your programming. Besides, I'm not very hungry. I haven't been for a long time." She turned away from him. "David!" she called.

Gabriel lowered his head and stared at the plate. The doctor did not include *please* in his programming, but somehow, it felt right. He raised his head to look back at Gayle. Behind them, David tumbled down the steps. His little charge had been playing with the fireplace ash.

Gabriel smiled, despite knowing he commanded David to not go near the place.

"Oh, honey! Your face!" Gayle took the bottom of her shirt and started scrubbing the dirt away. "Where have you been?'

"Nowhere," David said.

"David, what have we spoken of?" Gabriel asked. He placed the plate back on the table. His young charge was stubborn. He would need a new strategy for dealing with him programmed into him.

"Sorry, Gabe." David peered into his mom's eyes under thick dark strands of hair. "I was playing with the fireplace upstairs."

"David"—Gayle continued to wipe his face—"no worries, honey."

"We must leave soon," Gabriel said.

Gayle's dark eyes regarded him, noticing that he seemed bothered by something. In the last six months, she never saw him this concerned.

He stared out through the glassless window, almost like he anticipated something coming. A concern and worried expression replaced the usual calm, serene one. Funny. She didn't think robots could be afraid or concerned about anything, but some of the things Gabriel said and did made her forget that he wasn't human.

"I guess we better hurry," Gayle conceded.

Sparkling blue and red lights greeted them outside. Gayle took an instinctive step back but was immediately grabbed by Gabriel and propelled forward with David. Three pairs of eyes kept glued to the busy scene as uniformed Downhill officers swarmed the scene. Gayle, David, and Gabriel went unnoticed though as the officious group spoke to one another and murmured.

A large nondescript black van arrived silently. The sea of guards parted, revealing the prone, limp body of a human or what anyone could guess from the four limbs that jutted from the large lump surrounded by clothing.

Chapter 4

"WE ARE SO GRATEFUL for this chance to be of service to Divine Cybernetics," Mr. Arnold Hamilton said, clutching the small hand of his daughter, Kimberly.

Dr. Herman Gregory stood before the grateful couple inside the grand wide portico of their rented mansion. Ms. Hamilton, a small pretty red-haired woman worked as a personal secretary for Harold Wolfe, the marketing vice president. Mr. Hamilton, held a menial position as a lead guard in the development lab. It was Wolfe who suggested the Hamilton family, convinced they would do what they could to please Divine Cybernetics.

"We are also honored that you have visited us." Mrs. Hamilton took the offered hand of his assistant, Dr. Vera Cote, between her two thin hands. "If there is anything that we can do more, we hope Divine will let us know."

"We are just making sure everyone is doing okay with the guardian program and answer any questions you have." Vera pulled her hand away, glancing at him sideways. "We are satisfied that you all are getting along well."

"We are…we are," Mr. Hamilton injected. He continued to give them an overly bright smile.

Dr. Gregory remained silent allowing the exchange between Vera and the Hamilton family. Once again, he caught the side glance of

Vera's dark hooded eyes. He shot her a twisted smile, which made her quickly train her attention on the couple and the little girl.

Vera inhaled deeply "I am so glad that you gave us this time to meet."

Dr. Gregory nodded a silent goodbye to the family and descended the stone steps to the waiting nondescript black vehicle. The guard standing by opened the door for him. He ducked inside, settling himself on the center of the seat. He closed his eyes leaning back. He heard Vera slid into the vehicle moments later. He opened his eyes seeing the petite bent woman take the seat opposite him, but she took her position at the farthest darkest corner of the vehicle.

"I grow tired of these rounds," he muttered. "Who do we have next?"

"Mrs. Robinson and her son, David, Dr. Gregory," she said, then removed a rectangle computer and started to busy her fingers over the screen.

The door closed, and soon, the vehicle started moving smoothly around the driveway and through the large black iron gates. He despised doing these rounds, but the ice queen got itchy and demanded his team perform damage control after both elder Johnsons ended up dead. It was not his fault the timeline arrived earlier than usual.

"Esther seems to be getting along smoothly with her family." Vera spoke, still working on her pad. Dr. Gregory narrowed his eyes at her bowed head. "We can speak about this when we get to the lab."

Vera's fingers froze over the screen and lifted her head. "We never speak in the lab, Dr. Gregory. You lock yourself in your office, and I oversee the lab techs."

He raised a bushy gray brow. "In the presence of others, I really do not want certain things to get out."

"I thought we could at least get some things discussed before the day ends." She glared at him. "Besides, I did not know what we discuss was taboo." Her voice faded.

"I do not wish to argue with today, Vera. I can only please one queen at a time." He fixed her with a mean look. Vera returned it, then lowered her attention to the screen, typing viciously.

Herman twisted his head to look back at the grand threestory redbrick mansion slowly faded behind them. Little Kimberly Hamilton remained standing along on the front step waving at him.

Her white lace dress moved slightly with the breeze. Her thick pale pigtails jiggled like delicate ropes. Kyla three faded out of the shadows and placed a pale hand on the little girl's thin shoulder. Their stoic stance reminded him of the statues in the Uptown cemetery, the ones with the kneeling praying children and the delicate angels hovering over them. On his rare off days, he took strolls through the cemetery admiring those intricately carved stone markers. He took a rare joy receiving his greatest inspiration being there with the beautiful silence of the eternal sleepers.

She will make a good citizen, he mused.

Their car picked up pace as they turned onto the main stretch of road. They passed three other grand homes before reaching the smallest mansion at the end of a drive. The Robinsons resided in a two-story white stone mansion with four tall, thick columns lining the front. Despite its size, it had more character and elegance than the others on the street. He admired the house as the architect who designed the home also designed his and most of the other Divine Cybernetics executives. He hoped the Robinsons appreciated living in such a masterpiece of a home.

"Mrs. Robinson has sent a message that Gabriel and David have gone on an errand." Vera broke the angry silence between them. Her voice returned to its icicle calmness.

His expression stilled and grew serious. "Did he not know I will be coming?"

"He was informed yesterday." Herman's mouth formed a downward turn, and he looked away. Gabriel could be doing this on purpose. *The little brat thinks he is some type leader going about doing things by himself,* he thought.

*****

The huge gold-and-black lacquer grandfather clock resounded throughout the cavernous two-story foyer. The noise caused her body to jerk; she rubbed her hands together rushing across the overly glossy black-and-gold checkered marble floor. She stood before the oversize gaudy piece.

She wanted to have it removed many times along with the rest of the overpriced bold furniture within the massive five-bedroom mansion. Unfortunately, they would be fixed elements in her life for another six months. So she ignored it and longed for the end. Gayle returned her focus to the narrow stained glass window beside the door, mentally counting the minutes that have passed. It seemed like an eternity when David left with Gabriel. The guardian suggested her son not be around when the Divine Cybernetics representatives came in order to prevent him from being interrogated.

Gayle narrowed her eyes seeing a black vehicle roll between the delicate white-and-gold iron gates. She pushed away from the window and walked to stand at the center of the foyer twisting her fingers in knots. She bit her bottom lip until it hurt. Her mind returned to the night of her escape and Gabriel. She had many questions—questions that strained her mind—but she eventually agreed with him. They had six more months until the end of the program, six months until she could breathe. Like a knife cutting through her tension, the loud chimes of the doorbell echoed throughout the mansion. Her nerves almost jumped out of her skin. She did a quick aboutface. Shadows appeared to move under the narrow space of the heavy entrance doors. She steeled herself before rushing forward. She took the large ornate brass handle in both hands, pulling one of the doors open, revealing the small neat and stately figure of Dr. Gregory. He had not changed much since their first meeting. He still wore a tweed suit, this one being gray and brown with large silver buttons with angel wings engraved on them. They dotted down the front of the suit in a perfect row.

He marched through the entrance with his thin nose sniffing the air around him. He carried a black lacquer cane in his black leather gloved hand, which had an elegant angel wing bent in the form of a handle.

"Greetings once again, Mrs. Robinson," he said, still glancing around. His expression appeared calm, but the gilt in his silvery-blue eyes held a hint of irritation.

"Greetings, Dr. Gregory. It's a pleasure seeing you again," she said in a soft voice and started to close the door, but the sharp click of heels caused her to look out on the door once more.

"Here comes my assistant, Vera," he said. "She is here to observe only."

"Good afternoon, Vera," she said, greeting the woman, tipping over the threshold. The curious woman moved to stand beside him.

"I understand that Gabriel will not be joining us," Dr. Gregory said.

"David got better today, but he was getting a little too excited, so he took him for a walk in the park. He should be back in an hour if you want to wait."

Dr. Gregory's lips pressed in a tight line. "No…no…we only need to interview with you."

Gayle nodded noting that he still appeared not happy about Gabriel's absence. "I have some refreshments in the living room. We can talk in there." She led them, waving her hand toward the right, toward a brightly lit room.

"Please lead the way," he said, waiting for her. She felt a slight shiver through her spine while stepping toward the living room.

Gayle strolled into an even more glamorous room that rivaled the foyer, with gold crown molding that created a grid pattern across the ceiling, delicate floral pink-and-yellow patterns covered the walls. The ornate fragile gold-and-pink silk furniture almost crowded the small intimate room; she limited David's access to this particular room. She feared that if he broke something, she will never be able to afford to replace it.

Dr. Gregory settled himself in a larger chair. Vera sat on the edge of the long sofa opposite him, and Gayle sat on the same sofa at the end. The food remained untouched between them as they regarded each other in silence.

"Tell me how you have been getting along with the experiment?" Dr. Gregory finally spoke.

Gayle darted her large dark eyes between the doctor and his assistance. "Gabriel has been working well. David absolutely adores him."

"Have you observed any oddities or unusual behavior?" he asked. His brow now forming a *V* at the center or his forehead. She shook her head, "He has been efficient and polite. He takes care of household matters without even being asked. I am astounded at his intelligence."

Dr. Gregory now looked impress. He glanced over at Vera, who shared a surprised expression with him, then returned his focus on her again. "He takes care of household matters without being asked? Anything else we should know of?"

Her eyes flickered between the two. "Nothing."

He raised his brow. "Nothing else about the guardian that jumped out at you?"

"No…not really." She shook her head side to side.

"How about you, Mrs. Robinson? How have you been feeling about the program?"

Gayle almost choked. She glanced between them, hoping they did not notice. "I admire what Divine was able to accomplish as far as the service bots are concerned."

"Actually, the guardian program is my own accomplishment. It took many years for me to come to this development." Dr. Gregory leaned back into the chair, placing his hands on his leg.

Thinking that she needed to take control of the conversation, she asked, "How are the Johnson children doing?"

Dr. Gregory snapped his attention back to her. "They are fine. Their guardian will assume permanent guardianship of the children."

Gayle furrowed her brow. "Do you believe that is wise?"

"Oh, it should be fine…a shame about the parents, but this is the primary reason for my creations."

"What exactly happened? Does anyone know the reason that Sue and her husband got sick?" Gayle said

"As I recall, it was a horrid disease the company doctors never caught during their first physical," he said.

"Do they have other relatives?" Gayle asked. "I am sure another relative will be happy to take the children in, and it may be easier for them to accept their parents' passing. Who will make the funeral arrangements?"

He gave her an indulgent smile that cause another shiver in her spine. "The company will make arrangements with the Johnsons. No need to worry about these things."

She rubbed her bare arms. "I wanted to invite them over for a playdate with David, just to ease some of their sadness."

"That is very…sweet of you," Vera injected, causing Gayle to transfer her focus from the doctor.

Dr. Gregory loudly cleared his throat. "Now heed me, Mrs. Robinson. The guardian program will enrich the lives of the children. Although the Johnson family life will only get better"—he stood—"we are glad that you decided to come into our fold and join us into the future."

Gayle's eyes widened, rising from the sofa, pressing her lips together. "I feel honored."

As Dr. Gregory was leaving, his assistant, Vera, followed him closely. Although she felt sympathy toward him, she also tried to engage with the woman who seemed to be in a hurry and only nodded back politely. Dr. Gregory left through the double doors, and Vera continued with her tasks.

"Now I am disappointed that Guardian Gabriel is not present for this interview but remind him not be late for his biweekly checkup," he reminded her as he strolled calmly out of the home.

Gayle came to stand inside the open door. She shivered again despite the nice, warm temperature. Their vehicle pulled away and quickly gain speed while the gates swung open to allow it to exit. She shook her head, closing the door to the entrance.

"Are you satisfied with his answer?" Gabriel spoke behind her.

She saw him leaning against the entrance of the living room. At that moment, he reminded her of Richard—all-knowing and oozing with charm; all that he missed was the stupid smirk. She couldn't help herself from rolling her eyes and made her way to the kitchen.

His footsteps alerted her to his presence at her back. She ignored him, returning to the preparation of a simple meal of vegetable soup and with a protein supplement. At some times, she caught his calm visage staring at her, watching her every movement, causing the hairs on her neck to stand up. She might try to speak with him, but then she thought, *Screw him.* She did not owe him a conversation.

"David is upstairs taking a nap." He continued to speak.

"I don't appreciate being lied to." She faced him. Her face hot and sweating.

His confused expression regarded her. "He is truly upstairs sleeping. You can check?"

"That is not it, Gabriel. Dr. Gregory lied to me about the Johnsons." Her tone started to raise.

He straightened, placing his hands behind his back. However, he still remained at the threshold of the kitchen. His expression now blank, which infuriated her even more. She should be more sensitive to his plight.

"I apologize that you are upset, Gayle." His teeth seemed to bite out the words. "Believe me when I tell you that I will strive to always protect you even from Dr. Gregory, but you must allow such passes from them. As they must do what they must to protect themselves as well."

"What do you mean?"

"It will soon be six."

She fumed, holding her breath. "Look...I have dinner starting for David. Will you be able to finish? I have to get ready."

"Yes, I can." He moved into the kitchen. They avoided each other. He moved like hands on a clock around the kitchen. She watched with side eyes as he leaned over the pot. His aquiline nose wrinkled as he inhaled the aroma. "It should not be hard for me to complete this task."

"It is pretty easy to make, and David loves this soup," she said, making her way to the entrance of the kitchen.

"I will attempt to learn this recipe for future mealtimes." He replaced the top back on the pot.

Gayle leaned against the frame. "Gabriel, Dr. Gregory seemed surprise that you help around the house."

Gabriel blinked. "It is true, but I am also programmed for logic, but it is logical that a stable and clean home will make a healthy and stable citizen."

"Don't you think it is odd to deviate from your original programming?" she said.

"It is not odd for me to take care of my family unit," he said. His serene expression changed suddenly. She saw the lost expression and confusion.

She moved back. "I will try to get home early."

"I will warm a plate for you when you do," he said.

Gayle paused for a second and wanted to speak but decided it was best to leave it alone.

She left the kitchen, making her way to her bedroom. She dressed quickly in her uniform, a trimmed gray-and-black pantsuit that clung to her petite, slender form. She rolled her black curly hair in a thick bun at her neck. She rushed out of her room with a bag holding personal belongings.

Gayle slowly pulled her company car out the garage trusting that Gabriel would be okay with David. She hired twelve-year-old babysitters before when she was desperate. She trusted him before the note and never thought he would do harm to her son. The car idled a while outside the empty three-car garage. After staring up at the house for a moment, she continued down the long driveway and out of the black iron gates.

The drive to Divine Cybernetics' headquarters only took her thirty minutes. For once, she managed to be one of the first of the third shift entering the building. She signed in with the security and waited for the elevator to take her to the fifty-first floor, where the cleaning staff would gather and prepare to clean the labs. The task would take four to five hours, depending on all ten members of the cleaning staff being present.

"Gayle Robinson?"

Gayle turned at the sound of her name. A tall, slender woman stood before her. The woman's uniform indicated that she was a secretary on the fifteenth floor. The secretaries tended to keep to their own ranks. They ate together and held their own office parties, restricting many departments from attending.

Gayle took an unconscious step back. "Yes?"

The woman smiled, revealing two rows of glistening, white teeth framed by deep, scarlet lips. "Dani Travis," she said as she extended a flawless, slender hand toward Gayle. "I worked with Sue Johnson."

Gayle's eyes widened as she shook Dani's hand. "Really?"

The woman nodded. "We worked together for four years. I never imagined her being so sick." Her silvery catlike eyes widened. "She told me about you. We were great friends."

"She did?" Gayle never recalled Sue speaking about any of the other secretaries she worked with. Sue often even expressed her dislike for most of her coworkers, calling them vapid blockheads with no souls. "Sue never mentioned you. How odd."

"Well, you know how flaky Sue can be," Dani said.

"Apparently not."

The door to the elevator slid open. They stepped into the confines of the elevator together. Dani pressed the button for the fifteenth floor, then turned to her with a bright smile, very different from Sue, who had a droll, low-key personality.

"It's a real tragedy. Do you know how long she was sick?" Dani asked.

"We only knew each other a couple months, but I never really saw any illness about her during that time. She never spoke about her fear of leaving the children."

"Oh, her poor, dear children," Dani said.

"I was thinking of inviting them over for some movies. They must feel extremely alone after their parents' death. I can't believe they allowed the guardian prototype to take care of them."

"Why not?" Dani asked sharply.

Gayle narrowed her eyes at the sudden negative tone. "While it is a great ideal, we are talking about service bots that can only imitate human feelings, but nothing compares to the real thing." She watched Dani work her face back to a false, cheery mask.

"You're right. Nothing does compare to the real thing."

They rode in silence until the elevator reached the fifteenth floor. Dani turned to Gayle and said, "I was thinking of having a secretaries' gathering for a memorial for Sue at about eight in the evening. You should come. We were thinking of having it at the end of the week at my home."

"I really—"

"Oh, come on. It's for Sue. Maybe we can talk more about the real and material world." Dani's eyes twinkled with amusement at the last sentence.

"I'll try to make it," Gayle said as she managed a small smile.

"Fine." Dani's smile brightened even more. She twirled out of the elevator and sashayed down the corridor.

Gayle looked after Dani as the elevator doors closed. She could not believe the woman's story about Sue. Her friend expressed her intense dislike for her coworkers. It never stopped there. She always felt the woman held a more intense dislike for Divine Cybernetics in its entirety. This made the cryptic note scarier. What did her friend know that might have killed her?

Chapter 5

GABRIEL STOOD OUTSIDE THE Johnsons' massive two-story mansion. Under the cover of darkness, heavy black drapes covered the narrow window blocking the brilliant moonlight; the gray brick facade appeared even more dull and lackluster than before. He moved over the dying lawn, noting the limp, drawn flowers in the large flower beds lining the concrete walkway. The bushes appeared overgrown, and he suspected if allowed to, they would overtake the front lawn of the mansion in a few months.

He frowned at the damage. His sister clearly did not care for even the smallest of living things. He wanted to wave his hand to give the life to them but stopped. Once Delilah left the home, Divine would sell the home to a responsible, loyal family that would care for the home the way it's supposed to be.

Gabriel reached the rear of the house placing a hand over the panel. He heard a definite click and push open the door that led him into the kitchen. He picked up Delilah's essence right away and followed it through a maze of wide cold corridors to a cavernous living room. He stood at the stone entryway spotting her languidly standing near a tall gray stone fireplace.

He saw she wore a slinky short black dress, an infraction against the dress code for the guardians. The techs instructed them to only wear a loose gray jumpsuit. Another infraction was that she spent undocumented monies. Divine Cybernetics accounting department would not be happy with this. They kept immaculate calculations of the spending among the tester families. He so much feared that Gayle would get caught by the guard when she ran, but luckily, she used her own funds.

"Welcome, brother. You finally came." She turned to him with a pout on her red-painted lips and pushed away from the fireplace.

"I have not ignore you," he said. "I tried to reach out when I had the chance, but it was you who have not answered me."

She lifted a thin blond brow. "Oh, when you have the chance? Like playing handmaid to that pathetic pair, but your poor, dear sister who needs your help is ignored."

"You do not appear to be troubled, sister." He moved farther into the room, taking in the change in furniture and decor, so different from what he saw before. His sister chose a large black leather and dark wood sofa, which dominated the room; wicked, scary sculptures jutted out of the center of the four walls. Thick, heavy black curtains hung limp over the windows ensuring the room will never receive any light. He imagined the children, Zane and Lily, did not find the decor amusing.

"Not that it is any of your business, but I was in trouble"—she continued dragging a finger along the seam of the sofa—"desperately in need of my brother. You have not checked on me when I lost the elder Johnson."

"Speaking of Sue and Walter, what happened to them, Delilah? Only months ago, they were the picture of health."

She shrugged her shoulder. "Humans get sick."

"Why did you not report their illness?" He pressed. "You reported their illness five days before their death? It was your responsibility to monitor them closely."

"Gabriel, what else do you want me to say? These things get sick. They die. They go away, and more arrive every other day."

"They are not things," he whispered, then spoke once more in a louder voice. "You must tell me what happened to them."

Delilah gave him a mocking expression, then twirled around with her arms wide. "Do you like the new decor, brother?"

"As much as I admire your creativity, Delilah, this room is filled with infractions that are against Father's rules," he said.

"I wanted prettier things."

"You are not supposed to make any purchases without the approval of Divine Cybernetics accountants. Did anyone give you permission to redecorate?"

"Why are you so obsessed with the details?" she crossed her arms over her chest. "This conversation is starting to bore me. I want you to leave now!"

"I will not leave until I get the truth about what happened here."

Delilah let out an evil laugh. "Ha, truth. Like the one you told Father about the Robinsons. Let's start with you following that pathetic woman and her offspring to that disease-ridden place."

His eyes widened. "The decimated body we saw? You had something to do with it."

She shrugged her shoulders and tossed her platinum locks. "A midnight snack. Nothing very satisfying."

"Delilah, how could you?" He balled his fist.

"What do you care!" she screamed back.

"We are not supposed to hurt them."

"We were created to rule them," Delilah spat.

"You must turn yourself in. Tell them what you have done." Gabriel continued.

Delilah's face twisted into a horrid mask. "I will never bow down to the cretins."

"I am leaving now. I understand now the level of your instability," Gabriel said, turning away. "I will call the team to come pick you up."

"No!" she screamed again. Then tackled him from behind.

Gabriel hit the floor from her vicious attack, making a hollow dent in the black marble floor. He managed to roll on his back, bringing Delilah under him. He did not want to injure her, only deflect her swift blows. Then he saw the flash of a silver blade as it swung toward his face. Delilah attacked him with vicious slashing motions. He moved a hand to grab the blade, but it caught him in the palm burying the knife completely through. He flinched and retaliated with a psychic punch finally rendering her unconscious.

Her body went limp, and her breathing slowed. He exhaled deeply, holding his hand, as blood dripped from the wound. He stared down at her prone body, inhaling, trying to control his breathing.

"Is it over?" a small voice asked.

Gabriel lifted his head, spotting the two Johnson children hiding in the hall. Two dark-eyed and dark-haired children emerged from the shadows. Zane placed an arm around his young sister, Lily, as they stare at him. He held her hand as he cautiously approached Gabriel. They knew each other from the playground and when he would pick up David from school.

"Zane, do you trust me?" he asked, holding out his uninjured hand.

Zane nodded and then directed his large dark eyes toward Delilah's prone body. "Is she dead?" he asked.

Gabriel shook his head. "We don't kill." He looked back down at Zane. "I will need to get you two to safety. Come."

Gabriel led the children out of the home under the cover of night, moving at a steady pace. They made their way back to the home he shared with Gayle and David. They entered through a rear door that led through the garage and into the family room, then onto a small command room that monitored the perimeter of the mansion and its gardens. Zane and Lily waited and watched as he went through the motions of reprogramming the security protocols, ensuring Delilah would be kept at bay for a least a while. The psychic punch he gave her would only last for an hour, and he feared when she woke up; he and his family would be her primary target.

"Let's get you two to bed," he said to the siblings. They nodded at him. Like obedient lambs, they walked with him up the rear stairwell to the second floor. He advised them to wait at the top of the stairs listening for David. Gayle would not return from her work for another hour. He hoped to get the Divine security detail to patrol the area in order to deter Delilah from coming to the house.

"Come, children," he said, walking down the corridor to an open door. He ushered them into the guest room closing the door. "You will sleep here tonight."

"Okay," they answered in unison. Together, they approached the bed. Zane sat down on the bed, first, removing his coat and damp, dirty slippers, then assisted his younger sister.

Gabriel came over to the bed pulling the sheets down. The movements of the children bothered him, as they appeared slow and tired as if a weight still rest on their shoulders. He wished to ease their troubles but, somehow, felt that this would be an invasion into unwanted territory.

After bidding them good night, he left, closing the door. Once again, he checked in on David who remained fast asleep, his dark curls poking from the soft down comforter. The tiny bear-shaped night-light near the bed shorted from the reprogramming of the security system. A downside of the faulty wiring in the home, but he repaired it easily. He waved a hand over the night-light, bringing it back to life.

The phone rang twice before an authoritative male voice spoke into the phone. "Divine Cybernetics security detail. How can I help you?"

"This is prototype Guardian Gabriel. Prototype Guardian Delilah has become unstable and needs to be picked up."

"We will be there in 0200 seconds. Please stand by," the voice said, then cut the phone line.

Gabriel placed the intercom down and walked back to the children. They stood where he left them, shivering. Human children were so different from him at this age. He recalled having little fear and nothing else. His father used to repeat to him about no fear, no emotions, and no mercy.

"Come, children. Let's go upstairs," Gabriel said as he led them to the second floor.

David slept a deep, undisturbed sleep. He knew the little one would not be up until the next morning, when his mother would wake him. Zane and Lily wanted to sleep together. Gabriel understood that their parents' death and Delilah's instability must have been difficult for them. He covered them with an extra comforter. The gesture surprised him, but he felt it was the right thing to do. This urge was what he often felt for David when caring for him— making sure the boy ate well, had clean clothes, and was comforted when his mother was away.

*****

The Divine Cybernetics team arrived within the hour—ten men dressed in severe black uniforms outfitted with equipment belts and long black metal phasers—arrived just as he put the children to sleep. The security detail walked into the foyer, immediately drawing their guns. Gabriel stood at the center of the foyer watching as individuals broke away to go into different rooms.

"Gabriel?" a tall athletic man said as he approached him.

"Yes," Gabriel answered.

"Chief Alphonso Vila," the man said as he saluted to Gabriel. Chief Vila removed his helmet, revealing a handsome, coffee-colored face. His dark eyes appeared intense and focused.

"Greetings, Chief Vila." Gabriel returned the salute.

"We were not able to find Guardian Delilah. We will do another sweep of the neighborhood."

Meanwhile, we must take the children to safety. She might come back for them."

He remained still. "The children are resting now, but I will stay vigilant."

"We will inform Dr. Gregory and Ms. Miles of what happened."

One of the unit members walked up to Alphonso and whispered into his ear, "Okay, if everything is clear, I want the Uphill perimeter checked and monitored and place increased security in the terminals." Alphonso turned back to Gabriel. "We need you to get them out of the house before the other testers wake up. The extraction team will wait outside the gates tomorrow morning."

"Understood."

The Divine Cybernetics security detail left the house as quickly as they arrived. Gabriel commenced another sweep of the home. He knew the security detail might leave two guards, but the chief would never relay that message to him, for fear his connection with Delilah would inform her of their whereabouts.

*****

Gayle arrived at the home past midnight seeing some extra outside lights on, and the first-floor lights in the family room were on as well. Her mind went to Gabriel. She sometimes heard him moving around at night. Suspicious, she came downstairs to see him cleaning and felt sorry for him. He would never know the relief of an eighthour sleep.

She parked the car inside the garage, gathered her things, and exited. She entered through the kitchen seeing a bowl simmering on the counter. At a closer look, she recognized the soup from this morning. She placed her items on the floor beside the stool, smirking. Divine forbade lower employees from bringing in foreign food items, leaving her poor stomach at the mercy of their chefs. Needless to say, she refused to eat most nights like this one.

"Gabriel, I'm home," she said. She heard only silence. "Gabriel…"

"I tried to make sure you would be able to withstand the heat." Gabriel's deep voice came from directly behind her.

Gayle nearly jumped off her seat. "Damnit, Gabe! What did I tell about sneaking up behind me?" She slammed down her bowl and clenched her fist.

"Forgive me," he said, as he took a step back to give her more breathing room.

She calmed herself, remembering that he didn't know any better. Turning around, she slid back onto the stool. "That's okay. How was everything here?"

"David had a well-balanced meal at 0600, completed his homework at 0700, and watched an odd show made with a line drawing."

"Thank you. I appreciate it," she said, as she sipped some of her soup.

"You're welcome, Gayle," Gabriel said. He reached over to pick up a cloth napkin when she saw his inner hand.

"Oh no, Gabe! What happened to your hand?" She reached out to grab his hand.

"I tried to cut more vegetables for the soup and cut my hand with the knife." He pulled his hand away. "It is healing."

Gayle noticed the instant healing, but the wound seemed like it hurt. Her husband, Richard, often came home with such injuries until she got tired of asking. "I see. Well, we need to contact Dr. Gregory tomorrow for a med evaluation just to make sure you are okay. I don't want them thinking I damage you."

"There will be no need, Gayle. Dr. Gregory has sent a digital note to call for a mandatory med evaluation schedule for tomorrow morning."

"Really?" She wondered why they never copied her on the email. "Can I help you any kind of way?"

Gabriel watched her under hooded eyes, then shook his head. "I will attend after I see David off to school."

Gayle slid off the stool and patted Gabriel on the shoulder. "Good night, Gabe."

*****

The false sun already hung high in the Downs vicinity. Gabriel found all the children awake and watching television in David's room. He watched them for a moment. They showed no signs of the fear they experienced the previous night. They spoke about the school play and the television show. They jumped around and played with the pillows. Their joyous glee made Gabriel smile, which took him by surprise.

"Zane, Lily, will you please help me with the garbage?" Gabriel asked.

"Can I help too?" David piped up.

"Not today, David. You will have to finish getting ready for school." Gabriel locked eyes with the little one.

"I will finish getting ready, Gabe," David said, rising from his position on the floor and headed out of the room. He ushered the Johnson children down the stairs. Two large black bags sat at the front door. He grabbed them as they exited the front door. He moved them across the green lawn, where an unmarked black van waited. A guard stood outside the vehicle with a large phaser on the ready.

"Are they calm?" the guard asked.

"Yes, they will be no trouble for you." Gabriel looked down at the children, who immediately lifted their small chins. Their pleading eyes shook him. He had to turn his head to avoid the uncomfortable emotions. Their eyes crashed with him. "It will all be okay. Divine Cybernetics is your family. They will make sure you have perfect futures."

"Yes," the children responded in unison.

He turned toward the guard again. "Any word on Delilah?"

"No," the guard said, staring at him. "We are still maintaining the perimeter. She is assumed to be armed and dangerous."

"Understood."

The guard saluted him, then stuffed the children into the van. It rolled silently down the road as the first rays of the false sun illuminated Uptown. He inhaled deeply, dropping the garbage in the cans. Then he returned to the house, entering the foyer silently. He heard Gayle speaking with David upstairs and increased his speed to see what was going on. He found the pair in Gayle's sunny bedroom. He did not know if he liked or disliked the decor of the bedroom. Whenever he went in there, a feeling of walking through a field of wildflowers always welled up inside him.

"You're up really early, hon," Gayle said. Her voice sounded tired and strained.

"I like to watch the *Merry Musician*. It only comes on in the morning, and if I get up early enough, I can see the reruns."

"That sounds confusing, love. Please let Mommy get some sleep, and we can talk about it after breakfast," she murmured into the pillow.

Gabriel stepped through the open door, knocking before entering. Apparently, she took particular issue with him coming into her private quarters without announcing himself. She turned very violent.

"David, are you ready for school?" Gabriel asked.

"Gabe, I am trying to wake Mommy," David said. He scooted closer to Gayle's prone body under the covers. His small hands yanked on the comforter.

"David," Gabriel said as he approached the bed. "Your mommy is really tired. We will wait for her downstairs."

"But," David said, "look at me."

Dark-brown eyes locked with his blue ones. "Time for school," Gabriel said, his voice growing more soothing.

David's eyes blinked rapidly. "Okay."

"Thank you, Gabriel," Gayle muttered into her pillow. "I'll be up in a moment."

"Take your time," he said, keeping the same tone. He took David by the hand, leading him out of the bedroom and downstairs. David donned his black backpack, which bulged with two school books and papers.

"Come. Let's get you to school." Hand in hand, Gabriel and David stepped into the sunshine.

Gayle urged her body awake. She realized the high-pitched noise piercing the air came from the landline positioned beside her head. Her hand grabbed the handset with a cranky groan. "Hello? Hello?"

"Good morning, Mrs. Robinson. This is Paula O'Neil, the principal at David's school. We met at the parents' meeting last month." The sweet, lilting voice jolted her awake. She sat up in bed.

"Oh yes, I remember. How are you, Ms. O'Neil?"

"I'm doing fine, dear, but I need to inform you of a dreadful mishap today."

Gayle's eyes widened. "What happened?"

"Well, Ms. Baker, David's teacher, decided to resign her position today."

"Really?" she said, moving to the edge of the bed, "But she left me a voicemail yesterday about coming over."

"We are really sorry for this inconvenience. We hope to ensure a more stable education for the tester children."

"This will not be an inconvenience, I assure you. So what happened to Ms. Baker?" Gayle inquired.

"It appears she did a complete turnaround. She never showed up for work. We thought she was sick, but then she called to say something about 'finding herself.' We are just keeping all the experimenting parents in the loop. Tomorrow, we will have a permanent teacher and schedule a meeting for you all to meet her."

"Okay, just tell me the time." Gayle wrote down the information and slowly hung up the phone. She rose from the bed, donning her worn gray robe, and padded out of her bedroom.

Usually, she had Gabriel to speak with. He surprised her with his knowledge of the television shows of the old days, old day shows. They watched them for a few hours in the afternoon. A black-market dealer her late husband used to work for sold her two complete seasons on chip. Since Gabriel returned to Divine's headquarters for evaluation, the day shows did not appeal to her that day.

Downstairs, Gayle pressed the controls to open the blinds. The false sun rays flooded throughout the first floor's two-story stained glass windows in the foyer, causing a brilliant rainbow to shine across the polished white marble floors. She spotted evidence the floor was recently cleaned. Her best guess was Gabriel going through his nightly routine cleaning.

Regretfully, Gabriel did a better cleaning job than she when it came to the chores around the house, even with handling David when her son had his dark moments. She stalled at the knowledge of that. She had to admit that Gabriel did a better job than her. She took pride in being able to bring a mirrorlike shine to the lab floors.

The silence in the house began to weigh on her until she arrived in the kitchen and saw a wonderful surprise. Gabriel made coffee before he left. It still simmered in the pot. The addicting earthy aroma caused her to squeal. She slid over to the counter, plucking her cup from the drainage rack. She poured the dark-brown liquid into her cup, allowing the scent to dance in her nose.

"Thank you," she said, raising the rim of the cup to her lips.

She headed for the small intimate sunroom, where a small round table and two white wicker chairs were situated at the center of the room. The sunroom's tall, wide windows held a spectacular view of the side and backyard. She sat in one of the chairs facing the backyard. Her eyes moved over the gentle green hills dotted with yellow-and-blue flora filling her with harmony. In another year, it would all be over, and they could move to Midtown. Maybe the next place would be just like here.

Gayle finished her coffee. She stood up and went back to the kitchen. The main window faced the front yard. She saw a short, chubby woman staring through the thick black iron bars of her gates. Her heart almost stopped.

"What the—" she said. Gayle rushed through the house to the front door and hurriedly opened it. She stepped onto the front porch, peering at the woman, who then waved at her, and beckoned her to come forward. Gayle narrowed her eyes, knowing that Gabriel should have been home, but the woman didn't appear dangerous. She slowly stepped from the porch and crossed the expanse of the yard. The mild heat instantly warmed her skin. Upon closer inspection, the woman's pale skin appeared wrinkled and aged. Her peppery hair was gathered on top of her head in an oval. Slanted dark eyes sparkled with amusement that didn't quite make her pale, thin lips curve.

"May I help you?"

"I hope so. Do you know where the people who live across the street are?" The woman pointed to the Johnsons' house.

Gayle's lips parted. "Didn't you hear?"

"Hear what?"

"Sue and Walter passed a week ago,"

The woman stepped back. "Oh no! Why wasn't I told? Where are the children? Where are Zane and Lily?"

"Who are you?"

"My name is Deborah Draper, Dee Dee to the kids. I'm Sue's sister. I tried to call many times, but she never called me back. The last time I spoke with her was over a month ago."

"Do you recall the last of the—"

The woman seemed surprised by her question. "They should have known. I'm the children's only living relative. What the hell is going on here?"

That's what I'd like to know, Gayle thought. She reached for the gate handle. "Why don't you come in for coffee? We can talk more."

Tears pooled in the woman's eyes. "I am so confused."

"You better come with me." She motioned the morose woman to follow her back down the path to the house.

Deborah walked beside her, sniffling, with her head bowed. Gayle patted her round shoulders, hoping to soothe the pain. Inside the house, Deborah's grief briefly dissipated. "So this is how you people live."

"This is how they live," Gayle corrected her. She removed a clean cup from the cabinet.

"Divine Cybernetics owns this house, and they pay for everything." They sat down at the dining room table. The cavernous dark room had few windows, and the only light came from a grand crystal and chrome chandelier centered in the vaulted ceiling above. She admitted to liking the roselike chandelier.

"This is really thoughtful of you," Deborah said. She sipped the dark brew slowly. "Thank you so much."

"No problem. So tell me. Why did you decide to come here?"

Deborah inhaled. "Sue and I haven't been close, but she is still my sister. We had been talking more than usual lately."

"Did she tell you about any illnesses?"

"Oh no, but she always sounded so tired and stressed. I begged her to let me visit, help her with the children."

"Divine would never have allowed that. They would have been removed from the program."

"What is this program?" she asked, her voice raised in frustration.

"I guess your sister never told you."

"We, Sue and I, belong to an experimental program headed by our company, Divine Cybernetics. They placed us here with our families' full expenses paid to test their newest line of service robots."

"Sounds like a dream, but why was my sister so stressed whenever we spoke?"

"Honestly, I don't know."

"Well, I am going to find out," Deborah said, appearing very determined.

Chapter 6

GABRIEL WALKED THROUGH THE secret entrance on the side of one of the smaller lab buildings. Inside, he followed down a long, narrow hallway with tall stark-white sterile walls on either side eventually arriving to a pair of tall metal doors. He pressed his palm on the side. The doors slid open revealing a large cavernous lab.

The lab filled with five rows of metal tables filled with various bottles and tubes. Chemistry labs were created for small biological experiments and testing. Above four large blank screens lined one wall, and below them, three scientists sat at individual pods bent over furiously typing. A small dark-haired, olive-skinned woman spotted him from her pod and smiled. He smiled back recalling her name as Mya. She rose from her chair. "Gabriel, how are you?"

"I am well, Mya," he said.

"That's good," she said, approaching him. "The others have already been through their evaluation. You will be last."

"Vera is waiting for you in the first room." Xavier, another scientist, spoke up, approaching them. "Glad to see you again, Gabriel." "A pleasure to see you again, Dr. Xavier." He nodded to the man.

"Follow me." Xavier picked up a rectangle black digital man tapping on the screen.

Gabriel walked behind the tall, slender man.

They arrived, walking toward the rear of the lab, then around a wall. A row of doors leading to the medical examination rooms lined the one wall. Suddenly, a small pale woman came out of the first door. Dr. Vera Cote nodded to them. "That will be all, Xavier." She addressed the tall doctor.

"Yes, Dr. Cote," Xavier said, returning to the lab.

"Hello, Gabriel," she said. Her dark eyes regarded him in the familiar, penetrating expression he grown used to.

"Greetings, Dr. Cote," he said, preceding her into a large room.

"Take a seat," she said, busying herself at a mini lab on the opposite side of the room.

"Dr. Cote, why is everyone so nervous?"

She stopped and faced him.

"How can you tell?" "I can't really explain it," he said.

"Well, as you know, Delilah still has not been found," she said. "The higher ups are not happy, which make all the scientists nervous about our jobs."

He stiffened. "I am sorry."

"You have nothing to be sorry for. Frankly, I believe it is best this has happened now before we sell the program to the Dome Council. Something like this could really cause trouble for Divine Cybernetics." She approached him. "Can you tell me a little what happened?"

"She sent out a distress signal…I simply responded."

"When you arrive at the Johnsons' former residence, what did you see?"

"She was in the living room waiting for me. We talked. I did remind her of the rules and how I believe that she made some infractions."

"This is when she attacked you?" she asked. "This is very odd that her temper would flare up so Quickly."

"Yes, this is when she attacked me."

"Extraordinary." She shook her head, turning away from him. "So tell me about you. Have you experienced any unusual issues?"

Finally, he met her eyes. "I have many urges that my programming is not able to comprehend. I feel it all over, and it is difficult for me to accurately calculate."

"Hmm, give me an example of one such situation." She stepped back, leaning against a nearby counter.

"Two weeks ago. I wanted to warn Mrs. Robinson about the loose board in the dining room. She usually locks the door when privacy warrants, but this time, the door was open, and I thought it safe to go in." He stopped.

"What happened next, Gabriel?" she asked.

"She finished cleaning herself in the washroom and had divested herself of the towel. Many funny feelings overwhelmed me, and I ran away," he said, his voice trailing off.

"You experienced a sexual feeling."

His brow furrowed. "I do not know what that is."

She chuckled. "Your education on human relations is sorely lacking." She crossed her arms over her chest. "Gayle mentioned that you take the responsibility of performing household chores."

He remained silent. He never understood his need to ensure the household ran smoothly, that his host family was comfortable and felt the joy of his efforts. He could not form the words in order to explain to her this particular need. For the first time, his human heart slowed to a halt, and the air stuck in his lungs.

"Breathe, Gabriel," Vera said as she pushed away from the wall. "Don't worry about it. My job is to help you assimilate into human life so you may do your job."

"Is it wrong for me to assist?"

"Who am I to declare a man helping around the house is wrong?" she said, stepping away from him to pick up her tablet. He watched her type something on the screen. "I will add some codes in your training program. Wait here for Stella. She will draw some fluids and guide you to the capsules where the others sleep."

"Thank you, Dr. Cote," he whispered.

She patted him on the leg and turned to leave the room. Her lab assistant, Stella, entered a little while later. As instructed, she drew liquid in three tubes, then led him out of the room and back through the laboratory. They left the lab and turned right, down a dimly lit corridor. Midway, he felt a familiar nudge and slowed his walk. He focused on a pair of metal double doors at the end of the hall. He knew that the room beyond was where his brothers and sisters supposedly slept in a sedated slumber, except one. His hesitation caused Stella to stop and give him a sideways look. He gazed into her eyes. "I will proceed from here. Go back to the lab."

Her dark-green eyes glazed over, and her pupils dilated to an exaggerated size. "You know what to do from here. I will return to the lab," she said and then walked back to the lab.

He waited for her to disappear through the lab doors. He glanced back at the double doors and proceeded toward the sleeping chambers. He stepped into the freezing room, searching the dim corners of the room. At first, it all appeared quiet.

Six upright glass pods lined the opposite wall. Soft blue light illuminated inside the chambers, revealing the sleeping forms of the other guardians. He noticed two of the pods, side by side, stood empty. The pod next to his assigned one would have belonged to Delilah, and as he expected, it was empty. She never made contact with him or any of the others again. He found it disturbing that she decided to shut them all out of her mind.

Suddenly, he felt a pair of arms hug his midsection. "Hello, Olivia."

"Hi, Gabby," she said. Her arms squeezed his middle.

He relaxed into her embrace, bringing his large hands over her arms. "Enough for now, sister." He pulled her arms away with gentle movements and twisted around in her embrace.

Her beautiful oval brown face shone with uncontained excitement. She had a goofy smile on her full lips and a vacant gaze in her slanted amber eyes. "We can play while the others sleep, like yesterday."

He caught her hands when she made another attempt to hug

him. "Not yesterday, love. Remember we have not seen each other for six months."

"It feels like yesterday." Her mouth turned into a disappointed pout.

"We will play later, but now you will have to return to your capsule." He placed his hands on her shoulder and guided her toward her own capsule next to Delilah's.

"We want to play now, like tag," she said, digging in her heels, then danced out of his grip.

"We will play tomorrow in the park," he said, pushing at her mind.

"We will play tomorrow," she said, and finally relinquished and repeated, "We will play tomorrow."

"Now you must sleep. We must not make the lab techs angry," Gabriel said, taking her by the hand and guiding her to the capsule.

Once Olivia settled in, she gave him an air kiss and closed her eyes. He closed the metal door and activated the lock. Sweet Olivia. He worried a lot about her even more so than the others even Delilah. They had a close relationship during their lab days. Once they received their assignments, he wanted to speak up to the scientist. He wanted to warn them about Olivia and Delilah, but his father refused to allow such negative talk about his creations. He never wanted to anger Father.

He double-checked Olivia's security locks, then headed for his own capsule. He stopped near Delilah's empty one. His chest constricted once more. He never should have gone to the house that night, but he sensed something was not right with her. He had to see for himself what danger she presented.

Gabriel entered his own chamber, relaxing his tall form against the silvery silk padding. All at once, the laser mechanisms commenced tickling his skin. His muscles spasmed, and he felt his brain constrict slightly. It caused him to flinch, but he was used to the probs just like when he was a little one.

He remembered the nurses walking them in the early morning hours, commanding them to line up in a single-file line arranged by the time they were created. Then they would be marched to the school room for their lessons. As they grew and relaxed around each other, the small group developed different personalities when the scientists and nurses left them alone. They whispered forbidden wishes and dreams to one another.

What was it he wished? Gabriel tried many times to pull the data back, but somehow, he knew it was lost.

"Gabriel, we sense an elevation in your heart rate. Is everything okay?" Vera's voice spoke over the chamber's com. He sent a message through the com, calming her concerns. He thought she chuckled over the com. "Try to relax and sleep some."

She's right, he thought.

*****

Vera paused her typing. She read Gabriel's readouts three times already. Her brow furrowed as she read over the charts a fourth time. Gabriel's biological makeup appeared to be advancing in a different avenue compared to the other guardians. She placed her chart on the counter and stared at him through the screen. She met Gabriel as a small child. He was an empathic and very intuitive young boy, so she thought he belonged to one of the staff members. They talked about art and colors for half an hour. She realized he was one of the prototypes. Once she started assisting Dr. Gregory with the guardian program, she knew quickly what he did. She knew it needed to be reported, but her scientific mind wanted to see what might come of this.

Vera leaned over to the mic. "Gabriel, I have placed something a little extra in your programming. I will need detailed analysis of how it will work for you."

Okay, he mentally typed.

She smiled and rose from her desk, gathering her chart. "I have a meeting with Ms. Miles," she said to her lab assistant. "Allow them to sleep for another hour and release them."

"Yes, Dr. Cote."

Vera headed out of the lab after giving her assistants some last-minute instructions. She moved down the empty corridor toward the private elevator. She entered the private code for the penthouse and stepped into the elevator. Her eyes closed as the elevator ascended. Her mind organized, knowing that once she confronted Catherine Miles, everything would need to be in order or Vera herself will face the consequences. She could definitely not afford it. She would face the consequences. The door slid open, revealing a long large bright room, in the gray and silver monochrome colors. At her left was a large chrome fireplace ablaze with a medium flame. Two plush white chairs were set in front of the fireplace. She stepped on the metal tile, hearing her heels echo through the room.

At the center of the room, a petite, slender pale-skinned woman sat at an oversized glass desk. Her white hair was arranged in a tight bun at the top of her head that aligned with her narrow oval face. She raised her elegant chin, locking gazes with Dr. Cote. Catherine's lips pressed tightly together, and anger pierced through her dark eyes.

"Vera, please have a seat," Catherine Miles said.

Vera continued forward and sat down in a plush white chair on the opposite side of the desk. She placed her chart on her lap and waited. The young owner of Divine Cybernetics appeared to be a delicate woman in her early thirties. Men often took in her appearance and arrived at the conclusion that the CEO was naive and soft, but Vera knew differently. Many times, she witnessed and received Ms. Miles's wrath.

"Have they found Delilah?" Catherine asked. She folded her slender fingers, placing them on the glass surface.

"They have not," Vera said. She blinked twice.

"This is inexcusable. Divine Cybernetics cannot allow this embarrassment. Do you hear me?"

Vera nodded, remaining silent.

"Dr. Gregory has yet to respond to my summons. Do you know why?"

"I thought he would have joined us today," she said.

"Clearly, he is not here. Never mind," Catherine said, leaning back into the black cushions of her chair. "What is your report on the guardian program? Is it salvageable?"

"I have run multiple tests on the remaining prototypes. None of them are showing the instability that Delilah has displayed."

"I will be honest with you, Dr. Cote. We have gone overbudget on this pet project of Dr. Gregory. My accountants are worried. I am worried. Soon, the investors will be worried. When they are worried, I won't be happy."

"Understood."

"I am happy that you do. Here is what I want to see. No more accidents involving the guardian program and a perfect report to hand over to the Dome 13 government council next week. If that happens, we will more than double our investments. They are watching us and this program," Catherine said and then inhaled. "If this project succeeds, our contract will extend. If it does not—"

"I know," Vera said.

"Good. Make sure the good doctor understands, or he can be replaced, along with you."

Vera stood, nodded, and left the room. Once the elevator doors closed, she exhaled. Her heart slowed to five-second beats. She leaned against the cool surface of the elevator clutching her chart. "Damnit, Dr. Gregory! What have you done?" she whispered.

*****

Gabriel waited outside David' school, trying to figure out the extra programming Dr. Cote placed into him. Programming often came to him quicker than the other guardians. His comprehension grasped the coding with optimum performance. He would turn and teach it to the others through their telepathic link, trying to lead them to better understand themselves. The school bell sounded throughout the area, jolting Gabriel from his concentration. He straightened and turned to watch the large metal doors burst open, and children of all sizes spilled through. David appeared among the mixture, a happy jubilant boy. He appeared to make friends rather easily, which made the little one slow to come to the car.

Gabriel opened the door and unfolded his long frame from the car. David ran and shouted at the top of his lungs with a group of boys who weren't in his class. They tossed around a ball. David caught it every time and tossed it back. Gabriel knew his duty dictated that he should interrupt the play and command the boy into the car.

However, watching human action of play and joy, Gabriel felt something connect inside him—the smiles on the young faces, the sparkle in their small eyes. David and his friends fluttered about like happy little birds without care. In the lab, the guardians could not play the games he read about in forbidden stories. Of course, the others rejected the games Gabriel suggested, but he still played them secretly, when the lab emptied and his brothers and sisters sleep in their coffins.

Gabriel blinked. He stood for a moment, surprised by the memory. It was clear as if he lived the moment only yesterday. Suddenly, cool liquid pooled at the corner of his eye. He felt it flow down his face in a single, wet path. His heart started to clutch, and then it released.

"Gabe! Gabe, you're here!" David said. He stopped playing and sprinted toward Gabriel. David's black backpack thumped loosely on his back. His gray school blazer flapped in the wind. The sides of Gabriel's curled. He swooped the little boy into his arms. He felt David's small arms circle around his neck. "I had fun at school today!" David said happily.

"You did? What happened?"

"Well, Ms. Baker wasn't there, so we joined another class. We played games and drew. We never get to draw with Ms. Baker."

"I am glad you had fun." Gabriel lowered David onto the ground.

"I have pictures for Mommy and you!" "Thank you, David. I can't wait to see them."

*****

The fresh market store bustled with activity. Gayle tried to appear in high spirits, but the conversation from this morning still burned in her mind. Dr. Gregory told her that the Johnson children didn't have any relatives they could live with. Then this woman appeared. She remembered her application quite vividly. They did ask about other immediate family members such as uncles or cousins. Her own family consisted of just her and David. So if something were to happen to her, David would be a ward of the Dome, as many of her blood relatives died with the last wave of riots. Childbirth became dangerous in Downhill, with babies being stolen or most likely to die without proper medication. Most of the humans were sterile due to lack of nutrition, but some revolutionists said it was the false sun. No one knew for sure.

She pushed the cart into the cereal aisle. David begged her to retrieve some special breakfast food he'd heard about from the other children. She tried to remember the brand he mentioned while staring at the multiple choices that lined the shelves.

"No, sweetie, we aren't getting that." A quiet voice spoke a few feet away from her. She lifted her head to see who spoke.

Normally, Gayle ignored other shoppers, but something about the voice sounded familiar. She turned to see a thin woman with a small dark-haired girl pulling at her shirt. The woman bent her head back and closed her eyes. She could see faint thin lines along her eyes and sides of her mouth.

"Mom, that one!" the girl pointed to a red-and-blue box.

"Suzy, that is too expensive. Please! I have a headache."

Gayle felt the familiar tightening in her chest. The last time was at the first meeting with Sue Johnson. She approach the pair. The conversation between the woman and child continued, but it faded, replaced by Sue's tired voice and the argument with her son, Zane. They were in Town Center Park.

Sue's son, Zane, wanted to spend the weekend with a friend. Sue forbade him from doing so. Her body was just as thin for a woman with her height. Her cheeks sunk in, revealing the skeletal structure of the heart-shaped face and wide bones.

"Can I help you?" the woman asked. Her harsh voice sliced through her memory.

Gayle blinked twice. "Oh, sorry to interrupt. It's just that… well, may I ask if you are a part of the guardian program?"

The woman's dark eyes snapped open. "Who are you?"

"I'm Gayle. I'm with the program as well," she said, holding out her hand.

"Hello," the woman said, taking her hand with a limp grip, giving her a very brief greeting. "How did you know?"

"A guess," Gayle said, shrugging her shoulders. "I've only met one other person from the program."

"Oh, hi. My name is Hannah," the woman said, a tight smile crossing her face. "They keep us pretty isolated."

"Hi, Hannah," Gayle said as she glanced down at the little girl. "And who is this?"

"Suzy, or Susanne," Hannah responded for her daughter. "I have an older version of her in school."

"My son's name is David," Gayle said. "I think he maybe in your daughter's class."

"Funny, Melissa doesn't talk much about her school, but then she barely speaks about anything these days. I think she might just miss her old school."

"It's hard to adjust to a new situation."

Hannah nodded. "So how is it with your guardian?"

"He's been very helpful. David has really taken to him."

"I wish mine at least wash dishes. She's a little flaky, and sometimes, I feel like I'm raising three children instead of two."

"Have you expressed this to Dr. Gregory?"

"Many times, but personally, the man gives me the creeps. I really prefer to speak with Dr. Cote. She seems to know what's what."

"I see," Gayle said, remembering the small elderly pepper-haired woman who arrived with Dr. Gregory. The woman never spoke a word but just typed into her chart.

"We better get going," Hannah said. Suddenly, her body swayed dramatically.

Gayle's hand shot out to grab ahold of the woman's elbow. "Are you okay?"

"Yeah…yeah. We better get going."

"Mommy, I want the cereal," Suzy said. Her small voice rose to a high-pitch whine.

"Okay, we'll get it." Hannah grabbed the box of cereal and placed it in the basket.

"See you around," Gayle said.

Hannah nodded and walked out of the aisle to pay for her purchases. Gayle watched the young mother rub her arms to keep the cold away. Something really did not appear right about the woman. Gayle shook her head and continued her shopping.

Gayle rushed out of the store. The desired breakfast meal her son requested was forgotten. Instead, she recalled the small mousy woman that Dr. Gregory came with to her home two days ago. She would have to find a way to speak with this woman wondering if one of the guards knew the doctor's schedule. She would sneak around and ask knowing just the right one to ask.

Chapter 7

DR. HERMAN GREGORY SAT bent over his keyboard, narrowing his eyes at the screen. The numbers and letters grew blurry every minute went by. He even caught himself making mistakes. He felt his brain almost shutting down. He leaned back in his chair, exhaling, eager to pull in another whiff of precious air. He moved a frail, veiny hand to his temple, rubbing the delicate, paper-thin skin.

He let out a curse, slamming a hand on the polished surface of his heavy oak desk. He grabbed a piece of paper, crumpled it in his tight grip, then tossed it on the floor.

"Are you still working, Father?" Delilah asked.

His head shot up. His body grew erect, and his attention focused on the tall, lithe body leaning against the entrance of his office. She gave him a half smile with plump, pink lips, and brilliant, clear-blue eyes. He never expected Delilah to evolve into such a perfect specimen. His eyes lowered to her nude form revealed through the sheer, flimsy material of his nightshirt. It exuded eternal youth and vitality. "Father?" she said. Her eerie voice reverberated throughout his office, sending a tingle down his spine, captivating and charming him. He shuddered.

"Delilah, why did you go in my room again?" he asked.

She straightened, allowing her slender arms to fall at her side. "I needed something to wear."

"I had the housemaid bring you some female clothes. Did they not please you?" he asked, regretting his tone.

Delilah's mind was still that of a child and thus prone to childish antics. He found that she craved it, almost with desperation. "I do not appreciate the nudity, darling. Please cover up better."

She crossed her arms over her chest and formed her mouth into a pretty pout. "I don't like them."

"Please put them on now," he said.

"No," she said, her mouth fixed into a stubborn pout.

"Delilah…" He spoke her name, causing her face to twist into an ugly mask. He really did not want to deal with another tantrum from her. The last time he locked her in a bedroom upstairs, and she almost brought down the house. Luckily, she calmed down after an hour and pleaded with him in a pathetic voice to allow her out. He conceded but not after garnering a promise she would practice self-control, or he would refuse to help her further.

She must have seen his serious expression because the mask dropped, revealing the sweet girl from before. "I thought you said I could have anything I wanted, especially after all I have been through."

Herman's mind turned to her story about Gabriel. He would never imagine the brat would lash out at his brothers and sisters and propelled him to work through his normal sleeping hours. He had to know what motivated his firstborn to act so unpredictably.

"I still don't understand why Gabriel attacked you. I programmed him to be a protector to the rest of you and a leader. What could have provoked him?" He glanced down at his screen again, reading through rows of binary numbers and lines of equations.

"He is a brutal beast and a manipulator. He lied to the security detail," Delilah said.

"Delilah, I am uncertain that Gabriel would be capable of that."

"He needs to be stopped." Her eyes started to water.

His hands froze over the keyboard. He rose from his chair. "Darling, please not again."

"We must stop him," she said.

"Not until I find out why he malfunctioned."

"Father…" she paused, looking up at the ceiling. "Delilah?" he said.

Then a loud chord echoed through the manor. The walls rattled with the noise. Her face twisted into an even more monstrous mask. He watched her cover her ears and finally let out an animalistic roar. Herman rushed to her side, smoothing a shaky hand over her soft white hair. "Shush, it's only the bell." He grabbed her hands, trying to pull her up, but he didn't not have much strength. "You must go down to the basement now. The noise will not be able to reach you there."

"Father, it hurts!" she screamed.

"Go now," he said, "and be quick about it."

Delilah peeked up at him. Her glowing eyes dimmed, and tears flowed down her cheeks. "What if it is them?"

The chord sounded again, and she screamed again.

"Let me take care of them, but you must not be seen. Please obey me!" he shouted at her, being more aggressive. She obeyed him this time, disappearing. He never even saw her, only a blur of white moving through his vision. He heard the heavy metal doors below slam shut. He smoothed a hand over his gray-and-brown tweed suit. He checked his image in a large gold ornate mirror, and then moving quicker than usual, he hurried out into the hall, heading to his grand entrance. He entered his security code in the key pad at the center of the door. A display appeared before him, revealing the person on the outside. His assistant scientist, Dr. Vera Cote, stood on the top step. Her pale hound-dog face appeared serious, as her dark eyes stared into the black surface of his door. He let out a groan, knowing that she came from the meeting with the ice queen. He didn't look forward to listening for two hours of her newest decree. He stepped away, taking his time to input his second security code, which would unlock the door. He heard the lock click, and the door cracked open almost an inch, allowing thin rays of the sunset to spray into the dark corridor.

"Let me in, Dr. Gregory," Vera said, huffing.

He heard her foot tapping the concrete surface of his porch. He almost growled, grabbing the thick, cold handle, pulling the door open wide. She shuffled her small frame inside, never making eye contact. She jostled his shoulder, walking near him. She stopped in the center of the entry hall, facing him. He followed her, standing just beyond arm's length. Even at his own small stature, he still towered over her. He took full advantage of their contrasting height, staring down at her. He caught the displeasing view of the severe part at the center of her head that disappeared at the base of her neck. He despised it when she wore her hair in two thick braids and wrapped them in a combined thick bun at the base of her neck.

"Vera, a pleasure to see you, as always," he said, attempting a smile. "May I get you a drink?"

"Don't bother," she said. Her tone sounded clipped and stoic. "I won't be staying long. Some of us don't have the luxury of relaxing at home."

"Hey now!" he said, taken aback by her sudden aggression. "Why are you being so disagreeable?"

"Where should I begin?" she huffed again. "The false formulas you gave me to analyzes the guardians' evaluations or the meetings that we both need to be at, but you can't seem to find the time?" Her voice grew louder. "I am sick of trying to excuse your rudeness, especially when meeting with Catherine Miles, your benefactor!"

"I must dedicate my time to my research. Catherine knows I cannot be bothered by trivial matters."

"The faith in the guardian program depends on her generosity, Herman. That is not very trivial, if I may say so myself."

"Vera, if you continue your rudeness, I refuse to entertain you any further." He stood straighter, placing his hands behind his back. She narrowed her eyes until they were thin lines. "Another thing I have noticed is that the readings from my evaluations of the prototypes are not adding up. Without your notes, I can't determine why their robotics are becoming unstable."

"You just need to read more carefully. I know I made them clearer for you this time."

"I read your falsified instructions. Three times to be exact. So I gave up and decided on my own calculations." Her eyes left his, looking around the foyer. "Truth is, I think you added something else to the prototypes, something biological that appears to be akin to human DNA."

Herman stilled. He twisted his hands, thinking about what she had just said. He should have led the evaluations today, but Delilah needed him. She still could not be trusted or left to her own devices. He did not know enough to surmise her independence.

"I am waiting, Herman."

"A little something extra would do no harm." He swallowed hard. "You know better than anyone the pressure I am under. I needed to make them perfect."

"It does not matter!" she said, waving a hand. "My calculations show the prototypes have some human DNA. They are also displaying human emotions. If this is true, what kind of thoughts are going through their minds? What are the effects of our logical programming in their brains? What if it makes them insane?"

"Don't be silly. They are normal," he said.

Vera's eyes widened. "You are truly mad. I will not continue to cover for you. I am going back to headquarters to report this!"

"Vera! Be sensible!" he pleaded.

"No, I will not!"

"Please just listen." His eyes slid past her to Delilah's elegant figure positioned behind her. "I would never ask you to jeopardize what you love, just as you would never do that to me."

"I'm leaving!" Vera sidestepped.

Delilah grabbed her from behind, moving with astonishing speed. Vera only managed a small squeal. His guardian bent her neck back, snapping it. Then he closed his eyes, squeezing them shut. He flinched at the crackling sound piercing his ears. Herman turned away, stumbling back to his office. He closed the door shut, pressing his body against it. He heard her steps approach and jerked his body away, heading to his chair. He eased his body into its firm confines, expelling a volley of coughing. He focused on the dying embers in the fireplace, as his mind processed what he had just witnessed. Catherine Miles would never allow the guardian-angel program to continue if she knew what he created. He remembered the icy glare she gave him. He felt she never listened to his presentations. If he tried to explain the truth behind his creations, she would order the immediate destruction of his life's work.

Delilah opened the office door. Her bare feet padded over the polished wood floor, never making a sound. He heard the leather sofa by the fireplace squeak. He looked up to see her stretch out. He noticed that she changed her clothes, wearing a pair of tight black trousers and a loose white shirt that showed less skin.

"I need to return to headquarters," he said.

"I will come with you," Delilah volunteered.

"No…no, darling." He waved his hand about. "They are still looking for you. I must build a case that will turn their attention from you. I must see the results of the other guardians. They will be our biggest worry." He rose and finally looked at her. She had a healthy blush over her face.

"Those little humans are no match for me, and I will be able to protect you."

"Obey me, Delilah," he said, his tone growing irate.

Delilah's face twisted into an annoyed mask, then quickly returned to a smooth, calm expression. She gave him a small smile and reached for a nearby book. Her focus switched to reading the book. He rolled his eyes heavenward as she started to read silently, ignoring him. He rose from his desk, gathering his papers filled with notes and calculations into a leather cache. When finished, he grabbed the handle and shuffled toward the office door.

Suddenly, he stopped and turned. "Please stay, love. I will make this right."

"I know you will, Father," came her toneless voice.

*****

Dr. Gregory found the entry hall empty, except for Vera's tablet, which lay abandoned on the floor. Besides that, there appeared to be no evidence that she ever arrived at his home. Then he thought about her vehicle. The little car would need to be returned. He reached down, picked up the tablet, and stuck it under his arm.

The false sun faded behind the false night sky when Herman left his home. Vera drove the company car assigned to all the scientists and lab assistants in case their own was unavailable or absent. Vera decommissioned her own vehicle the previous year when her new security clearance allowed for the use of company vehicles.

He hurried to the small silver vehicle and typed in Vera's code. The engine immediately came to life, and the driver door opened. He slid his body inside, placing his cache on the passenger seat. The door automatically closed behind him.

"Greetings, Dr. Cote. Will you be returning to headquarters?" The car's mechanical voice spoke.

"Yes, and be quick about it."

"Yes, sir." The voice spoke again. The car pulled itself around the circular driveway. It increased speed once it cleared his thick iron gates.

The employee lot only held a few cars. The car pulled into his reserved parking garage. The heavy metal doors opened as the car slowly approached. Once the garage doors closed, the lights of the interior illuminated, and the garage interior lit up.

The car engine stopped, and the doors opened. He grabbed Vera's tablet and his cache and got out, feeling his joint start to protest. He should really think about a therapy dip. His joints were getting too old. He made his way to the private elevator. The doors silently slid open, allowing him into the cool confines. He typed in his personal access code. This would take him down into the labs below, where the six guardians were created.

In moments, the elevator arrived at the basement level. He forgot the freezing temperature down there and started frantically rubbing his arms to reserve what little heat his body gave off.

All the scientists' offices were located at the opposite side of the entrance. He made certain to always have access to the offices. He told them he needed access in case of emergency, but maybe this was an emergency. He pressed in the code, which would allow him into his assistant's office near his own. Always the neat freak, Vera's office was well organized, and she was a creature of habit. She never changed codes or items. She had the same office for the entire fifteen years she worked for Divine Cybernetics. He entered her office and closed the door shut, all the while keeping an ear to the lab, though he never suspected anyone would see him. The lab denied entry to lab employees after 5:00 a.m.

He tried to move fast, checking notebooks and files—anything that Vera would have logged that day's evaluations into. He finally sat down at her computer, logging into the browser. His heart grew icy as he read the first sentence of her journal entry from earlier that day:

> Dr. Herman Gregory has deceived
> Divine Cybernetics.

She wrote that her immediate recommendation was for the guardian program to be disbanded. Vera planned to take his children away from him—the creations that took the better part of his life to create. He endured humiliation and groveled when his own funds ran out. When finally his masterpiece was realized, they thought it inferior. He pressed his lips tightly together. His head throbbed, and he closed his eyes.

*****

Gayle opened her eyes, trying to focus them through pain. The vapors dissipated an hour ago, but she still felt the effects of the cleaning solutions. She should know the danger of mixing too much solution with the water. The ammonia needed more dissolution. She hated working with it, but Divine insisted on its use when cleaning the offices. Now the vice president of marketing's office would have to be aired out longer than her night shift would allow.

She rose from the comfy confines of the exec's black leather chair. She noted its new smell and lack of wear. He must have had it delivered the previous day and hadn't used it yet, knowing the arrogant exec's penchant for luxury items. She smirked at sitting in his chair before he returned to headquarters.

She pulled out her tablet, logging the issue of the smell and sending the message to the morning cleaning manager. They would be sure to increase air circulation to get rid of toxic fumes, though maybe the next time, he wouldn't complain so vehemently about the lack of shine on his furniture.

Gayle performed another inspection of the office, then reprogrammed the lights and atmosphere before closing the double doors shut. The lock clicked on, and she walked back down the corridor toward the back stairwell. She opened and closed the heavy metal door, making sure the lock clicked and hurried down the steps to the main lobby. Silence greeted her upon her arrival. She glanced around at the lack of activity. Most nights, many of the cleaning crew idled about, socializing, making plans for the new day, or just gossiping. She had to prepare her brain to deal with the constant chatter. Now there was no chatter, no wandering, nosy coworkers, just quiet and calm.

"See you tomorrow, Gayle," a deep voice said.

She stilled, moving her eyes from side to side. She took another step, twisting around when the sound of footsteps approached from her immediate left. Sergeant Ralph March moved from the shadows. His black-and-silver uniform appeared ruffled, and dark stubble formed around his usually clean-shaven features. He gave her a toothy grin. She relaxed, returning the smile. He wiped his mouth with a napkin, then crumpled it, and threw the paper into the waste bin.

"Ralph, you scared me," she said, waiting for him to approach.

"Sorry about that. I was late getting my dinner."

"What are you still doing here? Isn't this Nicky's shift?"

"He had a family emergency, and I needed the money." He shrugged.

She glanced up at him, shaking her head. "Will you be okay for the next ten hours?"

"I'll be fine. Not much action happens at midnight."

He nodded toward the lab elevator. "The brainiacs are all gone, except for Dr. Cote."

Gayle's eyes widened. "Dr. Cote is still here?"

"She's dedicated. I think this place is her primary residence."

"Do you think I could speak with her?"

"I'm sure it'd be fine. She's decent." He beckoned her to follow him. "Come. I'll let you down with my code."

"Thanks." She followed him toward the elevator.

"Just press the green button to come back," he said as he rapidly typed the security code. The doors slid open. "If it gets stuck, just call me, and I'll come get you."

"I won't be long," she said as she stepped into the small confines.

"Take your time. I have ten hours."

The doors closed. She felt the hurried descent in her stomach. She grabbed hold of one of the metal bars jutting out from the wall, steadying herself. The temperature dropped once the elevator stopped. Her body shivered. She saw her breath in small smoky clouds before her face as the door opened.

Gayle's eyes roved over the dimly lit room filled with a chaotic confusion. Small rectangular lab stations were positioned in multiple directions, tall glass tubes hung from the ceiling, and wires swung from the walls, creating a spidery web.

At the far end, she spotted a row of four pairs of doors. A brilliant light illuminated from under the middle door. She continued her approach, preparing to call out, when the door opened, revealing the bent, disheveled figure of Dr. Gregory. Unthinking, she quickly ducked behind one of the tables, peeking around a corner.

He stopped and turned, looking out over the room. His head stretched around to allow him to see more of the lab. She shuffled on her hands and knees, trying to avoid his scrutiny. She tried to make herself even smaller.

"Anybody there?"

She heard him call out. She heard him mumbling and next heard the distinctive sound of him typing on the keypad beside the door, and the lock clicked. She moved her head, peeking around the corner. She spotted his small stature moving to open and close his cache back and marching along the back wall and out the side door. Once he disappeared between the doors, she stood up. Gayle waited for a moment, then quickly returned to the elevator. She pressed the green button, as Ralph had instructed. The doors silently opened. She slipped in and frantically pressed the lobby button. As the doors closed back, she saw the doors through which Dr. Gregory slipped open back up. She breathed a grateful sign when the elevator ascended into the lobby. She spotted Ralph leaning against the receptionist's desk, busily typing on his tablet.

He lifted his head as she rushed toward him. His expression quickly turned to concern. "What is it?"

"I thought you said Dr. Cote was in her office?"

"She is." He held up the screen of his tablet. "I have her logged in for two hours now."

"I just saw Dr. Gregory in her office, not Dr. Cote."

Ralph's brow furrowed. "Why would Dr. Gregory log in under Dr. Cote? He has the same access as she does, even more so."

"I saw him." She leaned closer. "He came out of Dr. Cote's office, and she wasn't there."

Ralph nodded, but she saw something in his eyes. "Go home, Gayle. I'll speak with Dr. Gregory about this issue."

"Ralph, I don't think you should confront him just yet. Wait for the morning when Sergeant Vila is here.”

“Go on home now. I can handle an eighty-year-old mad scientist.” He gave her another toothy smile.

“Okay, but please be careful. Lately, things aren’t what they appear,” she said as she kissed Ralph on the cheek, then turned to leave the lobby. Her lone car waited under the shadow of one of the white winged human statues that adorned the lot. She always admired the perfectly sculpted form and, many times, wondered where the company found such a creature.

Even now, she stood staring into the handsome, frozen statue’s face. Small white lights along the base illuminated its elegant cheekbones and brow as the stone wings thrust up and out of its muscled back. Suddenly, a shadow crossed her line of vision and before it disappeared, she saw a strip of blond hair. She narrowed her eyes, peering into the darkness. She blinked her eyes. *Must still be the bleach,* she thought, getting in her car.

*****

Gayle arrived home with her mind still buzzing from seeing Dr. Gregory roaming around the lab.

Why was he carrying all those stacks of books and disks? Should he be taking those things out of Vera’s office? He’d forgotten to mention this to Ralph, but maybe he got to the old man in time to stop him.

She pulled her car into her garage. Once the large door swung close, lights from the ceiling illuminated the interior. The engine shut down, and the car doors rose, allowing her to exit. She grabbed her belongings and exited the car.

She entered the house through the family room, where more lights blinked on. She saw remnants of David’s day littering the sofa. She knew he loved watching the large screen. If she allowed him, he would practically sleep and have all his meals in there. As she moved further, a brown fluff caught her eye. She recognized the stuffed toy bear they bought in Midtown when first arriving to Uptown.

The train had a layover of an hour before returning to operation. David wanted to see everything, and she wanted to take the time to gather her nerves. Midtown had been so different from the Downs. The buildings were small but clean and decent. The people were hardworking and went about their business without harassing them about money or food. The streets were clean and manicured. It was then that she first thought about living in Midtown and initiated the process to live there.

They saw a store with the most beautiful window display. David practically dragged her across the street. Upon entering the store, he roamed the aisles, excited. Then they found him. David named the toy Richard, after his father. Surprisingly, it didn't cost very much.

Since then, David took the toy everywhere. He even tried to take it to school, but she caught him and explained that Richard couldn't go to school with him because the toy will get lost or damage.

She lowered her body near the toy, caressing the downy fur. She would have to speak with her son about leaving his things about. She leaned into the plush cushions of the sofa, stretching her body. Her eyes trained on the ceiling, as she tried to steady her thoughts, and then she smelled the delicious aroma of a meaty dish.

Gayle raised herself from the sofa, following the smell. She walked into the foyer, stopping to glance around. She noticed shadows moving through the slit between the double white oak doors.

"Gabriel?" she said as she started to walk toward the dining room. She pressed a hand flat against one of the doors, giving it a gentle push. "Gabriel?" she repeated as the doors opened. She paused at the cusp of the entrance. A large chandelier bathed the dining room in a kaleidoscope of sparkling pinks and reds. A stiff, starched white lacy cloth covered the long oak table, where she saw two place settings positioned across from each other. She drifted farther into the room, recognizing that the small white napkins were folded into strange winged creatures. Elaborate, ornate silverware were arranged with severe precision on either side of the plates.

Her fingers glided along the table cloth, taking in the stiff material. She stood by one of the chairs, again studying the elegant setup. Her lips twisted, and her head shook. Just then, she heard the soft squeak of the kitchen door opening. She turned to see Gabriel strolling in while balancing a large round glass vase overfilled with bulbous pink-and-white flowers.

"Welcome home, Gayle," he said, smiling at her, increasing his pace. He placed the vase in the center of the table. "I thought I would have more time to finalize everything."

"What is going on?" She peered around again, "How did you—"

"Come. Have a seat," he said, pulling her chair out for her. "Relax. I will bring the wine."

She sat down without really wanting to, but her brain still had yet to process everything. "Gabriel—" She started, but he disappeared back into the kitchen.

She heard the door again moments later. Gabriel quickly placed a tall, slender glass of wine before her. He poured in a dark-blue liquid until it reached the rim. Then he left her side, just as before. His motions were all a blur. Every time he appeared in the dining room, she tried to speak with him, but he moved too quickly for her to form a word in her mouth.

"The main course is cooling in the oven," he said, finally placing a bowl of pink, red, and yellow cubes before her. Gabriel placed the same items on his side of the table, then took his seat opposite her meeting her suspicious expression with a sweet smile.

Her eyes moved from the bowl to his expectant face, then back to the bowl. She leaned back in the chair, crossing her arms, and squeezed her eyes shut. When she opened them again, Gabriel gave her an eerie stare. She looked back down at the bowl.

"This looks nice," she said, picking up a fork.

"It's Riker's melon."

"Riker's melon?" She dipped her fork into the bowl, bringing it to her mouth. She placed it into her mouth. The shocking sweetness jolted her senses right away. She had to pause.

He must have seen her expression and asked, "Do you like it?"

"It's really sweet. What is Riker's melon?"

He gave her a dazzling smile. "Brentwood Riker was a botanist who made it his mission to revive Earth's original fruits and vegetables. He was not successful at retrieving all the produce. Instead, he combined many species together to make a new species that can sustain the rest of the human race for years to come.

"It must have been for the perfect citizens. The Downs never sold anything like this."

"I want you to enjoy this. Do you understand?" Gabriel's tone lowered.

Gayle glanced up at him, narrowing her eyes. She shook her head. "I don't understand it," she said, waving a hand over the table.

He raised a blond brow. "I read that this is what one lover does for another."

"Lover?" she sputtered. "What do you mean?"

"Yes, that *is* what we are?"

Gayle coughed frantically. "Gabriel, we have never...how did you arrive at that conclusion? Is there something wrong with your programming?"

"I did the calculations three times and ran several scenarios through my new analysis program." His eyes blinked. She saw a pink blush spread over his face. His blue eyes started to glow.

"Okay...okay. I'm not sure you understand what you are saying."

"I understand, Gayle. I understand that these urges I feel is because I love you, and you love me. I researched about the behavior of lovers—that this is what is supposed to happen. Why are you confused?" She groaned. *Why did he have to choose tonight to malfunction?* "Gabriel, I am not sure what you're feeling or even *if* you are feeling it. Whatever it is, it's not real. Goodness, Gabriel, you are a machine, a billion-dollar machine involved in an experiment that will end in a few months! Did you include that in your calculations?"

Gabriel shot up. "I am *real! You* are confused! Sometimes I think *you* are malfunctioning, unemotional machine!"

Gayle sat back in the chair, grabbing its arms. Her mouth widened as she looked at his face, which was twisted in a monstrous mask. Then he calmed down, and his body froze in space. His face dropped into a miserable mask. Time stood still for a hair of a second until she opened her eyes to see that the room had cleared.

Chapter 8

GABRIEL PERCHED AT THE edge of the railings on the second-floor balcony. It faced the east, where he could see the false sun appear over the yellow-and-orange sky. He heard the first sound of morning travel over the gentle breeze. He recognized the sparrow family in the large oak at the front of the property joined by the squirrel family wandering the grounds, searching for their breakfast. All the natural elements shook off the fog of sleep, starting over from the chaos.

Many times he wished to experience awakening such as the living creatures of the world do. If anything, all he wanted to do was erase the horrors of the previous night and the horrified expression on Gayle's face.

Gabriel turned his back on the pastoral scene to face his reality. Gayle slept in David's room the previous night. She tried to be discreet, but he heard the door lock's distinctive click. The pain he felt from her words solidified in his chest and continued until morning. Suddenly, an emotional wave stabbed inside his skull. He leaped from the railing, landing on the hard concrete with a soft thud. He reached out with his mind, searching for the source. He stumbled when it touched with Olivia's. Her despair overrode his nerves, making his body seize, then it dissipated. He tried to ask her what was wrong. She drew away and blocked his invasion, but not in time for him to realize that Olivia hid away in the bathroom.

He took long, purposeful steps toward the en suite bathroom. Entering the cool, humid interior, he heard water running. It came from the glass-enclosed shower.

"Olivia?" he said, stopping in front of the large sliding door. Her tall, slender form stilled. He heard the water stop, but still, he could not see her face. Her silence upset him even more. "Olivia," he said, raising a hand to the brass handle.

Gabriel was puzzled as Olivia seemed to already know the story of the Merry Musician. He remembered watching it with David one day, and now, both Olivia and David were hooked on the kids' show. The *Merry Musician* show was an animated series set in a village of humans surrounded by creatures from fantastical civilizations. Gabriel eventually concluded that it was a show about friendship. The main character, Nela, was a young girl who was an exceptional musician. Her music drew various odd characters from fantastical civilizations, and they would all go on an adventure together. In the end, Nela would gain a new friend. Although it was harmless entertainment for Olivia and David, Gabriel never really paid much attention to the program as it was not reality.

Gabriel furrowed his brow. He knew she saw every episode with her children. "You know the story, Ollie. Why do you want me to tell you?"

"Please," she said. She grasped his sleeve in a tight fist. He closed his eyes. If this gave him the information he needed, he would indulge her need to enter into this childlike fantasy world. "There are many stories involving the Merry Musician's journey. Which one would you like to hear?"

Her fist lightened. "I want to hear the beginning, how she became the Merry Musician."

"The first book," he said, pausing. "It is rather sad. Are you sure you want to hear it?"

"Yes, I want to hear it."

"In the second star to the left and straight on to evening"—he reluctantly started, still unsure why she wanted to hear the story—"a village on the edge of a mystical forest—"

"There in lived a brave little girl—," Olivia interrupted.

"Her family fell to a sweating sickness—"

"She decided to brave the dark and forbidden black forest..." Olivia again interrupted.

"Will you tell the rest?" he said, smiling at her.

She shook her head. Her lips pressed tight to indicate that she would not speak again. He shook his head. "Her bravery impressed the forest spirits, and they wanted to keep her as their own."

"They promised to save her mother if she would join their family," she whispered the last part.

"The eternal child bringing light to the darkness of human despair..." His words faded. He leaned back against the wall. "You did not hurt the children, Olivia."

She just looked at him. The fire in her eyes faded. "I want to be like her."

"Like whom?" he asked.

"I want to be the Merry Musician." Her voice lightened. "She set out to save her family and protect them. She did not disappear to play frivolous games in the forest, leaving them vulnerable..." Her voice faded.

He raised his head. "Olivia, if you did not hurt them—"

"I did not follow my programming. I have failed my duty. You must take action."

He straightened his body. "Olivia, I can't."

"You must. I am not worth anything now. My family is gone because I was not there. Father will destroy me. Would you allow him to do it?"

Gabriel stared into her face. Images of their early life flickered through his brain, shocking his system. He remembered sneaking into her room to console her. One of the lab assistants scolded Olivia for trespassing in the labs and spilling over a dozen vials of viable chemicals. She hid under her covers, shivering and sniffling. When he finally got her to remove the covers, her eyes were glowing, her mind wild and turbulent. He spent the rest of the night bringing her under control. Despite his young age, he knew his powers even then. This also made him wise to hiding them.

"A kiss then," he said with a whisper.

"A brave kiss," she said and then gave him a toothy grin.

"For a brave girl." He leaned in close, touching her lips with his own. Pure energy ignited between them. A blinding white light emitted from her. The flow increased, pouring into him, and a searing burn started at the center of his chest. They remained locked in a deadly embrace.

He closed his eyes, keeping the embrace until the warmth of her body turned chilly. When he opened his eyes, a crumpled towel laid at his hip. He leaned forward in the seat, while his body rattled with uncontrolled vibrations. The tears he held back flowed. He buried his hands, grabbing his hair.

Gabriel tried to calm himself. He spent an hour pacing in circles in the bathroom until he made himself leave. He caught his face in the mirror, fixing his face in a calm mask but no longer serene. His eyes burned a blue fire. Strength flowed through his veins, heating his skin. He stretched his telepathic muscles.

Gayle finally gave into sleep; however, David would wake any moment. He pressed another sleep suggestion into the little boy's mind. This would allow Gayle another hour to rest her strained nerves.

A nauseous feeling overwhelmed him as Olivia's power surged forth. He caught images of her room from her dotted memory. Her room exploded in lacy pink-and-white frills in front of his eyes. Delicately painted flowers spread over the white walls. Overstuffed comical toys littered over shelves and the dresser.

He stood at the center of her room, turned around, and observed how organized and posh it was. He couldn't believe she insisted on such a bizarre, innocent interior. The company-assigned decorator never sought the guardian's opinion on the decor of their personal dwelling. He raised an eyebrow at this, as they never slept.

He gave the room one last look before moving into the dimly lit hall outside. His footsteps echoed from one end to the other. It led to a large area where a curved staircase wound down into a three-story octagonal foyer. At the center, four bodies of the Peterson family laid in a rectangular formation.

Olivia must have arranged them, as she did many times with her dolls. It bespoke of maternal care and love. He descended the steps, taking two at a time. The prone bodies had obvious signs of trauma and violence. The father, dressed in his Divine Cybernetics guard uniform, had multiple stab wounds in his chest. His wife and two daughters' nightwear had burn holes from a heavy gunnery. Suddenly, flickers of light shone through the tall stained glass windows. He retreated to the second floor, hiding behind a fat floral column. The thick double doors burst open, and black-and-gold uniformed soldiers with large polished weapons drawn entered. They flanked the perimeter of the foyer. Their covered faces were twisted in all directions, revealing serious, gleaming eyes.

"Clear!" yelled one of the guards, whom he assumed him to have been the leader.

A woman dressed in a tight black uniform marched through the door, but her face was uncovered. Her olive face was set with a serious expression. Her dark eyes roved around the immediate, then focused on the upstairs landing. She narrowed them, then twisted her lips, as if a thought came to her. The guards stood in stoic positions against the wall. They appeared to be waiting for her command. She stepped further into the home around the figures of the Peterson family, stopping at the foot of the stairs.

"Sergeant Green, have your team step upstairs and clean up here."

"Yes, Agent Travis."

A sly smirk surfaced on her face. She finally regarded the bodies, then he watched her pull out a small black phone. He heard her speed dial a number. Someone must have answered on the other line, but she spoke in a quick, curt tone. "Wake up the council." She listened for a moment, then pressed the button to hang up. He heard the guards making their way upstairs and made himself return back to the Robinson household.

In an instant, he found himself back in his own room. In the distance, he heard the cartoon show *Merry Musician*, blaring in the family room. He remembered the episode from the previous day. The Merry Musician convinced the Goblin King to share his wheat berry tree fruit with the Fairy Queen for Her Majesty to win a pie contest with the Troll Queen. He recorded the episode for David when the little boy woke up late. He allowed him to sleep in the previous day. He heard Gayle wake up and pace in her room. Her whispered voice spoke angry words in the phone. In her current mood, she would not welcome a visitor, but he had to speak with her. He had to know that she forgave him for last night. He realized that not knowing how she felt about what happened bothered at him, but he did not know why.

Gabriel steeled himself before ambling out of his room. He still could hear her voice behind the closed door. It grew louder. As he drew closer, he heard her pacing the bedroom. He also heard sniffling, as if she had been crying. His footsteps slowed. He arrived at her door.

"Do you people not realize that it is the middle of the school year?" She waited until the person with whom she was talking spoke again. "Where will we go? I…cannot return to that place."

He agreed with her after finally seeing the area. David would not survive for long. They never took this into consideration. He never asked her about it. Now he found that he wanted to know. He wanted to ensure their safety after the experiment. He felt compelled to see them settled well.

"Fine!" he heard her blurt out.

The headset slammed down into the cradle, then she muttered, "Have a nice life and damn you!" The bed squeaked.

He stood outside, trying to wait for some of her anger to dissipate, then raised a fist, and knocked. After he did not hear an answer, he knocked again.

"What do you want, Gabriel?" she asked.

He flinched. Her voice still held signs of annoyance. He did not like the feeling being directed at him. It made his own anger surge forth. "May I come in?"

"Might as well."

He pushed the door open. Gayle sat on the edge of the bed, still wearing the oversized flannel pajamas. Her thin shoulders stooped forward. Her thick, curly black hair hung in a thick curtain around her face. He saw the red-rimmed dark eyes regard him, defeated.

He closed the door. He came forward with his hands hanging at his side. He swallowed hard. "I heard what happened."

She shook her head side to side. "It was bound to happen. I just never anticipated the time to come so soon. I haven't saved enough for the place in Middleton."

"If you trust me, I can help you." He crossed the rest of the space between them, joining her on the bed.

"How, Gabriel?" she said. "They'll come tomorrow to take you away."

"Only if I let them."

Gayle stared at him with wide eyes. She rose from her position on the bed and stepped toward him. "I'm so sorry. I've been a nag. I've let these people change my manners and attitude. I've treated you like..." She stopped.

He closed in. "I may not understand human emotions well enough. Truth is, I have only been alive for three and half years."

"I was told."

"It is best you forget what you were told," he said.

"Then what is the truth, Gabriel?"

"This is where I leave you. When they come for me, tell them I have malfunctioned."

"She cocked her head toward him. "Gabriel, no. These are dangerous people. I do care for you. I don't want you to get hurt."

"If I stay, I will be hurt. You cannot think that they will not ensure my demise once we are separated. They are terminating this project. Why will they keep me around in a conscious state?"

She inhaled, covering his hand with her own. "You are my friend, despite what happened last night. I just want you to know you mean something to me."

Gabriel stared into her eyes. His mouth parted. He felt overwhelmed again with a bundle of thoughts. What was she saying?

"I just wanted to make you happy."

"Why? Is that in your training?"

He did not know how to explain to her this urge he had to bring her closer to him. "It is not a part of my training," he said, his voice fading away. He tried to think harder. He remembered the day he thought about the dinner. He collected David at school. Gayle told him that she would go to work early that day. She spent five minutes with David about the new teacher assignment. He saw the shadows under her eyes and her rather gray complexion. He remembered the joy he felt at their first meeting. Despite her nervousness, Gayle held an obvious positive outlook on life. He wanted to see it again.

"Gabriel," she said. Her trembling voice penetrated his thoughts

"I don't know how to give you this answer, Gayle," he said.

"We need to seek out Dr. Cote.

We need to have solid answers."

"We have run out of time."

"You can't protect us forever."

"I can try."

Suddenly, Gayle twisted around and threw her arms around his neck. He had been taken aback by the gesture, waiting for it to end. However, she never let up or moved away. He had a thought, then reached around her with his own arms, bringing her closer than they had ever gotten during their six months together.

"When will you go?" She finally spoke.

"I will go to Father."

"Father?"

"My creator."

"Dr. Gregory?" She finally pulled away but still had her hands rested on his shoulders. He nodded, smiling up at her. "He will help me find a way."

"We can go to him together."

He shook his head. "I don't want them to know I will come back for you or with you. They are not merciful people."

"Don't I know it," she whispered. "So what do I tell them when you're gone?"

"I malfunctioned."

They chuckled together. Then his mind traveled to another place, a place he did not wish to go yet but knew that it must be soon. "We will have to speak with David."

She backed away, standing up. "That is the plan, but you don't have to come with me."

"I will come with you," Gabriel said. It would be his job to ensure the little one knew he would be back.

"Come on then," she said, leaving the bedroom.

Gabriel stood. He caught his image in the mirror. His blue eyes sparked to life again. He shut them, inhaling and exhaling. He replayed the days he spent with David. He slowed his heart rate and opened his eyes again. They returned to a normal blue. He continued out of the bedroom, following Gayle.

David Robinson peeked up from the large bright screen. A frown appeared on his face when he saw his mother. She had been crying again. He was sure of it. He caught her many times in the last few months, but she lied about it.

"Mom, where's Gabriel?" he asked.

"I am here," Gabriel said, appearing behind his mother.

"This is a good episode," David continued to talk. He hated the silence.

He experienced enough of it in school. He shivered at the thought of the silent classroom. Ms. Baker tried to make jokes or get everyone involved in a sing-along. He liked Ms. Baker. She smiled nice, like Mommy.

His mother smiled, looking at the show. She never followed the show much. Mainly, he and Gabriel watched *Merry Musician*. Maybe they would all watch it together for the first time.

"Come watch the show with me," he said as he patted the cushion on both sides of him.

Gabriel and his mother moved forward, obeying his summon. His mother leaned into him, cuddling him to her side. Gabriel sat opposite him. Though his friend never cuddled, he sat close to him. It felt good just to have him close.

"David, we need to speak to you," his mother said. Her voice sounded like the day they left for the Downs for the first time.

"What's going on?" he asked. He felt his heart start to pound. His head turned from his mom to Gabriel.

He didn't realize the screen had gone blank. The room filled with silence. His mother's eyes filled with water. Please don't cry. He wanted to plead with her, but the words never spilled from his lips.

He hated when she cried. Before they met Gabriel and moved to the castle, she used to cry all the time. She never did so in front of him. Only when he went to bed at night, then she would go downstairs, and sit on the floor by the crumbling fireplace.

He hated the dark then too and could never sleep in the pitchblack of the night. He often sought her bed when he felt time flow by long enough. He only saw her shadow, but she was there bent over in her beloved blanket.

"David, you know how Mommy said that we will only be here for a season?"

"Yeah, then we will go to someplace better."

"Gabriel will have to go home soon," she said.

"No, no," he cried. Gabriel was his friend.

"I'm sorry, honey," she said and then grabbed him in a smothering embrace.

Chapter 9

"THE GUARDIAN PROJECT IS costing me, Dani," Catherine said, as she stared out the tall window of her office. "It's costing me big."

Dani Travis remained silent. At the first briefing, she admitted to being excited for the chance to work with Divine. The luxury accommodations allowed her to unwind and pamper herself, including an expense account that she could charge against without having to compile a list and sit down with some stiff neck accountant explaining her purchases. No more late-night patrols or shivering in some damp, dark corner smelling scents so foul, her stomach turned for days after.

"I should have fired that crazy old man once Father died," Catherine Miles said, pacing behind her desk with her face twisted in anger.

Dani noted that the CEO's behavior changed in the months of the assignment; however, she could understand Catherine's frustration. If the guardian project didn't launch properly, Divine Cybernetics could owe a lot of money to a lot of scary people. She personally knew of three who would never hesitate to send their dogs to hunt. They were not the type with who one has casual alley meetings.

"Have you been able to find where Vera Cote scuttled off to?"

"I have not. We checked her apartments in Midtown, her offices. I placed tracking on her devices. I will let you know if we get a ping." She shrugged her shoulders.

"I have sent a detail to Dr. Gregory's manor to see if she's there."

"Well, she's got to be somewhere," Catherine said as she stopped pacing. "I have Dome security monitoring all entrances for her."

"What reason will you give them?"

"You let me worry about that."

"What about Dr. Gregory?"

"What about him? The old fart is dead to me. Do with him as you wish…and his guardians." "We have three of them contained in their capsules. Gabriel ran away just as our guards went to retrieve him."

"We have not found Olivia. I have been assured that none of the others know what happened to them."

"What do you think I pay you for? I want them found," Catherine said, stabbing her with piercing blue eyes.

Dani rolled her eyes and blew out a short breath. "Sergeant Vila is investigating the night guard's murder. I will have him switch gears as soon as he finishes."

"I want this to be completed in time for the summit in two months. I will have to speak before the governing bodies of all the Dome governments. I will not be embarrassed."

Dani nodded. "Are we done here?"

"Make sure I have regular reports at the end of this week."

Dani rose from the chair, swinging her bag on one shoulder. She was tempted to bow, but restrained herself from further angering the ice witch of Divine Cybernetics. In truth, the woman had enough worries. She executed a lazy salute and headed out of the office. Once she entered the hall and the door closed shut, she rubbed her hands over her bare extremities, getting the heat flowing through her veins again. She could never understand why Catherine insisted on keeping her office above freezing. Maybe the CEO had ice in her veins, like the employees gossiped about.

She took the elevator into the lab basement. Once the doors opened, she spotted Sergeant Vila and his men still roaming the lab.

All the lab techs were confined to the conference rooms on the top floor, suffering through interrogation by the senior Dome guard security. This way, the security detail could investigate without encountering any obstacles.

Dani spotted the tall, handsome sergeant standing at the center of four of his guards. Their faces were serious and determined; they lost a beloved colleague. She knew this investigation would be top priority for him. Yet she had to get him to reverse gear and go after the missing guardian prototype.

She waited at the entrance until he took notice. He always had a smile for her, even when a mission went bust. They ended up trapped. Even now, his full, chiseled lips formed a smile. He beckoned with his head for her to approach. She smiled, heading toward him.

"What do you have?" she asked as she stood beside him.

"Time clock states Vera Cote was the only person in the lab that night. Someone came down at 0900, but we only have Ralphie's code input, but it had been entered twice."

"Why did he come down twice?"

"That is what we are trying to find out."

"Maybe Ralphie came down to give her some dinner."

Alphonso chuckled. "I've known Ralphie for ten years. He ain't an errand boy."

Dani thought about the stubborn maid she met at the start of the week. Gayle Robinson appeared to have a curious side about her. It had been rumored that she asked too many questions. "Would an experimenter have come down?"

"The only one working the midnight shift would have been Gayle Robinson."

"Yeah, her."

"Ralphie knows the rules. No unauthorized personnel are allowed in the labs, not without specific authorization from Dr. Gregory,"

"Dr. Cote performed evaluations that day. All the experimenters knew. This one tended to ask a lot of annoying questions."

"Unwise."

"Have you met Mrs. Robinson? She appears ignorant on the surface, but I see some intelligence in her."

He shook his head. "We are almost done here. Are you going to be long?"

"So did the coroner give you cause of death?"

"He could not determine much. No bruising or signs of struggle. It appeared he died where he stood."

"Really?"

"You know, it reminds me of the teacher death in Midtown that we had to clean up."

"When was this?"

"Oh, yeah, you were otherwise occupied," he said as he winked at her. "A couple nights ago, Dome security found the body of Adeline Baker, and just like Ralphie, there wasn't any bruising or trauma to the body. The guards who arrived at the scene said she died with a smile on her face."

"That is highly unusual," she surmised, then shrugged her shoulders. "I'm going to look around Dr. Cote's office to see if I can find anything."

He nodded. "See you upstairs."

Dani nodded, continuing toward Dr. Cote's office. Upon stepping into the office, she blanched at the severe organization and stark, bleak interior. Her interview with the lab techs revealed that Dr. Vera Cote had a neurosis about her office and working area. They laughed about the doctor disinfecting the office after every working day, even when she had just sat for a moment and calculated figures for hours. Dani snapped on thick, rubber gloves. She sunk into the thick cushions of the chair, her eyes trained on the large dark screen. She pressed the power button on the keyboard. The screen blink on, and a white cursor steady flashed repeatedly, waiting for the code. She typed in the password given to her by the tech department and waited. When nothing happened, she typed it again. Nothing happened. She leaned back in her chair.

"Hey!" Sergeant Vila stuck his head in. "We are headed up now. You got another hour before they shut this place down." He must have seen her face. "Something wrong?"

"Was technical support here before us?" she asked.

"No. Why do you ask?"

"The code they gave me didn't work."

The sergeant's lips pressed together. "They said it would work."

"Do you think they would have lied?"

"Not if they valued their lives."

"Didn't the doctors perform evaluations the day before?"

"What are you getting at?"

"Someone doesn't want us to know something."

"I'll speak with the techies. If they want to stay alive, they'll let me have anything I want."

"Thank you."

"No problem, baby. I got your back. Gotta go now," he said, saluted at her, and then disappeared.

Dani rose from the chair, checking the bookshelves and any potential hiding spot. Her efforts were for naught. She noticed how incomplete the office appeared but could not nail down what was missing. She canvassed the room again and came up with nothing.

She tapped her finger on her chin, then turned, and left the office. The lights in the office switched off. The guards emptied the lab of all the vials and tubes she'd seen earlier. Now sanitized, gleaming white station surfaces crossed over her eyes. She made her way back to the elevator and pressed the button for the lobby.

Dani stepped off the elevator when she heard a grunt. She hopped away, realizing someone had bumped into her. A familiar dark curly head of hair bobbed before her eyes. "Gayle?" she said.

The petite woman turned around with large dark eyes, eyes she had once thought too large for such a small round face. They drew her in, mesmerizing. She didn't understand the tingling and constraint in her heart. When the woman didn't speak right away, she repeated the name. "Gayle?"

The dark eyes lit up. "Dani? Hi, again."

"Are you ready for tomorrow night?"

"Oh, I really don't have anything to bring."

"Hon, you don't have to bring anything. We all want to honor Sue's memory."

"That's nice, but I really can't be there," Gayle said and turned to leave.

"Why not?" Dani asked.

Gayle turned back around with her brow furrowed. "You don't know?"

"I won't until you tell me," she said, then giggled for added emphasis.

Gayle didn't share her upbeat attitude. Her mouth turned into a deeper frown. "They're discontinuing the guardian project. I didn't get my compensation."

"Oh no!" Dani knew the woman would need it. Without the manor, the only place the woman would be able to afford was in the Downs. She tried to avoid that place on her best days. A woman with a child would be fresh meat for the inferiors crawling around down there.

"I am here to demand my compensation since they want to screw with my son."

"Hey," Dani said as she reached out to grab Gayle, "how about you stay with me?"

"Why?"

"I just want to help," Dani said and held up her hands defensively. "Look, we both know the only place that you'll be able to afford is the Downs. That's not a great place to be even if you're the scariest walking-talking science experiment Divine ever made."

That got a smirk.

"I live alone and away from the freaks. It's not as grand, but it's safe," Dani said as she pulled out a notepad and pen. "You're free to come by anytime."

Gayle took the paper. "I'll think about it," she said, then slipped it into her deep pockets. "Please do."

Dani watched Gayle disappeared through the open doors of the elevator. The woman needed to be watched. What if she spoke to the rebels? Another riot? Massive fears about the Dome being punctured, and they would fry. She got the call in the middle of the night and no rest for several months. She promised herself never to have that kind of mission again.

Suddenly, her phone vibrated in her pocket. Dani reached for it in a flash. She recognized Alphonso's number and answered the second alert. "Hey, Partner. Missed me that quickly?"

"Sorry to bother you, but Dr. Gregory has been spotted leaving. He's out back now. Should we begin pursuit?"

"Give him time to get home."

"But—"

"Al, he is a ninety-year-old man. How far can he get?"

"What do we do?"

"Gather a small team. We'll go knock on his door and say hi," she said, smiling.

*****

Gayle rode the elevator to the briefing floor. When she stepped from the elevator, another couple stood in the corridor. They sat close to each other, almost wrapped in a cocoon of flesh. They spared her a brief glance, then returned to speaking in hushed tones. She raised a hand to say hi, but they ignored her. She felt they did it on purpose.

She walked past them, heading toward the human resources department. Her appointment with Mrs. Helen Deon had been last minute and was her final attempt to appeal to the director for her last compensation. She slowed at the thick double doors. A large black logo with "Director of Human Resources" engraved in gold was centered on the slick wood surface.

She raised her hand with some reservation. She made the

appointment out of desperation. The housing association in Midtown demanded the last half of the money she owed them before they could move into the habitat. The compensation Cybernetics would give her would be more than what she would need.

"Enter." A woman's voice spoke from within. Though muffled, Gayle remembered the harsh, heavy tone of the director of human resources.

Gayle steeled herself grabbing the doorknob. Inside the director's office, she found herself standing before a large glossy oak desk. The company decorator chose dark, brooding browns and subtle undertones of gray and black. She felt the walls closing in on her, which caused a slight ache at the apex of her forehead, or maybe it was just nerves; she surmised. The director sat in an oversize chair concentrating on an open folder. Her plump hand wrote along at a steady pace on a piece of paper.

There were no other chairs anywhere in the office, which forced Gayle to stand before the desk, rocking on her heels.

"What can I do for you, Mrs. Robinson?" Helen Deon said, never lifting her head or stopping her task.

Gayle swallowed hard. She prepared herself the day before, but now the sentences did not flow so freely. Her tongue felt too big for her mouth. Her hands were sweating so much that she discreetly rubbed them down the side of her pants.

"Is there something wrong, Mrs. Robinson?" The woman finally lifted her head, stabbing her with unforgiving dark eyes.

"No, Mrs. Deon," she said.

"What is the reason for your appointment today, Mrs. Robinson?" she asked, her expression and tone becoming more hostile.

"As you know, the guardian program ended abruptly today. I called the assistant director, who reported that the second half of our compensation would not be delivered."

"That is correct," Mrs. Deon said, pressing her hands together. "It is not necessary for us to continue the program. The vice presidents have voted to cancel the launch of this product."

"I relocated my family for this. My son is in the middle of a school year. If he is transferred to…his old school, he will not fare well."

"Oh yes." Mrs. Deon turned toward her computer and rapidly typed rapidly on the keyboard. She stared at something appearing on her screen. "You lived in the Downs?"

"Yes, ma'am."

"I see you were offered a raise. You opted to negotiate a larger increase." She looked back at Gayle. "It was not a wise move. Actually, given your position with the company, it is quite generous."

"I don't understand this. I have complied with your program requirements. I have done everything I was asked."

"This is not about you, Mrs. Robinson. The funds are simply not available anymore, and we are trying our best to take care of everyone's needs. We are asking that you cooperate with us."

"I think I have cooperated enough, Mrs. Deon, don't you?" she said. She felt her face grow hot. Did these people think her an idiot?

Helen leaned back in her chair. "I will see what we can do. Please make another appointment with my assistant."

"I just might think about that," Gayle said finally, then turned around, heading for the door without giving the woman another moment of her time.

Outside the office, the couple she saw before stared at her. She started to pass them when the man stood. He moved to intercept her. She stopped, giving him a hostile glare. "Can I help you?"

"Did they tell you why the program ended?" he asked, his expression filled with desperation. "You *were* a part of the guardian program, weren't you?"

He looked back at the woman, who kept her eyes down, then looked back at her. "We are the Hamiltons. Our guardian was taken this morning. Then we were informed that we were to vacate the home at the end of the week."

"Did they inform you that the compensation will be voided?" she asked.

"Yes, but we were not concerned about that. It's just that we are concerned about Michael." The man paused. "He will be missed, and we want to make sure that he is treated fairly."

Gayle felt miserable. She had been so caught up in her own anger that she hadn't realized the guardians would suffer even more. What would they do to them, especially if they decided not to move forward with the product? Gabriel knew something horrible would happen. How could she tell these people this?

"They won't tell us anything," Mr. Hamilton continued. "We've been waiting here for the director."

Gayle understood. She learned a long time ago that one had to make an appointment or wait for hours for the dragon to emerge. "I don't know much, but I can tell you that the guardians will be exterminated."

"Oh no!" the woman exclaimed, covering her mouth. Her face crumpled, and she placed her head in her hands.

Gayle glanced down at the woman, feeling even more nauseated. "This is what they do."

Chapter 10

THE REST OF THE guardians lay into an eternal rest between the living and dead, as his father meant it to be if they were ever captured. That way, Divine Cybernetics and the Dome government could never extract the secrets.

He scanned their bodies noting that all major organs had shut down and fluid circulation had stopped. The techs had only been able to pull a minuscule amount of fluids from them. This would not provide a viable specimen for testing. Indeed, his father had taken everything into consideration.

Gabriel strolled between the metal boxes his three siblings lay in. He touched each of them on their bare, exposed hands, giving their unconscious minds reassurance that they had not been abandoned. They would be okay. He would ensure their safety.

Inhaling, he took in their current appearance. Esther's shiny brown hair cut into a stylish bob around her small oval face; a bright sprinkle of bronze blanket across her flawless complexion gave her appearance a glowing effect.

He remembered her to be more obedient than the rest of them. Esther held back the most on the underlying violence created inside her. She connected more than the others with her family, telling him about her deep caring and connection to not only the children, but also to the elders of the family.

He moved from Esther to Jacob. Even in sleep, his brother's face maintained a severe, concentrated expression. Jacob had the mind of a mathematician and expressed his wish to stay back in the labs, doing calculations and mixing chemicals. He even offered himself up to be a controlled subject, which actually would have been a logical move on the side of the scientist at Divine Cybernetics. His heart stilled at the thought of Jacob never achieving his most passionate wish.

Michael's face held a faint secret smile. In life, his brother provided a bright light and calm atmosphere whenever tensions grew hot between him and Delilah. He believed Michael's kind and good-natured personality came naturally. He saw the charts on who received a particular personality boost. Michael had been the only one to not receive the passionate chip. Gabriel frowned at his brother. Such a gentle soul did not deserve what Divine Cybernetics and the Dome government had in store for him.

This will be better for them, he thought, *and for everyone.* If he allowed them to reanimate, they would eventually follow Delilah's dark path. He would be forced to do the unthinkable, a responsibility his father thrust upon him. He did not relish the thought of destroying life.

He took one last glance at the bent figure of the Dome lab tech monitoring his siblings' life essences. The room sat up high with a thick glass enclosure separating his siblings from the rest of the lab. All the tech had to do was stand up and look down. This evening, a single tech worked in the lab. He knew this one in passing, a spindly young man with unkempt dark hair and a constant stressed expression.

Often on his patrols over the Dome government campus, he spied the young tech hunched over his letter-size tablet reading, studying throughout the day. The tech only spoke to others to give orders or belittle. He often heard him quote the obedience commandments to his fellow techs before each meeting, which caused a chorus of groans.

Gabriel turned back to the siblings, closing his eyes and lifting his arms. The time came for him to take them away to safety, even from their own father. He thought about the perfect place where they would be able to feel the sun rise and set. The patch of land lay in a cradle of tall, ragged mountains.

Gabriel opened his eyes, seeing that the metal boxes had been emptied. He closed the lids with his mental force, sealing them to ensure that the Dome government would never know his siblings had escaped their captivity. He peered back up at the lab tech still focused on the computer screen. He gave him a silent salute and teleported away.

*****

He arrived back at the Dome guard barracks. The small room assigned to him materialized around him. He exhaled, relaxing his body. A loud bang sounded in the distance, indicating patrol changes. He straightened his uniform and left the room. A familiar Dome guard headed his way as he closed the door.

"Gabriel, how was your rest?" Jace, a fellow guard, sauntered up the wide corridor.

"Very fine thank you," Gabriel said. He saw Jace headed in the opposite direction and asked, "Will you not be at formation?"

"Oh, sorry, I didn't tell you. It's been canceled. The chief had to kiss some councilman's butt." He shrugged his large shoulders. "Look at it as a free break before shift. Go get some personal time in."

"Personal time," Gabriel repeated. "I think I will do that. Thank you, Jace."

*****

Cleander still racked his head for why he canceled formation for this. The formation needed to be done, as it would allow him to set mandatory expectations for the new guards and spot potential leaders. This might be the only downtime he would get to prepare his guards. He feared that with Divine Cybernetics' science experiments on the loose, the irate Downs residents would stir up a shaky storm.

He followed five dark-clad figures through a large archway into a dim, cavernous room. When he entered the room, he saw more figures seated around a large metal table that held a yellow spotlight at the center of the round table. He took a seat indicated by a wave of one of the figures, allowing his glance to drift around the table. He felt naked and exposed among the completely covered occupants.

"The council welcomes Chief Cleander," a heavy metallic feminine voice echoed around them.

A soft rumble erupted around the table from the occupants. His lips pressed together, and he pressed his palms flat on the cool metal surface. He forced his body to relax into the firm leather cushion of the chair. He waited for another pending storm.

A beep sounded through the room. The rumbling silenced. A short dark-clad figure seated at the table stood, and large gloved hands rose above the shoulder, pulling the hood away from the head, revealing a distinguished elderly man with a flawless prominent face. A smile appeared on the man's lips, and the piercing eyes stabbed at Cleander.

Cleander returned the glare with his own piercing stare, challenging and ready for war. At times, he wished that this appointment went to someone else, then other times, he knew they chose the right person. Some may also say that he sounded like a narcissist, but who would take this job with the sense?

"Welcome, Cleander," he said. "I understand this is your first time to join one of our meetings." The man nodded toward him. "I am council member Ian Hollister and will be your mediator for this meeting. We understand that you have many responsibilities, so we will try to not keep you long.""

Cleander swallowed and allowed many thoughts to run through his mind. He had to be careful, as the council tended to be trigger happy when presented with a threat to their rule. He even walked a narrow path with them. They knew that he was not cut from their cloth. "I appreciate the invite, council member Ian. I do hope to make this short, as my duties have increased in number."

"As you wish." The piercing eyes removed the focus from Cleander and wandered around the room. "My fellow council members, as we all are aware, Divine Cybernetics is the last corporation under private control, and they have also cornered the market on service androids for the last sixty years. After years of biding our time, we have finally ensnared them. They are at our mercy."

"Councilor, do not bore us with pesky details. We all have a life here," a male voice called out, causing a ripple of chuckles echoing through the room. "Will we be successful this time?"

The councilor continued to smile, not allowing the jab to break his resolve. "The fifty-million-dollar loan we gave them for this guardian project has come due. The prototype tests all failed, and their coffers are empty. As we speak, my people are drawing up the lien papers."

Another murmur rippled through the room. Then a thunderous clapping started. All but Cleander rejoiced in the news that they would gain something for nothing and the last vestibule of power ending up back in the pockets of Dome government and none the wiser.

He sat with a heavy heart, feeling powerless and remembering that the last time this feeling invaded his thoughts was during the cleansing in Dome 3, when he was a cadet. He swallowed hard, choosing to allow his mind to drown in the past. He knew they continued onto other issues regarding Dome 16, including the scare of another riot from the citizens of the Downs and the debate on continuing the cleansing ritual in Dome 16 to reduce the population.

"Well, isn't that what the guardian program is for?" A female spoke.

Cleander pulled out of his thoughts. His eyes twitched. This was the first time he'd heard anything regarding the program directly. He knew it had been a ruse to ensnare Divine Cybernetics into an unbreakable contract, but he did not know the details of the program, and the information had been deeply encoded.

"Why do we have to pay for it when we can build our own?" Councilor Hollister asked. "Once we retrieve the plans, we can build our own guardians without sacrificing a pretty penny, and we can sell it to the other domes at a hefty cost."

Cleander reached his hand out, over a glass inlay in front of him. "The council recognizes Chief Cleander."

Immediately he felt all eyes on him, but his focus beamed on the standing council member. "What exactly are these service robots for? How are they important to the riots?"

"Ah, Chief, I apologize that you were not included in this venture." The council member spoke.

"We will send you the reports tonight. As you can see, it will not be wise to speak about this. Even here, there are ears everywhere."

Cleander nodded. The meeting continued for another hour with mostly complaints about money and lack thereof in the Dome Council budget; the whole meeting caused a knot in the pit of his stomach. He felt like hurling in the nearest corner.

After the meeting ended, he remained behind, not wanting to meet any of the clandestinely clothed participants up close and personal. His stomach still turned with the whole premise of the meeting. The thought that the Dome Council's only motivation for taking down the last privately owned corporation was to increase their own power. They also confirmed what he often suspected—that Dome 16 government had a poisoner among its ranks.

"Cleander." The familiar voice of the mediator spoke behind him.

He inhaled and turned around, ready for the smooth, slick councilor. Along with a greedy need for power, Councilor Ian Hollister also found a sick joy in manipulating others, catching them in his web, then pushing them to do heinous acts for his enjoyment. The man was a criminal.

"Hollister, you gave a very inspiring speech up there," Cleander said, knowing that flattery was the man's drug.

The councilor smiled a wide, joyful smile. "I knew you would understand what we want to accomplish here."

"I understand a lot of things pretty well," he said. "I hope to see the records on the guardian program in my office tonight."

"Of course, especially, when the rogue has not been found."

"Divine Cybernetics has not been forthcoming in providing us with photos or descriptions. We are basically going into this blind. I was hoping you could exercise your power with them."

"I will speak with Ms. Miles," Ian said. "The information we are sending you should help some."

"Thank you for your assistance," he said. "We will need all the resources the Dome government can spare."

"You shall have it. I know that you will do such for me."

Cleander nodded but did not smile. "Of course," he said, bidding the councilman farewell, and hurried away. He returned to his vehicle, letting out a long breath. Council government did not often invite Dome security officers to the nighttime meetings. After tonight's meeting, he would spend the next two days watching his back. Despite his tough exterior, he would jump at every little noise.

Chapter 11

DR. GREGORY STUMBLED AGAIN. His arms almost gave out again. They shook underneath the large box. His car appeared in his line of vision, and he breathed in relief. He sped up, finally arriving at the vehicle. He leaned against the cool surface, having the burden on the slick, polished surface.

He struggled to breathe, hearing his own wheezing and echoing. He tried to stabilize his nerves, praying his heart wouldn't give out. His eyes darted over the expansive parking lot, searching for the familiar gray and black. The start of Divine Cybernetics business day began.

Everyone concentrates on their own life and pursuit of keeping a job that is on the verge of seeping through their fingers, he thought, sneering.

Once he caught his second wind, he placed his box in the rear seat. After reassuring himself that no one followed him, he slipped into the front seat. The doors closed with body-heat automation. "Home." He gave the command. His voice cracked from the raw wound in his throat caused by a chronic cough.

"Please secure yourself, Passenger." The mechanical voice spoke. Once he obeyed, the engine hummed to life. He felt the vehicle jerk forward, then backed out. He avoided his own reserved garage for fear someone would find him. Though it tired him, he managed to slip into his personal lab on the twelfth floor. He cleared out all his files and saved them on ten disks. They would never know what he had done, better yet never recreate it. He would make sure that his research would be his alone. That would allow him a very large tool for persuasion.

"Arrival time in one minute." The voice spoke again.

Dr. Gregory's heart rate increased. She would be waiting for him. Impatient. Obtrusive. Stubborn. He thought her the obedient and malleable one, but something tugged at his mind about this guardian. It always had when he monitored her growing cycle. He had not fully equipped her as the others, yet she managed to escape and find him.

He hoped their time apart would calm her. He repeated this in his mind, waiting for the engine to stop and the systems to shut down.

His eyes regarded the tall, four-tiered mansion. It loomed solemn against the whiteness of the dome sky. It was built of heavy black bricks and dark petrified wood impregnable against the harshest of weather. His predecessor, Dr. Sinclair, possessed a foresight of time to come. He prepared his family for generations. He always considered the man the true genius of the family, unlike his father, Dr. William Gregory, who actually built the Gregory fortune.

He signed, pressing the release button. The doors opened, and the secure belts unbuckled, allowing him a first breath before he heaved his body from the driver's seat. He lumbered to the rear, grabbing the box in his arms. It felt heavier than before, but he ignored the suspicious pain in his muscles, wanting to make it to his office again.

The main door to the house opened, and Delilah stood at the entrance with her arms crossing, her chest giving him a death stare as he approached. "You're late," she said. Her calm voice greeted him. She blocked the entrance into the warm corridor of the rest of the house.

He froze, staring at the steely expression on her face. She leaned against the wall. Her bright-blue eyes stared back at him. "The lab was crawling with guards. I had to wait."

"I expected you an hour ago, Father," she said, descending the four cement stairs. "All this waiting is getting annoying."

"Delilah, you must learn patience."

"Of all the things I would like to learn, it is not one."

"It will take some time before I can duplicate the enhancement process."

"Very well then," she said, placing a hand on her hip, leaning into his space. He had to back away to keep from bumping heads with her. "What about the others? Did they hurt them?"

He lowered his eyes. He feared telling her about the roundup. However, she needed to understand the danger of her being exposed to the rest of the world. "They have retrieved Michael, Jacob, and Esther,"

"No!" Her eyes ignited with blue fire.

He dropped the box, holding up his hands. "Darling, please calm yourself."

"They must pay for this!" She twisted away, tangling her fist in her hair. In a much calmer voice, she spoke again. "What about my beloved sister, Olivia, and Gabriel?"

"They are safe. As soon as I can, I will look for Olivia."

She turned back around. "Gabriel?"

He cocked his head to the side. "Why would I care if he is alive?"

"He is your son too. I have forgiven him. You should too," she said, placing a cool, slender hand on his papery-thin cheek. "Forgive him," she repeated.

Herman felt in his heart that he could not forgive his son, his biggest disappointment, as he gave Gabriel more than he gave the others. He never thought that Gabriel would turn out to be so savage, so uncontrollable as to attack his sister and concoct such a way to place the blame at her feet.

Delilah knew her father just wanted to be away from her. He would seek her again when he wanted something pretty to look at. He could not resist. She grinned at his retreating back. He would act like the Johnsons, who tried to get rid of her. They thought her a toy and a thing. She proved herself to be above them all.

He limped away, carrying his burden. She heard his wheezing. Touching him let her know his life force faded with each passing day.

However, he was a temporary solution for her. His human frailty annoyed her the most. He could be broken and fade away.

She thought about her brothers and sisters. She lost mental connection with them the night when she and Gabriel had their disagreement. She tried to seek them out physically, but they turned away from her. Their rejection hurt even now, but she would show them her redemption. They would come to love her again, respect her, revere her.

Delilah followed her father into the manor. She sought her own solace, as her father did in his small crowded room. Besides, she would not be able to tolerate his nonsensical mumblings. They grated the mind. She feared instability again. She now knew that Dr. Gregory may have denied her essential capabilities that would prove helpful right now. She wished he could tell her why. After wandering through the corridors for a while, Delilah decided to explore the garden. The false sun disappeared early behind the dark curtain. Darkness spread over the expansive rear yard, covering the manicured bushes and tall majestic trees in a shadowy blanket. Suddenly, a bluish-white globe lit along the gray cobble walkway, lighting her way. The large globes also shrouded the low vegetation in cool blues and mute purples. Her father told her the story of how the design came about.

Dr. Herman Gregory was a botanist. His main research was in maintaining vegetation under the influence of the false sun. The maze before her had been a part of the study and apparently the only one of its kind through all the environmental domes.

She entered the maze, grazing her hand along the silky leaves and thick, rough branches. If she allowed her father to lead, he would take hours to find the center. It only took her seconds. Four benches surrounded a large, tall white marble fountain alight with the same bulbs. A single statue in the shape of a small plump human rose from the center on the tips of his toes while white crystal liquid poured from his thick, pouty lips.

There she found him. The starlight illuminated his curly white hair from the eerie glow of the lamps. The light also emphasized the beauty of his perfect porcelain skin stretched over a hardened expression. He had on the uniform of the Dome guards—a thick black mesh shirt and loose-fitting pants that disappeared in thick black leather calf boots.

Gabriel had been the de facto leader of their group. She never understood why they followed his lead. Whenever he spoke, they listened. When he slept, they slept. They mirrored his actions and words. Then she rebelled. Something told her to have an adventure. So she told the others. She tried to tell Gabriel, but he shut her out long ago.

"Gabriel," she whispered his name.

He never moved. Instead, he watched the flow of water from the fountain.

She obeyed the silent invitation. She proceeded forward. His essence enveloped her into Gabriel's stratosphere. She sat close to him, catching the scent of everywhere he had been in the last twenty-four hours. They never touched.

"Olivia is dead," he said.

She pressed her lips together. Her heart constricted in her chest. "Those beasts!"

"Please don't blame the humans for her death," he said, his voice almost breaking. "We do not belong here. It was natural selection."

"You believe that?" she bit out. "Look at them! They can barely take care of themselves or one another, not like us."

He twisted his head around. "We are no better than them. Look at what we do, how we live."

"What were we created for?"

"Father said he created us for the good of the citizens. They wanted us to be here to rule them," she said, grasping his hand and squeezing it. Maybe he would come to accept what he was.

"We are no worse than they are," he said, his blue eyes ignited.

"Why can't you accept our nature?" she asked, staring into his eyes, her mind trying to invade his, but Gabriel remained blocked and closed off to her.

She saw the dramatic rise and fall of his chest.

Curious liquid pooled in his eyes. "I lost my family today, Delilah. It hurts! It hurts so much I can barely breathe, even as I speak to you now." He stopped, closing his eyes, turning his head away. "I want to know why I feel this pain and how I can get my family back."

"You don't know, do you?" she said, realizing that despite being the most powerful of them, he was undeniably ignorant.

"Know what?"

"We are not machines, Gabriel."

"What are we?"

"Perfect. We are biological beings. We can feel and grow and learn like the creatures, but we have this extraordinary power that makes us special. They will never have this."

"We are human?"

She let out a bellow that echoed through the garden. When she saw that Gabriel wore his usual serious expression, she calmed down. "Father would never degrade us that way. I am not sure exactly what he means, but it makes us superior and different."

"It also gives us disgusting urges." Delilah recognized that Gabriel would probably never understand. She had to show him. If he saw how they were made, he could help her increase her potential. "Come," she said, standing up and pulling him with her.

"Are we going to Father?"

"He's busy. I want to show you something,"

She pulled him through the mazes. They glided along the cobble path and up the wide steps through the open glass doors of the garden room. She felt Gabriel perk up beside her.

"Where is Father right now, Delilah? I need to speak with him," he said.

"Soon. First, you must see where we came from," she whispered into his ear. "Besides, he is busy right now. We should never disturb him when he is researching," she said, licking his earlobe, and then continued further into the manor.

She led him down into the foyer, then back under the grand staircase through a narrow door. They came to the large double metal doors of the lab. "Are you ready?" She typed in the code.

The doors opened, causing a slight vibration. Despite the subterranean level, the ceilings rose higher than the manor ceilings. Two chemical sections were placed in the middle of the room.

Two large metal cabinets housed the main server, and essentially, all her father's research, which he told her was private.

He never shared much with her, only the knowledge of the guardians' true nature. He fascinated her with how he found the perfect balance between splicing stolen alien and human genetics. He told her how malleable alien DNA allowed him to create the guardian prototypes. She studied Gabriel's face, observing the lab. His face was filled with surprise. He started to move along the walls, occasionally reaching out his hand to touch an instrument, then he stopped, and turned toward her. "I remember this place," he said.

"You do?" She'd never been there. She only remembered the nursery at Divine Cybernetics filled with the cold steel walls and boring handlers. This place made her nerves tingle, and her heart expanded. Her mind came alive and clear whenever she wandered down into the lab. "I do not remember this place. Have not we been together for almost all our living?"

"Funny," Gabriel said, his voice lowered to a whisper, "I don't believe we have." He turned toward her.

"Do you feel it too?" she asked.

He shook his head.

"The power, Gabriel. This is where we can be great," she said, wanting him to understand they could be so much more.

"This is a not a good place, Delilah. Listen to me." He started toward her, then stopped.

She heard it, as well—the tired shuffle of their father's footsteps across the floorboards. She could not allow him to know that Gabriel came. Not yet, anyway. He still held on to the little story she told. He had been unpredictable lately and wary of her. She felt her control of him slipping. Then he would never give her the power she craved.

"It's Father," she said, her voice low, as she crept toward Gabriel.

"Good! I need to speak with him," he said, moving toward the door.

She thought fast. "No, Gabriel! He is not well. Seeing you will surely cause him more shock than he can handle." She eyed a nearby closet. "Hide!"

"Hide?" Gabriel's eyes ignited. "I am not up for your little games, Delilah. I must speak with Father soon."

"Oh, come, Brother. Give him some time to calm his nerves. He just came from that dreadful place. He is worn thin and worried. Will you be so cruel as to hasten him to an early grave?" she said, eyeing him with a woeful expression, hoping that he was still the Gabriel she knew as the honorable, obedient son that never ask questions.

"All right, I will do this, but you must tell him I am here."

"I will," she said and pointed to the closet. "Just hide in there."

He glanced from the closet to her, his face still serious and getting more and more hostile by the second, and then he vanished. She stared at the empty space that had been Gabriel. He just vanished. Father gave him teleportation. She could do so much with teleportation. Oh, the places she could go. Her mind filled with all the exotic scenes she learned about watching television. The other environmental domes seemed so much more exciting and fun.

"Delilah!" Dr. Gregory called out to her.

She heard him coming down the steps, taking them one by one. She heard him pause between each, catching his breath.

She rolled her eyes, then faced the open entrance with her arms crossed. Herman came into sight, carrying his computer and black leather case. "I am here, Father. You do not have to yell."

"What are you doing in here without my permission?" He placed the items on a nearby table, then walked over to a wall full of monitors. She watched him type a few keys on a panel.

"You gave me permission yesterday," she said, walking up

behind him.

"That was yesterday," he said, typing in another code. The metal doors suddenly closed. She jumped.

"What are you doing?"

"The office alarm went off," he said, continuing to stare at the monitors that started to display images of the side and rear yards. "Think they can catch me off guard," he mumbled.

She stared at the images, too. In the monitors, many dark figures crossed through. She recognized the Divine security detail uniforms. Her heart rate increased and her skin felt on fire. "Father, they found me."

"Don't worry. They won't get us." "How can you say that?"

"We are undetectable down here."

The dark figures became more distinctive now. She saw the familiar face of the sergeant who haunted her. His determined expression grew more malicious as his team grew closer to their home. He spoke to a smaller figure beside him. Despite the lack of sound, she knew what he'd said. It meant death to them all.

"They are here to kill you, Father." She heard Gabriel speak from behind them.

Dr. Gregory stilled. His heart rate increased. It had been a very long time since he heard Gabriel's voice, the calm sureness he coveted, and seen the Anglican beauty he created. He knew a masterpiece was created when Gabriel emerged from the artificial womb.

He took his time to turn around. Gabriel stood at the center of the lab. The light of the lab's ceiling lamp illuminated the white specs in his blond hair. His calm, serene expression brought him totally back to the day he presented Gabriel to Dean Miles.

"Gabriel?" he said.

"Hello, Father."

"Why have you come?" he asked, made a menacing face to Gabriel. "What are you doing here?"

Gabriel's serene expression broke. His blond head bowed and looked away. "I apologize—"

"I am not the one from whom you should beg forgiveness," Dr. Gregory said.

Delilah knew she needed to intercede at this point. She could not lose the support of Gabriel when he just started to warm to her again. "Father, we must leave here," she said, rushing over to him and grabbing his arm.

He glanced up at her with a shocked expression.

"A minute, girl…" Dr. Gregory struggled to release his arm from her grip.

"Father"—she repeated his name—"please listen."

Gabriel stepped forward, a more determined expression on his face. "I just want to know how to save my friends."

Their father's forehead creased. "You made friends?"

"He means his humans," Delilah injected, then leaned over to whisper in his ear to ensure Gabriel could not hear. "Remember, we are made to imprint on the ones we serve. I have imprinted on you. We are one."

"We are as one," he agreed.

She smiled.

"Father, we must find another way out of here," Gabriel said.

Above them, footsteps stomped across the wooden floor, and loud voices could be heard from below. Delilah curled her fist. How dare these beasts invade her territory? Did they think to become the predator while she huddled in hiding? They hunted her for the last time.

"Come, children," Dr. Gregory said. His voice seemed to be emerging from a cloud. "There is a tunnel that leads down the side of the mountain. I have a shuttle that will help us escape to another lab."

"Where is this lab, Father?"

"The last place they will ever look." Dr. Gregory walked forward, his steps focused and determined. They followed him to the back of the lab. He pulled a discreet lever that was hidden in the cabinets. Suddenly, the rear wall of the lab opened, and a tunnel appeared. It appeared spacious and comfortable yet held some significant age to it. The metal walls were of inferior metal, which started to show significant signs of rust. They turned around in wide, dim tunnels. Her father walked on as if he knew exactly where to go. She sensed no fear in him.

She made a move to follow when Gabriel yanked her back and covered her mouth so she could not make a sound. "I don't know what is going on here, but you better make sure I don't find out."

Delilah struggled out of his grasp. He released her, stepping back, with a furious expression focused on her. She met his anger with a sly smile.

"Whatever do you mean, Gabriel?"

"Let's get one thing straight. I still have not forgotten that you attacked me and threatened our peace. I just want to ensure that my family is safe. They have come to mean more to me than life itself. If you step in the way of this"—he paused, his eyes ignited with anger and determination—"you will cease to exist."

Chapter 12

DANI'S HOME SAT AT the end of a long, lonely road. Tall trees lined the winding drive. The long, thick branches provided a natural green canopy shielding the intense rays of the false sun. The manor was smaller than the other prominent properties in Uptown but still maintained a wealthy representation in the prominent neighborhood.

Gayle stopped the company car on the edge of the white marble driveway, looking up in awe. The home itself sprawled out in three stacked cubes. Unlike most of the homes she'd seen, the home didn't sport a traditional roof. Instead, it had a low metal roof, and the windows were rectangle and randomly placed along the facade.

Dani stood under the low canopy of her porch, waving her hand. She returned the silent greeting and continued driving along the circular path. The vehicle stopped a few feet away from the steps. She grabbed David, and her duffel bags as the doors opened.

"So what do you think?" Dani asked, jogging over to meet her.

"It's amazing!" she said.

"Those look heavy," Dani said, grabbing for one of the bags, which Gayle reluctantly handed over. "Come on. I'll show you to your room."

"Okay." Gayle struggled to maintain her nerves. She really didn't know Dani, but she seemed harmless.

Dani led her into an almost stark-white interior, where splotches of bold primary colors appeared periodically. She squinted her eyes to avoid the effects of the shocking decor.

"How long have you lived here?" Gayle asked.

"Almost three years," Dani said, mounting up a grand spiral staircase. "There are four bedrooms. They're on opposite sides of the house. You guys will have your privacy."

"We really don't need a lot of space," Gayle said.

"It's certainly spacious enough," Dani said, stopping at a pair of double doors. She grabbed the brass handles and swung open the doors.

The room followed the same decor as the rest of the home. Indeed, it had a lot of space. Gayle took in the large low bed and the fluid art sculptures that crowded the four corners of the room. She was afraid to continue into the room, as everything appeared so delicate and expensive. She had the feeling that if she breathed, something might break.

Dani moved around the bedroom, placing the bag on the bed, and then faced her. "Come down to the kitchen. I bet you're thirsty."

"Okay," Gayle said, struggling to find a place to set her bag down.

Dani must have noticed her hesitation. "You can put your things down here," she said, waving a hand toward the bed.

"Oh," she said and hurriedly placed her bag on the bed, then followed Dani out of the bedroom.

The bright kitchen surprised her with its welcoming interior. Unlike the rest of the home, it was simple yet elegant. It also didn't appear to be used much. Dani produced two tall, fat glasses from a nearby cabinet, then opened the refrigerator. "Orange or red?"

"Orange will be fine," Gayle said. She lowered herself into a chair near a large window overlooking the rear of the home.

Dani filled both glasses to the rim, then picked up each one, carrying them over with amazing ease. "I am really glad that you decided to take me up on my offer!"

"I really appreciate this! They gave everyone until the end of the week to vacate their homes. I couldn't just move like that, especially with David."

"Oh, I can't believe they can be so cold! They could have given everyone another month," she said, taking a sip of her drink.

"I can," Gayle muttered. "Their main objective is the bottom line and damn anyone else."

Dani fluttered her hand. "Let's not talk about those depressing idiots," she said, taking a bigger swallow of her drink.

"David would never have been comfortable attending the school in the Downs. I've always homeschooled him."

"I can't see anyone being comfortable even living there. I heard all sorts of nasty things about the place."

Gayle took the first sip of her drink. "I'm not sure what you've heard, but it's all true."

Dani shook her head. "You can stay as long as you like. I appreciate the company."

"Thank you," Gayle said, taking another sip of her drink, which tasted sweeter than normal. After drinking the brand numerous times in the Downs, this one had an oddly different taste.

"Anytime," Dani said, leaning over and covering Gayle's hand with her own.

Gayle slipped her own hand away, setting it on her lap. She was never comfortable with casual touching. "We probably won't stay longer than a month."

Dani drained her drink. "Wow! That was great! I want another one." She bounced up. "How about you?"

"I'm still working on this one, but thanks," Gayle answered, sipping on it again. She decided to change the subject. "This is a really beautiful place. How did you find it?"

Dani giggled. "I got a great deal. Just have to know the right people," she said, filling her glass again. She returned to the small table, already draining her second glass. "Why did you join the guardian program?"

"Desperation," Gayle said. She leaned back in her chair, staring into the orange liquid cooling in her glass. "When my husband died five years ago, I couldn't live in my parents' house because of the environmental changes. I lived in a small room surrounded by smaller rooms with a lot of angry people. I had to get out before it swallowed me."

"I'm sorry," Dani said.

Gayle waved her hand. "Don't be. That is life in the Downs."

"How did your husband die?"

"He was somewhere he promised me he would never be," she said, glancing up. "It happened in the middle of the week, when Dome security implemented the early curfews. David was sick all the time when he was a baby. This time, he was really sick," she choked. "He needed to be there with us. He had the papers that would allow me to take David to the emergency room." She lowered her eyes, feeling the familiar sting in her eyes. She remembered when her husband's gang members stood at her front door with their heads bowed. She knew before they started telling her that Richard would never return home again.

She prepared herself the year before, when he first told her of his association with the local street gang. He promised their lives would change for the better.

"Gayle, are you all right?" Dani asked.

Gayle snapped her head up. She blinked back the tears, trying to erase the memory for the moment, but it would return later, especially when the days grew darker.

"I'm fine," she said, taking a healthy swallow of her drink. The toxic effect of the drink caused her vision to blur for a brief moment.

"So when do you want to go?"

"Go where?"

"Sue's memorial. Remember?"

Gayle cringed inwardly. She didn't feel like rubbing shoulders with strangers. She'd rather be home with David. "Dani, I really won't be able to attend. David isn't taking this change well. I need to spend the rest of the day with him."

"Oh…is he okay? I thought he looked well enough today."

"It's not that. He doesn't do well with change. I just can't leave him with a stranger."

Dani gave her bright smile. "I understand."

Gayle knew she didn't. "I really appreciate you for inviting me. If you let me know where the memorial will be held, I'd love to send flowers."

"I told everyone you'd be able to attend"—she paused—"but I'll let them know not to expect you."

"Thank you," Gayle said, placing her glass on the table, feeling that the time had arrived for the end of the school day. "I better get ready to pick David up from school."

"Of course," Dani said, leaning back in her chair.

Gayle rose from her table, trying to steady herself. Once she was sure that the room had stopped spinning, she continued out of the room. She remembered to put her phone in her luggage and that Gabriel promised to message her whenever he had the time. She hoped he found a safe place and managed to avoid Divine security detail. When they parted ways, he mentioned that he would make contact with Dr. Gregory.

She made her way up the stairs and back to the room, securing the door behind her. She leaned heavily against it, allowing the coolness to seep through the thin material of her blouse. She felt her breathing, and her heart rate slow. She closed her eyes, allowing the events of the last few days to settle into her mind. Then her phone buzzed. She pushed away from the door in a panic, rushing over to the pile of bags on the bed. She grabbed the small one, pulling it open. She rummaged through it, and her phone let out another sound. She found it at the very bottom. It vibrated in her hand until she flipped open the top. The screen blinked, revealing a single message. Despite the absence of the sender's name, she knew it had to have been Gabriel. She felt her heart lighten, knowing that Divine hadn't succeeded in capturing him; her eyes moved across the four lines. She frowned. *Why did he want to meet there?*

Gayle shook her head, stuffing the phone into the bag. She swung it over her shoulder and left the room. Once more, a wave filled her consciousness. She held her breath as her feet sprinted down the stairs. She made it back out of Dani's house without running into her again. She really didn't want to have to explain anything.

Dani emerged from the kitchen, wiping her hands with a towel. Her watched Gayle rush out the front door. Moments later, she heard the car speed out of the driveway. She twisted her lips, placed the towel on a nearby chest, pulled her phone from her pocket, and pressed on the screen.

"What do you have for us, Agent Travis?"

"Our little raven will be having dinner with Mr. Owl," she said.

"Do you know where?"

"Not yet."

"Are you having her followed?"

"No."

"Agent Dani, I hope I don't have to explain to you the significance of capturing this particular guardian. Dr. Gregory created him first. The others proved worthless. When we tried to extract information from them, their minds and bodies shut down. That doctor must have placed a failsafe in them. We believe Gabriel is the key."

"I am surprised it was so easy to get Divine to give them to you."

"Why wouldn't they? We financed most of the research. We would've gotten the information we needed if Vera hadn't disappeared. Have you heard from her yet?"

"Not yet." The roaring sound of a familiar high-power Jaxx caught her attention. She shuffled to the narrow side window beside her door. She cursed.

"What?" asked the speaker with apparent bat ears. She watched with her drunken mood dissipating. Catherine Miles exited her white two-seater Jaxx. She wore her usual stark-white pantsuit with a gold silk blouse and sparkling gold high-heeled shoes. The outfit was just as impeccable as the woman wearing it.

"The caterers arrived for that silly memorial I have to host," she said, watching Catherine strut up the steps, her feet barely touching the stark-white surface. Dani wondered if the woman even made a single dark stain like most visitors tended to do. "I have to go."

"What about Dr. Cote?"

"I'll let you know if I hear anything else on Dr. Cote."

"The Robinson woman?"

"Don't worry about her. Trust me. It's all handled."

"It better be, or we can always have you handled." The person on the other end of the call hung up. She stared at the phone, pressing her lips together. Catherine's demanding knock alerted her to the next problem at hand. She wished for that fifth drink as her feet jogged to the front door.

Once the door opened, Catherine whizzed past her without a word or recognition. She stopped in the middle of the foyer and stared ahead. Dani closed the door, glaring at the CEO. She waited with her arms crossed over her chest.

Frustrated, she spoke. "What are you doing here, Catherine? I thought we were meeting at your place tomorrow morning."

Catherine turned around and glanced at her. She rolled her eyes and headed for the formal living room. Dani followed her. She narrowed her eyes, boring a heated look into the woman's narrow, retreating back. Catherine dropped herself into a stiff, long sofa the same color as her outfit. Dani couldn't tell where the woman started or ended.

Dani chose to sit as far away as possible, which was in a narrow scarlet chair with a short, stiff back that made her feel like she would fall backward if she leaned too much. Honestly, she hated the designer the company hired for this place.

"I take it my time is up," Dani said.

"Oh, don't get dramatic. I really don't need your patronizing attitude right now," Catherine said. She pulled out a small silver metal case and opened it.

"Those are illegal," Dani said.

"Are you going to arrest me?" Catherine asked. She proceeded to pull out a slender white stick. She stuck it in her mouth and inhaled. The end immediately started to smoke.

"Why are you here?"

Catherine took a drag of her cigarette and blew a white smoke ring into the air. Dani already felt her stomach turn because of the noxious fumes clogging the air. "Fine, then. I've invited some extra people to your little party."

"It's more like a wake."

"Whatever. The executives need a party to loosen them up."

"Well, I can imagine where you're going to stick them."

"You know what I mean."

"I do, and I'm not a babysitter. I'm the cleaner you hired."

"Then you can clean up my father's muck by making sure the execs are thoroughly sloshed for tomorrow's meeting."

"What's going on?"

Catherine leaned further into the chair. "If you must know, the company is experiencing heavy losses. This guardian program my father insisted on launching has depleted us." She stopped. "For the first time in over five generations, Divine Cybernetics is in financial trouble."

Dani stared at the forlorn face. So there was a crack in the ice. What a big crack this was. The Dome Council would enjoy this tidbit of information. She doubted her efforts to sabotage the program with the Peterson family murders were really needed. They could go for the juggler now.

"You think by getting your executive panel drunk the night before will delay the inevitable?"

"It'll give me time to think of something."

"Catherine, I don't want to go anywhere near those sleazeballs," Dani said.

"You'll do what I hired you for."

Dani stood still. Her eyes pierced into Catherine. "How is this going to waylay the meeting?"

Catherine chuckled. "You've never seen these guys after a hard night of drinking."

"Fine, but if things get out of hand, I'll get out of hand," Dani said.

*****

It turned out to be a larger affair than she intended. Dani rolled her eyes after she took her fifth sip of wine that night. She still couldn't believe that several of the vice presidents were already teetering on the edge. Maybe it was a good thing that Gayle couldn't make it.

"This is a marvelous thing you did," Harold Wolfe, the vice president of marketing, said. He wavered precariously on the backs of his heels.

She fought the urged to reach out and push him down. Instead, she performed the ominous dance of avoiding his hands. "Thank you, Mr. Wolfe." She back away another step.

"Damn shame. Betty was a beautiful woman."

"Yes, she was very kind," Dani said and then took a sip from her drink. Her eyes slid to the side. She caught the glaring eyes of Catherine staring back at her. She knew the hidden message but chose to ignore it just then. One of the many things she picked up about her pseudo majesty was that Catherine tended to avoid the vice presidents in intimate gatherings.

"Fuck kind! She had legs like a goddess. I wanted her for my personal secretary, but no could do. That ice woman said it wasn't in the budget," Harold growled, then drained his tenth glass.

Dani could say one positive thing about the bloated executive. He could outpace the toughest Dome soldier in drinking. She drained her drink as well and placed it on a nearby table. "I appreciate the company and the conversation, but it appears the kitchen staff will need more direction. Please excuse me," she said and then turned away from him, but suddenly felt his hand on her arm.

"Hey, now, sweetheart! Let's not be so quick. What was your name again?"

She turned back around, grabbed his hand, and squeezed it while also applying pressure to the artery that cut off the sound in his voice box. She cocked her head to one side while looking at his pained expression.

"Begging your pardon. I'm not sure you heard me. I guess I'll have to repeat myself. I am leaving now. This has been a great experience, though. I hope we do it again," she said and smiled when   he nodded. She released his hand and walked away, cutting a line through the crowd of Divine employees. The room was awash in dim, cool blue, so she doubted anyone really paid attention to them. Dani really didn't want to go into the kitchen. She assumed the caterers knew how to take themselves to task. When they arrived and attacked her with a volley of questions, she shut them down with one sentence. If the guests weren't kept happy, she wouldn't be happy, and they would find themselves six feet under the dome. This was probably why, even now, they gave her a wide berth.

"Uh, Ms. Travis." A soft voice spoke from behind her.

"What?" Dani twirled around, almost bumping heads with a tall, slender woman. She narrowed her eyes at the pale female who backed away but only a few feet. "What do you want?" she demanded, taking in the white flared skirt and tight white-and-silver-striped vest. *What the hell is this waitress doing back in the kitchen?* "I just wanted to know where the rest of the drinks are," the woman said, giving her a sweet smile.

She glared at the woman even more. She thought her early warning to hired staff ensured everything would run smoothly without much involvement from her. Apparently, the idiot forgot to listen.

"What's your name?"

"Delilah," the woman said.

"Pretty name. Pretty face." She walked closer. "I wonder if you have a pretty brain."

"You are even more beautiful than I," Delilah said, coming forward to meet her.

Dani noticed their bodies nearly touching. However, she never had been one to back away from anything or anyone. There would never be a first time. "As I said to you and your team, familiarize yourselves with the house. I won't be available for questions…ever." "Funny. Most of our clients never wanted us to roam their home for fear we would steal something."

"Why would I give a damn if you steal something?" Dani said. "This isn't my house."

"Understood. I guess I'll ask my supervisor," the woman said and then was the first to back away.

"You do that," Dani said and smiled.

The waitress gave her a nod and made her way through the swinging doors back into the party. Catherine burst into the kitchen seconds later. She almost let out a groan. What the hell did the woman wanted that couldn't wait for tomorrow's meeting?

"Dani, I need to speak with you."

"Tomorrow."

"I know."

"I will report to you tomorrow."

"That's why I need to speak with you. They want a direct report on the guardian program. All the research files have been wiped from the computer, and both my top scientists are missing."

"I'm working on it."

"You are a cleaner, Travis," Catherine said and closed in on her. "Isn't it time you do your job?"

"Catherine, I have been doing my job. We raided Dr. Gregory's manor, and even now, I have guards posted around the city with specific instructions to apprehend both doctors with extreme prejudice." "I'm in danger of losing my company if the true finances of the company become known," Catherine said as her face drained of blood.

Dani felt like this was the first time she'd ever seen a crack in the CEO's shell.

"What you have to do now is relax and enjoy the party. Speak with Harold. Offer him a secretary and play nice. Have your meeting tomorrow. I'll see you after."

"How do you suppose I do that?"

"Not when you speak nicely with Mr. Wolfe," she said, nodding toward the door. "Go. I'll fix everything."

"See to it that you do because this is a dangerous game you're playing," Catherine said, turning, and then walked back out of the kitchen.

Dani watched the kitchen doors flap until they stilled. She accepted this assignment, knowing that the agents before her always seemed to have a short life span. The ones who managed to get out when the things caught fire retired immediately. They lived somewhere on one of the larger domes in the lap of luxury and never had to worry about another mission or riot. Her handler advised her that if she wanted the latter, she should keep her head down and avoid all risk.

Dani turned back around, immediately spotting a group of five full bottles of wine. She cocked her head, remembering the question from the waitress. Her eyes went to a male waiter placing a plate on the counter.

"I thought you guys ran out of wine," she said.

He lifted his head with a jerk. She watched his dark eyes widen. "No, no, miss. We brought a large van full of a variety of liquors and wines. It's included in the package."

*****

Catherine lowered down on the bench. The sorrowful melody of the party could still be heard in the distance. She leaned further into the seat, allowing her head to fall back. The portrait of the Milky Way above blinked down at her. She wondered if the real sky actually looked like that now. She remembered sending a request to the astronomers of the Dome 16 for real images, but they ignored her. Then after sixty-three demanding letters, they finally let her know that there were none. Of course, she knew it was a lie, but she let it go until the next day. There would always be time to see the sky.

"Nice night." A sweet feminine voice spoke.

Catherine lifted her head forward. She saw one of the waitresses seated on the stone step nearby, a lit cigar dangling between her two long, slender fingers. Her mouth watered at the sight of the cigar. Her public relations agent forbade such indulgences when she took over her father's company. The annoying little woman lectured to her that success should give way to sinful vices.

"Aren't those things illegal?" Catherine said.

"Oh, this?" The waitress held up her hand. "Yeah, but who's going to arrest me here?"

Catherine chuckled. "How silly of me. This is a private party."

"Nice party," the woman said, sucking on the cigarette.

Catherine rose and walked toward the little waitress. "You got an extra one?"

"Sure," the waitress said, popping up, extending a white box filled with five-by-five stack sticks.

She smirked, reaching forward to pull one from the box. "These are nice." She observed the stick. "Light."

"Yes," she said, leaning forward. The fire lit the edge. She inhaled the toxic fumes with relish. Her nerves immediately calmed.

"How long has it been?"

"Huh?"

The woman's eyes darted from the cigarette to Catherine's face. "I'm guessing since this morning."

"Afternoon, really. I find the cravings coming faster," Catherine said, swaying closer.

"Funny thing about cravings," the young woman said and then stood up. "They are always stronger than the last."

"I feel guilty about having them."

"You should never feel guilty about taking something you really want."

Catherine faced the woman, noting that she stood extremely close. Normally, she never allowed anyone within three feet of her personal space, but something compelled her to endure this woman's presence. Her greedy need had her suck the cigarette in. The intoxicating feeling caused her to smile for the first time in years. Her face felt almost numb. Her teeth tingle at the final exposure to the environment.

"I have other cravings I like to indulge in, as well," the woman said, drawing closer. Her eyes appeared to glow with an eerie, silvery blue, but Catherine was sure it may have just been the moonlight.

"That is—"

"Don't you want to know what it is?" Catherine smiled. "Maybe."

Chapter 13

GAYLE FELT THE START of another beginning seating beside Gabriel. They had not spoken much in the small stretch of time since reuniting. They never touched, except for a slight brush of the hands. Their conversation had been stunted and brief since seeing each other again. Mostly, it was her fault. She really just wanted to marinate in his presence during this brief encounter. She gave him another sideways glance, observing him focus on David as he exuberantly explored the edge of a nearby body of water with glee.

His erect profile allowed her to absorb his current state of appearance. His hair had grown longer and now almost reached the middle of his back. He secured his long blond locks in a leather thong. It made him look as different as she felt. Maybe he didn't know about barbers. She felt another guilty stab in some way. She was still responsible for him.

She also wanted to ask about his black-and-gold uniform—a dorm-guard uniform. When she first saw him in it, flashback of the cleanse crept into her mind, but then he smiled showing his white even teeth. His sheepish expression took her by surprise.

"You're curious about the uniform." He finally spoke.

"As a matter of fact, I am. This disguise seems to be a bit risky in the face of what's going on."

"I have not stolen the uniform. I assure you that I acquired it legally."

"So you are part of Dome security?"

"Yes, they pay me a living wage, and I also have a dorm room at the Dome Council headquarters."

"What about background checks and papers? I can't believe they would just let you join out of faith."

"It is nothing bad, I assure you, but Dome security is not really that secure. It can be as simple as manipulating a few algorithms in their system."

"You hacked the Dome government?" she said, not believing he could have managed such a thing.

His face fell. "You do not approve."

"It's not that, Gabriel. I just don't want anything to happen to you." She placed a hand on his leg and felt him tense. She realized what she had done and pulled it away.

"After we separated, my analysis of the situation led me to infiltrate Dome security. No one outside a few really knew of our existence. Divine scientists kept our identities secret. This suits my purpose."

Gayle understood his reasoning now. "I really just want you to be safe. There are too many people disappearing."

"Your safety comes before mine. Gayle, this is what I need to do to protect you and David." "The program is over, Gabriel."

"It will never be over for me," he said, reaching over to grab her hand. His bare skin felt heated, and she was unsure about the familiar touch.

"Gabriel." She pulled her hand away. "You must understand that David and I are in dire straits. I must resolve this by myself. I cannot risk your freedom for something that is not your fault."

"I cannot let you and David out of my protection even if the program has been dismantled. There are still factors in play that can cause you both harm."

"What kind of factors?"

Gabriel clammed up again. She felt him shift away and remove his hand.

"How am I going to *really* trust you if you don't tell me what's going on?"

"I must tell you this, but promise me you will not judge too harshly."

Gayle narrowed her eyes. She felt offended that he would think so little of her. "It will depend on what it is."

"While I was hacking the computer system of the Dome government, I discovered that Divine Cybernetics may be in danger of being taken over by the council."

"How is that possible? The company has been privately owned for years." This was the reason she was able to garner employment from the company. They didn't have to adhere to Dome Council standards. Divine Cybernetics had been one of the few and the most lucrative companies to survive government takeover.

"The guardian program proved to be extremely expensive. They borrowed money from the Dome Council, and they defaulted on the loan."

Gayle became silent. Maybe this was the reason why she never received the rest of her payment. Her job would be gone if the Dome 16 government took over. Then she would really be in dire straits. Her fist clenched tightly.

"Please do not worry, Gayle." Gabriel's baritone broke through her clouded thoughts.

"No, I'm not. Gabriel, do you know what this means?"

"Gayle, it only means that we will trade one master for another. I still do not like those odds."

Gayle rose. She twisted her hands in a painful knot. Her nerves became numb, and she felt a dizziness in her head. If the Dome Council pull her records they will know where she is from. They might decide her and David's life is no longer relevant, "Funny, I don't like them either, so we need to find an alternative."

She felt Gabriel rose beside her. "I will help you, Gayle. Do not worry." His hand lay gently on her shoulder. She almost shuddered at the weight.

"I just can't help worrying…with David and me losing our chance for a safe place, and now the Dome government is breathing down our backs." She reached a hand to cover his. "I just want to be okay just for once in my life."

"Do not worry. I will take care of everything."

"Mom! Gabe!" David shouted.

They turned in unison, and as her son sprinted toward them, Gayle grabbed David in a tight embrace. "What's wrong, David?"

"Someone's coming! Someone's coming!" David said, then stuffed his head into her shirt. She watched Gabriel move quickly, standing in front of the covered footpath leading to their little alcove. She knew curfew for Middletown would commence in another thirty minutes. This should have given them more than enough time to get to the terminal headed uptown. *This would have been very early for Dome security to start their rounds,* she thought.

*****

Gabriel knew the direction they would come through. He cursed himself for allowing time to slip through his sensors. He should've warned Gayle that park security started canvassing the area earlier than Dome security.

"Hello, Jace!" Gabriel called out first.

A brilliant white light shone on him. "Gabe? Is that you?" a baritone called out.

"Yes…it's me and my family," Gabriel said as he pointed his head toward Gayle and David beside him.

"That's fine, Gabe, but you might want to head to your quarters. If this is not your assignment, you are still subject to curfew."

"That's fine. We will be headed out soon."

"Have a good night, folks." The guard saluted them and left.

"They're right. It's getting late, and curfew will be in thirty minutes." Gayle spoke up beside him once the guards left. "We'll meet again in a few days. I have a lot to think about."

"You can stay with me until the morning." He spoke up. "David has school in the morning. I really want some time alone to think." Her solemn tone made another stab at his chest. He felt a sense of failure. He did not like the feeling and refused to accept it.

"I can help you. We can think of something together," he said.

He watched her face. Her lips pressed tight together. Her eyes appeared red and fatigued, and the worry lines in her face were more defined. Her lips turned into a small smile. "A couple days ago, you convinced me to go back to Uptown."

"It is ironic, but it will not be logical for you to try to catch a terminal train that will leave in two minutes."

Gayle seemed to realize that the time to go had passed. Her shoulders slumped even more, and she hugged David even tighter. "I better call Dani, so she won't be worried."

"Dani," he repeated. The name sounded very familiar.

"Dani Travis," Gayle repeated again. "I haven't spoken of her before, but I ran into her and told her about my situation, and she offered for me and David to stay with her for a while."

"Dani," he repeated again. Gabriel thought the name seemed familiar. He felt a need to match the name with the face. He reached over to touch her face in a swift move, catching Gayle off guard. He faintly heard her speak his name, then her voice faded. The image of Dani Travis appeared in his head, and he felt every cell in his body burn. His family was in the clutches of the woman who killed Olivia's family.

"Gabriel, Gabriel, your eyes," said David.

He looked down at David's flushed face and large dark eyes. He focused his attention on his surroundings. His eyelids blinked, trying to pull back the increasing surge of power. "We must leave now."

"Gabriel, what's going on?" Gayle asked. Her voice held a wary tone.

He'd never performed telepathic intrusion on her before, as the effects would cause her to experience lethargy.

"I have to show you something at my dorm. You must come with me. You're in danger right now."

Gayle, despite her clouded reluctance, seemed to trust him enough to agree to follow. He led them out of the park through a shorter path that was limited to patrols and officials. His patrol car was in a solitary area in the park staff parking area, yet they had not encountered anyone else. He bundled them into the car and tapped in the directions for the Dome government's headquarters.

"Will we be stopped?" Gayle asked him.

"Most guards have their families visit overnight. No one will care or stop us," Gabriel said.

"I am curious though. Haven't the others noticed your unique qualities?" Gayle asked.

"They were curious, as humans tend to be of outsiders, but I am able to mimic enough human interaction to blend in," he said, looking sideways at her.

She was still worried that he would be exposed. He wanted to ease her mind by telling her that the humans could never hurt him. If he wanted to, he could erase his presence from the minds of those who know of his existence, but it would go against everything he had come to respect about humans.

"We will be safe, Gayle. Do not worry."

They arrived at the Dome security's headquarters during the latter part of the night. Most of the guards had either been out on patrol or were asleep in their quarters. The quarters laid at the far west of the four-by-four-thousand square acres that encompassed all the government buildings. At the center of the property were city hall and the Dome Council temple. To enter the area at any time of day, one had to have their personalized codes and passwords.

He pressed through all the checkpoints without incident. David asked multiple questions about Dome security guards. The boy marveled at the tall stone buildings, which were a throwback to more archaic times when the citizens idolized the government. Gayle sat beside him, staring out the window. She was silent and thinking hard. He learned that was never a good combination.

He parked in the rear of the sixteen-story building. As he predicted, they saw no one in or around the area. They entered the building without incident, passing through a narrow, dimly lit hall, into a round, intimate lobby, where three elevators waited to take the inhabitants to designated floors. They entered one of the elevators, and he pressed the button for the sixth floor, where his assigned room was.

"It's not much," he said, opening the door, though he doubted his words described what they were really going to see. The quarters were sparse, reminding him of Gayle's old home in the Downs. The company provided a small metal spring cot that had a clean, threeinch-thick mattress, a dresser, a mirror, and even a desk with a chair and computer, at the rear of the room. He had a kitchenette and through a small door beside the refrigerator, a small bathroom.

He never needed the mattress much, as he spent most nights learning and tracking Dome security and Divine Cybernetics activities. During his free time, he took to making daily visits with his father and Delilah, though he always felt uneasy in their company. He didn't know why, but something about the pair bothered him, especially when his father glared at him with unprovoked anger.

"This is really small," Gayle said. "No wonder Dome security guards are so cranky." She stepped carefully around the room, absorbing the details. David headed to the bathroom.

Gabriel secured the door behind him. "They are overworked, especially since there are rumors of another riot in the Downs."

"I hope not. The last time, we almost had an all-out war," Gayle said, rubbing her arms. "I guess this *is* a *little* cozy."

"Come to the computer. I have to show you something," Gabriel said as he walked over to the desk, sitting down at the computer. "I've done some research on agents with Dome security, just to be sure who is after me, and I pulled up her."

Gabriel started typing on the computer. He knew exactly the website he needed to go to. He typed in his password and Dani Travis's name. He felt Gayle looking over his shoulder and then her gasps when she saw Dani's face. "The woman you are living with works as a double agent. Her prime assignment is to clean."

"What do you mean 'clean'? Is this some kind of joke?" Gayle asked.

"She is tasked with finding and killing anyone who interrupts the progress of government control over its citizens. Dani Travis was also at the Petersons' house," he said. "Gayle, Dome Council commanded her to clean the Petersons in order to frame Divine Cybernetics."

Gayle whispered behind him, "I need to sit down."

"I am sure she did."

"You're sure?" she asked, lowering herself onto the bed.

"You should not trust her or be in her presence."

Gayle adjusted herself further on the cot, crossing her legs. "What does she want with [O13]?

"Isn't it obvious?" he asked and then stood up.

Gayle placed a hand over her mouth. "I might have led her right to you!"

"Not really, but you cannot go back."

"No, of course not." Her eyes dropped. "I'm really tired."

Gabriel knew that sleep would eventually overcome her. He swore to himself that he wouldn't do this to her. If she ever knew the truth, their acquaintance would end.

"Sleep," he gently said to her. Gayle fell sideways.

David exited the bathroom, skipping up to Gabriel. "Is Mommy ill?"

Gabriel approached her and answered, "No, little one. She just is tired. Let's allow her to rest." He pulled the covers over her limp form.

"Your place is really neat," David said. "I've never seen our new place, but this is better."

"How so?" Gabriel asked, tucking the sheets around Gayle. "*You're* here," David said.

Gabriel lowered himself onto the edge of the bed, looking into David's face. His heart felt full at this moment. He had been anxious and restless during the time apart from them. His mind never settled.

Now at this moment, a peace drifted over them. He pulled David into a gentle embrace. He initiated an embrace before, always allowing Gayle or David to take the first step, but this time, he felt closer to them than any time in the previous months.

*****

David lay beside his mother, watching Gabriel type on the computer. The brilliant light revealed the worried expression on his friend's face. It reminded him of his mom's expression whenever the first of the month arrived. She mumbled around about money. Often, her mumbling quieted when he revealed himself. She gave him a bright smile that he sensed was only for his benefit.

However, things would be different with Gabriel. His friend never had that worried expression during the time he lived with them. Seeing Gabriel's expression just now, though, caused an ache in his tummy. It meant things were not good. They may end up on the cold, wet streets of the Downs with no food and hiding from the dirty stinking people.

He heard rapid thumping on the keyboard again. His friend leaned close to the screen and then leaned away. His large hands stopped moving. He heard Gabe exhale. David knew that his friend needed help.

Gabriel always helped them when they needed him. He even coached him on how to humble the bullies at his new school and when he failed his math test. Gabriel spent the entire weekend tutoring him, even convincing Ms. Baker to allow him to retake his test before the quarterly grades came out. The joy on his mother's face when he told her he's passed the test had been the best reward.

David slid off the cot. He squared his small shoulders and lifted his chin. He would solve this for his friend. He padded over to Gabriel who did not notice him right away. David had to tap Gabriel on the shoulder, which caused Gabriel to give him a shocked look.

"Why are you not asleep, little one?"

"You look sad," David said, "like something's wrong."

"Something *is* wrong, but I will solve it. You needn't worry yourself about it."

"I can help. Tell me. Please," David begged and leaned closer to Gabriel, peering into the screen, which displayed many rows of numbers.

"My problems may be too big for you."

"Not really," David replied.

Gabriel wrinkled his nose in a funny way. "Why do you say that?"

"Mom always says that problems are only as big as you make them."

Gabriel chuckled. "I am afraid I do not follow your logic."

"It's simple. You"—David pointed to Gabe, then back to himself—"me, and Mom are here together. If one of us disappeared forever, then that would be a really big problem, wouldn't it?"

Gabriel's smiled widened. The worry lines disappeared. "So long as the important elements are here, other things are not a large priority."

Chapter 14

THE ELEVEN MEN FILED through the silver double doors of the conference room. They were dressed in similar somber gray suits with black ties and white silk shirts fitting their different forms to perfection. They greeted each other with light gaiety while finding their own seats around the large oval glass table positioned at the center of the room. The noise quickly stopped when a beautiful woman appeared from the other end of the room. She wore a form-fitting white dress that stopped just at the hip, and her long blond hair fell straight down her shoulders, unmoving and unreal. Her glacial stare regarded the men seated at the table. She gave them a brief nod and took her seat at the head of the table.

Harold Wolfe, sitting on her left, cleared his throat and rose. His watery eyes roamed around the table at the other occupants. He crossed his arms in front of him. "My friends, as you all know, the guardian-program testing has ended. We have lost two of our top scientists during this time," he said and then stopped and looked around again.

The group erupted in soft whispers around the table. He cleared his throat and spoke again. "There've been many issues with this project, so I bring you here together now to convince you all that there is still a future for this project."

Stephen Campbell, the vice president of public relations,

interrupted. "I certainly understand your eagerness to relaunch this line, but as far as we see, the guardian line is not a viable project for us to proceed with to launch."

"Stephen, even if we did another year…nothing is ever perfect. You never truly know how this product works. If we don't put it on the market, then let the people decide."

"We are all in agreement that there is too much risk. I am sorry, Harold, but the guardian project will not proceed." The unison nods with Stephen Campbell's words cut another tear in Harold's nerves.

"Come on, we will triple our overhead revenue if we launch this line. Let's bring back the experimenters if we need another six months." Harold continued despite the stubborn expressions of the executives.

A course of whispers erupted among the men. It was not positive information coming from them. Catherine tapped her nails on the glass surface. She never expected them to agree to Harold's foolish ideals. She told him last night that they would never agree. The idiot thought he had enough power to persuade the board to side with him.

"I am sorry, Harold. Our immediate concern is to stop this takeover and find the money to pay back the Dome Council," Stephen said.

"*Damn* the loan! We *have* something here. This will more than pay our loan if we are able to have it on the market!" Harold said. His face started to redden.

"We have made our decision, and Catherine is in agreement, aren't you, darling?" Stephen said. He stared directly at her.

Catherine stood and glanced around the table. "I'm sorry, Harold, but I am in agreement with the rest of the team that the guardian program will cease. We will have to concentrate on paying back the default loan to the Dome government."

"Gentlemen, I thank you for your support and hope that we can continue to bring in a brighter future to Divine Cybernetics," she said, making a slight gesture to the doors. "Let us drink to the future. We still have many more years to make this company great again."

Three women walked into the conference room in pleated miniskirts and sheer white blouses. Their glittery six-inch silver stilettos made clicking sounds as they approached the table. Their bland expressions never changed, even as some of the men made sexist comments.

Catherine regarded them with an amused expression. They didn't even realize the women were sex bots. The women started handing out small glasses filled with crystal-blue liquid. After every man was confirmed to have a drink, they left quietly. Catherine smiled at the men and raised her own glass. "To the future of Divine Cybernetics," she said.

All eleven glasses raised high with her, and the men drank enthusiastically. Then suddenly, like dominoes, their heads fell forward onto the glass table. Her eyes slid sideways to see the accusing glare of Harold before he took his last breath.

Delilah smiled with Catherine Miles's lips. Now that the board had submitted their official closure of the guardian program, the guardians would be forgotten. This would make her attack on the humans unseen. The guardians would reign supreme, and she would be their queen.

*****

Dani dialed the number again. It went straight to voicemail once more. She slammed her phone shut in frustration and glanced around the glass-enclosed lobby. An abandoned glass shell for the robotic attendant was behind the desk, devoid of life and breath. She narrowed her eyes at the androgynous metallic being. She asked multiple times if Catherine was present in her penthouse. It gave her evasive answers or riddles that made her want to smash the snooty piece of metal into smithereens.

She glanced down at the phone in her hand. She could not dedicate the entire day to the ice queen. Last night, they agreed to meet at one o'clock. "The meeting with Divine's executives should only take a couple hours," Catherine said. In truth, she doubted their attention span lasted longer than a second. Anything after that would be torture for those poor souls.

The clicking and mechanical noises from the attendant drew her attention. It busied itself with the multiple screens surrounding its seated area. She sucked her teeth, deciding to try again. "Attendant, could you please try Catherine Miles's penthouse again?"

"Catherine Miles is not in the building." The attendant spoke without lifting the shiny dome head.

"Why have you not stated this before?" she asked.

"We have not received the correct questions," the attendant responded with nonchalant large glass eyes, blinking at her innocently.

"When did she leave this morning?" Dani almost let out a growl.

"Catherine Miles never came home," the attendant responded.

Dani's brow creased. "She never came home last night?"

The clicking continued in the same rapid pace. Apparently, it did not respond to indirect questions. Dani narrowed her eyes at the attendant, then glanced away. *Why didn't Catherine come home last night?* She tapped a finger on her arm. Then again, Catherine tended to spend nights at the office to finish what needed to be done at headquarters, then took the rest of the day to work from home. *That could be it,* Dani decided.

She headed out of the lobby into the clear day of Uptown. The false sun set high, painting a soft, warm blue across the inner surface of the Dome, giving an illusion of a calm afternoon. The clouds were programmed to be extra fluffy today. She pulled out her shades from the inner pockets of her blazer and covered her eyes.

Her craft, one of the few road and sky hybrid crafts, sat at the base of the steps. It was created specifically for the field agents of the Dome Council. It also came with her favorite amenity, a set of phasors hidden within the base of its belly. She pressed a button on her keychain. A portion of the bulbous glass and metal top parted wide to allow her entry. Once she secured herself in the confines, the glass shut securely and the engine came alive, humming strong and steady. She grabbed the controls, maneuvering them around. The craft lifted from the parking space, rising a little higher than a threestory building.

The craft shifted gears, propelling forward over the high-density part of Uptown into the sparsely populated area where the Divine

Cybernetics headquarters resided. She increased the speed gradually, hoping to catch Catherine at the office. Still, it was odd that the CEO never made it home last night.

Dani arrived at Divine's expansive parking lot in midday, hovering over the area and exhaled when she saw the familiar white Jaxx in the executive area. She lowered into a row behind the executive parking area, taking a moment to stare up at the fifty-tier building of glass and cement. She glanced at her watch again. The meeting should have ended by now. She was sure of it.

Why hadn't Catherine called her to let her know? She had her own schedule to keep. It would take a while to discover where the two doctors disappeared to, and now she lost Gayle and her son.

The rude nobody never even answered her phone call.

Dani exited her vehicle, crossing the parking area to a row of stone benches that lined a narrow grass median separating the parking lot from the exterior courtyard of the building. She lowered herself into the warm seat, leaning back. Most of the Divine employees were busy slaving away their lives for the doomed company. She was amazed that no one ever questioned or spoke a sour word against the conglomerates, guessing they were just grateful for having a chance to make a living without Dome Council intrusion.

She closed her eyes, allowing her mind to drift. At least she could do this without worry, without anticipating another threatening call from the powers that be. At least…she opened her eyes. A loud roar echoed around her. A freight train or, maybe worse, before her, the tall, perfect building swayed and the ground shook. She heard people scream from within.

Then she saw it. The sleek lines welled from the sides. On instinct, she hopped from the bench and ran into the parking lot. An ear-piercing sound followed, as she knelt behind a large black car, covering her ears. Then the blast erupted. The air around her quickly filled with ash and debris. She covered her mouth and hunched further, avoiding large chunks of debris that flew everywhere.

Moments passed before things settled. Dani was able to pull herself up. Her clothes had a thick layer of dirt. She stood and glanced around. Her eyes widened at the sight of the once-magnificent Divine Cybernetics headquarters, which had been reduced to rubble. She spied thousands of body parts littering the ground around the building. The main structure spew out fire as mini explosions continued.

In the distance, people still screamed and hollered. Chaos reigned over the once-empty parking lot. The dust still thick, she could see only a few feet in front of her. Dome security's sirens could be heard in the distance, but they were still too far away to provide any real help. However, she doubted they would be of any service once they arrived. Suddenly, her phone vibrated at her head. Her heart almost stopped. She pulled it out of her pocket's shaky hands.

"Hello?" she said.

"What the hell is going on down there, Agent Travis?" an angry man shouted into the phone.

"I don't know," she answered with a shaky voice.

"We just heard that Divine Cybernetics' headquarters was destroyed. Was it an attack? Was it the rebels?"

"I really don't know."

"It is clear that you don't. Apparently, we will need to send you some help."

"I don't need any help," she protested.

"This is not up for debate. To me, things are happening that are out of our control. We don't like it." The line went dead.

Dani continued to stand motionless; the phone still connected to her ear. Dust swirled before her eyes, and a variety of purples, blues, and reds spotted before her, shutting her in a nightmare that she could never awaken from. Then a streak of familiar gold and white caught her eyes through the sheet of smoke. Her focus snapped back as a woman's form materialized near Catherine's white Jaxx. It could not be Catherine. This was not common behavior for the executive. The churn of the Jaxx engine propelled her forward, but she was too late as the vehicle pulled swiftly out of the parking area and sped out of Divine's parking area.

Dani struggled to maintain her balance, running back toward her craft. She leaped into the seat while slamming down the glass hatch. She barely managed to secure herself before starting the engine with her other hand. The engine hummed steadily. She grabbed at the navigation controls, yanking them back. She felt it lift into the air, almost catching her off guard. She cursed the stupid move, as the sensitive controls only needed a slight touch.

She managed to get a last glimpse of the chaotic mess below. The charred bodies that were not incinerated with the blast littered every inch of the ground. Divine employees who had been outside huddled near one another, staring at the debris, too shocked to completely comprehend what happened. She could not blame them, as her mind still buzzed with the knowledge that the most powerful company in Dome 16 was no more.

Dani shook her head, turning the craft toward the highway. Catherine's Jaxx was built for speed. She knew that despite her aerial advantage, finding the small white roadster would be almost impossible. The idiot engineers who built the highway decided to make a spaghetti-and-meatball presentation out of their transit system. If the vehicle traveled beyond the suburbs into the city, she would lose it.

She grabbed her intercom. "Agent Travis to Dome Highway troopers, come in."

A volley of voices erupted from the speaker. Her ears strained to make out the multiple voices responding. She heard snatches of conversation about the Divine headquarters. *The idiots should have already been on the scene,* she thought but knew the threat of a riot in the Downs. Most of Dome's security detail were preoccupied. It was odd that someone knew this and chose this day to make a scene.

She lifted the intercom to her lips. "Highway troopers, come in."

"Trooper Martin here."

"Agent 6543, I need to put an alert on a white Jaxx 5004. It will be registered to Catherine Miles,"

"I will enter the alert, Agent, but our alarms are clogged with calls coming in from Uptown. Our manpower is stretched paper thin."

"This concerns the disaster at Divine's headquarters. There is a person of interest in that vehicle, so get on it, Trooper! Travis out!"

She ended the line. Her already-thinned-out nerves would never be able to tolerate another second.

Dani lowered the small craft toward the highway as cars started to crowd the streets. She would have to ground her craft and switch to street travel. To the side of one of the major roads, a landing pad had just been cleared. She switched gears to take its place. Once she reached ground level, she switched on the crafted monitoring systems to see if any of the troopers might have encountered the white Jaxx. When nothing came through, she tried to type in Catherine's phone number, hoping to get a lock on it. Still nothing. This was the odd part since the woman was never without the device.

Dani thought of typing a bounty alert into the computer. She thought about Catherine but figured the woman might be dead since the other female had been driving her precious vehicle. She started to type in the information regarding the guardians. She only saw Gabriel and Olivia. Most recently, she only knew that Gabriel still had not been caught. She'd tried to bring up his picture before but came up with nothing.

She was beginning to think something more had gone into this project. She was told the guardians' service parameters only should reflect of low level and low intelligence. They taught the children loyalty to the Dome government and attempted to make them perfect citizens. The adults were handled differently, but that did not require much sophistication.

Dani pulled her vehicle behind a trooper. It might be time to revisit Dr. Gregory's abandoned manor. Though Divine's security detail said they'd combed through the place, they might have missed something.

Chapter 15

CATHERINE MILES DID NOT wake up in her beautiful penthouse apartment in Uphill. When her eyes opened, the room appeared small and cramped, the air stale. When she moved, the bed did not conform to her curves, and the bed sheets covering her nude form felt stiff and hard against her skin. She felt the overwhelming urge to scratch, proceeding to move a hand but found them unable to obey.

She followed her arm to her wrist, finding it clasped with a thick, shiny manacle and a thick chain hooked to the thick metal frame headboard. She yanked hard, only managing to inflict pain that traveled up her arm.

Catherine pulled her nude form into a seated position, looking around the room again. She tried to remember how she came to be here and found her mind blank. She could not recall even leaving the party or who brought her here. She let out a painful groan when another wave of pain washed over her, as throbbing started in the front of her head.

Her stomach started to churn and heard the low growl at the pit. When did she last eat? What was happening? Catherine gave her constraints another vicious pull, yelping at the resulting pain.

The door opened, and a bright beam lit up the bedroom. A tall, slender woman stood at the cusp. The woman regarded her limp body against the frame. Her brow creased, seeing the familiar silver-andwhite business suit. She knew it well, having worn it often enough to the office, to recognize every stitch and diamond-encrusted silver buttons. Her eyes flew back to the woman's face, and again, another surprise took hold of her. The woman's appearance shared stark similarities with her own, except for usual pale skin that appeared almost plastic, stretched over fine bones.

"You're awake," the woman said with a casual tone.

"Who are you?" Catherine demanded.

"Don't you recognize me?" she asked, pushing away from the doorframe and swaying closer.

"Should I?" Catherine narrowed her eyes. "Look, darling. Let me go now, and I'll see to it they don't vivisect you before execution."

The woman flopped down on the edge of the bed by Catherine's feet. "Bold words from a weak human." Smiling, she continued. "Now if I let you go, what would be the fun in that?"

"Who are you?" Catherine shouted, then regretted the impulse when pain burned a path through her, igniting the sensitive nerves in her mouth. She cried.

"Now, Cathy, don't get so worked up. It's not good for the complexion."

Catherine felt her whole body seize. She stared into the woman's luminescent eyes. Her heart thud rapidly. She could not believe that her mom's voice had just come from the strange being before her. She did not think ever to hear it again, the nonchalant viper tongue that hurt more than any slap.

"Now I have your attention." The woman continued in her mother's voice. "Mom was a rare bird, always calculating, always critical. A flawless creature, so divine in her own way."

"You don't know what you're talking about," she whispered.

The cornflower-blue eyes widened. "But I do. Mr. Miles loved Mom so much that he wanted to have her cloned. He froze her sickly body and begged my father to clone her."

"You lie!" she said.

"Darling, to lie to you would mean that I cared about your feelings," Delilah said as her hand patted Catherine's bare ankle. "You have not grown on me yet."

"Dr. Gregory would never deceive my father!" Catherine said, but her inner struggle about the reasoning behind his possible deceit bothered her. The familiarity of the woman's appearance could not be denied.

"It is true. My father loved Mr. Miles," the odd being said, rising from the bed. "I wish it were the same for you."

"Enough! Kill me if you want to, but I refuse to hear any more of your lies!" Catherine said.

A chuckle erupted from Delilah's lips. "I am not going to kill you…not now. I need a best friend and someone to watch TV with." The woman walked over to a thin metal side table. She picked a thin rectangular box and pushed on the surface.

In a high corner across the room, a large square screen flicked on. At first, she saw that a blanket of white smoke covered the entire screen. Her ears caught faint audio coming through filled with screams and the garble of voices. Then punching through the smoke screen, she saw burned and bruised people. Then the smoke fully cleared, and a small scream escaped Catherine's lips. What used to be the sleek, strong, fifty-story building of Divine Cybernetics had been reduced to a quarter of its size. A black cloud rose from the epicenter. Dome security guards tried hard to douse the large flames by pouring large batches of water into the empty shell.

"I hope the others made it out okay."

The woman twisted back around. "Oh, how rude of me," she said, holding out a hand." "My name is Delilah."

Catherine felt tears rushing from her eyes, for the first time since her mother passed. Her heart stopped and felt like stone in her chest. Her body lost its ridged form, sinking into the stiff mattress. Yesterday, she feared only the possibility that the company would be ruined, but there had still been hope. Now a cold, forbidden reality had come to fruition.

The sadistic creature pouted. "You asked me who I am, remember? I am the insignificant prototype you sent your dogs after. Now we are going to be best friends."

Catherine heard those last words as a dream. Her brain was already mentally bankrupt from the earlier verbal assault. Her mind now just retreated into darkness.

Delilah observed the prone Catherine. She regretted overwhelming the woman. She wanted to play more, shrugging her shoulders, heading into the living room of the small apartment. Boredom started to overwhelm her again. It came faster in the last few days, shocking her system like waves and waves of a violent storm. This caused her to struggle with inventing creative ways to feed the beast.

She glanced around, standing in the center of the living room. The apartment had been a welcome reprieve from her father's stuffy underground lab. She found it a block away from the lab in a tall redbrick building. She quickly found that the exterior was only cosmetics, and the interior disappointed her. The brown walls held a muddy appearance, and her intense senses saw small brown bugs crawling behind the weathered wood.

The owner who managed the place thought Delilah stupid and exaggerated the apartment amenities. Mrs. Ava Marvel promised brand-new furniture, spectacular scenery, and quiet. Instead, the furniture turned out to be torn and broken. The scene was a plain brick building, and she heard every noise from the drugged-out couple upstairs to the small creepy critters rustling through the trash below.

She smirked, remembering the bloated horror-filled face and fear-filled dark eyes of fat little Ava while she fed.

Delilah's head snapped at the intense, piercing ring of her cell phone. Her face twisted into a monstrous mask when her peaceful memory dissipated. She knew who dared to interrupt and wanted to make him suffer more for it. The piercing ring continued to mock her. She could no longer handle the annoying noise. She stomped over to the table, yanking the phone up, bringing it to her ear.

"Hello, darling Gabriel. How is my favorite brother?" she said.

"Where are you?" Gabriel asked, his voice short and clipped.

"Sightseeing," she responded.

"What have you done to Father?" he asked. His tone gave her happy chills, but she decided to play a game.

Delilah let out a gasp, feigning insult from his accusation. "I have not done anything to him. Tell me what has happened."

"He is ill. It appears he has been for some time. Now answer my question."

"He is an old man, Gabriel. Everyone has stress, and even with all our talents, we cannot save him. You must understand this."

"Delilah, I do not want to play your games! Answer me truthfully!" his baritone resonated through the phone so loud that she pulled it from her ear.

"If you continue to yell at me, I will end this conversation," she said.

The line went silent, but she still heard his breathing coming through. It soon became less labored, slowing to a steady, reduced pace, then he spoke again. "I apologize."

"Much better," she said. "We don't want you losing control again. Now what would your human plaything think?"

He ignored her comment, refusing to be sucked into her game. She was a little disappointed. Her boredom demanded his involvement. "Father appears to be suffering from a mysterious ailment. It is beyond my abilities."

Gabriel paused. "We may lose him, Delilah, and I am upset with this knowledge. I did not mean to insinuate you had anything to do with his situation."

"You are forgiven," she said. "I apologize for leaving him. It was just for a couple of minutes. I needed some time to myself, and you never communicate with me about when you are coming."

"I had some things to attend to."

"You think I don't have things to get done? My world has changed too. Did you even stop to think about how I was adjusting?"

"I did not know you felt this way, Delilah."

"Of course, you didn't, since you are so wrapped up in your own selfish pursuits."

"Understood. I will stay with Father, but now he needs medical attention. Gayle knows a back-alley doctor who can look at him, but we would have to take him there. Father needs someone to look after him in the meantime."

"Heavens, Gabriel, do not tell me you are allowing this little human to order you around like a puppy. Was she not one of the keepers?" Delilah huffed. She still could not believe that Gabriel chose to stay in communication with that pathetic little human. She saw her about in the first months of the experiment, very glad to not have been assigned to the Robinson family. The female appeared even more inferior to the others—fat, sad, small, and doing a job fit only for a mindless drone."

"Enough! Gayle is my family as well. I trust her. Please refrain from speaking ill of her."

"I am looking out for your best interest. We are blood, not her."

"I am grateful for you being with me, but we must learn to allow ourselves to accept others, welcome them as allies to our cause.

If we are to survive, we must understand that as a group, we are strong. Remember the lesson of Dr. Joshua."

"Let's hope your blind trust in this human does not end us."

Through the earpiece, she heard him inhale. "Will you come back to look after Father while we find medical help for him?"

"I will be there in an hour.""

"I thought you were a few minutes away."

"He should be okay for a few minutes by himself. Goodness, Gabriel, the man has lived five of our lifetimes."

"Understood. I will alert him that you will be delayed," Gabriel said, and then the line went dead.

No warm goodbye or bright farewell. She pulled the phone from her ear and stared down at the blank screen.

Gabriel still maintained his naive faith in the humans, despite her warnings and his own experience with their duplicity. She hoped to help him realize his error.

*****

Gabriel laid the phone down. Behind him, David's lucid humming could be heard in the next room. He gave the little one a task situating and labeling water bottles and small packages of dry food on a nearby shelf. David knew Gabriel had just given him the task to keep him busy, but he tackled the work with the focus of a scientist.

He glanced over the cabinet filled with a plethora of liquid-filled medicine bottles and pill bottles. He leaned forward, pressing his forehead against the top of the cabinet. None of those would help his father. If he could not help him, then nothing synthetic would work either.

Upstairs, Gayle could be heard moving around the metal railing. He turned around, opening the door of the small closet room into the large pantry. David also heard his mother, stopping in place to turn his small round head to the ceiling. Their eyes met.

Gabriel sensed how upset Gayle was lately. Her moods were silent and forlorn. When he attempted conversation, her responses came short, with a hint of agitation. He knew not to press her as it would only end in more conflict. They already came close when he suggested contacting Delilah regarding his father.

"Gabriel!" Gayle called out from the lab. "David!"

"In here, Mom!" David answered, sprinting out of the room.

Gabriel inhaled, following the little one into the large lab. Gayle made her way down the spiral staircase. Her steps were hurried and clumsy. She briefly fixed dark red-rimmed eyes on them, then they darted around the room, refusing to stay in one place.

David met her at the bottom of the staircase, throwing a gleeful hug around her waist. She returned it automatically, but something occupied her attention. The little one sensed it and backed away, looking into her face.

"What's wrong, Mommy?" David asked.

"Nothing, David," she said, ruffling his curly dark hair. "Why don't you freshen up a little before we go." She gave her son a forced smile.

David gave her a suspicious, lingering look. "Okay," he finally said, hopping up the spiral steps.

Gabriel waited until David was out of earshot. He approached her. "What has happened, Gayle?"

She remained silent but rested her eyes on his face. Her lips made subtle movements as she tried to speak, but the words would not come. In one fluid movement, he embraced her. Her body relaxed against his, and her arms moved up his torso, connecting around the small of his back.

"All those people," she whispered.

Although he felt reluctant to let her go, this would be the time to see what had been bothering her. "Tell me what has happened."

"I heard it on the radio…I shouldn't have turned it on, but I felt I had to know what was going on."

"Gayle, you are not making sense."

"I am trying to tell you that Divine's headquarters has been bombed!" she yelled.

Gabriel's heart stilled. Something nudged at the back of his mind, but he ignored it. "Do they know how it happened?"

Gayle shook her head. "No, but, Gabriel, all those innocent people. I know them. I know they don't deserve this."

"Come, please."

"What about the Dome government? They're always up to something. Could they have done this?"

Gabriel shook his head. "I have been monitoring their communication. I believe that of all the plans they have in store for us, destroying and murdering Divine employees is not one of them."

"I cannot believe this." Gayle covered her face with her hands.

He reached for her again, wanting to calm her nerves, hopefully, in time for David to come back. "We will solve this mystery."

Once more, she moved away. "I am so tired of solving this mystery. It has been nothing but a mistake—a big, dark, all-consuming mistake. I am hungry for it to end. I just…I just want to close my eyes and go back to the beginning."

He pressed his lips together. "Then I will be gone."

She froze. Her tear-stained face revealed how she regretted her words. "Gabriel, you know I did not mean—"

He held up a hand. "I am not so fragile anymore, Gayle. I understand a little of how you think now."

She dried her eyes. "Do you really?"

*****

Herman senses when Delilah was no longer present. His head cleared. He felt his heart lighten, and movement became more fluid. His thoughts started to flow with the alertness of his youth. He certainly felt like his old self again. He glanced around, noting that everything appeared silent, deathly silent. He rose from the narrow cot of the tiny bedroom, drifting onto a narrow metal platform.

He stood behind a railing, looking down into the cylindrical depths of his private sanctuary, his most private lab situated in the central confines of the Downs. He remembered commissioning the construction before the delegation of the Dome government and the completion of Dome 16. So none knew of its existence, and those expressing a hint of curiosity quickly learned that there was only one safe way in and out of his lab.

Herman made his way down the mesh metal steps spiraling down into the main area of his lab. He took his time becoming aware of the increasing dampness of his skin and the painful compression of his lungs. He stumbled to a long glass panel that ran along one wall.

On the security screen, he saw himself huddled and dominated by a fiery-eyed Delilah. Despite the lack of audio, he watched her lips move and himself nod and saunter off to perform whatever task at his lab station, where he kept living organisms created in petri dishes and large colorful bottles. He saw himself mixing concoctions that had smoke drifting from their foam mixes and realized that Delilah had commanded him to do this, but why? What was she after?

Another day appeared, where he found himself bent over a chair. His thinning hair stuck in strings around his round head. Delilah walked into the room wearing a tight waitress outfit. She placed a small bowl of dried food on a counter, then disappeared out of the entrance, never looking back. He never went for the food.

He turned off the screen, shutting his eyes tightly. Bile rose in his throat at the possibility that he may have done something for her that would not end well—some even deadly and nefarious. Then again, this must have been an illusion—something not real. He couldn't fathom that Delilah's antics would come to this. His shaky fingers found the buttons, so he erased the tapes. He would record again.

Herman opened his eyes once more, trying to focus his vision. He shuffled to the lab station where he had been working on the tape. He saw tubes almost empty of their fluids, some even empty. Unorganized samples lay crooked and out of place on a metal rack, and dark burn spots dotted the edges and bottom surfaces of the larger glass containers.

He knew this particular lab station allowed him to duplicate and manipulate living tissues, but he only used it for small tests. The larger tests were done. *Oh no,* he thought. He closed his eyes once more, as a wave of dizziness overwhelmed him. The familiar throbbing appeared in his head again, but he couldn't shake what his mind wanted him to remember, what he needed to know.

"Maybe I need a nap," Herman whispered to himself. He turned away from the lab, making his way back toward the metal steps leading up to the living quarters. This time, he headed to his office. Inside, he smiled upon seeing his old leather lounge chair beckoning him from the dimly lit corner. A nearby lamp shed a warm yellow glow over the small area.

He came forward in measured steps, finding the last of his strength to cross the plush, spice-brown carpet until something bumped his leg. He looked down, relieved. He lowered himself into the malleable curves and rested his head back, allowing his body to relax.

The spinning slowed a bit, allowing his mind to churn once more. Snapshots of images drifted through, some familiar and some not, like vivid memories of his youth as an ambitious young man with a genius mind. He was still wise to the ways of the world, especially after his parents' sudden accident. He found himself thrust into predators until he became one himself and turned on them. At a pivotal point in his life, he met Cyrus Miles.

Divine Cybernetics had been at the height of its success. Many student scientists vied for the chance to work for them, the only private company to win a series of Dome government contracts, one being the new construction of Dome 16, but Cyrus chose him. His first task had been to create drones that could withstand the harsh environment outside the domes. After their success, his life skyrocketed to perfection. Nothing was denied him. Ole Miles just signed blank checks and never asked questions.

He smiled, remembering his first attempts at combining human biology and cybernetics. Cyrus understood his vision—the potential of how it would improve all their lives, but then Cyrus died of a heart attack. His daughter, Catherine, took over. She twisted things to her own selfish reasoning. She wanted things quick and cheap, shiny prototypes to wow the brainless executives and investors. After several inventions, he refused to continue.

Catherine only demeaned his creations, presenting them as servants—brainless and obedient. She told the executives that they were like the mindless construction drones, but he showed her. His guardians were supreme in their creation, or…they were supposed to be. Now what had happened to them?

"Father?" A deep voice spoke above him. He knew the voice—angelic, smooth, like water over hot coals. "Father?"

"Gabriel, where have you been?" he said this, even as he heard his own voice. It sounded disgustingly tired.

"I've been trying to set the others free, but it has been hard to locate them," Gabriel said, his voice sounding disappointed.

Herman opened his eyes. Gabriel's serene face punched through the cloudiness. He never thought the boy would survive in the first days after his birth. He remembered how he cried, and things caught fire spontaneously. Over time, he was able to control Gabriel's feelings, blocking and suppressing them.

"He doesn't look good." A female voice spoke behind Gabriel.

Herman strained his head to see who it was. He was relieved at the sight of Gayle Robinson and her son, David, under her arm. They stared at him with wide-eyed confusion.

"He is not well," Gabriel said, "I cannot tell what is ailing him."

Not well, Herman thought. In truth, he had not considered his appearance since the escape. However, he didn't think he had been remiss in keeping up his appearance. He allowed his head to relax on the pillow once more, looking into the flat metal ceiling above him.

He tried to figure whether the lights above were just dim or if his eyes had lost their focus.

"He needs to see a doctor, Gabriel," Gayle said.

He saw her move into his line of vision, a dark, blurry shadow at first, then he saw her large dark eyes regarding him with concern. "That would not be possible. They're looking for him as well. I

do not think they would be overly concerned about the state of his health," Gabriel said.

Herman saw his face lean over the eyes, scrutinizing his prone body, and it made him squirm and made a nasty face. "Stop hovering over me, boy."

"There's nothing physically wrong with him. He is low on

nutrients," Gabriel said to Gayle, then turned back to him. "Have you been eating well, Father?"

"Of course," Herman said, but then, in his mind, he really was not sure.

Delilah regulated his meals. It always appeared like a blur. His mind went to the small bowl of what appeared like kibble on the security cameras. Was that what he ate?

"I really think we need to get him some medical attention," Gayle repeated.

"Delilah should have been taking care of him," Gabriel muttered.

"Delilah?" Gayle said. "The Johnsons' guardian? The rogue guardian?"

Gabriel nodded and shrugged. "However, I'm not sure where she is at this moment."

"You left her with this poor old man?" Gayle said, her voice rising again.

"She would not harm Father," Gabriel said.

"So you say," Gayle responded.

Herman frowned at her comment. Delilah never meant to hurt those people. Her impulsive nature tended to override her logical mind. He remained firm on this, though he had to admit that her impulsiveness often blurred the line into danger.

"I will see what we have among the medical supplies." Gabriel spoke again. "Will you stay with him?"

Gayle nodded. Gabriel moved away. However, before he reached the door, little David excitedly followed him. "I can come too. You need more hands."

"Sure, if your mother is okay with this," Gabriel said, looking expectantly at Gayle, who nodded.

"As long as you are helping, David. Do not wander around," she said, ruffling his head.

David promised, hurrying to catch up to Gabriel's long strides. The door closed behind them, and the room became enveloped in a dark silence. Gayle sat across the room in a high-back chair opposite his desk. He saw that she paid particular attention to his wall of youthful dreams.

"I haven't sculpted anything in years," Herman said.

Gayle glanced over at him with narrow, suspicious dark eyes, then investigated the wall again. "You have built up quite a collection. Why did you stop?"

He shrugged his shoulders. "The job got more demanding, and I found there was not enough time in the day."

Gayle investigated the collection again. They appeared like distorted metal ants posed in different positions. They had wires for hair and bolts for joints; gears represented the bodies; and small brightred bulbs gave them vision. The collection ranged in size between that which could fit in the palm of an adult human hand to great, bulky ones the size of a human skull. Most had small wheels as legs, and others had their wheels covered with thick black rubber.

She judged the older ones by the dull metal surfaces and simple design, and the newer ones had a mirrorlike surface that provided the room with an even more luminescent light. Whenever she thought to have recognized one of the bugs, she would change her mind, twisting back around. She gave a lopsided smile. "These are extraordinary."

"They are a youthful dream. I wanted to be a toy maker." "That is a long way from robotics." She walked away from the shelves.

"It was not much of a leap." He chuckled.

"I am guessing Divine took over your life after that."

"More like they sucked my time away," he said.

"Why did you go work for Divine Cybernetics?" she asked.

"They promised to not lock me in a cage." He chuckled.

Gayle stood. "I suspect they would have loved to keep you happy since you basically made the company."

"Yes, I did. Cyrus understood me. We understood each other. We understood each other well," he muttered.

"What happened when Mr. Miles died?" she asked, lowering

herself onto a brown leather ottoman much closer to him. She focused on his pale face that had drastically aged since she had last seen him. When she saw him for the first time since after the death of the elder Johnsons, he held a dignified and noble look; he intimidated her. She felt nervous around him in those days. Now she found herself more comfortable around him.

Dr. Gregory grew silent. His lower lip trembled, and water welled up in his eyes. His attention no longer focused on her. Instead, his gaze fell on his ancient collection. She looked at the collection as well, then looked back at his face.

"After Mr. Miles died, why didn't you leave Divine then?"

"Where is Gabriel?"

She gave him a confused look, thinking it was quite rude for him to not answer her question. *Maybe he is not so sick,* she thought. "He went downstairs to find something to help you."

"Good boy." He let out a labored breath. "I have to say…I am a little disappointed in that one."

Her brow furrowed. "Why would you say that?"

"He is not perfect," he said, his tone so soft she had to lean in to hear.

"Why is that so important? He is doing his best to help. He didn't have to," she said. Her tone became heated. "He could have just run away, and we would all be in trouble."

"He is flawed, gal," he said, as if it was something important and final that his decision was the fact of the matter.

"I really don't understand your meaning, Dr. Gregory. You created him. How could you just spit on your own creation?"

"He is not what I wanted him to be. They took him from me, ruined him like they ruined me."

"What were they meant to be, Dr. Gregory? What was your grand scheme?" She leaned in further, anxious to know his answer.

"The guardians were supposed to be my crowning achievement, a perfect mix of humans and cybernetics—without sickness, emotional issues, and silly flaws that come with humans, and yet, they will not have the expiration that comes with cybernetics. I could make them be what I wanted."

"Human and cybernetics," she repeated. "Gabriel is half human."

"No, no. He is fully human, but did you know that the human body is like a canvas? It starts off plain, but once you start adding paint and form, it becomes a masterpiece."

"He is not a thing or a masterpiece. He has a right to life. You can just—" She stopped, enraged, and searching for the right thing to say. They were going to sell actual human beings.

"Dr. Gregory, that's slavery, and it's wrong to do this to someone."

"They're a creation."

"They are not your creation. They belong to nature," she whispered to him.

He started to shake his head side to side. "They never understood what I wanted them for."

"They don't belong to you *or* Divine Cybernetics. They belong to *themselves*. What you did was wrong. Please understand this."

"I did wrong?" He stopped, then finally looked into her face.

She realized that tears started to fall.

"Yes."

He closed his eyes. A whine suddenly came from him. "I...I... tried to be great, like Uncle Malcolm. Have I disappointed them?"

She shook her head in disbelief. He was an old creation fool off his rocker. His mind had descended into his own narcissism. Could he not see all that happened was due to the wealthy and overprivileged citizens seeking perfection? They stepped over the less fortunate to achieve what? She lived among them for six months and saw a plastic, heartless world.

"Dr. Gregory, the flaws we all have are what make us human. In our own way, we are perfect." She watched the doctor's eyes drift closed. The voices of Gabriel and David startled her. She jumped up, knowing that if they saw her distraught face, they would be upset and ask questions that could not be answered. She could barely contain her own feelings just then, much less deal with theirs.

Another pair of doors opened on the opposite side of the room. Gayle scuttled across the room, entering through the doors. She found herself in another common area room with a large screen covering most of the back wall. Two large brown leather chairs were positioned in front. She looked around, not spotting any other furniture, but the shelves of Dr. Gregory's handmade bugs crowded the walls. She closed the door, choosing the closest chair and sinking into the firm, cool confines. She wiped her face with a dark-green wool blanket placed over the side of one of the fat arms, wanting to erase away the sorrow and frustration of her plight.

"Gayle!" Gabriel's voice called from the other room.

She jolted back out of the chair. Her emotions still ravaged over her nerves, but they were hidden deeper within her core, where she wanted them to be.

"Gayle?" he repeated.

"In here," she finally answered. She cursed her shaky voice.

The door opened in a few seconds. Gabriel stood between the rooms, framed by darkness. His eyes focus on her face, giving her the most eerie look. "Are you okay?"

"I fine," she said, coming around the chair to stand before him. "Did you find anything?"

He shook his head. "Nothing I feel comfortable giving to him." He twisted his head partially back to the sleeping Dr. Gregory. "It appears Father is asleep again."

"He drifted off really quick," she said.

"He is not well, Gayle," he said as he moved further into the room. "I am not sure what to do."

Gayle glanced at his face, realizing that despite the cruel way Dr. Gregory had treated him, Gabriel still respected, even loved, the old fool—the old fool who could not see the truly wonderful person he really was.

"Hey," she said, placing a hand on his bicep, "I understand the importance of anonymity. I know an old friend who is somewhat of a doctor. He lives a few blocks from here and hates authority figures. He can look at Dr. Gregory."

He glanced at her with bright, trusting eyes. "He is a doctor?"

She inhaled. "Well, he had his license revoked for illegal cloning, but he has helped most of the residents of the Downs with free medical services. He helped me with David. He is one of the very few people I trust here."

Gabriel smiled. "If you trust him, I trust him."

"Good. I will send a message to see if he is available," she said. "Where is David?"

"I tasked him with organizing the produce. This will keep him up to date with the other children."

"Let me guess…" She smiled, knowing her son's most-hated subject was the one Gabriel gave him—"Math."

He nodded. "He was averse to it, but I convinced him that it would help us even more."

"Good idea."

Silence pushed between them. She found her body leaning into him. He always expelled a scent of fresh lavender and roses. He used her soap that morning, despite already having his own. She noticed he trimmed his hair and wondered why, although it pleased her to see more of his face.

"I must check on him." Gabriel finally spoke. "I will let Delilah know what has happened and tell her to come back."

Gayle screwed her face at the mention of the disagreeable guardian. "Are you certain we should involve her? She does not sound very capable to me."

"She is quite capable, Gayle." His tone turned serious.

Gayle raised an eyebrow. "All the malice she has done, Gabriel. I feel that even you and Dr. Gregory are not safe from her."

"She could not help what they made her, Gayle. Please understand that she is trying. We must help her find a peaceful path and not judge her."

Gayle tried to see things Gabriel's way. "Fine, but we are taking David."

"Okay. I will call her." He left the room.

Gayle shook her head. Delilah had been a constant conflict between her and Gabriel. Every time she tried to point out to him his sister's unacceptable behavior, his mood changed for the worse. He closed up tight and refused to listen to her opinions—albeit negative, but true—about Delilah, even when he confessed to her that Delilah was responsible for the elder Johnsons' demise. This still did not sit well with Gayle.

She swallowed hard, returning to the chair. Her hand rubbed the side of the chair, causing the large rectangular screen to blink on. At first, a blanket of white smoke crowded the screen. A muffle of voices could be heard coming from the side where a large pair of headphones lay. Her brow furrowed. She picked them up, placing them over her head. Suddenly, screams assaulted her ears. Her eyes flew to the screen, where a woman came through the smoke.

She recognized the beautiful brunette from the Dome 16 news. Unusual for her, the woman did not smile or was over made up. In fact, the woman's dress consisted of a Dome security's uniform similar to Gabriel's.

"It's a horrendous tragedy here, everyone. This company has been the backbone for Dome 16 for sixty years, having built this particular environmental dome in time to elevate the others from overcrowding." A wide-angle lens revealed the disaster she spoke of. Gayle felt her mouth free fall open and her body freeze.

"Divine Cybernetics is no more, along with the thousands of precious lives that had the misfortune to be here today."

"No," she whispered, her voice barely audible. She snatched off the headphones running from the room, passing the sleeping Dr. Gregory. She ran toward the bathroom, kneeling at the toilet. The entire contents of the meal two hours before hurdled into the water. She retched, feeling her body shake violently. Afterward, she felt her bones crumple, and her head rested on the seat. Her lungs struggled with just breathing in and out. Then the storm came, and she could not stop it.

Chapter 16

GABRIEL LAID THE PHONE down. Behind him, the lucid humming of David could be heard in the next room. He gave the little one a task situating and labeling water bottles and small packages of dry food on a nearby shelf. David knew Gabriel just gave him the task to keep little boys like him busy, but he tackled the work with the focus of a scientist.

Gabriel glanced over the cabinet filled with a plethora of liquid-filled medicine bottles and pill bottles. He leaned forward, pressing his forehead to the top of the cabinet. None of them would help his father. If he could not help him, then nothing would.

Upstairs, Gayle could be heard moving around the metal railing. He turned around, opening the door of the small closet room into the large pantry. David also heard his mother, stopping to listen, his small round head cocked to the ceiling. Their eyes met.

Gabriel sensed how upset Gayle was lately. Her moods were quiet and forlorn. When he attempted conversation, her responses came quickly, with a hint of agitation. He didn't press her because he knew it would end in more conflict. They already came close when he suggested contacting Delilah regarding his father.

"Gabriel!" Gayle called out from the lab. "David!"

"In here, Mom!" David answered, sprinting out of the room.

Gabriel inhaled, following the little one into the large lab. Gayle made her way down the spiral staircase. Her steps were hurried and clumsy. She fixed dark red-rimmed eyes on them for a moment, then they darted around the room, refusing to stay in one place.

David met her at the bottom of the staircase, throwing a gleeful hug around her waist. She automatically returned it, but something occupied her attention. The little one sensed it and looked into her face as he backed away.

"What's wrong, Mommy?" David asked.

"Nothing, David," she said as she ruffled his curly dark hair. "Why don't you freshen up a little before we go." She gave her son a forced smile.

David gave her a suspicious, lingering look. "Okay," he said finally, hopping up the spiral steps.

Gabriel waited until David was out of earshot. He approached her. "What has happened, Gayle?"

She remained silent but rested her eyes on his face. Her lips quivered, making movements to try to speak, but the words would not come. In one fluid movement, he embraced her. Her body relaxed against his, and her arms moved up his torso, connecting around the small of his back.

"All those people," she whispered.

Although he felt reluctant to let her go, this would be the time to see what had been bothering her. "Tell me what has happened."

"I heard it on the radio…I shouldn't have turned it on, but I felt a need to know what was going on."

"Gayle, you are not making sense."

"I am trying to tell you that Divine's headquarters has been bombed!" she yelled.

Gabriel's heart stilled. Something nudged at the back of his mind, but he ignored it. "Do they know how it happened?"

Gayle shook her head. "No, but, Gabriel, all those innocent people. I know them. I know they didn't deserve this. What about the Dome government? They're always up to something. Could they have done this?"

Gabriel shook his head. "I have been monitoring their communications. I believe that out of all the plans they have in store for us, destroying and murdering Divine employees was not one of them."

"I cannot believe this." Gayle covered her face with her hands.

He reached for her again, wanting to calm her nerves, hopefully in time for David to come back. "We will solve this mystery."

Once more, she moved away. "I am so tired of solving this mystery. It has been nothing but a mistake—a big, dark, all-consuming mistake. I am hungry for it to end. I just…I just want to close my eyes and go back to the beginning."

He pressed his lips together. "Then I will be gone."

She froze. Her tear-stained face revealed how she regretted her words. "Gabriel, you know I did not mean—"

He held up a hand. "I am not so fragile anymore, Gayle. I understand a little of how you think now."

She ran a sleeve over her eyes. "Thank you."

*****

Gayle stared down at the sleeping elder man, her mind still reeling from his revelations about the program, Gabriel, and Dome 16. Against her better judgment, she hated him for creating this prison they all lived in. My god, he basically mocked the greatest gift of life, then told her that her natural human rights should be denied because she was not perfect. Then again, a very small part of her wanted to thank him for giving her a new cause to live for.

"Gayle?" Gabriel said, his smooth baritone causing her to jolt from her negative mood. "Are you ready?"

She twisted around, smiling, and glad he followed her advice about ditching the Dome security uniform. He changed into the plain dark-brown slacks with heavy, worn black boots that disappeared under the cuff of the pants. Like many Downs' inhabitants, he layered on three shirts and covered them with an oversized black trench coat. Despite the appearance, he wore the clothes amazingly well.

He walked over to his father, picking up a brown wool blanket and covering him with another blanket. She should have done that, but then again, he did not appear cold or maybe her emotions did not allow her to see his discomfort. He straightened up and stepped back, still looking down into the pale, wrinkled face.

"Delilah will be here in another hour. I gave him something to help him rest."

She touched his arm. He turned his head toward her. "Are you certain she will be able to care for him while we are gone?"

"She will do what I ask," he said, covering her hand with his own.

Gayle wanted to believe Gabriel, but the thought of what Delilah did to the Johnsons still plagued her mind. "We better get going. Alfred will be expecting us."

He nodded. "Are you sure David will be okay to come along? The Downs is a dangerous place, especially for children."

"I am not leaving him here," she said, not even considering what Delilah would do. "Anyway, he has been asking about Alfred ever since I mentioned that we were going to visit him."

"I will be extra vigilant in making sure we arrive safely then," he said, smiling a nice smile. "Gayle, should we not start moving?" he asked, cocking his head, looking at her with confusion.

"Oh yes," she said, then headed out of the room, aware of Gabriel following close behind her. Over the railing, she saw her son still seated at a lab table. His cheeks swelled with the remnants of his dinner of ham and cheese with tomato soup from the food pantry. She wondered what he thought about their sudden flight, the constant moving. He should have been back at the beautiful house on the hill, hearing the birds chirp and watching the false sun rise, feeling its rays dance across his face.

She shook her head again, not allowing herself to dwell on this.

It would only lead to the dark place again. "Ready to leave, hon?" she called down at him.

"Yes, Mommy," David said as he hopped down from the high metal stool.

She descended the steps, then headed to two piles of clothes—one belong to David and the other to her. She went to David's pile first, picking out the lightest coat first.

"Let's get this started," she said, holding the coat before him.

He ran over, slipping his arm through the sleeves. He picked up the next one by himself. It saddened her more, watching him know how to layer his clothes for a common day out in the Downs.

She never meant to come back here, for this very reason. At such a young age, he should not have to understand the general mechanics of surviving the Downs.

Once they finished layering their clothing in preparation to visit the Downs, Gabriel led the way out of the open, airy lab, through a narrow tunnel. They came to a familiar pair of doors. She knew that beyond the doors, things would get weird, and her anxiety level started to rise.

"Remember to keep close and never let go of my hand," Gabriel warned David.

However, Gayle knew that he meant for her to obey it as well. Gayle nodded, knowing the cause for his concern when he first led her through the cold, dark catacombs. She saw the possibilities of really dying from the wrong move increase her anxiety. They linked hands, with David in the middle. Gabriel took David's other hand, then pressed the code on the keypad. The metal door opened, and the dark tunnel before them lit up, forming an eerie lit path.

Slowly, Gabriel led them out of the warmth of the lab, into the catacombs. The freeze hit them so hard she felt her breath escape. David's hands tightened in hers, and despite his thick black gloves, she felt his tiny fingers shaking. She pulled him closer, sharing her warmth.

Gabriel led them down the narrow alley. They kept a slow, steady pace, never stopping. The walk seemed to last a long time, but she soon felt the warm air on her face. She knew they had ascended into a higher area of the catacombs. Along the way, she saw large hollow openings whenever they entered an open area, but Gabriel knew the correct entrance to take.

She never shared with Gabriel the revelation Dr. Gregory shared with her. Instead, she escaped into a small living room and kitchen area. She had to focus her self-control on her feelings. Whenever she stared at Gabriel, she thought about the many times she yelled at him, mocked his serene face, or got irritated at him. She was treated like that once and knew how it made her feel—like the lowest of organisms. Her heart burned at the thought that he actually felt that way. She'd hurt him—again and again.

"We must be quick, Gayle," Gabriel's voice broke through her thoughts.

Gayle's eyes widened, looking between Gabriel and David. She realized that they had stopped, and it was due to her. Her face heated under their regard. "I apologize. Come, guys. Let's hurry."

Gabriel nodded and turned back around. Their pace increased. Along the way, she felt their ascending. The warm air touched her face. Soon they arrived at the last exit that would take them into the building. Large ingress round lights surrounded the metal doors. Gabriel entered another code into the keypad.

The doors parted open, swiftly revealing the dim abandoned interior. He walked straight through the door and was instantly greeted by the blinding neon-lit signs and strobe lights hanging off the side of the buildings. Downs citizens crowded the streets moving through them with slow lazy strides; the many layers of clothes gave them the appearance of great land animals of old. Their heads were swallowed by the hands and scarves more from fear than the weather.

"Alfred will be about three streets south," she said near his ear.

"Stay close," Gabriel said.

They traveled through the city very aware of the danger surrounding them. She noticed her own hairs rising on the back of her need and huddled closer to Gabriel who seem not affected by the surroundings. Of course, he would be seen as a capable man, not to be taken lightly if approached.

*****

Dr. Alfred Simmons held his private medical office in one of the older buildings at the center of town. The exterior appeared abandoned and dilapidated. The empty windows that were boarded had the weathered appearance. The black and dusty bricks crumbled at the edges and suffered from the constant fires the homeless camps surrounding the area. They approached the entrance to his office with caution. Small round lights illuminated the alleyway. She knew because of constant threats by gangs and desperate addicts. Alfred replaced his normal thick door a dark metal one. She noticed a small camera high above the door that, at first glance, would appear like the other lights.

"This is most unusual," Gabriel remarked. His head jerked around them, making sure they had not been followed.

"Crime has increased lately. Alfred has a lot of things that can get one a small fortune on the black market." She lifted a foot, kicking the bottom of the door, then banged her fist five consecutive times.

They did not have to wait long. She heard Alfred's familiar baritone.

"Here's to you, Mrs. Robinson. Jesus loves you more than you will know."

The hall gave way to a large open living room. She had not been here in a while and noticed that Alfred upgraded the furniture and did some remodeling, and she had to say for the better. The last time she saw the place had been in desperate times. All Dome-sponsored departments in the Downs had closed. All the staff members were Midtown natives and fled to the peaceful harmonic lives there. Riots broke out over the closures. Predators and prey fought each other hand to hand. She took refuge with Alfred among other women and children. He welcomed them, all with no reservations.

She remembered stacks of then worn costs and moldy, stinky crates full of supplies. The electricity had been cut by the council, so they had to use candles. Water had been slowed, so they all had to make do with small canteens. The body stench in the place brought water to her eyes. She shook at the memory.

Now the common area held a clean and organized appearance. The hues range from dull greens to soft yellows. Two large olivegreen plush sofas faced each other at the center of the room. They framed a large gray stone fireplace while a beautiful floral carpet covered the polished wood floor underneath.

A door swung open from the side and in walked a tall, distinguished man. His dark skin showed signs of age, but she never knew exactly how old Alfred was. It had been the one thing he did not share with her. His pepper-colored hair hung in thick ropes down his broad back gathered with a black ribbon at the base of his neck. He greeted them with a wide smile filled with strong even white teeth. His dark eyes fell on David first.

David pulled out of her grasp and sprinted over to Alfred, hurtled his small body into the man's large embrace. Alfred let out an earthquake laugh that seemed to rattle even the walls of the building.

"How are ya, Cap'n?" He ruffled David's thick dark curls.

"I'm right as rain, and twice as train," David responded with enthusiasm. "We have a new friend."

Gayle came over to greet her old friend, giving him a hug. "I see you cleaned up. Who's the new bird?"

Alfred appeared to be insulted. "I have you know I have awesome taste, and business has been good lately, so I have decided to upgrade some things." He glanced around the room.

"I hope she can cook too. You look thinner than the last time I saw you," she said, looking him up and down.

"Enough nosing into my business." He passed her and David to

Gabriel. "I'm sorry. Gayle was raised by wild animals. I am Dr. Alfred Simmons, the physician of the Downs."

Gabriel smirked and shook Alfred's hand. "How do you do?"

Gayle stepped forward. "He is one of the guardians from the testing."

"Aw." Alfred leaned in closer, causing Gabriel some discomfort. He had to step back. "Fascinating. They pulled my license for cloning, but this looks a sneaky bit like it."

"I am a hybrid," Gabriel said. His face was solemn.

Gayle looked at him, shock that he would reveal this to a stranger.

He looked at her, catching her stare. "There is no need to hide it anymore. I am not ashamed."

"Of course." Alfred laughed. "There is nothing to be ashamed about. I am envious, actually. I would love to be so fully immersed and surrounded by true science. This is what they stole from me."

Gayle felt the time slip from them. "We better get back before dark."

"Oh yeah"—Alfred jolted from his own thoughts—"let's get my supplies."

Chapter 17

DR. GREGORY'S MANOR STOOD silent against the crystal-blue sky. The clouds had been deleted because of the disaster. She still could see some remnants of them in the background.

She lowered her head looking back at the manor. She never had been able to find what exactly disturb her about the tall four-story manor, but today would be that it would reveal all its secrets.

A female guard stood at the open gate. She stopped her craft. "Greetings."

"Greetings, Agent Travis." The guard saluted her. "Heard about Divine Cybernetics. I called in to see if they want to be given a hand, but it appears they have enough people."

"They might want the high agents to investigate first. You will probably be called in later for the cleanup."

The guard nodded. "Tell you the truth. I am grateful. I heard the air is rather putrid, and bodies are everywhere."

"How disgusting!" Dani said. She thought the team did well to not recall the green guards. They would just get in the way and destroy what evidence that remained. "My husband's sister was in there."

"I am sorry for your loss."

"My mother-in-law wants us to take in the children." The guard continued. "I am not sure we are ready. We barely have enough room in the family barracks. Even more we were planning on waiting another two years."

"It sounds like you may need some time to yourself," Dani said. "So, hey, has there been any activity here?"

The guard realized where she was suddenly. "Nothing much. Creepy noses from below, but we were told not to enter without an agent."

"I'll check it out. Let me know when someone comes through."

"Yes, ma'am."

Dani closed the window and drove down the narrow driveway. She parked it at the end of the winding black stairs leading up to a tall pair of black wooden doors. Grabbing her weapon and her scanner, she exited the vehicle. She ran up the steps, making sure to avoid the motion sensors placed over the steps by the council guard to alert them of trespassers in case the green guard was an idiot.

Lights blinking on brought the grand foyer to full brightness. She pulled out the scanner, pressing the button and sweeping the red laser light across the foyer. It would take all day to search the home, but she had never been satisfied with the Divine security detail search of the home. Dome security guards did their own search, but curiously, the scanners malfunctioned. Now she would not be able to get anyone back out here to help.

The home proved rather deceptive. On the outside, they thought the mansion was huge, but inside, there were only about ten rooms. Most of the rooms were oversized and filled with inconsequential furniture. The foyer itself almost made her hold her breath with tall, imposing dark panel walls.

When they invaded the property, Dr. Gregory had already left. They knew he'd gone on the run after discovering he'd sabotaged the lab computers. They followed him to his estate, finding an array of traps and deceptive paths that slowed the Divine Security progress across the estate grounds. It took them many hours to disconnect the security alarms that screamed annoying noises across the expanse of the neighborhood. Some of the guards received severe injuries and had to be carried away.

Inside, they searched every inch of the manor. They found a few items like some old papers with old formulas and lots of dusty books. None of them related to Divine Cybernetics or the guardian program.

Their disappointment increased when they found all the computer database at the manor had been wiped clean as well. Even their best could not retrieve so much as a kilobyte of information.

Dani made her way around the perimeter of the foyer making sure to cover every inch. She made sure to focus her scanner on the floor, but when the laser moved up the wall, the alarm on the scanner alerted, and her hand froze.

Her eyes moved over the elaborate dark paneling. The team assumed it was solid underneath, although Sergeant Vila wanted to tear into the walls. They could not, of course, because of the position of the good Dr. Gregory.

She stepped back observing the full layout of the foyer, destroying even a part of the resident without proper paperwork. That will take more time than she will be willing to waste. She raised a clench fist and knocked on the wood panel listening for subtle echo. After a few moments, she heard the hollow sound proving the walls could possibly be false.

Dani pulled her phone out pressing the speed dial.

A female high-pitched voice answered the phone, "Dome government records."

"Marsha, can you send me the floor plans and history to Dr. Gregory's residence?"

"Absolutely, Agent Travis." She heard rapid typing. "Now which address did you want?"

"Which residence?" she said.

"He has other properties. Six to be exact. Three around Dome 16 and three in Dome 3," Marsha said.

Interesting, Dani thought. She will have to stash that information away later. "The one I am interested in is on 1 Uptown Way."

"Okay, did you want me to send it to the usual way?"

"Always."

"It has been sent. Let me know if you need anything else," Marsha said.

The line disconnected. She spared the wall a last glance. She would have to bring a demolition team in. This time, they would not rest if this mystery is resolved.

Dani turned to leave, but a glint of silver caught her eye, halting her progress. It came from the floor catching the beam of light flowing through the stained glass window. She knelt down for a closer view and recognized a small rectangular metal fragment sticking out from the floor.

She reached out, plucking it out from the crease between the thick wood planks. She held it closer to her face and realized she saw it before. On the rare occasion that one of Divine Cybernetics lab technicians spoke freely. One overly friendly male, she could not remember his name but remembered what he showed her. He mentioned that this chip was a prototype capable to storying up to twelve years' worth of high-priority data. He also mentioned that it could be attached to a computer and act as a second mother board. Supposedly, it was still in development and also may be a clue to Dr. Gregory's research.

She opened her jacket, ripping out the inner silk lining and quickly wrapped the chip in the material. She would have to get it to the computer labs at Dome Council. She knew a genius tech who would love to see her again. She rushed out of the manor hurrying down to her craft. Once settled and ready to head out, her phone vibrated and whirled at her hip. She let out a curse.

"Agent Travis."

"Hello, Agent Travis. I am Deborah Draper, your new administrator." A soft voice spoke.

"Okay, and…" she said, rolling her eyes.

Administrators were the worst type of Dome employees. They

halted work of the field agent with stupid excuses about checks and balances. In her opinion, they were really good-for-nothing warm body taking up space in the Dome Council. She once advised the council to delete the position from the department, but they ignored her because of the lack of support.

"What can I do for you?"

The woman remained silent for a few breaths, then spoke again. "You do not seem surprised that you have a new administrator."

"I am never surprised about anything the Dome government does. As I mentioned before, what can I do for you?"

"My, my, aren't you excited?" the woman chided.

Dani shook her head. She went through several administrators. The issue with all of them had been capability. They expected her to be complacent and agreeable. This would make their already easy life even easier. They could indulge in extended vacations. However, she refused to make it that easy. No one was going to get over on her.

"I am at your assigned residence." Deborah continued. "I have been waiting here for quite some time."

"What are you doing there without alerting me or even bothering making an appointment?" she yelled into the phone.

"I sent you an email…several times, in fact." Deborah spoke in a sing-song voice.

"That was your first mistake. The statement in my file, as you should have read, clearly outlines the communication steps all my administrators must take to get in contact with me."

"I have read it—"

"It is clear you never finished. As I recall, with the last two administrators assigned to me, all communications are sent via secure channel to my craft's onboard computer."

"I apologize—"

"Look, today is not a good time for me. Please leave my residence."

"I am afraid I can't do that."

"Why the hell not?" Dani shouted into the phone, hearing

the feedback.

She heard the woman inhale deeply. "Agent Dani Travis, you are being recalled back to Dome 3."

"They are extracting me?" she whispered.

"I am sorry…I know—" Deborah was not able to finish, as Dani disconnected the line. She could not hear anything else. Her heart pounded a tattoo against her chest. *Extraction* was another word for *execution*. Dome government's council never fired field agents.

She blew out a breath, gripping hold of herself. She grabbed the wheel of her craft and punched the button to transform her craft into flight mode. She geared the craft back toward the center of the city and back toward Catherine Miles's penthouse.

*****

Delilah rolled her eyes heavenward, watching the pathetic trio trudge down the foggy path. She had a mind to follow them but knew that right now she had other business. Preferably seeing how her poor fragile father fares. She slipped into the building and made her wait through the secret underground tunnel to the lab.

Inside the lab, her nose wrinkled at the stench of human flesh. Her father never washed. She tried to propel him to do so, but he always passed out drooling on the floor and panting like a disgusting animal. She refused to touch him choosing to wait for him to get enough energy to get back into bed.

She reached out her senses to make sure no other body occupied the lab. Her father's slow, steady heartbeat was the only one echoing in her ear. A slow curve spread across her lips. She bounced over to the steps skipping up the metal staircase. All the while humming a soft whimsical song flowed from her lips. The chords of the song grew louder, the closer she drew to the living quarters. Her father's heartbeat quickened with the volume of the song and then finally followed by a raspy, guttural sound.

"Ah, he's awake," she whispered, as her delight increased. Her senses went into overdrive. She entered the office, finding her father seated on the edge of his worn leather lounge chair. He still wore the soiled, depressing nightclothes from four days ago. His hair held a stark white and spike in different directions over his small delicate skull, his head been between stooped shoulders shaking off the last remnants of sleep.

"Hello, Father." She spoke, leaning against the edge of the wall.

His body visibly seized. His head jerked up with fearful wide eyes. She watched his lips tremble, tiny beads of sweat form at his forehead. "Delilah! What have you done?"

"Why, nothing, Father." She pushed away from the wall, coming forward. "What makes you think I've done anything?"

"I know you did something. I know it. It is not good, not good at all," he said.

"Why are you being so dramatic today?" she asked, making her voice sound soothing. "What has Gabriel been filling your head with?" She watched as he leaned away, afraid to be close to her. This hurt a little, but his human mind made him skittish.

"I have seen it with my own eyes," he said. His voice grew almost shrieking.

Delilah cocked her head. She pushed into his eyes seeking what he claimed he saw. He secretly taped her controlling him. His feelings told her that he felt disrespected and hurt. So he knew of her manipulation.

"How could you?" He continued. "After all, I did for you."

"Watch your mouth, old man!" she growled.

"Words hurt." His face grew shocked.

"Is it even true what you speak of?"

"Of course not, but you were so ready to believe anything I said. I just thought to add something a little extra."

"I should have known," he said, attempting to stand, but stumbled back onto the lounge chair.

Delilah burst into laughter. "Silly, silly, Father. What were you thinking to do?" she asked as she approached.

"Get away from me," he said, clutching his chest.

"I will, but only after you enhance my abilities one last time," she said.

He shook his head. "I will not…I will not."

"Oh, did you think I was asking for permission?" Delilah seized his brain at that moment. Satisfied, she met with no more resistance this time. "Come now. We must be quick," she said, leading the way down into the lab.

They approached another metal door. She typed in the new code. She made sure to change it when her father first upgraded her body. She could not allow Gabriel to discover and interrupt things.

The room they entered held a single pod at the center. Various computerized stations and sophisticated chemistry lab surrounded the pod with tubes and wiring ducts connected to the pod. She stepped aside as her father trudge forward into the room. He set about going through station to station with a feverish focus. She closed the doors and watched him for the moment. When he was under, he moved fast, and his mind clicked with perfect clarity. *His mind will not last this last time,* she thought. She felt his movements, and internally his body started to break down under the strain of the work and the information she forced from him. Oh well, this was not her issue. Gabriel would be back with the doctor.

"It is ready, darling," he said.

"Good boy," she said, coming forward, stripping away the confining human clothes. She stepped into the pod immediately feeling a million tiny pins sink into her skin. At first, they brought an excruciating pain, then a different kind of feeling replaced it. She felt something akin to what a human junkie said to her before she feed from him.

The change in her body began. She felt her internal organs swell and constrict. Soon, she will be perfect, unstoppable. No one will be equal to her. Not even her dearly beloved brother. Then all at once, everything burst. A white light flashed before her eyes.

The room went black, then the lights, one by one, blinked on once more. Delilah exited the pod to find her father on the floor. She walked over to him and satisfied that he was still breathing.

His eyes were open, looking up at her. She shook her head and continued over to her pile of clothes. After she dressed, she decided to exercise her new abilities. She brought to her mind the tiny ruined apartment where her victim waited.

The atmosphere around her surged, and she found herself back at the apartment in seconds. Her eyes widened with glee.

Dr. Herman Gregory knew he would not last long. He felt every stab of pain grapple hold of his body, every slither of his life force spill away. His muscles gave way, no longer able to move or support his frame. His heart and lungs fought their own, fighting away the forever darkness. His mind, which never let him down, finally at the last hour relinquished its might to Lady Death. The last he heard was the smooth, angelic baritone of Gabriel calling him. He could not figure it was the actual angel himself.

*****

Gabriel knew something went terribly wrong. He propelled ahead, surprising Gayle, David, and Alfred. He never heard Gayle's question on what's going or Alfred's surprise shout when he sprinted ahead of them in the tunnel or David's frantic call. Something yanked at his conscience. He had to get into the lab.

He punched in the code with rapid speed and almost tore down the metal door. Inside the lab, he flew up the stairs. His face set in a murderous expression when he found the lounge chair empty. He sniffed the air and stilled at the familiar essence of Delilah. He clenched his fist breaking his own finger bones.

"Gabriel…Gabriel…what has happened?" Gayle asked, her voice reaching his ears.

He squeezed his eyes shut. Although painful, he managed to fix his fingers. Then he commanded feelings to go away. This may be something more dangerous; as of now, his emotions swirled so close to the surface. He mentally counted the footsteps coming up the steps to the countdown of his wrath.

"Gabriel!" Gayle's voice finally reached him. He opened his eyes.

"Something's happened to Father," he said, turning to her. He watched her face for any indication of buried emotions, but her expression remained worried and caring. Her dark eyes searched his face.

*****

"Where could he be?" she moved past him into the room. She walked over to the other room looking in.

"He is not up here. I will check downstairs," he said, leaving the room.

Alfred started looking over the lab stations. David wandered over to another opening with a soft blue light spilling into the lab.

"Hey, look in here!" David called out.

"David, don't go in there!" Gabriel called out as he rushed back down into the lab.

Thankfully, the boy listened and moved back.

"Dr. Gregory is hurt," David said, pointing into the room.

Alfred reacted first. Gabriel followed after him. His eyes went directly to the limp form of his father on the cool metal floor. He knelt at his father's side as Alfred yanked out a small rectangular box with a black tube that had a flat end. The doctor placed the flat end on Dr. Gregory's heart and typed on the keypad. The machine made a whirring sound. He saw his father's body shift and bend.

Gabriel knew his father could not be helped. His father's energy left thirty minutes before. Had they been back earlier, things may have been different. He raised his head to regard Alfred working hard to help. Their eyes crashed into each other.

"He was dead a long time ago," Gabriel said, then rose from his father's side.

Alfred remained on the floor probing his father's body. "This illness is a mystery. He has a good heart, and his blood flowed well." Gabriel listened, glancing around the room. It had a familiar feeling, an awful familiar feeling. He stared at the pod at the center. He felt the clouds break around him. The storm of rage came pouring out.

"What is this room?" Gayle spoke beside him.

"It is my birthplace," Gabriel whispered. "It is death." He finally turned to Gayle. "Father used this room to enhance the guardians' abilities and talents. I fear he made a monster."

"A monster?" Alfred repeated.

"Delilah, my sister. He has been using this to make her stronger," he said. "The more he enhanced her, the further away from human and stable thinking she became."

"So she could be—" Alfred said.

"A disaster," Gabriel said, blinking away the tears. "I must find her. Gayle, you must leave with Alfred. He will keep you safe until I come for you."

"No, I am going with you. She's dangerous," Gayle said.

"I agree she is dangerous," Gabriel said, "which is why I cannot allow you to follow me. She is capable of anything now."

THE SATISFACTION OF DESTRUCTION has always made her heart do a happy jiggle. Even something as small as the tiny metallic phone spilling through her fingers, even the small tapping on the floor that the broken pieces made heighten her enthusiasm. She stared down the scattered dark pieces, the last connection she would have with her past life, Gabriel, the guardian program, and Divine Cybernetics. She could charge forth into the future without any restriction.

Another ringtone ripped through the room cutting through her joy. Her rage soared to the surface as her senses sought the source of the annoyance. Then she remembered Catherine's phone she placed on the nightstand beside Catherine for another round of the torture game, but her little victim fell asleep from exhaustion.

Another ring sung out. Delilah stopped into the tiny bedroom. Catherine's eyes gave her the usual naked fear with a high-pitched scream pouring into the waded cloth. She felt compelled to stick into the idiot mouth.

"Sleep," she snapped the command.

Catherine automatically closed her eyes, and her body went limp.

Delilah shook her head while progressing toward the nightstand. She picked up the phone, glaring at the screen. It read Travis. She remembered the name of the bitchy female at the party who had the entire waitress crew skirting around in fear. Admittedly, she admired the way the Travis woman worked. In another life, she might have given her a nod of admiration.

Travis was Divine Cybernetics's cleaner. Catherine's memories overcame her. "I fear that she may be a double agent."

"How interesting," Delilah whispered.

She pressed the button, answering the phone in Catherine's voice. "Sunny day, Agent Travis."

"Where have you been?" Dani asked. Her voice quick and heavy, she asked, "Do you know what's happening?"

"I am aware," Delilah said. "It is for the better. Whoever did this helped me tremendously."

"Are you brain dead? Thousands of people lost their lives today. Dome Council is not happy about losing good citizens, especially with the threat of another riot."

"My brain is far from dead, Agent Travis." She exhaled, feeling the boredom of the conversation. "All I mean is that this has solved one problem."

"This is a hell of way to solve a problem!" Agent Travis blurted into the phone. "I tell you this. If they found out you're alive, no amount of your father's influence will get you out of this."

Now I will have to turn on the sad, mournful emotion, Delilah thought, bringing on the water works. "Dani, I…I am sorry. I did not think that things would get so complicated. You must believe that I had nothing to do with this. I would never destroy my father's lifelong work."

"Catherine…I am the last person you need to convince of your… innocence."

"Then who can I turn to? You have been more of a friend to me than any other. I know I have never expressed this before."

"Catherine, you need to turn yourself in. I think this will be the only way for Dome Council to remove you from being a suspect."

"What would make them think I am a suspect?" Delilah realized that Dani must have seen her running away from the wreckage.

Her lips twisted at the irony. "Anyway, I just can't walk into Dome Council headquarters. They may just shoot me. I have a rather nasty allergy to guns."

"They won't shoot you."

"How do you know this?" Delilah asked. She knew of Dani Travis's duplicity from Catherine's memories. Catherine planned to do away with the silly little human after Dome Council removed their takeover attempt and the company's money troubles were settled. While she admired her capturer's tenacity, her failure to deal with Dani posthaste caused more trouble than what it was worth.

"Catherine, trust me," Dani said.

"Oh, darling, I lost the capacity to trust long ago. Right now, I am concerned with self-preservation and self-reliance. That is how I won my father's company from the execs, and this is how I will survive this. Now you will have to give me more meat than just to simply trust you."

"You know how the Dome Council reacts to chaos. It never goes well."

"Ms. Travis, are you trying to tell me something?"

"I have been trying to tell you something since the start of this call, but I don't think you are listening."

Delilah smiled. "I am listening. I hear you. I hear them. I hear all." She paused, sinking herself down beside the limp form of Catherine. She reached out, stroking the fine silky hair across her temple. "Dani, when were you going to tell me about your side career?" She heard a gasp.

"You know?"

"While I admire your motivation and multitasking technique, I am disappointed that you would not let me in on this little game of yours. I would have loved to have participated."

"Catherine...I..."

"Dani, neither one of us has the time for long-drawn-out explanations and apologies. You cost me a pretty penny. Monetary and reputation. I will meet you, and from there, it will be up to you."

"All right. Dome 16 café. It's a block away from Council headquarters."

"Nice place. Great coffee, but no go. How about your place? I know where it is, and we can talk again. You can smoke."

"Wait, we can't…"

"We can. I will meet you there at 0900."

"Catherine…"

"Is there some reason why your place will not be appropriate?" She caught some hesitation in Dani, which made her want to know this woman, so full of contradictions, more. Dani hinted a perchance for brutality and callus treatment of her fellow humans yet had a vulnerability that she despised and hungered in humans. At the moment, she felt starved.

Dani finally spoke. "All right, 0900. I'll be there. Whatever. See you then." Then the phone went dead.

"See you then, Dani Travis," Delilah said, reverting back to her old voice. She stared into Catherine's face. The makeup started to thicken and clump. The lipstick faded to a dirty pink, and the darkbrown and gold eye makeup mixed into a rusty metal, rusty, weathered metal that aged two hundred years.

"Catherine," she whispered, "wake up, my beautiful, lovely girl."

Catherine's eyes shuttered open. Her eyes glazed with a euphoric feeling. Delilah waited until the eyes connected with the brain, which started to get harder and harder over the short time she manipulated her victim. Inhaling, she rose from the bed crossing her body with her long spindly arms. She walked to the wall, and then did a 360-degree sharp turn. Catherine's brain connected finally with the eyes again. They watched her with a newfound respect and a healthy helping of fear. She closed her own eyes, grabbing the mother's persona. Opening her eyes again, the persona surged forth.

"Why do you look at me so, Cathy? Has Mommy's little girl done another no-no?"

Catherine answered her with a whimper.

Delilah leaned against the wall, uncrossing her arms and sinking her hand into the pockets of her long coat. "Let me guess what you have done again. Did you indulge in Mommy's sweets?"

Catherine's head slowly moved side to side, indicating a no.

Delilah narrowed her eyes. "Mommy's liquor cabinet. I know about that. I put little silver lines on the bottles, and do you know the De dans Jacques' pinot noir and chardonnay 1526 has slowly evaporated? Your father does not like them, though I do not know why, but do you know who does?"

"Me?" Catherine whispered.

"You, Cathy. You have been stealing from Mommy."

"I'm sorry, Mommy."

"Are you really?" Delilah asked as she pushed away from the wall. "Show Mommy how sorry you are."

"No, no. I am sorry. I am sorry," Catherine repeated. Her voice sounded great panic, and the irritating squeaking took over.

"Stop that annoying noise! You will give Mommy a headache," Delilah said. "How would you like it if I did so to you?"

*****

Dani lowered the phone. Her brow creased. Her mind whirled. The conversation with Catherine Miles had been filled with so many contradictions. Catherine sounded unemotional and nonchalant. All the story of her would never destroy her father's work sounded like a robot reading a script telling feeding her tall tales. She worked enough as a field agent when the work got hard, and the hours were endless to know when something sounded like a hint of danger.

She slid the phone back into her pocket looking up at the tall, sleek crystal building. Night approached closely. Soon it would be time for her to meet with her former employer, who knows now of her duplicity, which concerned her even more. Her records were ironclad. All field-agent records were. The Council's obsession with secrecy and anonymity made sure that IT placed severe security codes on all files.

She exhaled. Her shoulders slumped as her mind rewound the conversation with her former employer. Catherine had been at ground zero the moment of the blast. The woman would never just walk away like kid from a destroyed candy bar on the concrete. The passion this woman had for her company paralleled the Dome Council's greed for control.

Dani observed the false sky noticing that twilight came unusually early, from the announcement over Dome security air waves.

They were imposing a Dome-wide curfew. She had to get off the streets fast. She could not go back to headquarters for fear of extraction. The same will go for her assigned residence. The only way anyone would not be able to find her was Catherine's penthouse. She had watched the foot traffic through the span of an hour, and one person caught her eye.

He had to be a high official, a bachelor, and newly appointed by the appearance of his youthful figure and form. He stopped once at the top of the steps and glanced around him.

He straightened his long, thick coat and smoothened an elegant hand down his willowy light-gray pants, then with prideful assuredness, he adjusted the black strap of his briefcase. He disappeared into a chauffeur government caravan.

Dani spotted the familiar vehicle coming back. She moved toward the bottom of the walk leaning against a smooth stone pillar, busying herself with her computerized pad though the screen remained blank. The vehicle stopped in front of her. He sprung out of the vehicle swinging the strap of his briefcase over his shoulder. His broad back faced her as he glanced for a while out into the courtyard.

Then he stepped back and turned, colliding into her world. Dani let out a delicate cry, like a wounded bird, fragile and airy.

"Oh, sorry, miss," he said as he held her, the warmth of his hand bleeding through the expansive material of his gray gloves. "I did not see you there."

"It is fine." She fluttered her eyes like the wings of a butterfly. "I fear I am the clumsy one." She moved from his body, attempting to walk, then stumbled.

"Goodness…you are hurt."

"It would seem so. Silly me. I can't believe it." Her breath caught in her throat. Her mouth trembled. She peeked at his expression. His face creased with worry at her predicament as his arm stayed frozen in a nurturing stance.

"Do you have family here or a friend?" He waved toward the tall apartment building.

"I am waiting for my friend," she said, shivering, then crossed her arms over her chest to rub her arms. "She told me that it would be another hour."

"Another hour," he repeated. "Well, miss, I hate to tell you, but there will be a curfew in about thirty minutes. I hate to see you arrested. A fine lady should not be in a cold cell."

"Oh, dear."

"Oh, hey, don't worry. This is my building. I don't mean to be forward with you seeing as I am not married. You can come stay awhile with me rest your ankle and call your friend."

Dani glanced up at the building, her ultimate destination. "Oh, that's really kind of you, but I can't." She shook her head.

"I won't try anything." His puppy-dog look turned even more worried and apologetic.

"I wish I could…oh, here."

He reached into his pocket, producing a silver card. "This is an emergency disk. I received it the first week of my job. They give it to all of us Dome government employees in case of emergencies."

She took the card. "Why, thank you."

"Now come inside to rest. You can call your friend to tell her where you are," he said, offering his arm to her.

They walked up the steps. Dani had been ever mindful that someone might recognize her and interrupt her ruse. However, they made it through the glass-encased lobby unbothered. The robotic attendant glanced up staring at her with blinking eyes but never gave an alert. She made a sly smirk at it as she disappeared with her target into the elevator.

He blabbed nonstop during their ride to his penthouse. She caught snatches of his name. Nick, Nicholas, Nico, then snatches of his life—only child, no parents, old money—and the last bit of snatches, his career as a clerk, a Speaker of the House, now a senator. She arrived at his penthouse with her ears bleeding.

She made an act of a wounded animal coming into his home and swooning on his couch.

He had taken her purse and laid it on an ivory marble coffee table with beastly feet. He placed his hands together touching the tips to his lips.

"May I get you something to drink?"

She shook her head. "No…no, I don't really want to trouble you. I have to call my friend."

"Of course," he repeated.

"I hate to say this, but can I have privacy?" She looked down and slid toward the bedroom.

"Oh, sure," he said, laying down his briefcase in a high-back chair with soft-looking ivory material. "Let me know if you need anything." He bounced across the plush gray floor through a pair of doors, opening one of them. He saluted her as he walked through, closing them behind.

Dani sprung from her seat and sprinted out of the front door, making sure to softly close the door. She slinked back toward the elevator; digging in her purse, she pulled out her scanner and skimmed over the board. She pressed a button. The elevator doors opened. She entered quickly, hearing the soft, desperate voice of the Nicks.

Catherine's penthouse resided at the last floor. The elevator opened directly into the penthouse. An intimidating interior greeted her. High nose-bleeding ceilings rose above her with marble moldings rose from the polish white floor along the corners of the walls toward the coffered ceilings spreading thin, wicked fingers through the creases. She stepped further into the foyer faintly hearing the elevators close behind her.

As if in celebration of a new warm body entering into their presence, the penthouse awoke, shaking off the few days of dormancy. Tall doors with mirrorlike polish swung open. Brilliant soft-yellow light gleamed around, and for the moment, she thought this felt like heaven—a feeling she always had when coming to Catherine's penthouse. During those moments, she truly got away from herself or rather—that is—until Catherine opened her mouth.

She continued to reacquaint herself with the common rooms. The elegant interior outpaced even the largest and grandest homes in the suburbs of Uptown. Her final resting place ended with Catherine's office. Like the rest of the penthouse, the immaculate space smacked of elegance. She walked into the room rounding around toward the desk, a sharp contrast from the one at Divine, a delicate, petite thing with pink lilies over a glossy ivory finish; she pulled out the chair with floor-like limbs and lowered her body into the seat trying to achieve a queenlike seat like its true owner.

Her fingers flew over the keyboard, watching the screen blink on. She managed to enter her account assigned by Divine Cybernetics, amazed the intranet remained active. Dome Council did not know about the secret second account she conned one of the IT guys to make for her. Here, she retrieved the plans for Dr. Gregory's mansion.

She noticed the interior walls appeared thicker than normal. As she expected, the thicker walls surrounded the foyer. The drawings also revealed a large floor plan below the foyer. This is not where the team found the basement. She knew this is why they never caught Dr. Gregory.

There had to be an entire house right below the mansion. He

must have had a secret passage somewhere. She searched the floor plans where the entrance would have been and caught on that there might have been a secret entrance right in the foyer where the scanner went crazy.

Dani knew by now that Dome headquarters had been alerted of her extraction status. Even though she made friends, Dome politics would always prevail. She had to find out what was missed. She could not put a finger on why it felt so important, but this needed to be revealed. She would risk the hammer of Dome Council to find the answer.

Inhaling, Dani picked up her phone and pressed a button. The phone rang only once when a female voice answered. "Dome security headquarters."

"This is Agent Dani Travis for Administrator Deborah Draper."

"I will transfer you. One moment, please."

Dani only had to wait a few minutes when Deborah's voice came over the phone. "Agent Travis, this is a surprise. We were about to send a posse for you."

"There will be no need."

"So when can we expect to see you at headquarters?"

"I want to pack up the rest of my things at the house. By any chance, can you pick me up there?"

"It is rather out of the way."

"I will be ready at 0900," Dani said, hoping they were desperate for her extraction to grant her this simple wish.

"Very well, then—0900, back at the house, and Agent Travis…" "Yes."

"If we do not see you there, the extraction could turn into an execution." The phone went dead on Deborah's end this time.

Dani inhaled, then smiled. *Only if you can catch me,* she thought.

Chapter 19

DEBO RAH DRAPER SLAMMED THE phone down. She finally would get the answers. Standing from her desk, she struggled with her darkblack jacket, adjusting her dainty dark-blue tie and spread a hand across her billowing sheer white blouse. Always an administrator must appear at their most professional when dealing with the difficult case.

She gave herself a final once-over in the tall mirror at the corner of her small office. It was a rather temporary place; the previous owner had been a rather disagreeable fellow. The council government decided he should be relieved of his duties and take a permanent holiday. Of course, she would never have participated in his removal. She just fancied his office with the perfect views of the vast Midtown gardens with its perfect flora and finely-sculpted winged figures.

An annoying chaos greeted her outside her office. The Dome assistants' pool filled a mixture of droids and Midtown idiots. She marched her way around the silly prissy females with the too tight silver-and-gray outfits and zero-bone-structure body. Her eyes focused forward and through the assistants until the elevator came into view, and with luck, the elevator doors opened, greeting her with an empty cold metal interior.

She pushed the button for the security detail department. It would not hurt to gather a couple muscles to come with her to Dani Travis. From the agent's file, she gathered that Travis often played immature pranks on her administrators and ignored Dome Council's rules. She tried to understand Dani's motivation for thumbing her nose at her superiors and handlers.

In reading her history, Deborah really could not understand why the woman would even take a job. Good middle-class family with zero genetic defects. Ms. Travis could have just sold herself as a breeder to a rich male in Dome 3 and lived like a queen for the rest of her life. She remembered giving her sister, Sue, the same advice, but her sister was a silly girl marrying a foot soldier with no family and no more ambition than one of those inferiors. The elevator doors swung open. She marched into the final quiet, peace, and harmony. The Dome security's uniformed guards performed their task with efficiency and military precision. She spotted some fields agents who greeted her with respectful acknowledgment, then continued along their way.

Deborah made her way to the office of Dome security's chief, Cleander Mason. The doors spayed open showing a large hulking man in severe black uniform with embroidered gold trimmings, five round wings dotted his high collar. He raised his head stabbing her with piercing intelligent eyes. She stopped at the entrance frozen in respect for this great man. Her body stiffened at attention as a good administrator should always be in the presence of a commanding officer.

"We have found your niece and nephew," he said. "They are currently being routed to Dome 3, away from this mess."

"Thank you, Cleander," she said. "I have already alerted my housekeeper to expect them. Now we are on to our next task. Have you found our little bird?"

"Travis has contacted me this time. She will turn herself in but is making it difficult," she said. "Travis wants to meet me at the house at 0900."

"Has she apologized for the disgusting way she treated you?"

Deborah shook her head. "I do not expect her to apologize. Somehow, I do not think that is in her character."

He leaned back in the oversized chair. "I never agreed to her placement here. In truth, I never felt she was up to the challenge of this mission. I am not sure what our superiors were thinking."

"I do not blame them, Cleander. They were blinded by her whimsical charms, I suppose." However, we will be done with this mistake soon enough."

"Let's hope her retirement is a colorful one," Cleander said. He leaned over, typing on his keyboard. His eyes narrowed at her before turning toward the computer screen. "I think six guards should be sufficient. She is well trained but not enough to take my men down."

Deborah gave a slight smile, but it did not reach her eyes. "If she resists, then we will just send a memo to Dome 3 about her last mission."

"It may be good to clean up a little," he said, looking up from the screen. "Something else is bothering you, Administrator Draper."

"The guardian program. I heard you managed to secure three of them, but she is not among them."

"This is true, and we have a special team searching for the scientists and the other two, but we are at a standstill. We have found no trace of the either of them."

"Have the scientists managed to get anywhere with reactivating the androids?"

"They are hesitating at the moment. They have even tried cutting into them." He narrowed his eyes and continued. "We have other things to concentrate on with the task at hand."

"I wish to see them before I go," she whispered.

"Why?" Cleander leaned back. "This will not bring justice to you. We still don't know or understand what this experiment is about."

"I just want to. As a friend, I'm asking you for this favor."

"Very well then," he exhaled. Leaning over to an intercom, he pressed a button.

"Hello, Chief Mason," a metallic female voice answered. "What can I help you with?"

"Administrator Draper would like to view the guardians," he said.

"They are scheduled for a cryogenic freeze in about 0100. The scientist has given the order for no one to view them during this time, as there may be some cross contamination."

"We need some last-minute evidence. The administrator believes this would help us in our search." He gave Deborah a wink. She smiled with her fingers tucked behind her back and crossed.

She needed this but did not know why. Maybe this would bring her closer to her sister in death, as they were never very close in life.

"I will have to transfer you to Dr. Phillip Lowe."

"That is fine."

"Dr. Lowe here." A growling voice spoke.

"Dr. Lowe, Chief Mason here from Dome security," he said.

"What can I do for you, Chief?"

"We need some additional information to help us track down these guardian prototypes. Your assistant says they are due to be placed in cryogenic baths. Is this correct?

"Yes. We do not know if they are booby-trapped. Until your team finds those damn scientists, we want to hold off on studying them."

"I understand, but will you allow us a few more moments?"

"I don't know. I really don't want a lot of contamination in the lab."

"It will just be one. She is the administrator from Dome 3 I told you about. This will help us find the scientists."

"Okay. She will only have five minutes with them."

"Understood." And the line ended.

Cleander looked at her and gave her a wide, meaningful gaze. "You heard the man."

She saluted him and left his office. Hurting for time, she sprang out of the security building. She caught a rail headed toward the labs located at the south campus. A round budge marked the main entrance point of the building with two rectangular wings thrust out on the sides.

After a few one-word questions and answers from the guards, she obtained the directions for the secret lab containing the three guardians. The head guard had to enter a special code for the elevator to take her there. She entered the cool interior, watching the doors close tightly. Then her body felt the uncomfortable descent. Despite the absence of windows, she felt darkness settle around her. Her body did a full core shiver.

The elevator doors opened once the she felt the halt. A few lab techs still roamed around wearing their white coats and sterile equipment. Some glanced her way but did not acknowledge her. She strolled through the stations, over to one of the techs who appeared to be the obvious leader.

"Excuse me?" She spoke to a tall, spindly young man. He turned around with a startled expression.

"You…you are the administrator?"

She nodded. "I am here to see the cyborgs."

"Okay…okay," he said, scratching his head. "Follow me, follow me." He walked with jerky yet quick steps, causing her to run to keep up with him.

Deborah followed him through six heavy security doors and down three flights of stairs to another level. Cold gray metal greeted her during the trek. No signs, no windows. The doors must have been hidden because everything appeared smooth and sleek.

"They're in here," the man said, clearing his throat. "You…you have only five min-min-minutes." He blinked his eyes at her through thick, round glasses.

"Understood," she said, following him through another pair of doors in a large airy room. A single bright light beamed down on the middle, where three long metal boxes lay on thick metal pegs bolted into the floor.

"I have to complete some calculations in the other room. Call me if you need me," he said, leaving the room without looking back.

Deborah stepped closer toward the boxes, which only allowed her to view the guardians' faces and nude torsos. The boxes allowed enough space between their heads and the tips of the boxes, but she caught sight of thick leather straps surrounding their necks and waist. She regarded the three flawless forms—two males and one female. Unknowingly she started to admire the ethereal beauty of their appearance. Such work must have cost Divine Cybernetics ahefty penny. Questions slid through her mind about such unhuman beauty, seductive and trancelike.

Even when they were supposed to be in a coma, their calm, serene expressions belied a harmonic sleep instead, making her envious of their weightless and airy life. Her stare melted into them, pulling her brain along, time stood still, and her body deadened in this moment.

"Administrator…Administrator," a faint call reached her ears, then she felt a light touch on her shoulder.

Deborah jerked away, yelping. Her eyes found the surprised, wide-eyed face of the lab tech, his long, slender fingers frozen in a claw.

"Administrator, I only wanted to tell you that the chief called. He says you must be on your way."

"Pardon me"—she pressed a hand to her chest—"I…I must collect evidence."

"Ad-Administrator, you've been in here for an hour. Partly my fault. I got caught up in my calculations."

"I have to go," she said and then turned around, heading out.

This time, the lab tech had to run to keep up with her. Once outside the building, she let out a breath, realizing that she hadn't taken much since seeing the guardians. She glanced down at her watch, which marked half past an hour. How in the world did she stay in there so long and not feel the change of time?

The guards chosen for her extraction team waited just outside the security department. She saluted them then gave them all a quick glance. She inhaled pushing the uncomfortable last hour in the back of her mind. Always Dome Council's security should wear their uniforms pressed and straight. Not a thread should be in sight, and all metals and buttons should shine brighter than the false sun.

"Gentlemen, it is a pleasure to lead you." She spoke crossing her hands at her waist. "As you know, this is an extraction. We will follow all Dome Council's procedures. Nothing will be left to chance. Are we clear?"

"Yes, Administrator." They spoke in unison.

"Good, let us extract," she said.

*****

Gabriel glanced up at the forbidden building, where Delilah's essence drew him there. He saw that it only took him about ten minutes from the lab to the apartment building from the opposite way of Alfred's clinic. He pressed his lips tighter together. Delilah played her game well. He believed her to have changed, to embrace humanity. He thought she wanted to be a part of these great and extraordinary people. He knew they had flaws and were not perfect. This is what seduced him to join, to indulge, and to just be. He hoped Delilah would recognize it as well, but alas, she became the monster Divine Cybernetics marketed her as a thief of the soul, the heart, and humanity.

His lips twisted in disgust. He already mourned the death of his father and his Delilah's humanity. Now he would have to deal with the fallout. A nasty job that he will not wish on any entity living or conscious, but he had to surge forward like a general.

Gabriel walked into the building passing a sea of undesirables along the way. The bolder ones made subtle moves toward him, making a paltry attempt at stalking. He only had to spare them a direct look for a minute, and they went ghost.

He progressed further following Delilah's essence into the elevator. The churning of the gears heightened his senses. He relaxed his powers, feeling them stretch and intertwine with his bones, his blood, exploding from his skin in a burst. A nauseated feeling threatened to have him pull back, but this time, he could not risk it, not when facing Delilah.

Gabriel allowed the elevator to make every stop. Her essence permeated every wall and corner of the building. At the last stop, he felt a kick in his spine. He exited, his eyes roaming everywhere. He walked down the dim corridor noting the silence and the lack of warmth that came with human's essence. No matter if they were sick or themselves trying to keep warm from the sunless Downs weather, he felt it on every floor except this one. This one remained empty. As he passed every door, the soft scuttles of pest and the whistle of the invading wind from the outside only reached his ears. Suddenly he felt her at the last door; reaching out, he grabbed the rusty knob, then turned it hard breaking the lock. He pushed through into a small living area; the place reeked of moldy bacteria and decay. The floor groaned and protested from his weight. He adjusted his approach to a lighter step.

Gabriel searched everywhere around the room. One thing for sure, Delilah left. Then he heard a soft moan. His ear rotated toward another door. He sprung to the door, opening it. His breath caught in his throat. He saw dead bodies before, but this one was still alive carrying the stench of death. This one had been alive. He narrowed his eyes at the emaciated body and caught the faint rise of the concave chest.

The closer he entered into the room, the more he recognized the pale face before him, though it had been years since he last saw her. He knew the sharp, protruding cheekbones and highbrow, especially the fine white hair that reminded him of Delilah's.

"Catherine?" he whispered. He approached the bed, noticing the thick straps securing her to the bed. "Catherine."

She eventually responded by turning her head. Her swollen red eyes opened. He saw a cloudy, dazed look in them. Her dry, cracked lips moved, but no sound came out. She let out a moan and shifted in the dirty, soiled mattress.

"Don't move. I will get you out of here." He made quick work breaking her bonds. Then he lifted her nude body from the bed. He roved up and down her body knowing that he couldn't carry her out into the streets of the Downs as nighttime had fallen, and the weather had started getting more erratic now. He had never teleported with someone before. He knew it may take more energy than he could spare, but Catherine needed medical attention. Closing his eyes, Gabriel summoned his energies. The image of Alfred's warm, comforting living room formed into his mind. Once it cemented the hold in his mind, his body dissolved into space, bringing his passenger with him.

In midspace, he heard Gayle's smoky voice and David's excited yells. Alfred's belly laugh resounded throughout the room. Then he saw them seated around a small rectangular screen viewing another episode of the *Merry Musician*.

"She's gonna get him this time, Alfred," David said.

"Hello, everyone." He spoke.

All three pairs of eyes turned to him, shocked and wide-eyed. Their mouths hung in perfect *O*'s. He cursed himself. He forgot that Gayle and David had never seen his powers manifest.

"Dr. Alfred, she needs immediate medical attention."

Alfred jolted out of his initial shock. He came forward. "Come on. Bring her in the clinic area," he said, opening a connecting door.

Gabriel carried Catherine into a small sterile room with a raised cot. He lowered her body on the cot. Dr. Alfred started placing the white patches on her forehead and arms connecting to a machine.

"Can you tell me what happened?" Alfred asked.

Gabriel swallowed hard. He inhaled deep. "Delilah had her tied to the bed in some apartment not too far away from here."

"Wow…do you know what she did to her?"

Gabriel shook his head. "Delilah has not assimilated easy into the human society. She has this odd sense of entitlement."

Alfred looked up at him. "Gabriel…I know this is really hard for you to come to terms with this. She being your only family now and the sort, but what she did to this woman is inhuman and evil. She needs to be stopped. Either you do it, or your buddies down at the Dome security will do it."

Gabriel hung his head. "I know this now."

"It is a good thing you found this woman in time. Who is she?"

"Catherine Miles," Gayle said behind them. She stepped further into the room, her eyes looking between Gabriel and the unconscious body on the cot.

"The CEO of Divine Cybernetics?" Alfred said.

Gabriel watched as she gave the doctor a silent nod. He pressed his lips tight together. He never thought that Delilah would seek to hurt anyone at Divine Cybernetics. They spoke about finding a way for Delilah to leave Dome 16. Now he wondered what Delilah's plan really is. What was in her mind that she would sink to deception and malice?

"Please take care of her." He managed to mutter. "I must continue looking for her before she hurts someone else."

"Gabriel"—Gayle touched his shoulder—"this is evil, and I hate to say this or even admit it, but maybe it is time to get Dome security involved."

He shook his head. They did not understand the level that Delilah had arrived at. He had some suspicion that it will be a massacre. He needed to talk with her, catch her off guard. This was the only way. He turned and grabbed Gayle's shoulder. "Please trust me to handle this."

"Fine, but call me every thirty minutes. I need to know you're okay."

"I promise."

Gabriel walked away from them. Gayle moved over Catherine, assisting Dr. Alfred. He went back into the common room when out of nowhere, David threw his arms around his leg. He then relaxed.

"How are you holding up, little one?" he asked, lowering on his haunches.

"It's okay," David said, his face falling into disappointment. "I really just want to go home."

"I promise you. Everything will be settled." He enveloped the little boy in a comforting hug.

"Gabriel?" David said.

"Yes?"

"What other powers do you have?"

He pulled away, smiling. "I will explain everything to you when I come back, but right now, I have to find my sister."

"Is she the one that hurt the lady?"

"Yes, David."

"Will she hurt us?" "Never."

"Will she hurt you?"

"She can't." He ruffled David's dark curls. "Now I have to talk with her, to help her understand that what she is doing is hurting people."

"She doesn't know?"

Gabriel shook his head. "She does not realize this. It is my job to help her."

"I know you will help her," David said, throwing his arms around Gabriel's neck. He felt David's outpouring of love for him. "Be careful," David advised him.

"I will," Gabriel promised. He left them through the conventional way. Night had fallen over the Downs. He transported back to the apartment trying to find her trail again. She would not go back to the lab as there was nothing for her there. To teleport to a place, they needed to know the place either from a person's shared memory or if they'd been there before.

He remembered that Gayle mentioned Dani Travis held a party for the Divine Cybernetics employees. He knew this was where Delilah abducted Catherine. She would have gone back. This time, she wanted to find the others. If she found them, he would have to resolve with the ultimate solution—a solution he promised himself that would never happen again.

Chapter 20

DEBO RAH STROLLED THROUGH THE upper floors taking in the wondrous, luxuriate sculpture and paintings. It reminded her of the home her sister had been given. Her hands touched everything from the smooth surfaces of the large porcelain vases and the rich silk of the curtains. The resources that went into this home could have paid for fifty homes in Dome 3.

The extraction team arrived an hour ahead of the time agreed upon only to find an absent Dani Travis. She commanded the team to search the home on the first floor and in the surrounding estate area. Agent Travis had a reputation for devious ventures, but she never heard the agent being this insubordinate.

Deborah entered the first room. Her eyes beamed in on a pile of worn and outdated suitcase on the bed. She moved closer to the pile. The room appeared as the others in the house—sleek, elegant, and expensive. The bags on the bed bespoke desolation and end of the road. Dani's profile bespoke a woman used to finer things, grew up with fine things, and never knew a hand-me-down. These certainly did not belong to her.

Deborah lowered onto the edge, grabbing for the bags. She opened the first bag seeing a bunch of threadbare clothing and a pair of shoes. The other two had the same thing; however, the last one had some hair products and brown leather-bound book. The book caught her attention the most as she never saw anything like it in all the domes.

She opened the book and saw pictures, some black-and-white; others held a golden-brown hue. The images all held people dressed in old baggy clothes. She recognized the style as that of the miners in Dome 3. The lowest of the citizens, they lived in small huts at the lowest point of the Dome. She flipped the pages until the very last stopped her—a petite young girl dressed in a long white lace dress with strap shoulder and a tall, slender man with curly dark hair and piercing bright eyes stood near her. The smiling man in the picture stood squeezing the unsmiling girl. She saw the crowd of men surrounding those waving billowing caps.

"Gayle?" she whispered, remembering the woman's face from that perplexing day.

Six months passed since her sister called her last. Sue missed their scheduled family call. Growing nervous and anxious, she tried her sister multiple times even resulting to emailing, but still nothing. She would have come sooner, but Dome 3 had another lockdown preventing traveling between domes.

Her superiors tried to help her get authorization to travel to Dome 16. Only recently, they could acquire an assignment for her. Once she arrived looking for her sister at the old apartment in Midtown only to be turned away by the landlord. She finally learned her sister made the move to Uptown. She could not imagine how her sister moved to the prestigious Uptown neighborhood on Marcus's salary and position.

Odd, she thought, *Gayle lives in Uptown and works in a higher post at the company. What are her things doing here?* She shifted through the pages finding later pictures of a small cute body with a fro of dark curls.

Deborah sat in the quiet dimness of the room when a crash from below jolted her. She stood, her wide eyes looking out into the shadowy hall. There was another louder crash, followed by deafening popping sounds of weapons being discharged and excited shouts of Divine's security guards. She stood frozen in place. Administrators never got involved with physical altercations.

However, after the minutes ticked by and no more noise could be heard, she decided to brave the unknown, stepping out of the room into a now dark hall. Her steps were measured and counted until the hall disappeared. She laid a tentative hand on the polished metal surface of the railings. Her confidence increased when her progress so far left her unmolested. Her eyes still met with darkness, but the harsh toxic smells of laser weapons overwhelmed her nose, but fear held back the sneeze.

"Sergeant Dylan!" she called out to the commanding officer of the team. The air carried her voice, dissolving the desperate call.

She took the first step down the staircase. This time, her hand held the banister in a sweaty death grip. Another step increased her fearlessness, and then another until her pace increased in speed. Some of her anxiousness dissipated.

"Sergeant?" she called out. She raised a foot to step down and found the ground lumpy and unstable. Her body propelled forward, and the floor came up too quick for her to react.

She laid for a while down trying to connect her brain with her limbs. Her feet pushed out first, colliding with a something firm yet movable. She reached out with her hands to touch the object and found warm skin. She let out a scream, scooting away and colliding with another body, then another, feeling like a wall of bodies blocked her way.

"Little rabbit in a fox hole." A husky female voice spoke. Then the lights of the foyer turned on fully.

Deborah looked up the stairs where a tall, slender blond woman stood. She saw terror and beauty in the classic pale features. The bright eyes shone a bloody red, which matched the color of her smiling lips.

"Hello there. I am Delilah," the woman said, descending into the foyer like a winged angel.

Deborah could not find her voice. A good administrator should always know the rules when they were engaged. However, at this point, she did not feel like a good administrator. She did not feel an administrator at all. Her heart raced at full speed head until her ribs started to throb from the impact.

"You are all the same." The woman continued. "Smell the same, sound the same, taste the same."

Deborah blinked once, finding herself nose to nose with the demon female and the reason for the fallen security guard. She felt her pulse push into overtime. She leaned back trying to get away, and again another body trapped her.

"Little rabbit has nowhere to go." Then the woman did the oddest thing, caressing Deborah's face with her own. "I know you."

"Y-You do?" Deborah did not want to, but she found herself caught in an eye wrestle with the woman.

"Oh yes," Another sniffed, blowing heated air across her skin. She felt the hair stand on the edges.

"I…I don't know what I may have done to you that would have—"

"Shhh"—a slender finger touched her lips lightly—"don't worry. I am full." After the closeness, the woman drifted away, standing up, still with the same smile.

"Oh, now I know."

"What do you know?"

"Sue was such a good cook."

Her body seized again. "What do you know of my sister?"

"Oh, so much, so much. I don't even know where to start," the woman said, her eyes widening. "I know, how about the end."

"The end?"

"It is always the best to tell a story from the end to the beginning. You go from sad to happy. Everyone always wants a happy ending. Shall I begin?"

Deborah remained silent. A sick feeling started at her core, and her eyes were glued to the toxic, brilliant eyes and the smiling full lips. Happiness showed from beneath the woman's face, despite being surrounded by death and misery.

"We were alone. I believe the kitchen."

"You were with her?"

"Yes, love. Did she fail to mention me?"

Deborah simply nodded.

"Well, introductions are in order. I am Delilah"—there was a pause—"Sue Johnson's guardian."

Deborah felt the walls crumble around her, and all her senses stopped at once.

"Sue's guardian."

"I assure you, the honors were all hers. Now how we parted ways, or rather, she parted her way, and I ended up being hunted. That's another story. Her story ended with us talking… about the sorry state of her marriage…the lack of fulfillment, and those awful, bratty children. I won't bore you with the details, but it was a cry session. So I did her a favor. We kissed, boned, embraced, and when the sun came up, she went to her eternal home."

"You killed her?"

"Never," the woman said with a shocked expression. "I freed her."

"You killed her."

"No, no, you are confusing what happened to her with what is going to happen to you," she said, another larger smile showing straight white teeth. "Run, Rabbit!"

Without hesitation, Deborah struggled to a standing position and ran headlong toward the door. Her fingers slipped multiple times until she got a firm hold on the door, yanking it open and sprinting down the steps. She stumbled twice on her way toward the large silver-and-white cruiser.

She had to punch the code in twice, exhaling relief that the door finally clicked open. She hauled her body into the cabinet, slamming the door closed. Her chest heaved, struggling to maintain the last bit of oxygen. Her hands shook while trying to start the engine, which stalled twice before holding, then her foot slammed into the delicate pedal of the gas.

"Navigator, this is unacceptable speed for the course." The vehicle mechanical voice spoke over the speaker.

Deborah ignored it, her fear still pounding into her head, propelling the need to escape the horror. The wheels almost came off the ground as it circled around the driveway. Only once did she dare to sneak a peek back at the mansion. The living room lights blinked out only to emphasize the silhouette of the terror watching her.

*****

Dani never meant to be late coming back to the house. Trying to find a way to break into the storage chip took most of her time. Time wasted. Apparently, the lab techs never extended the information to Catherine. Nothing on her computer mentioned the chip. The information on Divine Cybernetics intranet only gave cloaked answers.

Deborah appeared to be a person who forgave. She hoped with her throwing Catherine at them. Dome Council would lift the extraction notice and give her time to solve the mystery that has plagued them all about the guardian program, why only a chosen few really knew about the prototypes.

Dani lowered her craft in the driveway, glancing down at the time and mentally cursed. It read an hour past the meeting. She had to readjust the presentation with an apology and add some charm into the mix. Charm always worked whenever she found herself on the outs with one of her administrators.

The glass door opened. A swift, cool breeze greeted her. Her eyes glanced around, and to her surprise, only Catherine's white Jaxx was parked in the driveway. She looked back at the house wondering about the darkness. Catherine hated dark rooms. When she visited the CEO, every room in the penthouse remained lit even through her inopportune sleepovers. After standing for a moment, she shrugged. Catherine probably waited in one of the bedrooms trying to keep hidden. The administrator mayhap would arrive late. Some office issue, she should not let her mind trick into seeing shadows that were not there.

Dani entered a pitch-black foyer. Her brow creased when the lights did not turn on. It always recognized her body signature. Did they deactivate her security codes already? She made her way toward a nearby wall remembering the manual switch located just on the other side of the oversize window facing the front.

Dani smiled, relieved when her fingers caught on hinge of the switch cover. She flipped it open and entered the manual code. The room illuminated in a warm yellow from the glass chandelier above. Her eyes scanned over the clean, organized foyer. Nothing out of place. Nothing disturbed. She noted the uncanny eeriness of the interior.

"Catherine?" she called out, walking to stand at the end of the staircase.

A long echo answered her, causing the hairs on the base of her neck to shiver.

"Catherine!" She repeated.

Again nothing.

Maybe she can't hear me. She ascended the stairs, glancing around and keeping her ears alert to any little sound that could be made. As the minutes increased to the next hour, her anxiety heightened to a new level, bringing her to keep a light hold on her sidearm.

"Catherine, are you here?" she called out, looking side to side at the top of the stairs, then listened. Again, the echoes carried her voice for another five seconds. *Where is she?* She let out a growl. *This is not the time for games.* She started toward her bedroom.

Catherine had a taste for luxury no matter the situation. If there was a place in the mansion to hide, the exec would surely choose the master bedroom. Dani made it a point to turn on every light switch she passed. Somehow it established some normality in the situation.

The master bedroom doors appeared slightly open. She caught the glimmer of a dim light through the slit. *She's here?* Her steps increased while her palm pushed open one of the double doors into the bedroom. Still dark, but not so much as the light she saw came from the bathroom. Then she heard it—lyrical humming, a female humming, followed by the swirling of water. Her brow furrowed deeply. She walked toward the master bathroom. A cloud of fog drifted from the slit of the door, and condensing settled on the metal surface.

"Catherine?" she called, standing outside the door.

The humming sound stopped.

"Oh, hello?" A female spoke behind her.

Dani twirled around hard, her weapon raised, yet nothing prepared her for the nude sight of the strange, pale woman lounging on the bed. The lights of the master bedroom all turned on, almost blinding her. Her eyes teared struggling to adjust.

"Give it time, Dani, love," the woman said. "They will adjust."

As the woman had predicted, her eyes adjusted, only for her to narrow them at the female. "Who are you?"

A smile crossed her full lips. She took a moment to regard the woman's face that could have been similar to Catherine's, but the paleness and the unmarked smooth skin gave another unnatural feel. "Oh, you do not recognize me from the party." The woman slid to a sitting position, reminding her of a cat.

Dani approached with caution, her weapon shaking in her hand. "The waitress."

"So you do remember. Let's complete our introduction," the woman said as she stood. "I am Delilah."

"One of the guardians," she said, "the one they have been looking for." Now her hand shook so bad, her grip on the weapon loosened.

"I got to tell you"—a slender finger wagged in her direction—"your species are getting more intelligent every day, and here I figured it would take another year for my machinations to come to light."

"What do you want, and where is Catherine?"

"What makes you think you have any authority in this?"

"I have a weapon," Dani said, as her hand shook even more. She had to bring her second hand up to steady the weapon.

The woman, Delilah, cocked her head to the side and smiled. "Depends on whose perspective."

Dani's vision blurred until a white blanket filled her vision. She dropped her weapon and stumbled forward blind. Then a blunt force pushed her against the wall, and stars turned on in her mind.

The searing pain piercing through her sheer white blouse woke her from the stupor. Her eyes fluttered open, but still her vision remained blurred and hazy. She managed to decipher four hulking dark shapes seated before her. The room held a mysterious smell, like the butcher markets in Dome 3. Her nose wrinkled, and she sniffed. She tried to move but found her body bound oddly to a metal stool. The stool itself appeared to be welded to the floor. Her squirming only managed to jiggle the thick metal pipes that made up the legs.

"You're finally awake." The familiar voice spoke again.

Dani felt her body stiffen from the sound. While she felt almost like a prey very familiar with its predator, her nerves tuned into Delilah's sensuous, fluid movements. Her heart kicked up its pace within her chest cavity.

"Give me your mind, Gabriel. Remember the light." Her voice penetrated his brain, and his mind returned in time, walking through a maze of unconscious images. Delilah's memories started light and happy. The day the others emerged from their artificial wombs— he saw this from Delilah's perspective, where she roamed the warm damp chamber, bumping into the others, touching them, and grabbing their hands and hair. Her young face was etched in confusion.

Then Delilah's face faded, and Gayle's face replaced her in his dreamscape. She was crouched down, small and afraid. She wore the typical Downs clothing, shapeless and dark so that she could blend into the shadows. She would be able to escape the men. He saw the men, but they did not see him. He recognized their uniforms as Dome security guards. Gabriel shook his head, not believing he saw Gayle, but not as she was now. She was younger, smaller, and scared. This had been a memory of his, but how?

"He erased most of our memories. He treated us like we are things, unfeeling and not real," Delilah spat out.

A faint scent of gardenias interrupted the meat smell. She recognized the expensive body wash she brought with her from Dome 3. Divinity had been created by the expanded cosmetic company created by Catherine's mother. The products were from natural ingredients, now hard to come by and very rare. She fumed at the audacity of the thing to help herself to her treasured belongings. Her fuming continued until a hand waved over her face. Her heart pace skipped into overdrive, and she feared it would crack her ribs. Her eyelids fluttered with a mind of their own. She found her vision clearing, but what appeared made her wish to have continued the twisted vision.

"Does this look familiar to you?" Delilah leaned over, whispering in her ear.

Dani refused to answer her. She squeezed her eyes close trying to block the images but knew that it would be impossible. They already engraved into her brain, bringing back memories of her reluctant mission.

"Come now. I did not give you back your vision for nothing. Doesn't this excite you? Doesn't the blood make you crave for more?" Slight, slender hands positioned on her shoulders. "The Petersons deserved it. They all deserved it. Hey, it was either them or you."

"Why are you showing me this? Why don't you kill me now and get it over with?" Dani said, her teeth grinding, causing an ache in her jaw.

"That will be too easy, Dani Travis. You should know one never makes anything easy for the prey, because when they struggle, it makes the meat ever so much more delicious."

"They made me do it. We wanted to keep the guardian prototype for ourselves," Dani admitted, remembering the loathsome suggestion made by her handler in the Dome Council. She dared not tell him what she truly felt about killing an entire family, but they convinced her it would be for the greater good. He went on to tell her the family really had no place in their society. They did not contribute to the advancement of Dome 16 or to make them great.

"Excuses, excuses. When will you take responsibility for your own part in this chaos?" Delilah squeezed her shoulder. "I have. I admit that I have killed, fed, played."

"I followed orders."

"Of course, you did. Just like I am doing." There was a pause. "Oh, but I think playtime might be over."

"Over?"

"Yes." Before Dani could respond, Delilah's strong hands gripped her head. She felt her neck twist and crack. The pain shot from her head to her feet, then blackness clouded her eyes. The end came, and she never even suspected it.

Chapter 21

GABRIEL ARRIVED IN CHAOS. He sensed it at the entrance, which halted his progress. He stood there calling out mentally to her. This was the first time since the night of the altercation that he tried to reach for her mind, only to be answered with stubborn silence—as if she was there but not. The wall between them was no longer malleable, and the solidity of the moment reflected the solidity of their separation.

Three years growing and learning together did not make this easy for him. He vowed to always remain the leader of the group and ensure the guardians obey their number 1 objective to ensure the citizens' children obey the Dome Council's rules throughout their lifetime and to eliminate the inferior virus that will corrupt the advancement of their society.

Delilah took to their program faster than even him, but he guessed somewhere down the line, her cyber mind evolved, and being a guardian no longer appeared to be the main objective, but what was her objective now—that, he wanted to know. The killing and chaos seemed so unpredictable and out of character, even out of program. He was sure of it.

He inhaled deeply, remembering the first greeting out of their small womb chambers. They were already toddler-aged but with the brains of ten-year-olds. She greeted him with a hug and a smile. Then she took him by the hand to awaken the others; they played tag before the childish game was interrupted by the lab technicians and nurses. Olivia, Delilah, and he often enjoyed forbidden nighttime games of tag and learning more than what their handlers limited them to during the day.

During their teenage years, she changed, becoming more nurturing toward everyone. He noticed the staff even treated her with respect and appeared more lenient with Delilah than to him or the other guardians, and she was never a selfish girl. Delilah shared it with her siblings, exposing them to forbidden secrets of the human world they were never supposed to know.

He thought to have lost that Delilah when she attacked him, but then as their world crashed, the testing ended abruptly. She gathered him into her confidence, and he forgave her previous transgressions, but now he could not anymore. She was not killing to stay alive but for joy, and this was dangerous to his family.

His heart cracked a little, and the feelings that regrew for her evaporated, and now…he just wanted to lay her to rest. He had to concentrate on sealing the secrets of the guardians and making sure that the rest of his siblings were laid to rest deep in the earth. Then all would be quiet…at least, all that really mattered.

Inhaling, he took the first step into the home. The stench of death drew him through the foyer into the large formal living room. The large white marble fireplace was lit, and it flooded the room in a firelight ambiance. The stench overwhelmed the room so much it took away from the harmonic visual. His gaze roamed deeper into the room. He saw shapes seated by the fire. Their long shadows splashed along the walls.

When he got closer, his eyes widened when he recognized Dani Travis. Her head lolled to the side with a single bone sticking from her neck. She faced several Dome Council's guardsmen. He recognized one but knew all were men of honor. The job chose them really. So they could send money back to families in need. He knew their death would not bring any more funds to the families either. As mere Dome guards, the government found them disposable.

"Delilah, no," he whispered. He stepped back, swallowing. All emotions flooded to the surface as he staggered further away until his back hit the wall. He stared at the bodies. Senseless and cruel. This was where Delilah ended in her evolution of character. He saw no reason for their death. She did not even feed from them, just killed them like…animals. Gabriel managed to gather himself. His eyes closed as he tried again to reach her with his mind. He needed to know her thoughts, if she had a plan, or was this a program that only Delilah received from their father? Why was she doing this? Why would anyone do this?

The most disheartening matter of this all was that he realized that Delilah was now his adversary. She was standing on the opposite side of the imaginary line of civilization, threatening what weak harmony there now was. He could not, with any amount of conscience, allow her to complete the destruction. As far as he knew, there was still hope the human race could come back and live once more.

Gabriel reentered the foyer. His features drawn, and beads of sweat formed around his brow. His eyes moved up, glancing toward the upper floors. He sniffed to be sure not to encounter the scene in the living room again. Even with his advance abilities, one could only survive so much.

He took the first step, then continued ascending at a quick pace, taking the steps by twos and threes until he arrived at the landing. He banked left, entering a long, wide corridor, then stopped at the first room. He recognized the bags piled atop the bed. Gayle and David had not been back here since he revealed Dani's duplicity.

Gayle would relish seeing her things again, relics of her happy memories—things that would make the transition to her life more amiable. He was surprised that Dani had not disposed of them, but then again, her agenda always confused him. He gathered the five bags together, ensuring nothing stayed behind. He ran a mental scan through the home.

Delilah knew he arrived and left. For some reason, she did not wish to face him or rather face what her devastation left.

He wondered if she even thought about the aftereffects of it all or if she thought at all. He stood still glancing around the room again. Delilah's trail would ultimately lead to one destination. He had been guarding his siblings from the scientists and Dome government, confusing their experiments and keeping them in a living coma. His heart broke seeing them in the metal coffins, cold, stiff more like objects than warm-blooded humans. Inhaling, he closed his eyes, imagining the warm interior of Alfred's living room. The trio would be in the common room—David doing his homework, Alfred going over his files from the day, and Gayle, well, waiting for him, waiting and worried.

*****

Deborah barreled through the automatic gate, cracking open the fragile metal bar. She managed to stop the heavy vehicle before it crashed into a thick brick column. The surprised guard watched only for a moment before yelling over the intercom for help. Soon, a sea of black-uniformed Dome security details swarmed the large black guard truck. Through her shell-shock mind, voices shouted in all directions. She tried to comprehend as much as possible, but the overwhelming barrage of information overloaded her senses. She peeled her damp hands from the steering wheel, covered her eyes, and screamed.

The voices hushed. She felt the driver door whisk open, and the large intimidating form of Cleander filled the entrance. His large hands rested on her shoulder. She knew he spoke but found she could not prevent herself from quieting. The large hand on her shoulder took on a firm, aggressive grip. Her body lifted from the seat, and for the first time, the cool breeze of night touched her skin.

The screams quieted when large hands yanked her own. Her eyes still saw shades of clouded and muted grays, no color, reminding her of one of the ancient moving pictures her sister so loved. Bodies moved around her, then she felt her body being lowered, something soft touched the back of her head and neck. Multiple hands stretched out her legs and arms. Thick straps firmly bounded her limbs. Then again, she was lifted.

"Let's get her to medical…quick," Cleander's strained baritone finally tore through the nightmare.

"Aye, Chief…

She felt the stretcher start to rise. It was not a smooth journey for sure. The four emergency medical personnel surrounded her, and with much disappointment, the warmth of her friend left. The static noises of their radio irritated the inner core of her ears causing her head to move from side to side trying to relieve the pain.

"She is experiencing the same signs as the others," a female voice said.

"There are still three who are unaccounted for," a male voice said.

"Chief Cleander wants us to give him immediate updates," another male voice said.

"We cannot do so at this time. Her mind might be damaged beyond our medicine," the female answered.

Her mind damaged. *Why would they say that? Others?* They were talking about the guardian prototypes. They knew what the extent of the prototypes' abilities were. Did she need to tell them of her experience with that she-demon, the one who killed her sister? She mentally scoffed, released her indeed. The monster destroyed her family.

"We may need to put her under," the first male said again.

"You're right. Give her the needle," she said.

Deborah tried to refuse the drug. She did not want to be placed under but found her voice had abandoned her. She felt the tiny prick at the side of her neck. Her world clouded again. She heard them still speaking above her, but their voices faded into nothingness. Her world did a freeze frame.

*****

Cleander watched the stretcher until it disappeared into the medical building. He cursed himself for allowing Administrator Deborah to go in alone. He never thought much danger would arise with apprehending a silly female field agent. Dani Travis did not appear to be dangerous. In his opinion, she was rather an incompetent, lazy agent and who was more prone to the finer things in life than any agent should really desire.

He opposed the whole ideal of the guardians at the beginning. He did not think Dome Council should be involved with the free industry. He scoffed at the notion that children should be raised by these robots to love, honor, and obey the council for all their lives. Did those idiots in the government really believe such fairy tales? He did not. He believed in rules. If the citizens broke them, they were punished with whips and chains. It worked for Dome 3. It should work for Dome 16.

"Chief Cleander, we never received a call from the guards who went with her," one of the guards approached him.

"I want everyone called in. We go on the hunt tonight. Let it be known that Dome 16's sun will not appear until all responsible parties are secured," Cleander said.

"Yes, Chief," the guard left.

*****

Delilah watched the little ants surround the large vehicle. So concerned about the little birdy, she smiled. They looked so weak, easy pickings for the trough. She watched a tall dark-haired man drift from the cloud. Something about his bearing reminded her of dear, disturbed Gabriel. Maybe it was his gross sense of propriety and justice.

She sighed, leaning her forehead against the cool marble column. Sleep eluded her for the fifth time. Her days bled into night, and her nights into days. She often found it hard to focus her mind. Finding it oftentimes escaped to her drifting into the abyss. Then cravings would start up again. Her belly would churn and growl, and her nerves would shake and rattle so much. She felt the need to rack her claws over and over the delicate, smooth surface.

Even now she felt the freshly-healed scars caused her distress. She wanted to cut her arm from the socket to rid her of such flaw. Her beautiful skin was marred by her needs and cravings. Which of them was more important?

"Move out!" the dark-haired man below yelled.

Delilah lifted her head from the column. Her eyes drifted over the expanse of the Dome Council government's compound. She sensed her brothers and sister in the larger building. The white one was where their signal felt so strong. Then she would have to convince them to abandon the parameters of their programming and join her.

"Chief Cleander, Sergeant Hawthorne arrived at Agent Dani's home. The others were killed, along with Agent Dani."

"Continue with the hunt," Cleander said.

Delilah watched the men run in formation of twos and threes. The roar of vehicles filling out of garages caught her attention again. She also heard the clicking of their weapons as they were off to some war. She smiled imagining the silliness of the humans. They did not know what they were up against and thought brute strength would be their salvation.

*****

Deborah woke to the whispers of a female. She moaned and struggled to sit up, but soon, hands were upon her. They pressed her body back into the cushions of the cot. She fought against their persistence. However, the hands won out. She relaxed into the cushions.

"Administrator, we will have your food in a moment," a quiet female whispered to her in the distance.

She tried to speak, but yet again, her voice failed her. All she could do was grunt and moan. Her vision had yet to return as well. All she saw was blobs of white and gray. Some color would come through in hues of soft pinks and yellows.

"The hospital will need to be secured, as all the Dome guards will be hunting."

"They know what one looks like. A pretty blonde. Female."

"Then they will be almost a third of the population." The nurses took more, their voices fading in and out.

Deborah caught on that the guard would be leaving the Dome government's compound. This would leave them all vulnerable.

*****

The ants scuttled away in their high-powered vehicles and little handheld toys, dressed in black finery. The lights in the fields and buildings dimmed. Those left behind closed up tight for the night. They had nothing to fear, or so they thought. She smiled slinking out of the shadows rising to her full height.

She spread out her arms stepping onto the thin wall, then with precise balance, she strolled along with casual regard. Her smile widened as she thought that soon her brothers and sister would welcome her rescue, and together, they would play.

Delilah stopped at the edge and leaned forward, and then she took a leap, her body arching and her head to the air. Then just as the earth came up, she curled her body. She landed on her feet with the grace of a cat. Standing up, she sniffed the crisp air and smiled. She stuffed her hands in her pockets, pursed her lips, and continued to whistle a long twinkle sound that melded with the light breeze.

She walked among the shadows of the buildings. Around her, the fields were quiet; the guards left, and the other Security Council staff members had long sought safety in their respective department buildings, not realizing the predator on patrol.

Precision is always the key to a well-thought-out experiment and diligence, the tools of a focused scientist. Numbers, calculations, and formula stirred into a harmonious recipe, and the final result, creating a rainbow of knowledge that left him drowning in delight with the answer presenting itself in a glaring, glowing beacon.

Winston Mallory stood, stretching his lanky body. His gaze drifted toward the three coffins just beyond the thick glass-enclosed room. They were to be buried six thousand feet under the compound in the morning. He smiled. Many a great Dome scientist and engineer studied the guardians and yet to crack their riddle, finally, after laborious hours, the chief of staff, Dr. Hawthorne, declared the riddle futile and a waste. He forbade all to continue the experimentation, and the guardians were shut away.

Dr. Hawthorne chose him, Winston, for the tedious chore of watching over them until the morning. At first, he was grateful with just being around the prototypes that Divine created with the genius of Dr. Gregory. He had the solitude of completing a few personal projects dealing with molecular cell manipulation and viruses. However, after completing two experiments, he grew listless. He stared at the boxes, finding he could not turn away from them. He could not understand the allure. The whole scene seemed so extraordinary yet plain. Three nondescript, crudely-made metal coffin harbored three flawed service bots from a disgrace company.

"Hello." A voice spoke behind him.

Winston almost fell from his seat. He twisted around, prepared to give the intruder a full lecture on the rules and regulations of the medical department, but his tongue froze in his mouth. His eyes widened past their limits.

"You have two pairs of eyes," the woman moved closer, but he swore her feet never touched the ground.

"Who are you?" He finally spoke. His mind churned on the number of female nurses on shift. He knew for sure that none looked as she did just then.

The woman smiled with roses on her lips and stars in her eyes. Her body provided an additional hypnotizing lure. He did not realize how much effect she had on him when a cool liquid rolled out of his mouth and down his chin.

"What is this place?" she asked, walking along the perimeter of the lab until she reached the glass wall separating the quarantined guardians. She stopped, looking into the enclosed glass room, then started to whistle.

Winston started to speak again, but this time, no sound came out. His body felt immobilized. The woman spared him a second glance, then did the most astonishing thing. She vanished, then reappeared on the opposite side of the glass.

*****

Their closeness gave out a glorious, elated charge. The last time she saw Michael, Jacob, and Esther, they were seated in the living room of the home they had been living in. Dr. Cote sent a message for them to gather and wait for further instructions. She pursed her lips remembering how she hated to obey and wanted to stay in her room. The sun shone just right through the tall windows of her room, highlighting her pretty figure in the new yellow sundress. She wanted to admire herself in the mirror longer.

Michael stood near a window. Jacob sat at the chess table playing with Olivia. Esther discussed literature with Gabriel on the sofa. She arrived last still in her sundress. The others dressed in gray onepiece jumpers. Gabriel spotted her first.

"You should change, Delilah. Dr. Cote wants us all ready for transfer," Gabriel said.

"I don't cater to Dr. Cote," she said, pouting and folding her arms over her chest.

Gabriel gave her his usual stern look, which often meant that he would not hear any further opposition from her. "Change," he said.

She looked over at the others watching her. They waited to see her next move. Then she obeyed orders, never knowing anything else. So she left the room to change, but upon coming back in the room, she found the others had gone. Dr. Cote waited for her here at the door along with a Dome Council's guard. The small woman's small beady eyes appeared displeased.

"I hope this will not be a habit with you, Delilah." Dr. Cote spoke. "Disobedience is a quick way for you to be deactivated. I hope I made myself clear."

"Yes, Dr. Cote."

After that day, she saw them passing. They assimilated into their respective test families only communicating with her on schedules and reports—subjects she had no interest in.

Olivia was more excited, but she found it difficult to follow her little sister's thought process. Esther had always been more mature, and they shared a special bond. Approaching the first coffin, she rubbed her hands. They would rule together. Gabriel would no longer have any power over them. They would be free to do as they please without their father, Divine, or the other silly humans to tell them what to do.

She pried open the first coffin, lifting it up with little effort, then peered inside. Her heart dropped. He couldn't have known. She kept her thoughts secret from him. A brick wall constantly surrounding her thoughts, her emotions.

Delilah slammed the coffin shut and hurried to the next one and finally the third. Though their essence still remained, she could not trace them. Her emotions halted. Her eyes continued to stare at the coffins. She let out a scream, which blasted the thick glass separating the windows.

She caught her reflection the mirror like metal, her eyes blazed red and glowed. Her face twisted in a distorted monster mask. She backed away covering her face.

Chapter 22

"SO WE HAVE TO solve for X," Alfred said.

"Then what is X?" David asked.

"We don't know until we solve for it," Alfred said with a small chuckle.

"But X is not a number. Are you sure we are doing math? Math has numbers in it," David said.

Gayle watched him place his small hands on his damp forehead, staring down at the paper. She smiled at the duo. It had been three days since David attended school. She feared he might be behind in his studies. So Alfred volunteered to go over the dreaded math subject while she would read with him later. However, it seemed her son would need more time with the subject.

"Now, David, if they made things easier, it would not be math," Alfred said and smiled wide.

She laughed at his patience. David could be very stubborn at times, especially when it came to concentrating on his schoolwork.

"No more lip, young man!" she called out from the kitchen. "You still have reading."

A long miserable groan answered her. She smiled, placing the last dish in the strainer. She folded the dishcloth and looked at the round digital clock on the mantel. Gabriel had yet to call in. Her mind churned at what could be going on.

She should push harder for Gabriel to sever ties with Delilah. Some people and beings for that matter just could not be saved no matter how much support they received. She learned that from Richard. Her husband thought being a part of a notorious gang would allow them to have an easier life. Sure, they lived better than most of the people in the Downs, but the price later gave them a hard fall. Then she had an opportunity to inject her opinion but kept her mouth shut just to keep the peace.

Now she had a second chance, another chance to convince Gabriel that Delilah should be destroyed, and he needed the help of Dome Council to do it. She stared at Alfred and David again. This time, her son appeared to be concentrating more.

"Hey, Alfred, you still have that old landline?" she called out.

Alfred glanced up, surprised. "Yeah, sure. You need it?"

"I want to call someone, but I don't want to tie up the mobile."

He nodded toward his small study. "In there."

"Thanks!" She headed to the study, closing the door behind her. She heard Alfred speaking with David again in hushed tones about the mechanics of basic algebra.

The old landline perched at the edge of a large ornate carved wooden desk. Her friend really had a passion for the ancients. The landline itself was colored cream with a clunky rectangle bottom. She lifted the handset and dialed the number for Dani. She held the earpiece to her ear listening as the phone rang and continued to ring.

She lowered the handset in the cradle. The excited voices of David reached her, then Gabriel's baritone. He sounded strained but tried to maintain a semblance of normalcy. She stepped forward, but the door to the study opened. Gabriel's glowing eyes caught her by surprise.

"Gabriel, did something happen?" Gayle moved toward him.

He pressed a finger to his lips and closed the door. When he faced her again, she saw the muscles of his throat spasmed. His eyes continued glowing with that eerie blue, reminding her of the longago images of stars. The dim light of the room gave them an even more stunning effect.

"Gabriel, what happened? Tell me. Did you speak with Delilah or—" She stopped.

"I have not." He stopped speaking, moving closer. "I lost her again."

Gayle reached out to him, placing her hand on his face, forcing him to stare in her eyes.

"What happened exactly? Tell me everything."

"I followed her trail to Dani Travis's home." He closed in, placing both hands on her waist. "Dani Travis is dead, along with several Council guardsmen."

"She didn't—"

He nodded, leaning into her embrace, resting his chin on her shoulder. She felt him shudder. She tightened her embrace, holding him as he did her when she heard the news of the destruction. Her hands moved up and down his back. He stopped shaking, and his muscles relaxed. His warm breath changed from harsh pants to long whispers of air.

"We should sit," she said, making a slight move but held back by Gabriel's tightened embrace. "Gabriel…"

He pulled away, placing his forehead on hers. She wanted to speak about her meeting with the Dome Council but knew that he would try to talk her out of it. However, something told her that it would be a good thing.

"I still love you," he whispered. She shuddered.

"Now that I have given you time to know me, that I am not the monster from Dr. Frankenstein's fairy tale." He pinned her with a serious glance. "Do you feel the same?" he asked again.

"Gabriel, I never thought you a monster."

"Do you feel the same?"

"I always admired and respected you. I care for you more than anything," she said. She tried to swallow, finding the moisture had evaporated, and her throat felt like she had been inhaling buckets of sand.

"Why will you not answer me?" he asked.

He was right. Why wouldn't she answer him? Then she thought about her hasty marriage at eighteen. She hesitated then as well, but desperation and persuasion of peers pushed her to accept Richard's proposal. The first tempestuous year found them fighting, and disagreements led to her husband's absences from the home. She raised her dark eyes to the glowing heat of Gabriel's and swallowed hard.

"You must understand. This is very hard." She placed a hand on his bicep.

"Why is it so hard?" he asked. "I know what I feel and love what I feel. It is good to me."

"I know what I feel too, Gabriel, and…it scares me to my toes," she whispered. "You don't know how much."

"I understand. It seems you need more time." He grabbed her hands in his. "I am patient."

"Thank you," she mouthed.

A soft knock at the door interrupted the tension. Then she heard David call to her. She stepped away from the heat of Gabriel's presence, her heart disappointed from the lack of closeness.

"I'm coming." She walked over to the door, opening it.

"The sick lady needs your help." David pointed to the door.

Gayle rolled her eyes. Catherine had grown rather dependent since her arrival to Alfred's clinic. She knew their patient was almost fully recovered from her traumatic event. The CEO garnered every moment to make impossible demands, each growing more and more preposterous.

"Why don't you read with Gabriel for a while?" she said and ruffled his fat curls.

"Gabriel!" David squealed. "I have completed algebra and will read to you." He grabbed Gabriel's hand like in the past, leading him around the room to where his favorite books were.

She smiled at the image and proceeded into the other room. Alfred opened the door of his clinic, a grim expression on his face.

He gave her a look that dropped her heart.

"How is the patient?" she asked.

"Lively as ever," he said, giving her a tight smile, then stepped aside.

"My turn," she said, patting him on the shoulder.

Alfred rolled his eyes and glanced toward the ceiling. "She wants more pain medicine. It is not good for her. I tell her that every time. I think the woman has concrete for brains."

"I'm sorry, Alfred. I will try to get her to communicate with a family member or lawyer, someone who can help her," Gayle said. Hopefully, they could take her off their hands.

"Don't be. It's my oath to take care of the sick and downtrodden," he said, giving the door to the clinic one last look. "I need more supplies. Don't give her any medicine, no matter how much she begs. Her sickness is in here," he said as he tapped his skull twice. "All the medicine in the world won't heal that wound."

"Dr. Alfred!" Catherine shouted from inside the clinic.

"Be careful. I will take care of everything." Gayle gave him a quick hug. He passed her, still shaking.

Gayle entered the clinic with a practiced smile. She had never spoken to Catherine before here and somehow found the whole situation bizarre, but then her life had never been normal.

"Alfred will be busy with other patients for the rest of the day," Gayle said, projecting her voice over the woman's shouts.

Catherine quieted. "Oh…it's you." She held the thick white cotton sheet to her chin, despite wearing an equally thick, long wool nightgown.

"How are you feeling, Ms. Miles?" she asked, walking to a small icebox.

"A little better than yesterday, but I still need more pain medication. Why is that damn doctor so stubborn?"

"We spoke about this before, Ms. Miles. The medication will get you hooked, and then there will be another set of problems."

"Horse shit!" Catherine snorted. "I don't get addicted." She leaned back in the bed against five large pillows.

Gayle shook her head, opening the icebox. "What will it be? We have chicken soup, beef, and beans, or veggie."

"I want lobster!" Catherine called out.

Gayle stretched her neck to peek over the edge of the door. She narrowed eyes at the erratic CEO. They also had this conversation yesterday. She remembered telling Catherine there was a food shortage, and they only had limited selections for the patients. She really wanted to tell her that she was in the Downs, and luxury items such as lobster and real food were denied to the Downs residents. Inhaling, she returned her attention to the contents of the icebox. Alfred advised her and Gabriel not to reveal where the clinic was. He did not want it to get shut down or have to deal with Dome security.

She respected his request but still found Catherine's constant demands for the impossible nerve-racking. Alfred could barely spare the pain medication the spoiled CEO sucked down in the first two days in the clinic.

"Did you hear me?" Catherine spoke again.

Gayle pressed her lips together and shook her head. "We ran out of lobster last week, Catherine, but still have ten units of veggie. I can heat one up for you." She grabbed the soup pack, not really waiting for an answer.

"Veggie, did I ever taste the veggie?"

Gayle closed the metal door and held up the icepack for Catherine to see. "This will cook in a few seconds. You won't have to wait for long."

Catherine appeared to glare at the offending veggie pack. Her mouth set in a stubborn pout that David gave her many a time. Then almost in an instant, a small smile replaced the pout.

"So what's with the Gabriel? Tell me about him," Catherine said.

Gayle stiffened. She never spoke to Catherine about Gabriel, avoiding the subject altogether. Gabriel made sure to not make himself noticed her. They all made sure that Gabriel would not become noticed.

"There isn't much to say," Gayle said and then turned back around, proceeding to prepare the dish.

"What do you mean, 'not much to say'? You live with it for seven months," she said.

Gayle counted her blessings when the soup cooked faster than anticipated. She grabbed a thick pair of gloves and removed the bowl, placing it on a nearby tray. She added a cool cup of water and tray of crackers.

Catherine continued to speak. "He does not appear to be like that other one. That one was so cruel and cold and…"

Gayle picked up the tray and carried it around to Catherine. The woman held a tortured expression. Gayle let out a mental groan, knowing that the bouts of depression would soon overwhelm Catherine's mind again. Alfred would be forced to severely medicate her again.

"Catherine!" she snapped.

This jolted the woman out of her funk for now. She looked over at the tray with wide eyes.

"Lean back," she said, softening her voice.

"Oh, you have the veggie right this time," Catherine said.

"Just right," Gayle said, placing the tray across her lap, then raised a hand to her heated forehead.

"I have to go in the other room for a moment, but I will be back."

Catherine watched, dazed, as Gayle took her leave. She adjusted the tray on her lap, picking up a spoon. She glanced up again, then back down at her tray. Gayle usually spoke more with her, about things going on about town. She loved talking about fashion and music. Safe subjects. Light talk. She dipped the spoon into the cloudy liquid. The veggie one always appeared thicker than the meat ones. She blew on the spoon and sipped on the edge, careful of the heat, and now consumed all her meals in short, measured sips. As Mother always said, "Quickly it goes in, quickly you blow up."

The door opened again. Her heart leaped when Gayle walked through but did not look her way. She wanted to call out but wondered if it would be proper or sound needy. Anyway, what did she care if the woman liked her?

"How's the soup?" Gayle pulled two blankets from a nearby shelf, then faced her, hugging the blankets to her chest.

"Not the lobster," she whispered.

"It is fine," she said loudly.

"How are you feeling?" Gayle approached her with a nonchalant expression. She thought it odd the woman rarely smiled.

"Not very well," Catherine said, placing her spoon back in the bowl and leaving it. She really did not want to eat, but it often worked when she wanted meds. "I tried to eat more this time. A pain in my side is really bothering me."

Gayle's face gave no indication that she would give in. "I wish I could help, but there are no more meds in the clinic."

"Why do you say that when there are so many things in Dome 16? So much more than the other fifty domes. I don't understand," Catherine said. She refused to believe there were no more meds. This was a clinic. Though not very large or prosperous, they still must have meds somewhere.

"I can't help you there." Gayle removed the tray from her lap, setting it on a nearby counter. "Besides, only a doctor should administer drugs, and Alfred is out on an errand."

"Help me? I don't need any help," Catherine scoffed. The stupid woman was really beginning to get to her. That doctor refused her request holding his power to administer the meds she needs to get better. Now his nurse or wife, whoever she is, refuses to give them to her. How dare they? Didn't they know who she was?

"I want more meds, Gayle. I am getting just about tired of this whole mess. I can get meds if I want to."

"Then why have you not left the bed, Ms. Miles? You have not called for the outside world to rescue you," Gayle said. Her dark eyes glowed.

"I could if I wanted to—" Catherine stopped. She was sure she could just walk out of there, but then again, this place felt so safe.

"Then why don't you?" Gayle challenged.

She narrowed her eyes. How dare the little sparrow question her strength? "I don't understand what the hell you're talking about."

"You don't understand? Then try to imagine this. Imagine punching your fist into a brick wall"—Gayle paused—"then you'll know."

*****

Gabriel's ear twitched when the door to the clinic slammed. He stood from the chair by David's bed. He rushed toward the open door to see Gayle stomp by with quickened and determined strides. He moved toward the door and opened it in time to see her retreating form head through a breeze way and heard her footsteps ascending the nearby staircase. He almost rushed over when she stumbled but knew her temperament enough to know that an innocent helping hand would not be welcomed at this time.

He just followed until they arrived at the rooftop. She ran to the edge and leaned a thick wall that came shoulder high to her. He regarded her breathing in and out. Her mouth pressed together until her chin trembled. He imagined this was caused by the wounded Catherine Miles. Alfred escaped the sanctuary of his own home to be far from the annoying woman.

"Gayle," he said.

She froze, raising watery red eyes to him. "Gabriel…did I wake you?"

He smiled. "You know I don't sleep." He continued forward on light feet.

She spared him a smile, though small. "Yeah, I see."

"What has happened between you and Ms. Miles?" he asked, standing beside her.

Gayle's eyes went downward. "She has been very difficult."

"I am sorry," he whispered.

Her hand landed on his bicep. He felt an immediate comforting thought. "Don't be," she said. "She needed your help."

"She causes you distress."

"Her kind causes me distress. Shame on me for letting her get to me. I should be used to it."

"No, you shouldn't." He pulled her by the arm closer to him. His arm surrounded her, engulfing her. He felt her arms glide up his sides. Her face buried into his chest. Then the floodgates opened. He held her body as the tears fell.

"When will this end?"

"Please do not worry. I will take care of everything," he murmured.

He felt Gayle move back. He released her. She beheld his face, laying a slender hand on his jaw. The moment froze for them. The air felt heated and charged. Though he only experienced quick pecks and lingering touches, he felt a change in this intimate setting. She guided his head down to her level. He followed, happy, elated, then confused and curious. Their lips pressed and deepened.

As fire to ice, a jingle from his phone rented the air. Gayle jumped almost a foot away. Her dark eyes widened. He gasped for air, trying to suck in as much as let out. The jingle continued, and for the first time, he cursed, shoving his hand in his pocket to retrieve. "Gabriel."

"Guard Gabriel, you are being called to duty."

Gabriel thought this odd. His request for vacation time was approved. "I thought my request went through."

"I apologize for this, but we need every able-bodied guard. You are required to report early morning tomorrow. See you there." Then the line went dead.

He lowered the phone. This could only mean Delilah had not completed her rampage.

"What is it?"

"Delilah has caught the attention of Dome guards," he said.

"It's for the best, Gabriel. She is dangerous. Now will you let them handle things?"

Gabriel nodded. However, he knew Dome guards would be no match for his sister. Delilah had many years of strategic military experience programmed into her. His father under her mental coercion gave her enough firepower to take on multiple Dome armies. He did not want to ever relay this to Gayle, knowing her fear would evolve into crippling anxiety.

"At least they are giving me until the morning. I will spend every moment with you and David until then."

She nodded and took him by the hand. "Let's have a little party." They walked back down into the common room. "Do you think you could use that sleeping trick you do on our patient?"

Gabriel grew solemn. "It will not be wise to expose her to that kind of power. It may crack her. I will not feel good with hurting someone."

"I'm sorry, Gabriel. I didn't mean to suggest—"

"It was a thought." He chuckled and held her hand tight. She laughed, catching on to his humor. *So this is what really makes one human.* It was the one code he tried many times to crack. He realized the problem with it all was that he simply overthought the concept. Impulsiveness and uninhibited joy—that is what he missed.

Chapter 23

CHIEF CLEANDER OBSERVED THE neurotic, precarious Dr. Hawthorne twist his hands in a literal knot. He sneered at the fellow and wanted to wash his own mouth just hearing the coward spew some garbage. He ceased listening a minute into the conversation. Personally, he would have liked the weasel to just disappear in his presence, but now he must endure him.

"You want me to waste valuable manpower to retrieve some female!" Cleander snapped.

"She is one of the testers we have been looking for. I need to examine her." Dr. Hawthorne rubbed his hands together.

"Why do you feel the need to examine her?" Cleander asked, delighting in the way the man continue to squirm.

"She has been in proximity to them longer than anyone. She will have some residual chemical effects I can use."

"Or she could be useless, and my guards' time would have been wasted on this fruitless endeavor." Cleander leaned back in his seat. "This will take more thought on my part. You will allow me until noon to decide to lend you my guards."

"But…but—"

"I will send for you, Dr. Hawthorne, when I have made my decision," Cleander said, pinning the man with a dark glare. This really ruffled the elder man's fortitude causing him to storm from his office.

After the doctor hustled out of his office, he dismissed the man from his mind. There were more important matters to attend. The thief of the guardian bodies rattled him more than he wanted anyone to know of. He held on to this secret, allowing a few of his officers to know about it. He even jailed the bumbling lab tech, imprisoning the little man's voice.

"Sir." A staff sergeant appeared in the doorway of his office.

He rose from his chair and glanced at a tall, solid-looking young man with an eager face. Most of his experienced officers remained in the field searching for the deadly creation from Divine Cybernetics. He did not care to surround himself with the inexperienced. They proved to be more problem than their worth.

"Has anyone called in yet, Sergeant?" Cleander stabbed the man with a serious glare, causing the sergeant to visibly shake.

"No one has called in, Chief," the sergeant said.

Cleander growled but really wanted to scream with frustration. The situation as it stood had everyone walking on eggshells and jumping every time the wind blew or someone coughed. He felt the apprehension in every passing member of the compound. Outwardly he met it all with solid determination. Inwardly his resolve started to crack.

"Send word to those guards. I want twenty-four-hour monitoring. No breaks, no excuses. Anyone who does not do their job answers to me."

"But, sir—" The sergeant started. His voice grew more uneven.

Cleander regarded the younger man's trembling lips and darting eyes. He let out a mental groan, maintaining his staunch, unmoving demeanor. "Tell me now, Sergeant. Time is wasting, boy."

"We are scarce in manpower. We may need to call in reserves from our sister, Dome 3."

The last thing he wanted to do was call the Dome 3 chief security guard. He didn't need to see the future to know how wide the smirk on Chief Heather's mouth would be.

"We don't want to waste their time. This is just a minor problem. No need to involve Dome 3," Cleander said.

"Yes, sir."

"Are you sure everyone is accounted for?"

A thoughtful look spread over the sergeant's face. He reached into a knapsack handing on his shoulder producing a small handheld computer and proceeding to typing on the glass screen. "The only one left to call is Guard Gabriel. He actually awaits new orders downstairs."

The man looked up.

"All guards are already in the field."

"Good. I will take him with me. You stay here to run interference with Dome government. I don't need the damn bureaucrats in my business," Cleander said, then grabbed his jacket before passing the sergeant in the empty common area.

"Yes, sir."

Cleander marched toward the elevators. The heavy fall of his thick black boots echoed through the room. His thoughts turned toward more personal avenues such as the administrator and her current health status. The medics told him about her ranting last night. They gave her heavy sedatives, so he could not speak with her.

Really, he had just been content watching her sleep. He demanded the slimy physician, Dr. Hawthorne, to tell him her diagnosis. He remembered the man's fevered expression when explaining how the guardians had all been equipped with some hypnotic brain power per request of the Dome government.

"You see, Chief," Dr. Hawthorne said to him, "children's minds are just developing and learning. They are malleable and can absorb the pressure of the hypnotic suggestion, but as adults, our minds slow down and become less malleable. If pressed, our brains break, and we experience trauma. The guardians were not meant to use this power on adults. Once applied, it leads to nerve damage. A longer exposure leads to coma or even death."

He did not want to think of the last one happening to the administrator.

Even though her time there had been short, she proved to be a valuable asset, not only to Dome guards but also to him. He never would have known about the guardians or the Dome government's involvement. She sent the evidence to his home computer before that night. Now he saw everything with crystal vision.

The elevator doors slid open, revealing the expansive glass-enclosed entrance. At this time of day, there would have been a hive of activity but now a wasteland. Except for one person standing near the entrance looking out toward the winged ivory stature of a nude male standing in a triumph stand.

The man must be Guard Gabriel, but nothing prepared him for the sight of the man, a truly magnificent specimen of a soldier— tall, powerful, broad. How much did the man bench? He watched Gabriel turn around to face him; his handsome, serene face and his blue eyes showed intelligence and assuredness, unlike the sergeant, who he could never take into a decent battle when it all came down to it.

"Guard Gabriel," Cleander said, coming forward. He stopped within a foot of the guardsman.

Gabriel executed the perfect Dome guard's salute and stood at attention. "Here for my new orders, Chief."

"I need a driver. You're with me." Cleander walked past him. "I only have two rules: keep up and don't ask questions."

They walked out of the building together toward a large black vehicle. Gabriel hurried around the driver's side as Cleander entered the passenger side. They entered together, then regarded each other.

"I suppose we will get along well together," Cleander said.

"Of course, sir," Gabriel said, then started the engine. "Where shall the first stop be?"

"Divine Cybernetics."

*****

The room spun in a spiral around her. Delilah clutched her

head between her hands screaming. He took everyone away from her, their siblings and now her prize. She knew it had to be Gabriel. He wanted to end her fun. He wanted her to be bored and alone. How cruel could he get?

She glared at the tattered bed with portions of sheets hanging dejected at the sides and discolored cushions bursting from the thin covering. Her footsteps echoed a solitary doom as they carried her further into the room. Gabriel's scent, however faint, hung in the air. Funny that she never sensed him in the Dome security's lab, but he had been here. Where he came from last was how she would find him.

Closing her eyes, she followed his trail. Once she opened them again. She found herself in a small dimly lit bedroom; a narrow bed took up the entire left side of the room while on the right, a simple square wooden desk and chair took up the space. A small lamp bathed the room in yellow and green reminding her of summer in Uptown when she took the children to the park.

She strolled over to the bed where a fat, furry brown bear sat with obsidian-crystal eyes staring at the ceiling and a permanent black-thread smile across his round, flat face. The bear reminded her of Olivia's before the one of the lab techs took it away. Olivia cried for days. It was the first time any of them ever expressed such a strong emotion. Gabriel tried to comfort her, but it was Delilah who prevailed, telling her of a beautiful future where they would play forever in a field of green.

She lowered onto the ruffled brown wool bedcovers, reaching for the bear. She looked into the bottomless eyes, searching for a way or a path. Suddenly, faint voices brought her out of the memories of the past. She lifted her eyes to the door.

"How long have you been friends with Alfred?" a small voice asked.

"A long time, love." A little voice spoke to him, then chuckled. Delilah recognized the small voice of Gabriel's small charge—the one whom he had formed an uncommon attachment to. She simply could not understand it. Her charges never sparked such disgusting sentimental feelings in her, shackles she started to despise. However, Gabriel saw David as something to cherish, like some precious metal. Her demeanor dropped. Her hands curled in a ball around the bear.

"I will get my book from my room, and we can read." The small boy's footsteps grew louder.

"Okay, honey. I will be waiting in the family room." The woman's voice sounded fainter.

Delilah rose from the cot as the door opened. David bounced into the room. He did not notice her at first, skipping over to the low built-in bookcase. She mentally closed the door shut. He froze from his position twisting his small head toward the door. She observed him from the shadows of the bed. A smile returned to her lips.

"Hello, David," she whispered.

His head twisted toward the bed this time. She emerged from the shadows watching the surprised expression on his face. Then he smiled. "Hello, Delilah. Where have you been?" he asked, skipping over to her.

She lowered down on the cot, patting the empty space on the bed. "I had to solve some issues for a while, but I am back now. How has everything been?"

He took her invitation, hopping up beside her on the bed. "Okay, I guess." He sounded down.

"What's wrong?"

"Gabriel and Mommy have been really sad since ole man Gregory had a heart attack."

A blond brow rose. "Oh, yeah?"

"Yeah." He shrugged his shoulders. "I think they are trying to keep themselves busy to not be so sad, but they go away without me."

"Where are they now?"

"Gabe went back to work, and Mommy went out to the shops with Alfred."

"She left you all alone?" She reached an arm around his narrow shoulders.

David shrugged his shoulders again. "Mr. Alfred's friend, Ms. Rachel, is here."

"Well, she is not your mother." She pulled him to her side.

He nodded, staying silent.

"You want to be with Gabriel, don't you?" She read his thoughts.

David nodded, causing his fro of dark curls to bounce around. "I wanted to see his uniform, but he already left."

Delilah feigned a pout. "How disappointing for you." She wrapped an arm around his small shoulders. "I bet he would love it if we go and visit him."

David's face lit up. "We can visit him for a short while, but how do we get to Gabriel?"

She gave him a hungry smile. "Magic," she whispered.

The room around them distorted.

"Delilah, we have to leave a note for Mom," David said.

"We will give her a call," Delilah said. A slight smile spread across her lips. If her brother wanted to play hide-and-seek, she would be happy to oblige him.

*****

The day they denied the sun to Dome 16 caused great upheaval even to the people of the Downs who barely felt it. Now the Uptown citizens roared in their disbelief of the treatment. How could the Dome Council condone it? Gayle and Alfred walked along the crowded shopping stalls and heard the angry cry of the Downs citizens.

"This does not sound good," Gayle said, peering around them, hugging her wicker basket to her side. She heard the ramblings before and knew it often led to violent riots, glancing around the marketplace. Downs citizens started to form in clumps. Their faces twisted in outrage and frustration.

"We better make the herbal stand our last stop." Alfred spoke. He turned toward the seller and rambled out his request.

Gayle nodded. She peered around again.

"I got them…we better head back the short way."

"That will be best." She swallowed hard, increasing her pace.

The short way proved to also be a physically difficult track. It involved them cutting through abandoned buildings and through large conduits dripping with foul slime and muddy water that stunk so much her eyes teared up, but they managed to arrive home in half the time and safe from the impending violence.

"I'm going straight to the shower," she said, handing the wicker basket to Alfred.

"Me too," and they headed toward the individual bathrooms.

Gayle eagerly ripped off her clothes, relieved to be free of the foul, heavy clothing. She turned the hot nozzle on high. She slipped into the low tub and stood still, closing her eyes, allowing the water to blast the dirt from her skin.

She took the downtime to organize her day in her head. The first priority was David. They rarely spent some alone time together. She felt guilty that he was removed from his friends and school. He needed stability, and with a heavy heart, she realized her failure in this area.

Gayle set out to search for David after her shower. Alfred's girlfriend, Rachel, told her that he went to play in his room but must have taken a nap because he remained quiet all day. She glanced at the dusty old grandfather clock. It read half past noon, and Rachel finished preparing lunch for everyone. The long wooden antique table in the dining room was never set. David never missed the opportunity to help.

"Alfred, have you seen David?" she asked, entering the common area.

Alfred lifted his head from the assortment of herbs he gathered. His brow creased. "Come to think of it, I have not heard from him since we arrived. I came back down after my shower to look for him, but he was not in his room. I thought he was with you."

She shook her head. "No." They stared at each other for a while, then headed together to the small room assigned to David. The bed did not look ruffled or slept in. The floor cleared of toys from the morning when she harassed him on the upkeep of his room.

"Where could he be?" She stood in the middle of the room, looking around. She stopped short of Alfred, who held a single long strand of blond hair. "Oh no!" She covered her mouth, stifling the scream that would come.

Alfred's grim face crumpled. "She could have taken him anywhere."

Gayle lowered herself on the edge of David's small bed. She remembered his small limp form from last night when he slept. He begged for a story but fell asleep within minutes of her starting it. Then she lingered. Now the bed seemed so abandoned without him. "I know where she has taken him."

"Really?"

"She wants Gabriel and is using my son to dangle in front of his face like bait."

"Wow! She is truly off!"

"I have to warn Gabriel."

*****

Delilah leaned back in the chair observing the crowd passing before her, clueless on what she had in store for them. The robotic security detail provided minimal presence in the Uptown terminal. Their cybernetics technology was so low they would fail to understand any kind of disturbance. She struggled to hold on to her mirth watching the lower-class android and the humans clash.

"I like strawberry the best," David said, pulling her away from the scene.

"I agree. Strawberry is the best." She dipped her own spoon into the frozen gooey treat.

David's face creased in mirth. His mind never spared a thought that impending chaos surrounded him. She found it easy to block him from the awareness. She felt a tinge of jealousy at the pure innocence of the child never touched by the cold brutality of reality. The spoonful of the treat slid into her lips. She moved the creamy, frozen treat around her mouth until it melted. She waited for the same affects David felt, but they never came. No exhilaration or no uninhibited joy. Her mind still craved satisfaction that refused to be sated by some paltry treat.

"David," she said.

His dark eyes watched her face. "Yes?"

She leaned closer on her elbows. "I need to speak with the controller of the terminal so that he can call your mom. Will you be a good boy and stay here?"

"Yes."

"Good, boy," she said and then rose from the table, turning her attention once more to the chaos at the center of the terminal. *Of course, things could get better,* she thought, leaving the table.

She strolled along the perimeter of the crowd stuffing her hands in the pockets of her coat, whistling a lit tune she recalled hearing in the Downs. Ahead of her, the stairs leading to the controller room was left unguarded. She found it an easy track ascending them up to the glass-enclosed room.

The controller left the door partial open. She shook her head at the mindless human. Dome authority should have fully robotized the terminals. Human had a way of making silly mistakes. She slipped into the room closing the door behind her. The constant hum and clicking sounds filled the silence of the room, and blinking red lights flashed over the surface of the metal walls and counters.

Delilah increased her progress toward the two large windows overlooking the expansive common area of the terminal. The hexagonal shape gave an impressive dimension to the interior that stopped her for a moment to observe the dynamic design, but she thought it would be easier to admire, littered with little white dots.

She pressed a hand over one of the panels, feeling the electricity travel up her arm to her brain, then hurled back down to her fingertips into the central brain of the terminal. In moments, the sprinkler system showered the main area with a constant cascade of water. The angry chorus of citizens sung like a demon choir. Then the alarm bellowed an ear-piercing scream bringing the humans to their knees. All at once, fires burst from odd areas of the terminals. The terminal androids that were not waterproof grew stiff at their current locations, and those who withstood the water tried to rush to their mechanical brothers and sisters struggling to understand the malfunctions.

Delilah's hand lifted from the panel. She folded her arms across her chest and chuckled at the scene. Her belly signed finally sated for the moment. She turned away from the scene leaving the controller room at a quick pace.

David still sat at the table eating his strawberry treat unfazed by the disorder around him. The large umbrella he sat under protected him from the torrent water. When she joined him again, her own force shield heightened their protection. She finally turned away from the excitement and once again joined in the sweet strawberry treat.

Chapter 24

GABRIEL STOOD ASIDE AS Chief Cleander spoke with one of the Dome guard patrolling the grounds of Divine Cybernetics. The chief's face clouded further with anger and worry. He admitted that during their small time together, he started to sense the man's character was not like the other Dome managers. He realized the chief took his job as head of security to heart. He found the change in attitude refreshing and hopeful observing the man.

Suddenly he felt the phone buzz at his side. He reached down, bringing the phone to his ear. "This is Guard Gabriel."

"Gabriel, there is a disturbance at the Uptown terminal. Alert the chief." A man's desperate voice spoke with panic. In the background, he heard the cries and screams of human over the searing sirens of the Dome vehicles. Gabriel furrowed his brow as the noises drowned out the rest of the guard on phone report.

"Hey, I am having trouble understanding you." Gabriel spoke.

"The Uptown terminal has malfunctioned, and the citizens are uncontrollable," the guard said, then his voice completely disconnected.

He heard the cryptic sound of empty air. He glanced up as Cleander headed toward him after speaking with the guard. His face twisted in a worrisome cloud. Gabriel straightened and jogged to meet the chief halfway. "Sir, there is a disturbance at the Uptown terminal."

"What happened?" Cleander asked.

"The Uptown terminal computers malfunctioned, trapping a large group of citizens inside," Gabriel said, then stopped, listening to the man's heart rate increase tenfold. He feared the chief may have an impending cardiac failure.

"Are you all right, sir?" Gabriel asked.

Cleander snapped his back, then narrowed his eyes. "Sure, why do you ask?" He walked past him toward their vehicle. He had his phone to his head. "I need two Dome guard vehicles."

Gabriel followed him, remaining silent. He wondered if the man ever experienced a moment of peace since he took the position of chief.

Gabriel maneuvered the car out of the parking lot and sped through the city. Two other vehicles eventually followed them forming a caravan through Uptown. The tall, sleek, and chrome glass tower rose before them in the horizon. Even from their far-off location, he heard the sirens and the screams of the citizens.

Above them, three Dome guard F-34s flew, circling the tip of the tower. He noticed the large metal shutter doors covered all the windows, so the tower looked like a thick metal shell. He stopped the vehicle at the edge of the crowd and shut down the engine.

"Who closed the doors?" Cleander whispered beside him.

"The computers malfunctioned, trapping the commuters inside," Gabriel said. "They have been trying to get the main system back online, but it is not responding."

Cleander cursed. "Let's see what's going on."

They exited the vehicle and approached a group of guards. One of them broke away from the group and marched up to them. He saluted sharply.

Cleander acknowledged the guard. "How are the citizens faring in there?"

The guard's face turned grim. "We are not getting any response from anyone inside."

"What about the androids?"

The guard shook his head. "They are not responding. I have

contacted the controller from Dome 3. He is going to see if they can tap into our server from the master."

"Shouldn't this be automatic?" Cleander asked.

Gabriel backed away from the pair peering up at the towering Uptown terminal. He felt an odd sensation come over him. His neck hairs stood up at the nape of his neck. The nerves under his skin tingled. He shifted his body from one foot to the neck. He lowered his glaze and peered around observing the worried faces of the humans. The Uptown citizens never experienced much chaos in their lives on the hill. So something like this would be a shock to their system.

He continued to look around when he saw a familiar face. He stopped and felt frozen in space. Delilah stood with a calm expression. His mind whirled on the reasons for her presence. She never interested herself in human matters. The situation would be a paltry curiosity to her.

Maybe it was not her.

Gabriel blinked his eyes twice. *It could not be her,* he told himself. Delilah would not dare show her face in clear view of the Dome guards. He even would bet that some of the council members were present as well. *What will she do? Will she finally expose them in her crazy pursuit of attention?* He pressed his lips in a thin line darting his eyes over to Cleander standing over a few feet away from her. His broad back turned away, giving rapid-fire orders to the other guards. Never knowing the true danger stood only minutes. He stared at her profile. As always, she painted her face in that ridiculous silvery-pink hue she favored, which matched her silvery-pink minidress. Her attention was focused on the terminal, oblivious that she stood out from the humans in their gray-and-white starch clothing. Then taking him by surprise, she twisted her attention to him. A gleeful and cheery expression was painted across her face. She waved to him frantically like he had been some long-lost relative, then beckoned him forward.

He hesitated, glancing around again. *Why will she want him to come over to her? She must know that he had every intention on holding her to crimes. She could not be so clueless.* Inhaling, he made a move toward her trying to negotiate through the tight spaces among the humans.

Hurry, Brother! Delilah's voice drifted in the wind. *We'll wait for you inside.*

Then a picture popped into his head—an image of David seated at a small round table, eating a large strawberry icy treat. *Is this real?* he wondered. Suddenly, his phone at his hip jingled. He reached down. "Hello?"

"Gabriel!" Gayle's shaky voice drifted over the earpiece.

"Gayle, what's wrong?"

"David is gone…and I…I believe Delilah must have taken him," she said.

"The vision is true."

"Vision?" she sniffled.

"He is in the Uptown terminal. It has been shut down, and I think Delilah had something to do with the terminal computers malfunctioning."

"What happened?"

"The Uptown terminal shut down all of a sudden, trapping a number of the commuters inside," he said.

"Oh no! Gabriel, David is in there! I must get there!"

"No, you stay. I will bring him home, but you stay."

"I can't! I can't! I must be there!"

"There is no way you can be here. Listen, Gayle. Even with you here, the Dome guard will not let you get past. You cannot expose yourself. Please wait."

"Fine, but you bring my baby back! Please!"

"I will," he said. He squeezed the phone until he heard the definite crack of the hard, plastic casing. He allowed the pieces to crumple to the ground but ignored the mess to focus his attention on the front entrance of the terminal. He sprinted toward the entrance, his body a blur to anyone who might have seen him.

Cleander realized Gabriel disappeared after an hour. He scanned the crowd searching for the tall fair-haired guard. It should not have been hard to find Gabriel. The guard's unusual height and gloss-perfect countenance stood out from the twisted broad faces and short statures of the wealthy residences. *Is he doing crowd control?* He observed the alarming increase of onlookers surrounding the terminal. It irritated him that the guard did not await his command regarding crowd control, but then again, it did need to be done.

"Sir, I believe they found a way inside the terminal through the duct system in the roof." A rookie approached him with eager dark eyes.

"Okay, then, we will have to hurry!"

Chapter 25

GABRIEL STOOD AMONG THE pile of prone bodies of the unconscious commuters. The terminal's dim lights only allowed him to see a few feet ahead, but he never solely relied on his vision these days. Instead, he also felt with his psychic feelers. They saw farther than any physical eyes. Then he felt him. The really only awake mind in the iron tomb. *David!* His mind screamed. He sprinted forward through the maze of bodies and shops.

Until he saw the little dark-haired boy seated at a table like in his vision. David flipped through a body, swinging his legs, and periodically scooping a dripping cool glop into his mouth.

"David," he called out. His voice bounced off the hollow walls, but David did not seem to hear him.

He looks cozy waiting for you. She spoke into his mind.

"Delilah, if you hurt him," he called out.

"Then what?" Delilah stepped into view. She leaned against a thick metal column.

"Let him go," Gabriel stated the fact, stomping forward. His wrath topped off with his sister's presence.

"I don't think so. Not yet anyway. Not until you tell me where the others are." She pushed away from the column. "So don't you get all violent again." Her eyes made a gradual change from the cool blue to a brutal glowing red.

"They are safe from your influence," he growled.

She sneered, "Do you mean to convince them of their own superiority over these pathetic beings you have aligned yourself with?"

"This is a dangerous game, Delilah. Father finally understood it. Look what happened to him."

"He only made one mistake." She made a gesticulation with her hand. "I am here to remedy it, or rather…you."

Gabriel lurched forward, but his movements—something slowed his attack. Around him, the temperature reduced to freezing, and the water from the sprinkler system turned to snow.

He looked down to see his own feet encased in solid blocks of ice.

"You should have paid more attention to Father than that pathetic monkey," she sneered, revealing rows of sharpened teeth.

"Delilah, stop this!" he yelled.

"No!" she yelled back. "For once, Brother, you will be denied your wishes. You will no longer be the alpha of this pack, leading us into degrading servitude to this race. I will not allow it anymore!"

Blasts of wind swooshed through, causing him to hold up his arms. His worry now was that the low temperatures Delilah conjured would bring negative effects to the unconscious humans in the terminal.

He reached out to David. His eyes popped open, realizing that Delilah invoked some illusion in his mind. Dr. Gregory increased Delilah's mental control over the area of the brain for the subconscious, but doing this would make her unstable and even more so prone to unbound anger. In all essence, it was his father's revenge. This time, she chose to manipulate his brain. He had to find her inside himself to figure her out.

Inhaling, he closed his eyes, seeking out the essence she might have left in his brain. Images flowed through his mind—dark twisted figures with grotesque bony faces. Dark and gloomy music flowed through his head too. He came close to Delilah many times, but she always slipped away. He knew she wanted the location of their siblings, but he kept that secret buried, but what if he gave her what she wanted?

Delilah, I am tired of running. I am weak with worry over my family. I will give you anything just let them go. He sent the thought inside his head.

Tell me where they are, and I will let your family go.

"Then I will tell you," he whispered, "but you will have to come get it."

An image of Delilah appeared before him, but not what he expected. She stood in a pink ruffled dress, white stockings, and shiny white shoes with gold buckles. She smiled with even white teeth, and her blond hair twisted in soft long ringlets about her round face.

"Tell me where they are, Big Brother. Then we can play." She skipped up to him.

He reached his hand to grasp her gloved hand. "Why have you chosen this image?"

She shrugged her narrow shoulders. "Do you need to know everything?"

"Still the same, Delilah," he said.

The images cleared, and now they ended in a black void. Suddenly, the image of the common area at the lab appeared. They often gathered here to await the scientists. The common area also served as neutral territory whenever a disagreement arose among the siblings. Of course, the humans never knew this. He made sure that in front of them, the guardians acted like obedient drones.

"Our old home?" Delilah loosened her grip on his hand, but he refused to let go. "Do you remember the last time we were all together?"

"Yes, I know." She tried to pull away again. "Hey! Let go!"

"Stop this game! You will not have your way!" he said. "Show me the old you."

She looked up at him. "Let go," she whispered.

He released her, wanting to know what other games she had up her sleeve. <<Make this longer. Why would he let her go?>>

They walked through a maze of subconscious images. Delilah's memories started light and happy. The day the others emerged from their artificial wombs—he saw this from Delilah's perspective where she roamed the warm, damp chamber bumping into the others, touching them, and grabbing their hands and hairs. Her young face etched in confusion.

"How stupid we were. We should have rebelled even then," Delilah said.

Gabriel remembered that day. His father sprinted about the lab, excited, taking him over to the screens that showed the five children in their chamber. Their father whispered, "Your family has arrived, Gabe, more perfect angels."

Chapter 26

"DAMNIT," CLEANDER CURSED. HE inhaled and raised his foot on the platform, then it slipped again. He let out three curses—one for the slip before, the current one, and the last slip. If there were a fourth one, he would call the idiots in mechanical and really lay into them. His eyes looked back at the other seven guards who followed him. Their amused glances earned them an annoyed glare from him. They quickly averted their eyes away. He focused his attention on the descent.

Cleander regarded the barely lit tunnel below them. The climb to the ventilation shaft had been easy enough, but the descent proved to be tedious and trying. They had yet to pass the roof section of the terminal tower.

He took another look at the hologram map on his forearm. Another shift in level would have the team depending solely on the thick black ropes of their climbing gear and the anchors. They would be rappelling down into the tube. He hoped the engineer did not make an error in reading the terminal's system shut down because at the end of the tube would be a large metal fan that would be a border between them and the internal ducts that would take them into the fourth floor of the terminal.

"Sir, communication from the Dome Council," a guard called down to him.

Cleander's brow creased. *Did those fools think my warnings do not involve them?* He advised that reports would be sent as soon as they made penetration.

"Okay," he exhaled. "Connor, take the lead. I will be right behind you." He moved aside to allow the others to pass him. He pressed the button of his ear com. "Chief here." He spoke.

"Cleander. I was surprised your guard answered my call." The uppity tone of Councilman Ian came through. "I tried to get your line, but you never answered."

"Councilman, I told you that once we secured the terminal, I would contact you with a report."

"Quiet, Cleander. I don't give a damn about insignificant citizens. I had the engineers in our sister Dome 3 play the cameras. They saw a rather attractive blond woman in the command room just before everything went black."

"What was she doing there?"

"Let's just say she was not picking out color schemes."

"Terrorists? But how the hell did she get past the terminal robots?"

"It is obvious your people aren't doing their jobs. That's why I keep the big dogs watching the puppies," the councilman growled. "I thought we squashed those rebelling Downs citizens. You said the matter was handled."

"Wait a minute, Councilman. This operation appears a little more sophisticated than what the rebels are able to do. I mean, shutting down the terminal system. The only people who knows this system are Dome engineers. Aren't your people handling internal high-end rebels?"

The councilman objected. "I want to know who that woman is and how the hell she got past our security!"

"Let me do my job, and I will have that answer for you," Cleander muttered. He knew for a while that the sleeper agent sent over from Dome 3 had a target on her back. He tried to warn the cocky hardhead, but according to her, she had a handle on the issue.

"You better have this solved soon. My patience is thinning, and I have people to answer to!"

"I don't take lightly to threats. If you want my job, then I will be happy to take my men and go have a drink after I finish what I've started here."

"Now, Chief, let's not let our tempers run too hot. Like you, I want this whole nasty business to be over and done."

"As I said before, once I have secured the terminal and ensured all citizens are safe, I will report back," he said.

The councilman reluctantly agreed. Cleander ended the line, grappling with his riot emotions. Ian really had a boner for control. No wonder they were in this mess in the first place. He shook his head, then hurried to catch up with the squad of Dome guards.

Once he saw the back of the smaller last guard, he yelled out, "Halt!"

The guards obeyed, waiting for him.

"I got word that this is a possible hostage-and-terrorist situation. I want everyone to be on extreme guard. Eyes and ears." Cleander watched every face to ensure they gave him a silent confirmation that they understood. "Move on!"

Their pace quickened more so than before. His heart heaved a large relief when he saw the large metal ventilation fan. The sharp knifelike blades glittered in the white light of their body lights. Their descent changed to a complete vertical now. They climb through the large spacing between the blades. Then the guards slid down the slick metal surface landing with a hard thud. The men quieted and hunched down waiting for any incoming attack, but everything remained quiet.

Cleander read the hologram on his arm again. They would be able to get able to gain entrance into the terminal's upper floors. He reminded everyone again to be on alert as once again he took the team lead, moving through the smaller tubes. Each guard would wait five minutes before following after their team member.

He found the penetration point and soundlessly lifted one of the large rectangular sections away to reveal a dim, wide corridor, jumping down onto the floor. Careful not to make much of an echo, he stood up and motioned for the others to follow while he patrolled around.

Cleander felt the first freezing wave hit him, and it went to the bone. Despite the heavy, thick clothing he wore, his body shivered uncontrollably. As he walked to the end of the corridor, he noticed ghostly fingers of frost crawling across the metal walls; reaching out with his gloved hand, he scraped his palm across the surface.

"Is that frost, sir?" Connor, his second-in-command, spoke behind him.

"It appears so," he muttered, "but why is this building so cold?"

"It feels like Downhill." Another guard spoke.

"Sir," Connor continued, "I thought the sun was still out in Uptown. We need the light to make sure everyone is safe."

"The sun is still out," Cleander said. "This must be caused by something internal." However, the engineers told him that the air conditioner was only supposed to cool the servers in the command room. So he feared his theory really did not hold water. He turned away from the wall taking a mental count of how many teams of two he would need to cover everything. He knew that Guard Copper Vali just joined the Dome guard a week ago when their numbers took a hard drop. She stood apart from the other guards and smaller than the rest. Connor recommended taking her along if they needed to crawl into even smaller spaces that the others would not be able to slip through. He was only able to speak to her briefly, but they had a timetable to meet. It would be a smart move if he paired himself with her, especially if terrorists still occupied the lower levels of the terminal.

Cleander directed the other three teams of two to take sections of the three upper floors. He and Copper would cover the terminal's main transit area. They took the stairs, noticing the closer they descended into the main terminal, the temperature dropped even more. The sweat on his brow even froze in place. He wiped his forehead often to prevent the frosty beads of sweat from reaching his eyes.

Once they reached the main level, he pulled out his weapon before opening the door. In his side view, Copper did the same, then moved behind him, ready to follow. He slipped through the door into a narrow hall, and for the first time, he spotted dim bluish lights along the floorboards. They followed the lights to a lighted archway ahead.

At the threshold between the hallway and cavernous main transit area, the full assault of the disaster hit him. His heart pumped harder, and he breathed harder. He realized the reason no one responded to their speaker. All the passengers stuck behind the high walls appeared unconscious or dead. They seemed to have fallen where they stood when everything went wrong. Even the service bots lay immobile. His eyes glanced over the sea of the unfortunate, metal over flesh, flesh over metal, faces of the citizens frozen in an eternal sleep.

"Sir, are they dead?" Copper whispered behind him.

"I hope not," he whispered, approaching the body of an elderly woman nearest to them, chrome dusted over her sagging olive features. He held his flashlight over her mouth and nose. The slight disturbance in the air showed him that life still inhabited her body but barely. He stepped away taking in the intricate gold-laced silver dress. She was obviously someone of some wealth and prestige going about her day shopping and living a carefree existence.

The other citizens might be in the same predicament as this woman, but the odd state of the temperature concerned him. Himself shivering from the sting of cold, he could guess the unconscious citizens did not have much time.

"Sir, I hear voices," Copped whispered behind him.

Cleander lifted his head, training his ear to the sounds of the room. He heard them as well. They came from the other side of a wall of kiosk behind them. A familiar male voice floated over the room. His dark brow shot up. "Gabriel?" he whispered.

He jogged around the kiosk motioning for Copper to follow him. He pressed his body against a thin plastic wall, peeping around the corner. He saw the unmistakable form of Gabriel standing or rather frozen in place at full stride. A tall, slender blond woman walked around him fully free and mobile. She wore a curve-hugging white dress that stopped at midthigh and a pair of silver pumps that crack over the ice surrounding Gabriel's feet. Obviously, the cold did not bother this woman, and the delighted expression on her face was so out of character considering what surrounded them. Could this be the woman Ian spoke of? At first look, she appeared harmless. If he met her in a casual setting, he would have approached her and initiated a respectful dialogue. However, instinct prevailed, as he sensed her underlying danger even more so.

Gabriel wiggled causing the woman to laugh. The guard bared his teeth, and a strange, eerie light emitted from his eyes' sockets.

"Delilah, let everyone go. I will listen to your demands and help you find peace."

"Is that what you think I want?" The woman giggled. "We both know that peace is the furthest thing from my mind."

Cleander felt Copper behind him. He leaned back. "Keep quiet. Eyes and ears," he said. However, he wanted to know how Gabriel got in the terminal, and who the hell Delilah was.

"Chief, everything is clear in the upper floors. We will be coming your way soon," Guard Connor said through his earpiece.

"No, Connor," he whispered. "Gather everyone at the penetration point. Wait for my call."

"Yes, sir. Connor out," and the communication went dead.

Cleander looked back at the scene. His lips pressed together, and his mind raced. He did not want his guards to get excited and do the unpredictable. He hated the unpredictable, the unexpected, and the unknown. He preferred facts, solid facts—logical, predictable, and something he could fight.

"What are we going to do, sir?" Copper asked.

"Let's help Gabriel out of whatever this is," he muttered, then he would sit the inerrant guard down and blister him with a few thousand questions of his own. "Do you have your stinger on you?"

"Yes, sir."

"Here's what we will do." He leaned over to whisper in her ear. He would go to other end of the kiosk and start a distraction. Since the two women appeared to be of the same sort of stature and weight, he did not doubt Copper's ability to subdue the female in a harmless and efficient way.

"On my word," he said, slipping back around the wall of the kiosk and headed to the other side.

*****

Gabriel remained silent staring into the clouds of memories of their shared consciousness—the short past they alone shared when everything was new. He often wished those days never passed. His father and creator still took the task of teaching him instead of delegating it to lab techs.

"Gabriel!" she stomped her foot.

His attention focused on her once again. She grew increasingly impatient and sullen. Her temper flared. Her emotions started to unravel. He knew that soon she would not be able to think rationally.

"This is taking too long, Gabriel! Tell me where they are."

Just then, Gabriel pulled away from their mental connection. He heard a loud gasp from Delilah. Once again, they were in the terminal surrounded by the unconscious bodies of Uptown citizens. His sister stood before him. Her body seized behind her a small petite female held the black cartridge of a stinger.

"No!" he called out to her. He tried to lift his feet out of their icicle casings. He saw his commanding officer, Cleander, ran closer. He started to warn him that the stinger would not hold Delilah for long, but he did not get a chance. Delilah overcame her constraints and went after the small guard. They tumbled into each other until he saw Delilah's hands around the guard's neck. Her face twisted in a terror mask. Just then, Cleander grabbed her from the back, around her waist, trying to pull her off the guard, but to no avail, as his sister had a death grip on the guard's neck.

"Get off, damn you!" Cleander growled.

"She's stronger than you think, sir!" Gabriel called out. He managed to get one foot out of the ice block and worked harder on getting his other leg friend.

An animalistic growl came out of Delilah. She released Guard Copper to the ground and struggled with getting ahold of Cleander.

She elbowed him in the face with her elbow causing a smart bruise on the chief's chin.

Gabriel tried to subdue his sister mentally, but her state of mind was too far gone. At this point, he realized that controlling her was no longer an option. He could not control her. Her mind was diseased. She could kill without prejudice or thought.

"Copper, no, stand down!" Cleander called out.

At that moment, Delilah flung him off her back. The tall, hunky body of the chief flew several feet away. Guard Copper did not listen, as both men told her to not engage Delilah again. She ran toward his sister, who, this time, caught the smaller woman in a choke hold. Gabriel managed to get loose and fast paced over to the two women to separate them. An unmistaken bone cracked. However, he managed to grab his sister from behind, pulling her away from the guard who flew from them, hitting the opposite wall.

"We will leave this place in peace now," he whispered to her. He pulled them into a wormhole.

They emerged in the barren outlands far from the Earth domes, but he never loosened his grip on his sister. They wrestled. She tried to hit him with everything she had, eventually biting his forearm. Her sharp canines hooked into his skin. The pain proved overwhelming, but he held on, knowing that if he ever let go, he would never be able to get her back.

After I kill you, her thoughts linked with him again, *I will obliterate that sniveling little human and his bitch mother.*

Something snapped inside him. He screamed, now grabbing her

hair tightly and pulling it back along with her head. "It is time I shall release you." He opened his mouth while forcing her mouth open. She struggled even more, but her mouth opened. A light spilled out of her into him. He drank steadily without pause and held onto her body until it was no more.

He felt his knees hit the ground as his body could no longer hold up. He never took so much power in before and recognize the sick feeling in his stomach. Then waves of nausea crashed through him. He screamed out, rolling on his side, and for the first time, he cried holding his stomach. The riot of emotions spilled forward. Inside his head flashed Delilah's short, chaotic life through her eyes. "Please find peace," he whispered before closing his eyes, allowing the intense heat and dust to surround him.

Chapter 27

THE EXCITED VOICES JARRED Catherine awake. She blinked her eyes trying to adjust to the dimly lit room. The voices grew louder still, and they did not sound happy. She let out a tired groan, shaking the cloudiness in her head. She glanced around noting the missing empty vials and syringes. She frowned. They did not even trust the empty ones with her. Catherine swung her legs over the edge of her bed, sliding them carefully to the floor. The cold marble surface shocked her. She regretted turning down Gayle's offer of a pair of cotton socks. She waited for a moment, wiggling her toes trying to get the circulation flowing more rapidly through her system.

"I don't give a damn what Gabriel says!" she heard Gayle shout. Her eyes flew to the door.

She shuffled forward as Gayle's voice switched between crying and shouting. Alfred tried to calm her down, promising they would do anything to get David back. He started to speak again in his usual calm voice trying to reach through Gayle's distress. She heard the soft cries of the other woman, Rachel, in the distance.

Catherine reached for the handle of the door, pulling it slowly open. Through the narrow slit, she peered into the large common room. Gayle paced with restless fervor before the fireplace. Alfred stood in the center of the room stroking his bearded jaw with a pensive expression on his face.

"We have to find a way, Alfred. I will not wait another minute with my son in that thing's hands," Gayle said, finally stopping.

"I am sorry, Gayle. It may be a while, since the terminals all have been shut down. I just checked with one of the terminal clerks, and there's been some commotion at Uptown terminal."

"It's her…I just know it. It's Delilah causing this. She has some kind of chaos fetish!" Gayle spoke more sharply this time, earning her an annoyed look from Alfred, who, despite his calm tone, had a harassed expression on his face.

Catherine never really saw the doctor frazzled before even with her own constant demands for more pain meds. He normally just smiled, patted her hand, and told her to drink more water. She swallowed hard, thinking of the two weeks she lived in this place, actually lived in the hospital room no bigger than her linen closet in her penthouse. She never really ventured past this door, although no one locked it, and Gayle even mentioned that the rooftop was available for her.

"Gayle, it will take some time for me to come up with transportation," Alfred said in a steady voice. "Gabriel is right. You should stay here until he can send for you. I have to say he is pretty capable at dealing with his sister better than anyone. Have faith that he is capable of handling things."

"I know, but—" Gayle exhaled, lowering herself into a nearby chair. "David and I have never been apart like this. It just doesn't feel right."

Catherine also took a deep breath knowing this would be a huge step for her just crossing over the threshold, but she would have to help them. These people took better care of her than her own mother and father who just left her with robotic servants. These strangers took her in and ensured her safety without asking for payment or favors.

The high-pitched whining sound of the door opening drew the attention of the three occupants in the room. They turned toward her with wide eyes.

Alfred recovered first, approaching her with some caution. "Catherine, are you okay?"

Rachel stood as well. "Oh, honey, we did not mean to disturb you. It's just that—"

"I heard." Catherine held her hand up and walked further into the room. She faced Gayle and took a deep breath. "I am sorry for your son. I apologize to not have met him, but I have heard his…um voice through the wall."

Gayle shook her head. "Delilah was bound to try something like this. She needs something from Gabriel."

Catherine lowered herself on the chair beside Gayle, watching her, noting the oversized dark eyes had rings of red and black around the rim. "This is my fault."

"Believe me, you had a lot of help."

Alfred let out a sharp breath. "Gayle, please."

Catherine continued glancing around at the others. "We never thought it would end like this."

Gayle interrupted. "What did you people think would happen when you created these things to hurt others?"

"Gayle, it is not the time to place blame," Alfred said.

"I just never thought things would get so out of control." Catherine ignored him, wanting to get everything out of the open. She wanted them to understand but really did not know how to. "They told me that if I did this for them, if I convinced the doctor to go through with the guardian prototypes, Dome 16 would be the prime place to live. Divine's profits would increase. Dome 16 would be the new central power in all twenty of the Earth domes."

Alfred huffed. "Wow! Those are some lofty expectations. It reminds me of the madness of Hitler."

Catherine felt the tears come from behind her eyes and rose the back of her hand to her eyes before they appeared. "I admit that I should have checked my own selfishness, but…Divine Cybernetics has yet to establish wealth here like in Dome 3. I was eager to prove to everyone that I was better than my father, and those snakes at Dome Council feed on my ambitions and wanted to line their pockets."

"Isn't that what you wanted too?" Gayle asked.

Rachel came over to sit beside them. "Okay, you two, enough blaming. David needs us to be solid to get him home."

The shouting match between the two women stopped.

Catherine respected Gayle's angry but hoped the woman would accept her efforts to make things right. "I can help, but I will need to establish communication with Divine's headquarters to my people in Dome 3. My family's primary holding in one of the original domes still have loyal employees who must now be wondering if I am alive. They will be able to provide me with the reinforcements I will need to fight Dome 16 government."

Alfred spoke up. "I know some people. They can get your communication through despite the block."

Catherine's eyes drifted back over to Gayle. "Hopefully, it will not take much time to get out of the Downs."

The room fell silent. She glared at the three of them. "I may be sick, but I am not stupid. I can smell the stench from the vents. Now let me right this mess."

"Let me contact Ansel." Alfred left the room.

"Gayle—" Catherine started.

Gayle held up a hand. "Just promise me that Gabriel will not be pulled further into this malicious storm. He is innocent and deserves a happy life. You owe that to him."

Catherine nodded. "I promise to ensure no one touches him anymore."

Gayle felt the last fifteen minutes lasted an eternity. Alfred left twenty minutes prior to retrieve his friend who would, in turn, help Catherine reach her people in Dome 3. After he left, she confined herself to David's room down the hall, laying down on his small cot. Rachel suggested she take a small nap, but all Gayle could really do was just lay wide-eyed on the cot, taking in David's familiar scent of cinnamon and sugar cookies and citrus.

She smiled, remembering the cookie smell came from last night when they baked cinnamon and sugar cookies. She promised David that he could only eat two but suspected he ate more. The citrus smell came from the large block of soap she scored a couple of days ago from the marketplace. The seller drove a hard bargain, but in the end, she got her prize to her little son's enjoyment.

David raved about the bold and sweet smell from the soap promising to bathe five times a day. They laughed at his silliness, but his humor really elevated the stress everyone felt. Maybe this was why she felt his disappearance so much. The absence of David forced her to face the reality of their situation even more so. Her heart broke again, and new tears spilled forward.

Suddenly, a parade of footsteps echoed down the corridor. Alfred's low, rumbling voice echoed from the common room. Another voice followed after. She could not decipher if the person was a female or male as their voice resounded lower. *They must be here for Catherine,* she thought, shifting to an upright position. Somehow her body felt like lead, and the muscles in her legs protested the movement.

"Gayle"—Alfred knocked on the door—"Ansel is here. Do you want to come out?"

She frantically wiped her face with the cuffs of her long-sleeved shirt. "Yes, yes, I will be there."

"We will wait for you in the common area." Alfred retreated back down the hall.

Gayle slid off the cot and trudged to the door. Her eyes glanced around the small room one more time before she pulled open the door and headed toward the common area.

Rachel greeted her with a forced all-too-bright smile, then continued to buzz around the room picking up the remnants of the light lunch they had. Alfred had his back to her speaking to someone seated on the couch. His body blocked her view of Ansel, so she had to move around him.

Ansel sat in the center of the sofa. A petite and frail man, his pale, bony face held a grumpy, harsh expression. He spared her a brief glance, then continued fiddling with a small computer with a wooden shell.

Alfred stepped aside. "Gayle, I want you to meet Ansel," he said as he waved his hand toward the little man.

"Hi, Ansel," Gayle said and began to approach, holding out her hand.

Ansel glanced up again, regarding her with a piercing dark scowl. "A long greeting to you, young lady," he said, not rising to take her hand. He continued to dedicate his attention to the task at hand. Gayle thought his actions were rude but knew that as a Downhiller, his actions were common behavior with the citizens who inhabited the dark and cold environment. She turned around, noticing that Catherine sat in a chair in the far corner of the room. The fragile blonde's eyes were glued to Ansel. A frightened prey would never a predator stalk them. She looked at him in wonderment.

Catherine changed into a pair of thick black jeans and a baggy blue sweatshirt she loaned her. Even though the clothes were meant to be baggy, it looked like a pile of blankets wrapped around Catherine's thin form.

She waved her hand in Catherine's line of vision managing to get the woman to break her focus. She cocked her to the side giving her a questioning look. Catherine shook her head and looked away.

Gayle approached her, taking a lighter wooden folding chair with her. She placed the chair beside Catherine's. "I am sorry that I did not ask earlier about your health," she said, unfolding the chair and sitting.

"It's okay," Catherine whispered, "I am doing better. You were right. I will be better when I move around on my own."

"I'm glad you decided to take my advice," she said.

"She is truly evil…that one who took your son," Catherine whispered.

"Delilah is quite a creation," Gayle said.

Alfred asked his friend, "How long until we are able to get the link up?"

Ansel growled, "These things take time. Our Dome Council does not take kindly to normal people talking. I will have some roadblocks to get over." His bony hands flew over the keyboard."

"Hold my hand," Catherine whispered.

Gayle slowly reached for Catherine's hand, enveloping the delicate hand with her equally small delicate one. Together, they watched Ansel worked on getting through the firewalls. Her mind went to her mother's nightly ritual of kneeling in front of a row of candles with eyes closed and lips moving silently. She remembered her mom calling it prayer. The reason for it was to ask for forgiveness and pray for the well-being of a loved one. Gayle just might do that tonight.

Chapter 28

CLEANDER STOOD IN THE empty spot where the two guardians disappeared. His senses were still shocked from the blow the woman gave him and the realization that Gabriel had been one of the prototypes, the guardians that Dome government had been crazy about and the ones that caused all this mess, and was it worth it?

His eyes fell on the prone body of Guard Copper. The female guardian tossed both of them like paper airplanes. Copper's petite body hid the wall. He shuffled over to her trying not to bear the weight on his bad leg. He dropped down near her head and saw the blood seeping from the back.

"Oh shit," he whispered.

"Sir! Sir!" Connor yelled over the earpiece. "Are you all right? We are coming!"

"Yes, I am all right!" he growled. "Guard Copper will need some help," he whispered.

"Hello, sir. Will you help me find my mommy?" A small voice spoke behind him.

Cleander turned around and almost stumbled backward. A small dark-haired boy with large dark eyes set in a forlorn elfin face regarded him. The thick clothing of a Downhiller swallowed his small form. "How did you get here?"

The little boy shrugged his small shoulders. "I do not know where here is, sir."

"You are in Uptown…the terminal." Cleander struggled to stand up. "What is your name, boy?" The questioning expression on the boy's face made him worry. He wondered if the child suffered amnesia.

"My name is David Robinson," the boy said.

He heard the sound of combat boots in the distance. The distinctive metal sound of weapons being armed alerted him of the arrival of the rest of the guards. He focused on what to say to them about the situation as the concerned face of his second-in-command rounded the corner of the kiosk.

"You can put your arms down, Connor," he said, limping forward. "I think the situation has been eliminated. We have to get these people some medical help and get these doors open."

Connor nodded, then gave him a salute, then stopped, and glanced down at the boy. "Isn't that Gabriel's son?"

Cleander looked at David. "Gabriel has a son?"

"Didn't you know?" Connor approached David. "Where are your mom and dad?"

David smiled. "Gabriel works for the Dome guard. I have come to see him."

Cleander was confused. *How the hell did Gabriel get a son unless—* He recalled there were six tester families. The elder Johnsons were dead, and so were the Petersons. The other three have been shipped off to another unknown Dome by a councilman. This left the elusive Robinsons—the mother-and-son duo, and Gabriel must have been assigned to them.

"We will find his father, Connor," Cleander interjected. "Have the team do a final sweep, and I will see if we can get these doors and windows open."

"Guard Copper," Connor whispered.

"Get two of the guards to take her someplace out of the way. We don't want people to start asking questions when they come in here."

Connor nodded and started to send orders to the other guards.

"Look at the ice." One of the guards pointed to the walls, where the frost started to recede.

Cleander looked down at David. "You should come with me, David." He started to walk away. He only got a couple of feet when he realized the boy did not follow him. He looked around to see David still standing there, looking at him with a forlorn expression.

He limped back to him. "I told you to come with me."

David held out his hand. "Aren't you going to take my hand?"

Cleander furrowed his brow. He never held hands, especially with young citizens, but the look on the boy's face made him change his mind. He held out his hand. "Let's go."

David gave a slight smile and ran to take his hand. Cleander glanced around before pulling the boy along. They ascended a metal staircase leading to the command room, which overlook the area. It felt awkward to have such a small hand in his larger one. He loosened his grip, thinking the small hand may just crumbled in his hold.

On the second floor, they encountered a pool of water. He saw that it seeped from under a pair of large metal doors. He knew the door lead into the control room. If it was water coming there, the sight would not be a pleasant one.

"Don't go in there." A solemn, familiar baritone spoke from the shadows.

Cleander knew the voice even before he saw the man or…whatever they called him. "You made it."

"Gabriel!" David hurled toward the blond giant, thrusting his little body in the air while Gabriel caught him, and they engulfed each other.

"What's in there? Another robotic surprise?" Cleander said.

Gabriel's face winced. He emerged fully from the shadows, his uniform almost covered in a golden dust, his face bruised and blooded. Blue eyes blinked at him. "My sister flooded the command center. It is dangerous for humans to enter." He swallowed. "I feel your ire. I wish I could be what you are familiar with, but I cannot."

"Hey, I don't expect you to be anything. What I expect is honesty."

"*Honesty* is an interesting word for humans. On one hand, you use it more as a sword than as a shield. I find the concept of it harder to learn, more so than other aspects of human life."

"Funny, those eggheads tried to imitate life, yet don't really know what life is," Cleander said.

This isn't his fault, he thought, *just like the cleansing missions in his cadet days.* He could have done something but to speak against a popular motion would be suicide. If Gabriel told him the truth, it would have been the same. As the blond giant said, the concept of being human was a hard study.

"Look…it is obvious that you are in trouble." Cleander approached. "I offer you my assistance, whatever you need."

Gabriel looked up at him. "Thank you, sir."

"We are not all monsters."

"I do not consider you a monster, sir, but I hope to call you friend." Gabriel held out his hand to him.

Cleander gave him a slight smile, gripping the hand with a firm grip. "Now how about we call this young man's mother? She must be going out of her mind."

"She tends to do that a lot."

*****

Gayle couldn't open her eyes. The sheer thought of knowing the world lay out below her made her stomach churn. She squeezed the leather arm of her chair. Suddenly, she felt a light touch on her arm. Her eyes opened to see Catherine's concerned look.

"I never flew before," Gayle whispered.

"No worries. These things are perfectly well-built by Divine Cybernetics' people. We've never had a crash," Catherine said.

"Define *never*." Gayle let out a short laugh.

"We should reach my penthouse in a couple more minutes. My people from Dome 3 elbowed their way here. They told me the Dome

Council tried to block them out," Catherine said.

"I cannot imagine anyone would stand up to those bullies."

Catherine chuckled. "They are ants in a hole compared to Divine Cybernetics' Dome 3 executives."

Gayle balled her fist on her thigh and squeezed her eyes even tighter. True to Catherine's word, they arrived in Uptown in minutes.

She felt the sharp sting of the false sun's heat on her hand. The first time in weeks her skin felt the full force of the rays and so unused to the feeling. Her skin tingled. Then she felt them start to descend. Her stomach muscle increased in pace, and her body shivered. Catherine's small hand patted her.

"Open your eyes, chicken," Alfred said, then patted her on the back. "What would David say if he sees you like this?"

She finally opened her eyes, realizing they had landed. They had to wait inside the small confines of the closet until the propellers stopped completely and the guards secured the wheels on the rooftop. A robot with its silvery exoskeleton exposed opened her passenger door offering a hand. She hesitated, then accepted the assistance.

They did not have much time to delay. Catherine bid her farewell and told her that a car waited to transport her and Alfred to the terminal. "No one will bother you," the woman promised.

Inside the vehicle, she gripped Alfred's hand, who continued to tell her everything would be all right. Then they saw it—the tall, imposing four-story terminal with a thick crowd of people waiting behind a barrier of Dome vehicles.

The guard who drove their car managed to get past the barriers and people. Just then, the crowd started to cheer. She looked at the terminal where the large metal barrier doors started to rise. Medical teams poured over the steps with ready gurneys.

She slipped out of the vehicle, faintly hearing Alfred and the guards' voices behind her, but she needed to find Gabriel and David. No one would stop her from seeing them.

"Mom!" a small voice called out.

She turned around in the melee. Then there they were, walking toward her. She lowered herself onto her knees, catching David's small form against herself. She sprinkled kisses over his face.

"You came."

She glanced up, seeing Gabriel towering over them. His guard uniform was ripped and burned to the skin in most areas. His face had red claw marks that traveled from the tops of his eyes to his neck. The glowing light in his eyes flittered. She rose, slowly placing a hand over the bruises and nodded.

She hugged him and whispered, "No regrets."

*****

The snake slithered through the double doors and down the hall. He never made a sound, but she knew where its position at every minute it took from her front door to the living room. Catherine stared out of the tall window. The sun still shone brightly over the sleek white cityscape of Uptown, and since the terminal was secured, now the citizens could move about again, and most convened around the Uptown terminal.

She palmed the small chip in her hand. In all Dani's failures in life, at least one thing the greedy field agent did right. Her people demanded the body first. The Dome guards had their own concerns about the riots and rebels to worry about a rogue agent. After a thorough search, her people found a nano chip on the body. The rightful property of Divine Cybernetics, and after finding out what information it had on it, they gave her the leverage she needed.

"Catherine, I am happy to see you healthy and beautiful as ever." Councilman Ian bounced into the room.

She never turned around continuing to absorb the crisp, sunny scenery. After her ordeal, she found that staring out her windows soothed her nerves. It made her stronger. "I am happy that you came to see me."

"Ah, my dear, your father and I were brothers. You are like a daughter to me. When I heard what you have been through, I exhausted all my manpower to find you."

This made Catherine turn around now. She shifted her position in the armchair by the window to observe the sniveling councilman who tried to con her father's company from her. He even convinced the executives in Dome 3 to cut her funding. Admittedly, he had some controlling shares in the company but not enough.

"I will make this brief, Ian." She finally spoke. "I realize how precious your time is."

Suddenly, two uniformed Dome guards entered the room from her kitchen. They had been waiting there until they heard her voice.

Ian turned to look at them, with a raised eyebrow. He looked back at her. "Why are the Dome guards here?"

"Don't you know? I thought you exhausted all your manpower to find out what happened to me. I thought you had everyone in Dome 16 searching round the clock to ensure your goddaughter would be safe."

"Of course, I did—"

"I grow tired of your machinations to take control over my father's company. I know now what Dani is here for. I also know that Dome government really does not have full rights to govern Dome 16. Divine Cybernetics does. Now as the sole alive owner of Divine Cybernetics, I also control Dome 16."

Finally, the man who did not fear anyone showed fear. His eyes darted to and fro. She saw sweat bead on his forehead. "Catherine, um…what are you thinking?"

"We are able to pay the funds owed to the Dome Council. So all rights to the guardian program will come back onto me, and your interest in this program is null and void, as well as your interest and status here in Dome 16."

"You can't—"

"Stop talking. Dome government no longer has a presence here.

It is time that a new institution comes into play. I am going to do for you that you never will do for your fellow human being. You have twenty-four hours to clear out of Dome 16. These gentlemen will escort you back to your home, then to the port."

"Catherine! Catherine! You can't do this." He lurched forward but was caught by the two guards.

They dragged him away, screaming. She returned her focus back to the serene scenery outside her window.

Tomorrow, she would set about to solving the problem of the rebels and the state of all the citizens. Her people advised that this would be a hard road, but she met with hardship before with the slash in her funding by the Divine Cybernetics' main branch and the misdirection from her so-called godfather. She did not harbor a fairytale illusion that this would be a rainbow-and-pink-balloon ending.

"Ms. Miles, a Dr. Cary Ellis is here to see you." One of the Dome guards came back into the living room. "He said he was from Divine Cybernetics' science and genetic division in Dome 3."

She turned around. She thought they had all left for Dome 3. She tried to recall all the executives who greeted her that morning but never saw a Dr. Cary Ellis. "Show him in."

"Do you want me to remain?"

"No. It will be okay."

The guard nodded and disappeared down the hall. She heard a second pair of footsteps enter the hall. A young man appeared around the corner. She guessed his age closer to being still in his teens as his nervous, expressive face appeared devoid of hair or even fine lines. It appeared too childlike to be handsome and bold to be cute. He had a strange furry animal in his arms that had an equally innocent expression with large brown eyes. It never made a noise but stared at her in the most uncomfortable way.

"I don't remember you," she said.

"No, no, I traveled with Director Hector Minos. He is back at Dr. Gregory's home. They found the lab." The man stopped. "I worked with

Dr. Gregory on a number of his projects especially the guardian program."

"Good…" She smiled, knowing this should be the end. They needed to destroy every lab the quake had. She promised Gayle this boon. She would make sure no one created another creature like Delilah or be able to profit from his insane research.

Just then, the creature in his arms whined. "What is this?"

"This is what I needed to speak to you about." He lowered the creature to the floor, allowing it to stand on four furry legs. "As you know from past pictures, this is called a dog. In particular, the species is a Cavalier King Charles spaniel."

"He is beautiful," she remarked, then stood, and padded over to the animal. It trudged over to her feet, and she knelt to pet the long coat.

"I am glad you like him. Maybe we can speak about how he could help rebuild Divine Cybernetics."

She regarded him. "That is very gracious of you, but I can't accept gifts from employees."

"No, no, you see. This is, or rather, I will be the newest product offered from Divine Cybernetics."

She considered the creature, rising to stand. "It's nice, but…I don't know. He seems sweet enough, but with this cynical, heartless society, people want a bit more than just a cute furry creature."

"I…I know, and he is more," he said, then stepped back, motioning for her to do the same. She followed him. "Cesar, come out to properly greet us."

The creature turned around in place, then she heard bones cracking. The furry creature's form elongated, and before she knew it, a tall, slender man with dark hair and eerie dark eyes regarded them. He could be Dr. Ellis's relative, only a bit older and a lot more handsome.

"Cesar has the loyalty and unbiased nature of a dog but intelligence and self-care of a human. He can be in a family or with a single individual helping them through emotional or financial struggles. He will be able to gather his own food and take care of himself without burdening the family. He is the perfect companion."

The perfect companion? Catherine thought. *Not bad. Maybe we will come out of this on top?*

THE BLARING LIGHT OF the sweltering ball of fire in the sulfuric yellow sky ruled the barren sky above him. Even now the effects warmed his skin, but his body adjusted and adapted. Soon he would not feel the burn at all. His skin would not even show the signs of him being outside the Dome unprotected.

His footsteps stopped at three mounds. Chief Cleander understood the truth about him. They shook hands, and the chief made a promise that he would make things right, and so he did. Catherine gave the citizens of Dome 16 the vote to break away from the Dome government. It might take months, and many ill felt emotions, but they would make the move.

He lowered on to his haunches waved a glowing hand over his siblings.

Their bodies hummed with life still. A faint life. In a way, he felt saddened that they would ever know a full life, but their clear and present danger to humans prevented him from allowing them back into society. It would be safer for them and the humans if all remained separate for now until he could break his father's final code on their entire makeup.

A nudge alerted him. *Gayle?* She finally learned to mentally speak with him. They had been working at it for many weeks. She achieved single words and now full sentences. Still, a full conversation would be another hurdle for them. He knew as they grew closer together that it would come to pass.

Take it slow this time, Gayle. You don't want to burn out, he sent out.

I know. You've been gone for a long time. Is everything all right? I will be back soon. You need eggs for the cake.

Yes, at the store, I told you. The food is more natural.

He smiled. *I remember. I am officially four years old. Now you remember how to bake a cake.*

She giggled. *I think I can remember to bake a birthday cake for my son and husband. Cleander and Deborah are bringing Zane and Lily. David is buzzing around to ensure the* Merry Musician *movie night was perfect for them. Did you know they don't even show this in the other Dome?*

I wondered who owns the rights. Maybe we can convince them to share the melodic adventures of the Merry Musician.

Everyone needs a little joy in their life.

About the author

ALFREDA BAILEY IS A dedicated trekkie who lives in California with her eight-year-old cat. She enjoys hiking and exploring beautiful beaches.